Praise for bestse
Elite

D0485162

"Has everything a good b
der, betrayal, mystery, a
do you come across a book that you can lose yourself in and *Midnight Sins* is definitely one of them. Lora Leigh is a talented author with the ability to create magnificent characters and captivating plots."

—*Romance Junkies*

WITHDRAWN

RENEGADE

"Leigh delivers . . . erotic passion. This is a hot one for the bookshelf!" —*Romantic Times BOOKreviews*

"Smoldering romance, suspense, and mystery. Add to that the cast of interesting characters—and their pasts—and you have the perfect recipe for one amazing novel."

—*Night Owl Romance* (4½ stars)

"Will have you breathless . . . gets your blood running hot with the physical attraction." —*Romance Reviews Today*

BLACK JACK

"Overflowing with escalating danger, while pent-up sexual cravings practically burst into flames."

—*Sensual Reads*

HEAT SEEKER

"Leigh's pages explode with a hot mixture of erotic pleasures." —*Romantic Times BOOKreviews*

MAVERICK

"A phenomenal read." —*Romance Junkies*

"Scorching-hot sex, deadly secrets, and a determined assassin add up to another addicting Leigh thriller. Leigh's ability to credibly build damaged characters who are both intriguing and intense gives her stories that extra punch." —*Romantic Times BOOKreviews*

"Sex and violence power the satisfying second installment of Leigh's Elite Ops series." —*Publishers Weekly*

"Full of wrenching emotion and self-flagellation by the hero, the new series of Elite Ops promises to be even better than the sexy SEALs at this rate."

—*Night Owl Romance*

"With her customary panache for emotionally intense, sensual characters, the author attracts readers into every world she creates. This fabulous follow-up to *Wild Card* is no exception to the rule." —*A Romance Review*

WILD CARD

"Highly emotional and addicting . . . an intoxicating first installment of a brand-new series." —*Romance Junkies*

"Ferocious passion!" —*Romantic Times BOOKreviews*

And Leigh's sexy SEALs series...

KILLER SECRETS

"A smoldering-hot, new espionage tale. This chapter of Leigh's SEALs saga reverberates with deadly danger."

—*Romantic Times BOOKreviews*

HIDDEN AGENDAS

"Treachery and intrigue combine with blistering-hot sensuality in this chapter of Leigh's SEALs saga. The title of this book is particularly apt, since many of the characters are not what they seem, and betrayal can have deadly consequences. Leigh's books can scorch the ink off the page." —*Romantic Times BOOKreviews*

"An evocative and captivating read." —*Romance Junkies*

DANGEROUS GAMES

"Lora Leigh ignites the fire . . . with steamy heat added to a story that makes you cheer and even tear up."

—*Fallen Angel Reviews*

"Leigh writes . . . tempting, enchanting romance[s] that readers are certain to devour."

—*Romance Reviews Today*

Also By
Lora Leigh

THE CALLAHANS

MIDNIGHT SINS
DEADLY SINS
SECRET SINS

THE ELITE OPS series

LIVE WIRE
RENEGADE
BLACK JACK
HEAT SEEKER
MAVERICK
WILD CARD

THE SEALs trilogy

KILLER SECRETS
HIDDEN AGENDAS
DANGEROUS GAMES

BOUND HEARTS

WICKED PLEASURE
FORBIDDEN PLEASURE
ONLY PLEASURE

Anthologies

LEGALLY HOT
MEN OF DANGER

ULTIMATE SINS

LORA LEIGH

NOTE: If you purchased this book without a cover you should be aware that this book is stolen property. It was reported as "unsold and destroyed" to the publisher, and neither the author nor the publisher has received any payment for this "stripped book."

This is a work of fiction. All of the characters, organizations, and events portrayed in this novel are either products of the author's imagination or are used fictitiously.

ULTIMATE SINS

Copyright © 2014 by Lora Leigh.

All rights reserved.

For information address St. Martin's Press, 175 Fifth Avenue, New York, NY 10010.

ISBN: 978-0-312-38910-9

Printed in the United States of America

St. Martin's Paperbacks edition / September 2014

St. Martin's Paperbacks are published by St. Martin's Press, 175 Fifth Avenue, New York, NY 10010.

10 9 8 7 6 5 4 3 2 1

To the Wicked Readers on Sinful Saturdays.
Thank you for your friendship and for the hours
of laughter for the past three years.
Your insights and your opinions have been greatly
appreciated.

And in loving memory of Dorothy Alta Marie (Few) Lucas
December 9, 1949–March 21, 2013
Thank you for the laughter, the love, and the memories.
And for being not just a generous
loving aunt, but a true and wonderful friend.
You will never be forgotten.

PROLOGUE

Amelia at eighteen

The file was far more than he had expected.

Crowe Callahan knew he shouldn't have been surprised. After more than fourteen years of harassment, nothing about Corbin County should have surprised him in the least. But this one did.

Wayne Sorenson, Corbin County's attorney, had actually managed to convince him as well as his two cousins over the years that he was a friend. Information had come to light in the past year, though, that indicated he wasn't as loyal to the Callahans as he wanted them to think. Only in the past weeks since Crowe had begun secretly seeing Wayne's daughter, Amelia, had Crowe learned his suspicions were more than true.

This file, though.

This file detailed Wayne's deception even further. That, added to the information Crowe and Amelia had uncovered, hinted at the hatred the county attorney harbored for the Callahan family.

It was information Crowe would have never learned without Amelia's help.

But what had begun as a mere flirtation, a game to learn the truth behind his suspicions, had turned into something far more emotionally serious.

Something far more physically dangerous than even the information found in the file she had provided.

Reading each page thoroughly, his gaze narrowed against the dim light spilling through the partially opened shades of the office, Crowe restrained the urge to curse.

It was nearly too dark to read, but using the penlight he brought with him could be far too risky. And not just for him. If the young woman who had slipped him into her father's office was revealed as having aided and abedded—abetted, he corrected himself—a Callahan, then her punishment could be far more than her father's wrath.

It could mean her death.

But had she not warned him of the file, had she not slipped him into her father's office, then he would have never known the threat that the Corbin County attorney represented to him and his younger cousins.

The repercussions could have destroyed them all without this forewarning.

Each page listed and described years' worth of circumstantial evidence that didn't prove a damned thing. But together, tied sequentially and argued effectively, that evidence could fry not just him, but also his cousins, Logan and Rafer.

It showed him, once and for all, that when they returned to Corbin County permanently, a certain power base would have to be established before anyone learned of it. They would have to return with the upper hand and enough support to ensure that it took more than a few dirty county politicians to destroy them.

"He's been building that file for over five years," Amelia

whispered as she stood next to him. "When I found it, I couldn't believe it."

Because her father played a damned fine game of pretending friendship and loyalty to the three cousins.

"Believe it," he murmured, slowly closing the file before directing his attention to Amelia Sorenson once again.

Wayne Sorenson's daughter.

Crowe Callahan's carefully hidden lover and his greatest secret.

God help him, she was fucking pretty.

Long, burnished gold-and-brown hair that fell between her shoulder blades. Soft, mesmerizing, thickly lashed turquoise eyes. Innocent. Fiery. Stubborn as hell she was, and filled with so much life.

"Can he trace the disappearance of the information back to you?" he asked carefully, hiding his concern.

There were whispers—not really rumors or gossip, but lifted brows, warning looks, and a shadow of sympathy—that certain citizens close to the Sorenson family were prone to give her. Those slight reactions indicated Amelia's father wasn't the doting, devoted dad he played in public.

"Everything's already been moved to the new offices." She looked around slowly, her gaze lingering on the worn couch then the wide, walnut desk they'd made use of more than once since the move had begun several weeks before. "It won't be surprising that the file has come up missing. And it won't be the only one to have disappeared."

She was slick, this one. But hell, that was something he had always known. Only in the past weeks had he begun to see just how controlled and ruthless she could be, though.

Weeks.

Six weeks. It wasn't near enough time, he thought

regretfully. Not nearly long enough to have amassed the memories he'd begun to realize he wanted with her.

"You're taking a heavy risk, fairy-girl," he growled as he actually considered putting the file in the drawer where she had hidden it after the desk had been cleaned out.

A little puff of air expelled from her lips at the accusation.

"The evidence itself has been dumped, and other pieces burned," she informed him with a triumphant quirk of her lips. "All electronic backups were taken care of this afternoon." Her brow arched in mock curiosity. "Too many hands moving too many things. It was really too bad those magnets were stacked on top of the PC, as well as his laptop. And of course there was that magnetic stack confiscated when the sheriff busted that Internet fraud group last year. Someone was just stupid enough to transport it along with his flash drives and SD cards." Her gaze glittered with fury. "I can't believe he'd try something so evil as to frame you and your cousins. As though you haven't been through enough hell. Those damned magnets have gone over the entire house, any possible hiding place, and every inch of his vehicle. I won't allow him to destroy an entire family with lies and suppositions." The smile she shot him was tight and mocking. "I've just been a busy little bee this week, Crowe, and every move I've made has been covered. No one could even guess that any of that information was deliberately destroyed." She shrugged. "None of it was important enough to risk allowing him to succeed in his plans against you and your cousins."

Son of a bitch.

She had actually found a way to erase the electronic files they feared he had. Not just the originals but also any hidden backups her father might possess.

Pride flooded his chest.

She'd done what he'd believed couldn't be done. She

had found the evidence that Wayne Sorenson was building to prove what Crowe believed could not be proven, because it hadn't happened.

Wayne was trying to bring him and his cousins to trial for the murders of six young women they had slept with seven summers before. Six innocent young women whose choice to sleep with a Callahan had resulted in their horrible rapes and tortured murders.

"You're certain this is all that's left?" he asked, lifting the file.

"I've looked everywhere I could think to look," she assured him, pushing slender, delicate fingers through her hair. She frowned thoughtfully. "His PC and laptop have been completely wiped. I've gone through every paper file myself and found nothing else. I've checked the house, the safe, this office, and every nook and cranny I could find. If there's another file out there, then he's far better at hiding it than I ever imagined."

Taking a seat on her father's bare, scarred desk, Amelia stared up at Crowe, her gaze somber.

"How did you find out about this file?" Shoving the folder and its contents into the small leather backpack he carried, Crowe narrowed his gaze on her, wondering what Amelia gained in betraying her father for the cursed Callahan cousins.

"By accident," she admitted, her gaze now so innocent he almost felt like a pervert for all the things he'd done to her lush body in the past weeks. "I overheard him discussing it on the phone with Aspen County's attorney. He's still trying to tie Jaymi Flannigan's murder to your cousin Rafe. He had to prove that Rafe knew she was considering a move to Aspen and leaving Corbin County to do it, though."

"He was building a case that Rafe had killed her out of jealousy." He nodded at his own deduction. "But none of us left the county that day. And we have witnesses."

"Wayne's trying to find someone to prove you were in Aspen and that your witnesses are lying." She bit at her lip before thinning both angrily. "He and Sheriff Dunmore was discussing how they could prove Thomas Jones was actually trying to help Jaymi, rather than being responsible for killing her."

Thomas Jones had killed her. There was no doubt about it.

Crowe, Logan, and Jaymi's lover at the time, Rafer, had heard her screams and raced to her location. They'd arrived in time to see Jones shove that knife in her side before jumping from her body and attempting to escape.

"What 'proof' did you destroy?" What the hell could that bastard have managed to find that couldn't possibly exist?

"Dunmore managed to convince a bartender to give the deposition you saw in the file, that you were indeed in Aspen. But he disappeared from town a week later, as Wayne's deposition states."

"Indicating that we possibly killed him as well to keep him quiet." God help him. When would it end?

If it weren't for the will their parents had left and the knowledge that if they left and turned their backs on the fight for what was theirs in Corbin County, then a serial murderer might acquire or inherit it, he and his cousins would have left years before now.

Amelia rubbed her hands over her face wearily before lowering them to her lap.

"There was a shoe belonging to another victim with Logan's thumbprint. A newly discovered glove with Rafer's fingerprints that, according to Dunmore, hadn't been easy to transfer after the prints were acquired from elsewhere. I'd really be careful about dishes and utensils used in the café, bar, and restaurant here in town," she suggested softly, her eyes gleaming with moisture. "Can't we stop him, Crowe? I'd testify about what I heard."

Crowe was shaking his head before the words were past her lips, reaching out for her as he stepped to the desk.

"Don't even consider it." Teeth clenched, denial raging through him, Crowe quickly pressed between her slender thighs, holding her in place before him.

One hand tangled in the silken strands of hair that fell down her back as the straining bulge of his erection was cushioned by the hot, feminine heat between her thighs.

"Hell no!" he snapped, glowering down at her; the need to take her, hard and deep, strained his patience. "You've taken enough risks in the past weeks. I'll be damned if you'll risk yourself that openly."

"But he's lying, Crowe!" she hissed back at him, her palms flattening against his stomach. "And you know he won't stop. This has been going on for years, and it was only by chance that I found it."

Her hands pressed against his stomach, but not to push him away. No true pressure was applied. Her fingers curled against his shirt, clenching the fabric, and Crowe swore he could feel her need to touch his bare flesh.

"We'll stop him," he promised her. "But you will not risk yourself any further. You will not draw Wayne's wrath down on you any more than you already have. Because I swear, Amelia, I'll kill him if I ever hear he's even dared to bruise you again. Do you hear me?"

Again.

Crowe still fought the need to kill the bastard for the bruises he'd already seen on her perfect porcelain-and-silk flesh.

Her lips parted and he could see her intent in the way her hands clasped in front of her, slowly twisting together as she leaned back from him.

Her expression, her voice, every part of her presented perfect truth and honesty. All but that one movement. A movement she only used when she lied.

"Lie to me, Amelia, and I'll take you straight home this instant," he warned her, his tone dark, forbidding. "And give me any of those half-assed excuses you've given everyone else and I won't be responsible for what I do to him."

She breathed out heavily. "He didn't hurt me, Crowe."

He knew better.

"And if he tries again, Amelia, then I'll hurt him a thousand times worse."

The throb of his cock and the slight flexing of her hips were beginning to affect more than his patience now. He'd been more than a week without her. Damn, that was too long not to have tasted her lips, her soft, soft flesh, the sweet heat of her need.

She made him hungry. Hungrier than he'd ever been for another woman.

Small, warm hands unclasped, then slipped beneath his shirt to find his bare flesh as Crowe watched her expression turn soft and dreamy, her gaze darkening with a feminine hunger that never failed to amaze him.

"Then we won't argue," she promised as she wrapped her free arm around his neck to pull him to her. "It's been too long since you touched me." Her soft, pink little tongue swiped over her lush lower lip. "Touch me now, Crowe. Please."

Touch her now?

He'd been dying to touch her again since five minutes after he'd last had her. He couldn't get this hunger out of his system; nor could he find a way to keep from holding on to the hope that somehow, some way he could keep her.

His lips covered hers. There wasn't a chance of denying himself the pure sweet pleasure of those tempting lips. Pouty, sensuous, the lush curves parted beneath his as her arms wrapped around his neck.

He'd taken her here in this room four weeks before. He'd laid her back on the leather couch across the room, knowing she was innocent, but completely unaware she was still a virgin. His first virgin, and the first woman to sink inside him in a way he couldn't explain, nor could he escape.

He'd not touched another woman since. He'd not wanted to touch another woman.

She parted her lips further, her adventurous little tongue tasting his, surprising him with her boldness. Pleasure shot through his system, drawing a groan from him as her hungry response grew hotter.

He'd told himself, more than once, that he wouldn't do this again. He wasn't going to endanger her further. He couldn't do it, because losing Amelia would destroy him. And it would kill more than his soul. His cousins would be burying him beside her if he were the cause of her death—

God help him, the guilt would follow him even past death.

"Amelia. Wait, sweetheart." He drew back, that thought flaying his conscience as well as his soul. "Baby, we have to stop this."

"Why?" Amusement colored the husky, sex-and-more sound of her voice. "I've been dying for you, Crowe. A week was far too long to not see you or talk to you. Too long not to be able to touch you."

Hell, his shirt hung open. His chest was bare to her eager touch, and she had moved to his belt and pulled open the first snap of his jeans.

Moving to catch her slender wrists as her fingers tugged at the next snap, he was immediately stalled by her hot little tongue curling over the flat, hard disk of his nipple.

In his entire sexual lifetime Crowe had never had a woman cover one of his nipples with her lips. To have Amelia do so, to have that pleasure explode across his nerve endings, was shocking. So shocking that he stilled, his teeth clenching as his fingers fisted in reaction.

The time it took him to adjust to the caress, she spent amplifying it. Her teeth raking over the disk, clenching on it as he fought back a growl of pleasure. That pause gave her the time and the opportunity to release the remaining metal buttons on his jeans and release the flesh throbbing for her touch. Her fingers curled around his steel-hard erection, and all his good intentions shot straight to hell.

There was no turning back. There was no denying her.

Seven days.

Seven days too long.

Unfisting his fingers, Crowe lifted his hands, spearing them into her hair and tangling in the silken strands as Amelia turned her attention to the sensitive flesh of his other, unattended nipple.

He'd never known the pleasure she was giving and he was shocked enough that an instinctive response against it just wasn't happening.

From there, like dominoes tumbling down an emotional line, any response to combat the pleasure or to protect her against what might be was instantly sabotaged.

Instead every sense, every emotion and physical response became instinctive, driving home the innermost knowledge that walking away from her would destroy part of his soul.

As he gripped her hair, the dominant sexual creature lurking just beneath his surface surged forward.

His cock was hard, throbbing, her soft, silken fingers teasing him with her touch. Teasing him with the knowledge that every kiss, every lick, every second she was in his arms she was learning what he liked first.

His fairy-girl, he called her.

His fantasy.

Guiding her head, her caresses, and her kisses, Crowe slowly urged her lower. Fiery little licks of her tongue tasted his flesh as she moved down the line of his body.

Imperative little groans and hungry, breathless little mewls had his testicles hardening, clenching in need.

"Crowe." The soft sound of his name was a plea on her lips as she reached the base of his hardened shaft.

Gripping his erection with one hand, she stared up at him, vulnerability marking her expression as Crowe eased her into position before pressing the engorged head against her lips.

"Just pretend it's your favorite treat," he teased her, fighting back the primitive urge to push past the swollen curves. "Just take me, baby, however you want to."

Her lips parted.

"Ah yes, sweetheart." he groaned, watching in shock, heat surging through him, as the fully erect crest slipped inside.

"Ah baby, hell yes." Breathing was becoming harder by the second. "That's it, Amelia. Just suck it inside your hot little mouth."

Ah, God.

Staring down at her, the feel of her lips, the moist heat of her mouth, her nimble, graceful fingers at his balls tore aside any last thoughts of not having her.

Of course he was going to have her.

By God, she belonged to him.

* * *

She could barely breathe.

Amelia sucked the engorged crest of Crowe's erection as deeply as possible, suckling it, licking it, loving it. The salt-and-heat taste of him was addictive. The throb and flex of the iron-hard flesh was an aphrodisiac she didn't want to fight.

With each draw of her mouth his hips flexed, pushing him deeper, urging her to take more, coaxing her hunger higher with each taste of him until she was certain the hard, ever-deepening clench of his shaft signaled the release she craved.

"Hell no," he suddenly groaned.

The first dark, salt-and-man taste that infused her senses had him suddenly pulling back, his fingers tightening at the base of his erection as her eyes flared open.

"Wait, Crowe." Her protest was instinctive.

It was time for his treat now.

"Come here, Amelia." Drawing her quickly to her feet, his hands clenched her hips, lifting her until she was reclining back on the desk, watching him impatiently.

Anticipation was exploding through her. It raced through her bloodstream, awakened nerve endings she hadn't known were so sensitive, before striking at her clit in electric pulses of deepening sensation.

As he laid her back on the desk, one hand cupped the back of her head, the other sliding up her thigh as his head lowered, his lips covering hers in a kiss that burned through her senses. He'd never kissed her with so much hunger, so much need.

His lips slanted over hers, his tongue licking against hers as his fingers found the curve of her breast, then one tight, hard tip.

The stroke of his thumb over her nipple sent crashing

waves of pleasure flooding her, drawing her body tight as a gasp tore past their kiss.

Crowe's head lifted, his gaze locking with hers as he watched her reaction this time.

Catching her nipple with his thumb and forefinger, tightening his grip just enough, he began milking slowly, rolling the pebble-hard tip as her lashes fluttered and a cry of pleasure escaped her lips.

She didn't see his head lowering. She felt his lips surround her other nipple. Moist, hot, his tongue curling over the tight tip as he sucked the sensitive point into his mouth.

Drawing on her hungrily a groan rumbled in his chest, his fingers leaving her opposite nipple to stroke down her side, her hips, before moving across her lower stomach and sliding between her thighs.

Her sex was freshly waxed just the day before, the trip to the spa slipped in during an errand Wayne had sent her on. The only curls left were those that grew on the upper curve of her mound, above her clit.

Crowe's fingers feathered through those curls, once, twice, before sliding lower, his hand curving, cupping the heated, aching flesh as his upper palm pressed firmly against her clit, rubbing against it far too lightly.

There wasn't enough friction.

Hips arching, desperation pounding through her veins and centering at her clit, Amelia gasped with the pleasure rushing through her.

"Crowe, please." Panting, fighting for breath as his lips moved from her nipple, she arched closer. Amelia could feel the driving desperate pleasure building through her senses.

Nothing mattered but his touch, now, always. No matter the time, day or night, the memory of it, the need for it, was always there.

Moving lower, his lips spread a wave of fiery pleasure across her flesh as her hands buried in his hair, clenching, tightening with the building tension ratcheting through her body.

His kisses feathered over her lower stomach, her hipbones, then drew a surprised cry from her as they brushed over the swollen, straining bundle of nerves driving her insane.

"Crowe, yes," she gasped, her thighs parting farther as she felt him settle between them, his hands pressing beneath her knees, urging them to bend, to give him greater access to the sensitive, slick folds between her thighs.

"Sweet Amelia," he whispered as his fingers parted the swollen flesh. "Now I get to enjoy my favorite treat."

Dipping his head, he slid his tongue through the narrow slit, pressed against the clenched entrance of her vagina, then licked slowly upward until he found the hard swollen bud throbbing for his touch.

Pleasure was a rush of electric flames burning in the wake of his tongue. Each lick, each stroke, each muttered growl of pleasure had her arching, moaning, begging for release as each sensation built, burning brighter, hotter, with each hungry stroke of his tongue.

"Oh God, Crowe, please," she begged, her hands buried in his hair, hips arching to be closer, to drive his tongue harder against her clit, the entrance of her vagina. Anywhere that would trigger the release.

Licking, stroking, his tongue circled the little bud as he pressed two fingers against the hungry entrance. They pressed inside, slowly stretching the inner tissue. Twisting his fingers inside her, working deeper as his tongue licked and stroked the pounding bud of her clit, he pushed her higher.

In the six weeks they'd been lovers, he'd done things to her that had her blushing to think about even as her need for him had encouraged him to teach her how to pleasure him as well.

Now arching and writhing at the strokes of his fingers inside her, Amelia could feel her senses threatening to come apart with the force of the steadily rising need for release. It pounded through her body, shot through it in wave upon wave of spasming pleasure.

And she was so close. So certain it was just a breath away, no matter how many times he pulled back just before she could crash into the rapturous abyss awaiting her.

His fingers slid deeper inside her, rubbing the nerve-rich flesh and flexing muscles that clenched around each penetration. His lips tightened on her clit, his tongue flickering over the little point, driving her so high, so close she tried to scream, to beg as his fingers curved inside her, reaching to a point in the uppermost depths of her vagina that sent a pulse of pure white-hot energy tearing through her.

Exploding through her.

It was cataclysmic.

Arching tightly against him, a strangled cry tore from her lips as he suddenly moved to his knees, his fingers stroking again, again. Rapid-fire pulses of release tore through her another time, causing her to jerk against each surge of sensation as his fingers slid free of her.

Not that she had a chance to accustom herself to the deprivation. As his fingers left her, the broad head of his erection was pushing inside. Working the heavy shaft deeper inside her as her flesh aided him with the clenching, milking motions that stroked the hardened shaft with each surging penetration.

Her legs curled around his hips, her pelvis tilting as he came over her fully, gathering her closer to his chest. His lips covered hers, his tongue slipping past to drive her crazy with need for him.

She was surrounded by him.

She was stroked inside and out by him, kept imprisoned in a whirlwind of growing, burning rapture that quickly escalated out of control.

Her release shattered inside her in a complete frenzy of explosions that stripped her to the very core of her emotions.

Lightning licked over her flesh, struck at her clit, the clenched depths of her vagina. Hard, clenching pulses of pure ecstasy struck at her womb as she became completely lost in the man who created the storm.

"Oh, God. Crowe." She jerked in his arms as the pulse and throb of his cock spilled his release inside her. "Oh God, I love you. I love you."

Don't leave me, she wanted to beg. The words locked inside her. *Please, please God, don't leave me.*

Don't let me go. The need remained locked in her soul.

She wouldn't beg him for more than this, and she would only beg when the pleasure was too painful to bear.

But she would always, always love—

The room was silent, the hands on the clock still hanging on the wall ticking ever closer to the moment when he'd have to leave her.

What the hell had he done?

She had somehow managed to slip into his heart, and Crowe knew he had no choice but to walk away. For her sake, he had to.

He couldn't allow this to happen again. Each time he held her, each time he took her, he was risking her further. Each time, she burrowed deeper into the heart he was certain he no longer had. The heart his training had ruthlessly pared down to essential function only. He could have sworn there was no longer the ability to love within it.

But Amelia was proving differently.

Thomas Jones's accomplice hadn't been found seven years before when Thomas had died with Crowe's knife buried in his side. The FBI was certain the mastermind of the operation was still living, still waiting, still watching.

That meant any woman the Slasher learned Crowe or his cousins were with became a target. Amelia would become a target if he didn't stay away from her. Because each time he held her the possessive, dominant male he was found that it was becoming impossible to release her once morning arrived.

Once this night was over he had no choice but to leave, to walk away from the only woman he swore he could feel even when she wasn't in his arms.

Three nights later

Standing beneath the heavily leafed branches of the tree outside Amelia's balcony, Crowe watched as she stared down at the pillow where the neatly folded letter lay. It took every second of training the military had put into him so far to force himself to remain still, to wait, to watch, to allow her to read what he'd written.

He could see her hand trembling as she reach out slowly, picked it up, then unfolded the paper and began to read. There was no hardening himself against the pain he knew she was feeling. He let it lance into his soul, let it burn through his heart. Once this night was over, he'd once again become the icy, emotionless agent he'd thought he was before he returned to Corbin County and gave in to his lust for the delicate fairy who had tempted him too far one hot summer night.

As she finished, a hand covered her lips and she rushed

for the balcony doors, surprising him as she pushed them open, stepped onto the balcony, then closed them quietly behind her.

Had she seen him?

He was ready to jump soundlessly to the ground when she slowly crumpled to the floor of the balcony, huddled into the corner, and let the sobs she'd obviously been holding back, free.

"No. No. Please, please God no," she whispered hoarsely as she sobbed, the words barely distinguishable as Crowe forced himself to watch, to listen.

He'd caused this pain.

He'd done this to her.

As much as he longed to escape it, as much as he needed to distance himself from it, he couldn't.

She was his heart, his soul, and seeing the pain he was causing was ripping his soul to shreds.

"Please, no. Oh God, Crowe, don't leave me alone . . ." she begged the night again, pressing her head into her knees as she wrapped her arms over it. As though somehow she could contain the pain, the driving agony of the words he'd left her.

"Good-bye, fairy-girl," he whispered as he watched her, agony burning through him. "Maybe next life."

Maybe.

Five years later

The funeral service had been small, but filled with friends of the late Clyde Ramsey. No one had foreseen this. For a man in his seventies, Clyde was amazingly—no, he *had been* amazingly healthy and in excellent shape. News of his death had therefore shocked the small ranching community of Gray's Falls, and sent his friends reeling in shock.

His friends weren't the only ones. The three young men he had assumed guardianship of, more than twenty years before, had sat silently in the back of the church, their heads lowered respectfully.

To give those friends credit, they had remained in the church and endured the presence of the three men. They had also remained polite and sympathetic as they all met at the small graveyard inhabited by only three other graves. Simple white gravestones marked the others.

David, Samuel, and Benjamin Callahan. Beside Benjamin's grave, Clyde now rested, bare dirt covering the finely made vault beneath. Atop the bare earth were the multitude of funeral flower arrangements, some artificial, some live cut flowers whose endurance was incredibly limited.

After the reverend had read Clyde Ramsey's final prayer from the Bible, he'd then expressed his sympathy to the boys he claimed Clyde had always called "his sons," said a final fond farewell to Clyde, then called the service to an end.

Nearly fifty close friends made their way from the ranch's cemetery to return to their homes in and near Gray's Falls, a small ranching and tourist community nearly half an hour from Aspen.

Now, still standing inside the wrought-iron fence surrounding the acre of land set aside twenty-four years before, Crowe Callahan stared at the wounded earth where Clyde lay, the icy purpose he didn't bother hiding now filling his soul.

He was a weapon. Born and bred in the fires of hatred, trained in the killing fields of a war on terrorism, and honed in the brutal, soul-destroying second that he'd felt one small woman's heart break.

"He was murdered." Clyde's only recognized blood relative, and one of two whom Crowe recognized, Rafer Benjamin Callahan spoke his suspicions aloud.

Lifting his gaze from the grave, Crowe stared back at him from beneath his lashes.

"I know," Crowe agreed, meeting his cousin's dark-blue eyes before he once again shifted his focus, surveying their surrounding with the intensity of someone who knew all the ways to kill a man.

He wasn't unaware of the concern that filled Rafe and their cousin Logan.

"He called me last week," Rafer revealed then, drawing Crowe's gaze back to him. "He said he needed to see me as soon as possible. He claimed he'd uncovered something about the night our parents were killed." Rafer gave his head a hard shake. "He was dead before I ever received the message."

"Same here," Logan revealed.

Both men turned to Crowe questioningly.

"I got the same call," he said. "Like the two of you, I was completing my final mission before discharge."

"Just after his message, Archer left his own message saying that they had found him dead," Rafer bit out with an edge of fury.

Murdered.

Even Archer suspected Clyde had been murdered, though he'd been unable to find any proof. Still, Crowe had managed to get his hands on the report, and the fact that the sheriff wasn't satisfied with the determination wasn't lost on Crowe.

"So what do we do now?" Rafter asked, anger throbbing in his voice.

"Now we take back what's ours," Crowe stated, that icy purpose inside hardening further. "And God help anyone attempting to stop us."

"He thought he knew who the Slasher was." Logan's statement had Crowe sliding him a thoughtful look.

"How do you know that?" Crowe asked, keeping his voice low.

He could feel the eyes on them, but he'd been feeling it since they arrived at the funeral, though he wasn't certain if anyone was close enough to hear the conversation. He'd let it ride for now, but he'd go hunting later, he decided. Sometime when his cousins weren't there to see.

"His message," Logan said. "His message said he needed to talk to us, that he'd uncovered something about that night. Something that explained everything and to remember what we were searching for when we left."

"We were looking for a possible tie between the Slasher and the person responsible for our parents' deaths," Rafe remembered as Crowe listened. "But we didn't find one."

They had searched hard enough over the years, though, relying fully on Clyde's certainty that the tie existed.

"If we're going on the supposition that Clyde was murdered, then based on the message he left Logan, we can assume he either found some evidence to support the theory of it, or had a suspect in mind," Crowe murmured, keeping his head down, ensuring his lips couldn't be read, nor their movement tracked.

"Then somehow the Slasher himself learned what Clyde had found." Logan frowned at the thought. "If Clyde had actually suspected someone, wouldn't he have left a clue to it somewhere?"

"We've torn apart every area of the house and property looking for the information we gathered ourselves before joining the marines," Crowe reminded them, knowing someone would die for it eventually. "We can't even find that, let alone anything else he left."

"His killer could have found it," Rafe pointed out.

The thought of that had the ice in Crowe's veins solidifying.

There had been more in those files than simply what Clyde himself had gathered.

Thank God the file Amelia Sorenson had given Crowe that summer hadn't been hidden with Clyde's information. Clyde had known of it, and several of the files he'd put together himself had included information regarding the county attorney. Amelia wasn't named in the notes placed in the boxes of information and evidence, either, but the possibility that someone could figure out that some of Clyde's tips came from her was a concern.

The possibility that the information they had could endanger Amelia had the ice that formed Crowe's soul threatening to crack.

If the Slasher realized she was helping them—she wouldn't survive it, and Crowe knew it. For five years he'd stayed away from her, kept his distance. He wouldn't let her face that fate now.

"Maybe Clyde contacted Wayne," Rafe suggested. "I know Clyde was working with him in regard to that rustling operation they busted in Gray's Falls last year. And Wayne always did keep in touch with Uncle Clyde."

That wasn't possible, Crowe thought.

His cousins had no clue about the relationship he'd had with Wayne's daughter, or that she had been voluntarily sending Crowe information since she was sixteen, but Clyde had guessed.

After Crowe had left, she anonymously sent that information to Clyde.

She would have known Clyde's friendship with Wayne was a hazard to her, he reminded himself; she wasn't a stupid woman. If she had been then she would have never survived her father or the man she had been briefly married to.

"We could contact Wayne," Logan said. "See if Clyde *had* talked to him."

"I don't think that's a good idea. He's tried more than once to frame us, and I'd prefer not to tempt him to try again." Crowe shook his head, their quizzical looks demanding an explanation. "Clyde may have trusted him in other areas but I really don't think he would, or we should, contact him about this.

"I think we should wait and discuss Clyde or what he might have known, once we're in the house," Crowe added softly. "Where the conversation is certain to be kept to ourselves."

"You could be right." Logan rubbed at the back of his neck in irritation. "Doesn't change how dirty Sorenson is, though. That family always was damned strange. Amelia used to be okay, until she married that bastard Stoner Wright."

Rafer frowned as they all moved away from the grave site and headed to the sprawling ranch house, keeping close, their gazes constantly moving over the area, their senses alert.

All of them sensed the eyes watching them and were taking precautions to keep their conversation to themselves.

"You know, I was home the week Amelia married Stoner Wright," Rafer said as they walked, evidently needing something to talk about. Crowe wished they'd find another subject. "Clyde received an invitation and attended the wedding. He told me Amelia had jumped from the frying pan into the fire. When I ask what he meant, he wouldn't elaborate. He wasn't surprised when Stoner came up missing, though. Clyde just smiled and said he knew that problem would get taken care of right quickly and that he was glad he hadn't been disappointed."

Glancing along the distance to the ranch house, his

teeth clenched, Crowe knew exactly what Clyde had been referring to.

Not that he was about to elaborate.

"Clyde could be damned strange himself, couldn't he?" Logan grunted fondly. "He mentioned the same thing to me when I asked about Stoner. And I swear he was amused as hell."

No doubt he was, Crowe thought, not really surprised that Clyde had figured some things out. Clyde had known human nature better than most.

"Yeah." Rafer glanced past Logan to Crowe, frowning. "We were both home the weekend Stoner was seen leaving the house with several pieces of luggage, weren't we? Some of Wayne's cronies at the bar were with Wayne when he dragged Stoner out behind the bar and threatened to kill him if he didn't pack his shit and leave. When Clyde heard that he had left the same night, I remember he muttered something about Stoner being scared of far more than Wayne. Do you think he suspected then who we were looking for and decided not to tell us until he had proof?"

Oh, Crowe really didn't think that was what Clyde had been talking about. Sometimes Clyde knew his charges far too well.

"He would have told us." Crowe shook his head. He wanted them off the subject of Amelia and Stoner as quickly as possible.

"Yeah," Logan agreed as they stepped into the ranch yard.

"I don't know who or what Stoner may have been scared of, but I highly doubt it was Wayne. I know Archer heard a rumor that either Wayne or Stoner had blackmailed Amelia into that marriage, but no one knew the leverage he used." Rafer's comment had Crowe's tension growing now. "If he could force Wayne to allow his daughter to be abused, then he had some heavy ammunition."

Crowe didn't even know that one.

After all these years, and the question's he'd asked, Crowe had never figured out how she had been forced into that marriage. He'd always assumed Wayne had been the one to apply the pressure, though.

"Anyone hear from Stoner since?" Rafe asked after several moments of silence.

"Archer mentioned Wayne has." Logan nodded. "Wayne's secretary, Carlotta, said a letter arrived sometime at the office last year, addressed to Amelia. She gave it to Wayne and hasn't seen it since. She said he was demanding money, and that either Wayne or Amelia receives a letter or phone call every six to eight months or so." Logan breathed out roughly as they stepped onto the porch and into the house. "I guess they keep him paid off to keep him out of the county."

Crowe remained silent. He'd heard the letters had been arriving; he just hadn't yet tracked them down. He had someone working on it, but so far they hadn't identified the sender.

"Stoner was beating the shit out of Amelia while they were married, according to Archer," Rafer stated in disgust as the warmth of the house welcomed them. "After Stoner disappeared one of the maids was gossiping about it. I just remembered Archer mentioning that when I came home last year. Archer stopped by the house one night after observing Doc Trynor's car in the driveway. Wayne had called him to check out Amelia after she fell down the stairs."

Rafer rolled his eyes.

Crowe could feel the killing ice beginning to build inside him. There were days he wished—

"And she was refusing to go to the hospital. When

Archer demanded to see her, he told her he'd never seen stairs leave the same bruises that a man's fist would. She just sat there, all ladylike with her hands clasped in front of her, and assured him it was indeed the stairs." Rafer shook his head as he moved to the counter and the coffeepot they'd prepared earlier. Flipping it on, he turned back to his cousins. "The bruises were bad, though, from what I heard."

It hadn't been the stairs. Crowe knew that for a fact.

"Why are we talking about two people who have absolutely nothing to do with the Slasher or our parents' deaths?" Crowe asked coldly, knowing this subject was guaranteed to push him into something damned stupid. Like killing the father who had dared to allow such abuse to continue as long as it had. "Weren't we trying to figure out what the hell happened to all the files and information he had gathered?"

Thank God he and Clyde had thought to scan a backup digital copy, in case anything should ever happen to the originals.

"Because one of them could know something," Rafer pointed out. "Someone sent all that information over the years, Crowe. And if the Slasher stole it before killing Clyde, then he'll make certain Wayne Sorenson receives those files once they realize the bastard is out to frame us as well."

"Wait." Logan paused as they each stood within the warmth of the kitchen, trying to make sense of a past and a present that simply had too many pieces missing. "You think Amelia would have sent that information?"

"Hell no." Rafer saved Crowe from having to admit to something they should have known about all along. "But she's not the only one in and out of that office."

"Why don't we just keep looking for the files Clyde hid

and see what he added to them?" Crowe challenged the other two men mockingly. "We still have the backup digital copy; all that may be missing is whatever he found recently. We have some things to finish ourselves anyway. We'll make it appear we're concentrating on opening Brute Force Security Services and getting the plans in place for the resort, Avalanche. While Clyde's killer thinks we're distracted by those endeavors, we'll see what we can do to make him show himself."

And while they were doing all that, distracting the Slasher, possibly another killer, Wayne Sorenson, and whoever else decided to watch, Crowe would continue to fight the urge to return to the only addiction he'd ever had in his life.

That of one delicate, far-too-beautiful fairy who tempted him to recklessness.

Amelia.

"We need this house and the ranch wired while we're at it." Crowe looked around the kitchen and open living room, his eyes narrowed as plans began to form in his mind.

Turning to Logan, he asked, "What did Clyde say our parents did when they first began to suspect the little accidents they were experiencing were more than accidents?"

Logan stared at him thoughtfully.

"He said they looked at the strengths and weaknesses of each of their homes then chose the one they thought would best protect all three families and moved into it together."

Crowe nodded as Rafe carried the coffeepot and cups to the table where they all took a seat.

"They all lived in town at the time," he reminded them.

"Yeah, so?" Rafer prodded.

"Listen to me, dammit," he growled. "They lived in separate areas, in separate homes, and Rafer's parents were here at the ranch more often than not."

"Yeah." Rafe rubbed at the back of his neck as Logan leaned forward, watching Crowe silently.

"Before, there were odd accidents, nothing too serious, but enough to cause them to become concerned for their children and move into the one house that Logan's parents owned—"

"But what they did was allow the killer to focus on one location, and on our families as a whole," Rafer guessed.

"Exactly." Crowe could see now exactly how they could further strain the enemy's resources. Especially if the enemy was limited in manpower. And the Stalker would have to be limited in manpower. The more people were involved, the greater the chances of discovery.

"Logan." He turned to his middle cousin. "Get your stuff together and move into the house on Rafferty Lane."

He turned to Rafer. "You'll stay here on the ranch while I make it appear I've moved into the cabin on Crowe Mountain."

Logan snorted. "Like you haven't been living there for years anyway whenever you've come back."

Crowe smiled with slow, easy mockery.

"But they didn't know when I was due to return," he reminded them. "So, they never knew when I was home, allowing me to move about freely whenever I did leave the mountain, as long as I stayed in the shadows."

"Because you weren't where you were supposed to be," Logan said thoughtfully.

Crowe inclined his head in acknowledgment.

"So, once again, we won't be where they expect us to be," he told them. "We've always stayed together whenever we've returned. This time, we separate. Let's make it harder for him. We wire all three places with cameras and sound and see who comes visiting."

"You scare me, Crowe," Logan murmured.

"I'm sure I do," Crowe grunted, catching the sarcasm in his cousin's voice. "Now, why don't *you* scare *me* and actually get your shit and get the hell out of here. We'll start wiring your place tonight. Rafe and I'll slip in after midnight and work till daylight."

"Hey, don't forget about that heated path along the base of the mountain behind the house," Logan reminded him, the widening of his eyes indicating his sudden memory of the path.

Crowe realized even he had forgotten about the geothermals their fathers had found and piped into.

They had created a path a few degrees above body temperature, allowing them to slip in and out without being seen should anyone attempt to use surveillance equipment.

"Hell, I'd forgotten that myself," Rafer admitted.

"I don't even think Clyde knew about the path. Let's make sure no one else finds out about it, either," Crowe murmured, finally finding a chance to sip at the coffee Rafer had carried to the table.

Finally, something in their favor.

For twenty-two years he'd felt as though they were constantly two steps behind whoever the hell shadowed them and the families that disowned them.

"We'll survive this," Rafer said, his voice curiously hollow as he made the statement.

"Damned right we'll survive it," Crowe told him.

"While we're surviving, let's try to make sure no one else suffers." Logan was the one to bring their deepest fears to the surface. "Because God help me, but I'm tired of watching innocent women die."

He wasn't by himself.

But what Crowe feared the most was that the Slasher would discover the one secret he'd fought so many years to hide.

The secret of the woman who held his heart.

The key to his destruction.

CHAPTER 1

Two years later

Sleep wasn't happening.

Too many memories haunted her, the knowledge of too much blood and betrayal echoing through her soul.

Amelia had known her father was cruel. She'd known he was a bastard. He'd proved it over the years in so many ways.

In ways that would scar her soul forever. Yet there were days, and nights such as now, that she thanked God he'd never treated her as though he loved her, that he'd never fooled her into trusting him.

If she had trusted him—

A swift, hard strike of terror had her breath hitching at the implications of such a mistake. At what she could have lost, when she had already lost so much.

When she had lost—

"What happened to your room, Amelia? It used to have life in it."

Amelia swung around, her heart in her throat, her breath suddenly trapped there, threatening to strangle her as she stared back at the man, standing so strong and sure as he slipped past the balcony door.

Amelia had known Crowe would show up. She'd known after she'd been dumped on his porch by Amory Wyatt two weeks before, naked, helpless—oh God.

She turned away from him, staring around the room, wondering what he saw to make him say such a thing. Trying to focus on anything, everything but the memory of him finding her like that.

God, he had changed. In the seven years since the last evening they'd spent in the county attorney's office, he'd hardened. He was stronger, broader. He was colder.

But then, so was she, she thought. The difference was that she knew the chances of ever finding the warmth she had once known with this man were nil to never.

Amber-flecked brown eyes, emotionless, stared back at her from a face with a harsh, savage male beauty that still had the power to steal her breath.

He owned her heart. He owned the young girl she had once been and fought to forget until the second she'd whirled around to see him standing inside her room. The epitome of every dream she'd ever had—of every nightmare she never wanted to remember—staring around the room that once held so much more than it did now.

The full-size bed was neatly made. It hadn't really been slept in for years.

She always dreamed of Crowe when she slept in it.

Once, there had been lace on what were now plain sheets. Decorative pillows and the big stuffed mouse he'd given her weeks before he'd disappeared forever.

The small chaise in the corner of the room held the single blanket and small pillow she used when she did sleep. On the table beside it sat a glass of water, half empty, her phone, and books.

That chaise once held lace scarves, magazines, a pile of books. The table had held pictures of herself with the few friends she'd believed she'd never lose.

There were no pictures now, not of herself or of any friends she might have once had. She had learned to never reveal a weakness. A picture was the same as an arrow pointing to a weak spot, someone or something she may love.

She followed Crowe's gaze around the room.

It was nearly spartan, with few adornments or keepsakes. It resembled a hotel room more than it did someone's home.

"Is it over?" she asked.

Had they finally found what they needed to prove her father was the heinous evil behind the identity of the Slasher?

The question hung in the air as she fought to distract him from the sterility of the room.

The sterility of her life.

"It's over," he stated, not bothering to hide the satisfaction in his tone. "All we have to do now is catch him."

Amelia brushed the shoulder-length strands of hair back from her face and watched him carefully.

"Surely, he can't hide for long," she whispered, hating the trembling of her voice, the fear that wanted to rise sharp and painful inside her.

"I won't let him hide for long," he answered, his lips twisting into a sneer. "But he doesn't want to hide, does he? He wants to destroy us."

No, her father wouldn't stay hidden for long. She knew Wayne, and she knew the demonic killer known as the Slasher. She'd spent most of her adult life trying to avoid both, only to learn they were one and the same.

Unfortunately, she hadn't been certain of that until the night her father had forced her from her bedroom, rendered her unconscious, then transported her to the cabin where he had already raped and killed more than a dozen young women in the past fourteen years.

She was forced to shake her head slowly as she met his gaze once again.

"What now, then?" she asked. "How do you intend to make him show himself?"

She couldn't shake that overwhelming fear that the shadows twisting and churning beyond the stark balcony outside her window held something far more sinister than just the darkness now.

"I intend to offer the perfect bait," he stated, his tone icy, his expression hardening.

But what, Amelia wondered, confused, was the perfect bait?

Pure male arrogance tautened each plane and angle of his face. The sharp, high cheekbones, the aristocratic blade of his nose, the deliberate thinness of what she knew was a passionately full lower lip.

He was enraged though it was buried behind that veil of icy indifference. But she could sense the volcano beneath the ice, churning, ready to erupt—not with heat, but with frigid, remorseless fury.

Which way would the explosion radiate, though, without the object of his hatred to catch the fallout?

Wayne had disappeared, and Amory Wyatt, his partner in the bloodletting, had escaped without a trace. He was gone without so much as a follicle of hair to be found in the house he had lived in for more than four years.

Amory had become an indelible part of the county as director of social services. He had been seen as kind, compassionate, and generous. Yet, he was made of the same brutal cloth her father had been cut from.

"You don't seem overly upset that Daddy Dearest is gone, Amelia." Powerful arms folded across a broad chest, stretching the material of the black T-shirt he wore over the hardened muscles beneath.

Amelia could only shake her head as she fought past

the trepidation rising inside her. "It doesn't seem real," she finally answered, terrified to believe in it. "For so long I prayed—"

Another hard shake of her head and she cut the thought off.

She hadn't meant to say that. She hadn't meant to reveal so much.

And of course Crowe had no intention of letting it go.

His eyes narrowed, long, thick lashes lowering over his gaze as he paced closer to her, his arms dropping from his chest, his hard body tense, as though prepared to defend himself every second of his life.

"Prayed for what, fairy-girl?" The jeering reminder of the nickname he had given her so long ago jarred her senses.

Once, he'd whispered the pet name with arousal thickening his voice. The rasping cadence had been a part of memories guaranteed to leave her aching with longing, even now.

"To be free of him." Forcing back what she'd nearly said, she shoved her hands into the hidden pockets of the dark-gold broom skirt she wore as she hunched her shoulders against the chill building beneath her flesh.

"You knew who he was." He made the accusation suddenly with knowing silkiness.

Amelia shook her head desperately, her hands immediately leaving the comforting warmth of the pockets to bury into the sides of her hair as she clenched in the strands. Fighting her fear had always been the worst part. She was such a coward, and always so terrified that her own actions would result in a friend's persecution, arrest, or, even worse, Crowe's imprisonment.

"I didn't know!" she cried out, feeling the heat of his body as her eyes jerked open to the sight of his chest far too close to her.

Immediately her hands were against the softness of his shirt, desperate to push him back, to force back her own aching needs and the dark fears she couldn't rid herself of.

Or the shadowed rage building inside her.

"Then why pray for your freedom?" Broad, callused fingers wrapped around her arms, the warmth of them sinking through the cashmere material of her sweater.

"Because he was desperate to destroy you." She had to escape his touch. "I had to pretend you didn't matter. That none of you mattered. That no one mattered. I had to search for evidence against you." Tears filled her eyes. "I had to lie through my teeth and make it sound convincing whenever I asked if the Callahans could be part of those atrocious deaths while he pretended to defend you." Her voice broke as agony rushed from the dark, once hidden depths of her soul where she had pushed it so many years ago. "I had to hate you just to be able to save you. And God help me, yes, I just wanted to be free of it."

She had sacrificed everything she was, everything she had ever wanted to be, to save him. To ensure her father couldn't destroy him.

"You knew he was the Slasher," he repeated, slicing deeper into her soul.

"You know that isn't true." A sob escaped her lips as she pulled back from him, tried to pull back from the heat searing into her flesh. "If I had known in time, I would have warned you."

Had she suspected? Was that where the fear had come from for all those years? That terrifying knowledge that something dark filled the soul of the man she was supposed to call father.

Crowe released her, but rather than backing away to give her space, he continued to move closer. She retreated until he had her back against the wall.

"I didn't know," she repeated, agony resonating through her as he caught her wrists, anchored them in one hand, then brought them slowly above her head, forcing her to the tips of her toes as she strained away from him. "What are you doing, Crowe?"

"He didn't want to kill Logan, Rafer, or me," he told her. "He wanted us imprisoned. He wanted us out of the county for the year the trusts our parents left us specified as the amount of time we could be out of Corbin County before we lost everything they wanted us to have. He wanted to watch us suffer."

"I didn't know what he was doing," she protested again, though she feared he was deliberately ignoring it, just as he would ignore any proof she had that she wasn't lying.

"He wanted to destroy everything we loved." Fury throbbed just beneath the hard growl of his voice and echoed in the silent fire beginning to blaze in his eyes. "He and his fucking partners raped and murdered any woman we touched and did everything they could to frame us for those murders."

And they had nearly succeeded more than once.

"I didn't." She had to force the protest out, because he was touching her. Whether in anger, hatred, or the intent to harm, still, he was touching her and God help her but she had ached for so long . . .

A whimper left her lips as his hard chest pressed against her breasts, his hips into her lower belly, and the raging erection beneath his jeans angled at her navel.

She could feel how hard he was, remember how hot, how intent he could be while pushing inside the wet, aching depths of her body.

"He almost took everything we cherished, Amelia," he reminded her, his eyes brilliant in the darkness of his face, in the sudden arousal that suffused it. "He nearly destroyed Rafe and Logan and the women they loved, and he made certain he tracked down every woman we may have even considered having as a lover."

"I didn't know!" she cried out again as his free arm wrapped around her hips and pulled her up his body until he jutted his hips between her thighs, the denim-covered erection notching against her sex. "Please, Crowe, I would have stopped him if I could have. I swear. If I had known, you would have known."

"He dangled you beneath my nose like a fucking piece of steak before a hungry wolf, Amelia," he told her, his tone brutal. "He was daring me to take you."

She couldn't think about that; she didn't dare.

"Please, Crowe. Let me go." The plea was whispered but no less desperate for its lack of force.

Her loss of strength against him was terrifying. The feel of his body, all lean hard muscle and raging male hunger, was more than she could deny herself.

She had ached for so long.

Ached for his touch. Ached for the perfection of pleasure she had found in his arms so many summers before.

"Let you go?" His head lowered, his lips brushing against the line of her jaw. "Do you really think that's going to happen, Amelia? After all this time, after the effort he went to in teasing me with you?" Strong teeth nipped at her jaw before the warmth of his tongue eased over the little ache. "Dared me to take you. Have you considered why? Have you considered the punishment he had in store for you if I ever dared to take what was so subtly offered and he learned of it?"

She couldn't—

"Please don't do this to me." Her head fell back against the wall, tilting to the side as his lips moved slowly down the sensitive column of her neck.

So slowly.

His tongue licked against the nerve-ridden flesh, his

teeth scraped against it, sending pleasure racing with fiery force along her tender nerve endings.

He was going to break her in ways Wayne had never been able to break her. He would destroy that last dark, hidden place where she had stored the most important memories, the deepest depths of her love for him.

"Don't do what to you, sugar elf?" he whispered, one hand sliding beneath her skirt to her bare thigh as his hips rolled, the hard wedge of his cock pressing against her suddenly swollen mound. "Don't pleasure you the way I've been tempted to pleasure you? Don't take what I was offered every fucking time you stared up at me with those pretty eyes?"

A moan escaped her lips as he gripped the flesh of her neck in his hard teeth, his tongue lashing at the skin there with exquisite hunger. He refused to give her a chance to catch her breath, or a chance to deny him. Just as he refused to allow her to place any distance between them.

"God, I've hungered for you." His fingers slid farther along the inside of her thigh, finding the elastic edge of her panties and rubbing against it erotically. "Have you been hungry for me, Amelia? Have you been wet for me, baby?"

Wet for him? She had been so wet for him over the years that it had been all she could do to keep her panties dry.

His fingers slipped beneath the elastic edge of the silk-and-lace panties and found the slick heat covering the swollen lips of her sex.

Amelia froze, her lashes immediately rising, focusing on Crowe's as he lifted his head and stared down at her.

Lust burned in the dark depths, predatory and filled with a heat that seared her to her soul.

"Crowe . . . please . . ."

Suddenly his fingers were no longer just caressing her; the tips of two pierced her entrance, sending heat raging through the intimate flesh. Spiraling, brilliant arcs of pleasure tore through her system as her hips jerked forward, her inner flesh now desperate for more.

"Oh, God, yes." That moan couldn't be hers, could it?

It was, she knew it was.

"Like that, elf?" he whispered at her ear, his teeth raking against it as her hips rolled against the penetration. "Do you want more?"

"More." She was ready to beg for it. "Oh God, please, Crowe . . ."

Brutal, shocking heat tore through her.

She remembered the night he had taken her virginity, the searing, white-hot pleasure and pain that had engulfed her, and knew that sensation again. His fingers filled her, stretched her, piercing her with dominating strength.

"So hot," he growled at her ear as his fingers moved inside her slowly, stretching her, making her ache for more even as her flesh burned and protested the invasion. "Sweet, sweet Amelia. So hot and wet."

She was falling again. Amelia could feel it, knew what was happening, and knew it would destroy her. It had happened like this before. Crowe's touch, the power of his hunger combined with her own overwhelmed her, only to rip her heart from her chest when he walked away from her.

"Don't," she cried out, shocking herself as well as him. "Please, don't . . ."

Don't destroy her. Don't own her again only to toss her away.

"Don't?" The snarl in his voice ripped another cry from her soul as she forced her hips to still. To stop the needy roll, the outward thrust into each penetration that forced his fingers deeper.

"Let me go."

"No . . ."

"Please, Crowe," she cried out desperately, pushing against his shoulders, feeling the orgasm beginning to build as his fingers found that sweet, sweet spot deep inside her. "Oh God, please let me go."

She was free so fast she nearly crumpled to the floor.

Slapping her hands against the wall behind her to catch herself, she stared up at Crowe as his own hands braced against the wall above her head.

"This time," he snarled down at her, fury raging in his eyes, darkening his expression until every plane and angle was suffused with it. "Just this time, Amelia. But you better fucking pray you can convince Wayne I'm actually sharing not just your bed but also your body. Because if you don't, then I promise you . . ."

His head lowered until they were nearly nose-to-nose.

"I promise you, if you don't convince him we're lovers, then I'll make damned sure we become lovers. I'll do whatever the fuck I have to, to ensure he shows himself."

Amelia stared up at him with a sudden, horrifying knowledge.

He would use her, however he had to, to draw Wayne from wherever he was hiding.

He wasn't there for her.

He wasn't there because he ached for her, or because he needed her. He was there because he wanted vengeance.

He needed it.

He ached for it.

Crowe was hungry to make someone, anyone pay for the lifetime of hell he'd been forced to endure, and if he couldn't find Wayne and make him pay, then he would make her pay instead.

A harsh, pain-filled sob tore from her throat. Shock and misery filled her until she swore she couldn't hold more, only to feel it building inside her further. Tears slipped from her eyes as she stared up at him.

Oh, God, how she loved him.

She loved him until the knowledge of what he could do to her, what he was already doing to her, sliced at her soul like a dull knife. The pain caused her stomach to pitch, the coffee she had drank earlier churning in it.

"I can't . . ." She couldn't survive this.

She couldn't survive his pain, the agony of his knowledge that a man who had once claimed to be his friend had all but destroyed his and his cousins' lives.

She couldn't survive knowing what she had come from, whose genes she shared and what the monster who had helped create her had actually done.

She could feel the blood on her own flesh now, the iron bite of it in her mouth, gagging her.

"Amelia." The rage was gone now. He reached for her again as she tore away from him, unable to bear the agony resonating through her a moment more.

The thought of him touching her, of him taking her, of staring into his eyes and knowing she was judged by the actions of her father had her heart ready to explode, her mind racing in terror.

She couldn't let him do this, to her, or to himself. The world would soon know who had terrorized the Callahan cousins. Everyone would know, and when Crowe had to face her, when his disgust with her could no longer be hidden, it would kill her.

"Don't you walk away from me again, damn you!"

His curse forced her to acknowledge the fact that she was moving. Turning, she raced from her bedroom, down the hallway, desperate now to escape the house.

It was cold outside, the brutal mountain air carrying the certainty of snow, but she didn't pause, didn't think of what she was racing into. Only what she was desperate to escape.

He was so close. She could feel him as she neared the front door.

Reaching out for it, her fingers within inches of the knob, she was suddenly grabbed, swung around, and forced against the door.

"Let me go!" Amelia screamed as he pulled her against his harder body, one hand burying in the hair at the back of her head and angling her head back until he could stare into her eyes.

"The hell I will." Releasing her hair, he gripped both arms and lifted her to the tips of her toes. He glared down at her, fury pulling his lips back from his teeth in a silent snarl. "I want him dead, Amelia. Fucking dead. And you'll help me draw him out. Whether you want to or not." He gave her a hard, furious shake. "Do you fucking hear me? You will help me."

"And what makes you think I can help you?" she screamed out, the pain destroying her. Yet somehow she had a feeling she knew exactly how he expected her to help him.

"Destroying our women seems to be his favorite sport. How do you think he's going to handle it when he thinks his daughter has become my woman?" Pushing away from her, Crowe flexed his fingers, fighting to ignore the need to touch her again, to feel her silken flesh against his fingertips.

He swore he could feel the heated warmth of her flesh, even in his dreams. Swore his fingertips ached with the need to touch her when he awoke deep in the night searching for her warmth.

"You would do that to me?" The betrayal in her eyes slapped at his conscience, but strangely, her voice lacked any hint of the anger he'd been prepared to deal with.

Still, her soft turquoise eyes stared back at him with bruised betrayal.

Betrayal?

How had he betrayed her?

All his life he'd dealt with her father's betrayal and had never known where it originated. He'd had no idea Wayne Sorenson was the monster stalking his family.

But Amelia hadn't known, either.

Hell, he knew she hadn't known. He knew she'd had no part in it, but the rage burning inside his soul was like an entity all its own, its only ability that of striking out at one of the few people he knew would always forgive him.

But that didn't mean he wouldn't use any means necessary to achieve not just her future safety but also the safety of his cousins and their wives and children.

"I would demand this of the fucking Queen of England if it meant ending Wayne Sorenson's reign of terror over my family, Amelia. If that hurts your feelings, then by God I'll apologize once I see his ass six feet under."

He watched as she turned slowly away from him, the weariness in her expression punching him in the gut. Because he knew it was his fault. He had put that look in her eyes, and he hated himself for it.

What the fuck was he doing, not just to her, but to himself as well?

That bastard had all but destroyed him over the years, but that was no excuse for what Crowe was doing to her. For hurting the innocent sweetness that had always been such a part of his fairy-girl.

"Very well," she said softly, her back still to him. "I'll play the game." But when she turned around, the pain that had filled her eyes was gone. The weariness pushed away. Staring back at him was just . . . emptiness.

An emptiness he swore he'd see replaced, soon, with heat.

As soon as Wayne was dead.

"I won't let him hurt you again, Amelia," he vowed. That vow was all he had left to give her until the bastard was out of both their lives.

"I swear, I'll never let him hurt you again."

Somewhere inside her soul a scream was echoing. Her entire spirit felt wounded, and Amelia had no idea how to make the pain stop.

"You didn't let him hurt me the first time," she said, her voice distant. "That was my choice, Crowe. Just as it's my choice this time. Remember that."

As his eyes began to narrow on her she turned away from him and slowly opened the front door.

She was exhausted. It took everything she had just to survive this chaotic storm of anger, pain, and memories. She couldn't deal with him, couldn't deal with the guilt and hunger he added.

"You should leave now." He had to leave, before she completely shamed herself and begged him, pleaded with him—

"Amelia." The warning tone of his voice had her back and shoulders straightening.

"You will leave. Now. I said I'd play the game, Crowe. But only the game. Once you've decided the rules, then come find me. Until then, get the hell out of my life."

She didn't like the smile that curled his lips or the blatant promise that filled his gaze.

"I'll do that, for tonight." She had a feeling his agreement had very little to do with her demand. "Be ready tomorrow, sugar elf. Because bright and early, you'll have the rules. But once this game is over, all bets are off."

Without explaining the statement he left the house.

The second he cleared the door, Amelia closed it behind him, locked it firmly, and set the alarm.

Moving hurt, but she forced herself up the stairs to the balcony. Stepping outside she collected the key she'd always left hidden for Crowe before stepping back into her room and locking the door behind her.

She'd tried.

She'd tried so hard to ensure that Wayne didn't carry out his threat to have Crowe arrested and imprisoned when he'd learned she'd helped Crowe destroy the files seven summers before. At the same time, she'd placed herself in danger more times than she could count by ensuring he could never again build another case against the Callahans. And all the while, she'd lived with the horrifying fear that Wayne or, God forbid, the monster trying to destroy the Callahans, would learn her greatest secret.

Instead, she had begun to suspect the most horrific evil she could have imagined. And it had all begun with the lie she had overhead Wayne telling Archer Tobias. The lie that he had no personal involvement with Amory Wyatt.

Six days later she learned the truth of the monster he was.

Amelia had begun following her father the night she'd overheard him deny knowing anything more about Amory than his identity. That night, she'd waited and watched as Amory slipped into the house, then she'd tried to follow them after they left.

She'd tracked their movements in a journal and took pictures with the small field camera she'd bought.

She had gone to the scenes where many of the young women who had been murdered over the years had been found, and she'd stolen and copied files of the investigations from the sheriff's and county attorney's offices.

But she had no more than her own gut-wrenching fear and suspicion.

She hadn't had any evidence. All she was the knowledge Wayne had lied about his whereabouts the night Katy Winslow had been killed.

He hadn't been at the house that night, and he hadn't been ill as he'd told the sheriff when he was asked why he hadn't answered his cell phone that night.

Wayne had claimed he had taken cold medicine and hadn't heard the phone.

Somehow, though, he'd known she was following him. That she was trying to find even the smallest kernel of evidence that supported her suspicions.

How had he known what she was doing?

Was it the look on her face when he'd walked into her room and her head had jerked up from the computer?

Had she looked as terrified as she felt when she looked up the stories of the young women whose deaths were attributed to the Slasher?

Or had he been watching her as she had been watching him?

Whichever, he'd paused, staring at her, then smiled with chilling evil. "Ah, Amelia," he'd sighed. "And here I'd hoped to spare you."

Amelia had to cover her lips with her hands to hold back a sob as she fought against the memories of that night.

She didn't want to remember. She didn't want to relive the hell she had visited until Amory Wyatt had carried her from the cabin and drove her to that mountain clearing below Crowe's cabin.

She didn't want to remember.

And now Crowe was making her remember. Even worse, he was making her agree to walk through hell for him again rather than running for the freedom she'd dreamed of.

A freedom she knew she'd never realize until Wayne was dead.

Yeah, she would play the game. And she would even play by his rules, if possible.

And when it was done, she wondered, would she be free of the past, and the memories? Would she be free of them or would she only create another nightmare she didn't want to face when morning came?

Amelia had a feeling she was only going to create another nightmare.

Especially if Wayne had his way. Or if—God forbid—he learned the one secret she would give her life to keep hidden away just a little longer.

Most especially if Wayne ever learned what she had hidden from him.

CHAPTER 2

By God, he was going to kill her.

He should have killed her when he had the chance. Before she had done this to him.

Before Amelia had betrayed him.

Wayne Sorenson leaned forward, his arms braced against his stomach as panic rushed through his system and threatened to send him into a furious rage.

All his dreams were shattered.

Lifetimes, generations of searching, and he had lost it all.

He watched as the cavern beneath Crowe Mountain was breached, the artificial wall his ancestor had created to hide the legacy he and his son had amassed over the years turned to brittle stone and dust. And inside, a fortune of gold, jewels, and priceless artifacts gleamed dully beneath the cameras' light.

Found.

A week after Wayne's partner and then his daughter had betrayed him, and now, the Callahans had it all. They'd taken everything.

His dreams.

The dreams of Clavern Mulrooney's direct descendants

had fallen into the hands of the hated Callahans. The descendants of the bastards who had stolen the land and murdered the captain and his son before their fortune could be reclaimed.

Where was the fairness in this?

"Ms. Sorenson, do you have a statement? Your father hasn't been found yet, nor has his partner. Do you think they're watching?" A whimper escaped Wayne's lips at the journalists' excited questions as he watched the attention shift from the fortune to those watching the revelation.

His precious daughter.

She stared back at the cameras, satisfaction gleaming in her turquoise gaze as she addressed the journalists.

"Wayne's watching," she said with a tight smile as she stared back at him through the television screen. "He won't be able to help himself. And I hope he knows this ends it. It's over, Wayne," she stated softly. "And you lost."

The camera turned from her to one of the journalists who somberly nodded as he faced the camera's eye once again and gestured back to the once hidden cave with a jerk of his head. "The treasure, as per an agreement with the state of Colorado as well as the federal government, will be split with fifty percent going to the Callahans for the generations of persecution by Wayne Sorenson and his ancestors. The Callahans will place the treasure in a museum that will be created on the coming resort property Avalanche, which will be overseen by the Callahan family. The other fifty percent will be auctioned off to benefit the families of the young women murdered by Wayne Sorenson and his partners, Thomas Jones, Lowry Berry, and Amory Wyatt . . ." Excitement suddenly transformed the journalist's expression. "And here's the spokesperson for the Callahan family, Crowe Callahan. Mr. Callahan." Microphones were suddenly thrust into Crowe's face as more than one journalist now vied for position. "Mr. Callahan, do you have a statement? What would you tell Wayne Sorenson if he were here at the moment?"

Wayne watched as Crowe reached out and drew Amelia to him. Lights were suddenly exploding as Amelia turned her face into his broad chest.

"What would Sorenson think of your relationship with his daughter?"

"Mr. Callahan, can you verify the rumors of a relationship with Ms. Sorenson stretching back to the summer she graduated from high school?"

"Mr. Callahan, can you comment on the rumors of Sorenson's murder of his daughter's ex-husband?"

The questions were flying, and all the while, Crowe stared back into the camera with an expression that had a scream building in Wayne's throat.

"It's over," he stated, and Wayne knew the message wasn't for the journalists or the world that would see it. "This ends it."

He pushed through the microphones, journalists, and cameramen to make his way from the caverns that led from beneath the mountain he had always called home to the lake that lapped gently against the sheer cliff rising from the edge of its waters.

Fury rode Wayne hard as he picked up the unregistered cell phone he'd acquired from the rough table in front of him and punched in the number he knew by heart.

"Callahan," Crowe answered immediately.

"It isn't over," he snarled, teeth clenched. "It isn't over, Callahan."

Crowe laughed.

That laughter struck at Wayne, enflamed the fury burning through him.

"Then come get me, Wayne," he chuckled, pure amusement racing across the line. "Because it's all mine now. The treasure you could have had if you'd just asked for it, the daughter you tormented, the town you tried to destroy. It's all mine."

Wayne disconnected hurriedly, the faintest hint of a click over the line assuring him the call was being traced. Pulling the device from his ear, he stared at it for a long moment, his chest heaving, fury tearing through him, before he suddenly threw it and watched it hit the wall across from him and shatter.

"It isn't over!" he screamed in fury, jerking from his seat and pacing to the window that overlooked Sweetrock.

The hunting cabin was well hidden; he'd made sure of that. It was the only haven he had left until he could arrange his escape from the States.

And there would be no escape until Crowe Callahan suffered. Not until Amelia lay dead and bleeding while Wayne watched that bastard take his last breath.

It wasn't over.

They had committed the ultimate sin of stealing the last dream Wayne could cling to. And he had committed the sin of infecting his daughter with his filthy touch.

It wasn't over . . .

A smile curled at his lips, his gaze narrowing as he considered one last play he could make. It was iffy, he admitted, but workable. It was a last-resort maneuver, but he needed a miracle at the moment. And he'd planned for just that to aid his escape. Instead, he'd use it to aid the Callahans' destruction. Yes, it just might work.

Three days later

It was almost over.

That mantra had been all that had kept Crowe from going insane over the past ten days.

It was almost over.

Now it truly was almost over.

The discovery of the cache of pirate gold and lost treasures in the Colorado mountains had stunned not just the Callahans, but the country. Televising the moment the cavern was breached and allowing the world, allowing Wayne, to see it first, had accomplished his aim, but in a way that, Crowe admitted, he hadn't expected.

He'd expected Wayne to come after him, not the actual treasure as it lay under close guard in a secure safe room at the offices of Brute Force.

That one, he'd surprised Crowe with.

Surprise or no surprise, Crowe had been waiting for him. The son of a bitch hadn't even made it out of town before Crowe was on his ass in the powerful sports car his partner had loaned him. Just in case the need to chase Wayne to ground arrived. Now, maneuvering the powerful little car as it headed into the mountains, Crowe could see the end in sight.

Sirens blasted from behind as the sheriff followed closely, racing behind Crowe's and Wayne Sorenson's vehicles while a news helicopter tracked the chase.

The car Ivan Resnova had loaned Crowe took each curve beautifully, hugging with expert precision. Crowe couldn't have asked for a more powerful ultra-performance vehicle to race through Corbin Pass and torment the other man with his inability to lose him.

The three vehicles were heading up the winding, dangerous pass road that wound its way up Callahan Peak, then continued to Aspen. The former county attorney was taking the sharp bends as though they were child's play in a tan sedan that had obviously been equipped with a hell of a motor.

Crowe knew Corbin Pass and Callahan Peak well. He

knew better than to drive this road at the speeds they were currently clocking, but he'd be damned if he'd let Wayne get away now.

"Son of a bitch," Crowe muttered as his borrowed sports car held the curves at ridiculous speeds while the car ahead of him nearly slid over the side of the mountain at the sharpest angle in a turn.

That sedan wasn't going to hold itself on the road for long unless the other man slowed down significantly.

"Call from Sorenson, Wayne," the feminine tone of the Bluetooth announced over the earbud. "Accept or deny?"

God how he wanted to reject that call.

"Accept," Crowe finally barked.

As though anything he could say or do could ever make a difference at this point.

"What do you want, Sorenson?" Crowe growled when the call connected.

"Should I prepare a list?" Wayne asked, his voice calm, sad, despite the effort Crowe knew it was taking to control that damned vehicle.

"Forget your list, Wayne," Crowe said, fury and cold, hard mercilessness spreading inside him. "If you survive this mountain then you'll still have to deal with me. And you know what I'm going to do."

"Kill me?" Amusement laced Wayne's tone. "So sorry to disappoint you, Crowe. Well, perhaps I'm not. But I can't allow you that pleasure, though I very much hope that should I indeed go over one of these cliffs, I'll have the pleasure of taking you with me. Too bad Amelia isn't here as well."

"Keep hoping, asshole," Crowe drawled, ignoring his mention of Amelia. "It's not going to happen."

A hard breath echoed over the phone.

"Every time I see you, I see your mother, do you know that?" Wayne asked, his voice hollow. "All the fury of a woman betrayed mixed with the disbelief, horror, and shattered trust that comes when you believe a true friend was the one to steal the hopes and dreams harbored in your soul. That was my Kimmy as her eyes filled with tears, her lips trembled, and she begged for the life of that whimpering brat she held to her heart."

His mother, Crowe thought. The son of a bitch had killed his own parents and his cousins' parents during one of the worst blizzards to ever rage in the area twenty-four years ago. All that had saved the newborn Kimberly Callahan held in her arms had been her pleas and some demented emotion the bastard had felt for her before her marriage.

Crowe clenched his teeth, forcing himself to listen, hating the bastard, but knowing the confession in the recorded call would be all they needed if Wayne somehow survived.

"I thought baby Sarah Ann would ease my pain," he continued, speaking of the infant sister Crowe had believed was dead for so many years. "I knew she would be the image of her mother, and she is. But I never really see the heart and soul of my Kimmy in her."

Silence filled the line.

"Are you there, Crowe?" Wayne asked softly.

Crowe didn't answer, only clenched his hands tighter on the steering wheel.

"Yes, you're there. I can feel the fury, and hatred. The pain," Wayne said.

Crowe's teeth were locked tight, clenched to hold back the rage building inside him.

Clenched so tight that his jaw felt as though it might crack.

"It wasn't Sarah Ann that held her mother's heart and fire, though. It was you, Crowe. I think that's why I couldn't kill you in all these years. I couldn't kill your cousins, either. Kill them and you might actually leave. You might turn your back on everything here and never return. It took me until last night to realize why I hadn't killed you. That's why I couldn't do as I planned and just kill you after—"

Silence.

Crowe had to laugh.

It was a bitter, furious sound as he rounded another hard curve and watched the back end of the sedan fishtail again, dangerously, before righting itself.

"You can't even say it, can you, Wayne?"

Wayne snarled back at him.

"Then allow me. After you put a fucking bullet straight through my mother's heart and killed her in cold blood—"

"Never!" Wayne suddenly raged furiously. "God no, Crowe. Never. I had already killed the others, even her precious David. I was blind with rage and jealousy. I had to make myself finish it. I had gone too far."

"You didn't have to do it," Crowe snarled. "You didn't have to kill any of them."

"They knew!" Wayne screamed. "You don't understand! Somehow they found out about everything. My past, my wife's death. The location of the treasure. They knew it all and they wouldn't even tell me where it was. I had to kill them before they made it to Sweetrock and the Corbins. They would have destroyed me."

"Sucks to be you, Wayne," Crowe bit out furiously. "And now you've lost it all. All we have left to find is your wife's body, right? Then I have no doubt Colorado will reinstate the death penalty just for you."

"I won't let that happen." Wayne's voice was guttural, furious.

"You don't have a choice," Crowe told him.

"Tell me, Crowe, how will you continue to take my

daughter to your bed, knowing my blood runs through her veins and will run in the veins of her children?"

"I'll handle that far better than you'll handle knowing I've always had her loyalty. Freely. From the time she was sixteen, Wayne, she would get hold of us and tell us everything you and our grandparents were up to," he reminded Wayne. "I had her complete loyalty while you've had only her hatred."

"No—" Wayne began.

"Yes," Crowe snapped. "She has always been mine, Wayne, and you didn't even have a clue, did you?"

"You bastard!" the other man screamed.

Crowe watched as Wayne forced the car around the next bend without so much as hitting the brakes.

The car fishtailed, but rather than recovering like before the back end slipped farther, the driver's-side tire hitting the narrow shoulder.

Adrenaline raced through Crowe's veins. His gaze narrowed as he watched Wayne fight to recover.

Fought and failed.

Sliding, aware of Archer doing the same behind him, Crowe watched as the sedan slipped over the cliff.

Wayne's scream over the Bluetooth connection was cut off as the sound of the metal smacking stone reverberated through the canyon.

Increasing his own speed, Crowe raced around the next curve before twisting the wheel and sliding into a turn that put him on a dirt road leading to the canyon floor.

Sorenson wasn't the first victim Corbin Pass had claimed.

As the sports car straightened and headed toward the canyon floor an explosion rocked the cliff, causing the little car to shudder and nearly slip on the dirt road, throwing it sideways before Crowe could compensate.

A quick flip of the wheel, a harsh curse, and the car's tires bit into the dirt, pulling it back quickly as a fireball suddenly swept above the small canyon, nearly reaching the edge of the road before retreating.

"Burn in hell, bastard," Crowe muttered as the sports car slid into the narrow canyon, rocking to a stop as he stared at the flames engulfing the sedan and the body that could be seen still sitting behind the wheel.

Crowe stepped from the car, standing next to it as Archer pulled in behind him, barely missing the back of Ivan's sports car.

Before the vehicle had stopped shuddering from the abrupt stop, the driver's-side door was flung open and Archer was out of the powerful wide-built jeep he drove and striding up to him.

They watched as Wayne's car and Wayne himself burned.

The flames were intense enough that Crowe suspected they were fueled by more than the violence of the crash into the canyon.

"He was fucking crazy." Archer sounded shocked. "You know he patched me as well as that news helicopter into that call, don't you?"

Crowe hadn't known that. He was damned glad he hadn't said more to Wayne.

"Then you heard his confession?" Crowe stated.

"Me and every person watching on television," Archer agreed.

What did it matter? It was over now.

The Slasher was dead.

"Nash and John are on their way," Archer said. "John's going to be glad it's over. Maybe now he can relax and stop killing himself trying to watch over two sisters he's terrified he can't protect effectively."

Amelia being one of those sisters. Hell, it was hard to

believe the undercover agent was actually a son to the bastard.

"Yeah, it will be a hell of a relief," Crowe agreed.

It just didn't feel right, and he couldn't figure out why.

The hairs on the back of his neck rose while a sense of foreboding had his shoulders tensing. Something wasn't right.

Wayne watched the vehicle burn. Somber, regretful.

He'd imagined one day getting to know the cousin now burning in the car he had rigged with an explosive.

As far as the cousin had known, he was being paid simply to draw Crowe up the pass where Wayne could assassinate him. He'd been more than eager to take the job, no matter the risks, just to have the money to pay the medical bills from his daughter's illness.

The other man hadn't even suspected what was coming.

Wayne had helped him don the latex mask that ensured Crowe would believe he was chasing Wayne. He had then given him precise orders.

Orders that had been followed implicitly.

Hell, maybe he should have considered partnering with that cousin rather than Thomas Jones all those years ago. Wayne had a feeling he'd have been the perfect partner if he'd chosen him before the birth of his daughter sixteen years before. Unfortunately, he had cared so much about that daughter that he hadn't considered the drawbacks or possible deceptions.

It had been too late to change the plan, though.

No one knew about the cousin, Jimmy Bowers, or his connection to Wayne. The man's DNA would be close enough to Wayne's to get the FBI off his ass, hopefully.

At least long enough for Wayne to take care of his daughters and Crowe Callahan.

Him and those arrogant cousins of his.

His only regret was Amelia.

Had she simply stayed away from Crowe as he'd warned her to do, then she would have been safe. Had she not betrayed him for Crowe, then Wayne would have just let her be after Amory's betrayal.

She could have lived.

But he couldn't allow her to live now. Not after a Callahan had defiled her body. Still, if he wasn't mistaken, he knew his enemy's greatest weakness. He only wished he'd known earlier how much his daughter had meant to the other man over the years.

Wayne knew how to destroy Crowe Callahan now.

He'd seen it in the recorded broadcasts of the news stories. He'd heard it in the bastard's voice.

Crowe was in love with Amelia, whether he realized it or not. Taking her from Crowe would destroy him.

CHAPTER 3

Wayne was dead.

Or so it appeared.

Leaning forward in the large, dark leather chair, Amelia watched the chase up Corbin Pass for what had to be the hundredth time since it had actually occurred six hours before.

Eyes narrowed, she focused on the tan sedan as the news helicopter recorded its race up the mountain.

From the moment Sheriff Archer Tobias had called in the sighting of the suspected serial rapist and murderer, chaos had reigned. News helicopters, reporters, and journalists had flooded Corbin County, Sweetrock, and the Ramsey Ranch in Pitkin County, Colorado.

Then they had all but surrounded the house Amelia had lived in during her marriage years before, next to her father's property, searching for her. It hadn't taken them long to learn she had moved back into the main house after her husband's desertion five years before.

Amelia's life had gone from bad to worse when the media arrived. As if it could have gotten any worse after her father had kidnapped and almost killed her weeks before.

Like he had killed so many other young women. Like he had killed her mother.

"Admitted serial rapist and murderer," the reports always stated.

Wayne had admitted to his atrocities as he spoke to Crowe and Archer, just before going over the cliff. He had admitted to years of murders in an attempt to destroy the Callahans, steal their land, and recover a treasure that had been hidden for generations.

Wayne hadn't had to admit to it, though.

She had known it was Wayne and Amory the night she was kidnapped. The night he'd attempted to kidnap and kill Crowe's sister, Anna. Not just because his partner, Amory, had mentioned Wayne's name, but because she had heard his voice herself. Because he had stood over her that night as she lay drugged and helpless, stroked his hand down her arm, and in that low, deep tone that always sent fear racing up her back assured her it was going to hurt when he allowed Amory to kill her.

It was all she could do to swallow back the bile that rose in the back of her throat at the memory. God. How had she not known—how had she not at least suspected him for the monster he was?

When the car exploded on the television, the fireball reaching nearly to the top of the canyon wall, Amelia's fists clenched as a sense of satisfaction filled her.

And a sense of trepidation.

And suspicion.

"Too easy," she muttered, covering her face with her hands as she fought the panic building in her chest. "There's no way he would have 'let' that happen."

"Where did you see him let anything happen?"

Amelia was on her feet, swinging around as adrenaline surged through her system. Coming face-to-face with Crowe was a shock to her senses, she realized. It always had been. Her heart beat faster, her body became primed, her mouth dried out—but farther down, that sensitive flesh between her thighs became far too wet.

She had been expecting him, yet still the effect he had on her was instant. From the moment she heard that the chase was occurring, she had known he would be there soon.

That didn't mean she had to like it. It didn't mean she'd known when to expect it.

She clasped her hands in front of her, preparing herself to weather this meeting as she did every other meeting with him. Without fracturing from the inside out with the pain of what she had lost over the years.

Those predatory amber-flecked brown eyes followed the movement, the hard line of his lips quirking with some unspoken humor.

He really had changed since the night she had helped him steal that file from Wayne, she noticed again. The dark, hard planes and angles of his face had matured and hardened. The compassion and warmth that had once filled them was no longer apparent. His wolf-colored eyes blazed from within his face, giving him the appearance of a warrior while his hard body assured her he had the power to be just as lethal.

There were a few lines at the corners of his eyes. *Life lines,* she liked to call them. The unsmiling curve of his lips, the hard, strong line of his jaw, his stubborn chin.

He was tall, nearly six and a half feet, without so much as an inch of fat on that hard body. Dressed in jeans, boots, and a long-sleeved white shirt under a black leather jacket, he could have been a gunslinger or a Native American chief from decades past.

And he never failed to steal her breath, making her heart race and saturating the flesh between her thighs with her need to be possessed by him.

In the weeks since the discovery that Wayne was the Slasher, Amelia had pretended to be Crowe's lover. She had been at his side during the discovery of the treasure Wayne had sought and remained quiet whenever it had been suggested that they were involved in a relationship.

Those were the only times she had seen him, the only times he had touched her.

As she watched, he slowly shrugged the jacket from his shoulders. Her gaze was drawn to the breadth of them, her senses to the memory of the feel of them beneath her sensitive palms as she scraped them with her nails.

Those shoulders had rippled with strength, and tightened powerfully as he moved above her.

"You seem doubtful that he's dead," he stated as he laid the jacket over the back of the old wingback chair next to the family room entrance.

Doubtful? Was that what she was feeling? No, she was feeling terrified. "Excuse me for being skeptical, Crowe. I may not have known he was the Slasher until the night he kidnapped me, but I did know how calculating and ruthless he was. I won't believe it until the DNA tests prove it's him."

She couldn't take the risk that he had somehow managed to fool everyone.

She had far too much to lose, and far too much to protect.

Releasing the hold she had on her own hands, Amelia fought to restrain the anger and the pain that had built over the years. The hunger, the need: They were all tied together, one and the same, and tormented her each time she was around Crowe.

"Archer had the body transported to the morgue, and Nash will be sending out for DNA tests. The county hasn't purchased the equipment for it yet," he informed her.

She was well aware of that. "Wayne blocked the purchase three years straight," she remembered bitterly. "No doubt to ensure that he, or his partners, would have the time to escape or for Wayne to corrupt any samples."

"No doubt," he agreed, hooking his thumbs in the front pockets of his jeans as his gaze roved over her body slowly.

Her breasts swelled immediately, her nipples rasping against the lace of her bra as his gaze paused at them.

Remembering?

Did he remember how sensitive he could make them? How they responded with such intense pleasure to just the thought of his touch?

"Why are you here?" she finally asked nervously before realizing she'd once again clasped her hands protectively in front of her. "How did you get in this time?"

The smallest curl of mockery pulled at his lips. "That lock on your balcony door upstairs isn't nearly as secure as you think it is. And the alarm is so easy to trick that a three-year-old could do it."

Wonderful.

"So you're just checking to make sure I'm safe?" she questioned him, before taking a moment to stem the anger threatening to override her control. What had made her think he'd be there for any other reason? "Why, thank you for your consideration, Mr. Callahan. Shall I see you out?"

See him out when she wanted to scream, to rage because she couldn't have what she needed, she could never have what she ached for. And not just because of Wayne. Once Crowe learned the true extent of her deception, he would hate her.

A low, amused chuckle vibrated from his chest, stroked over her senses, and had her clit throbbing harder in need.

Hell, her whole body ached for his touch. Every cell was on high alert and straining toward the warmth of his flesh.

He made her want to hope, when she knew better.

"Do you really want to see me out?" he asked, his head inclining quizzically as mocking amusement filled his gaze. "With all those reporters outside?"

Amelia glanced toward the windows, her lips tight in displeasure. The shades were pulled, the heavy curtains tightly closed against the glare and flash of cameras.

Even before she had been released from the hospital after the twenty-four hours of observation, and an intense interrogation by the FBI, Sheriff Archer Tobias, and the Callahans' lawyer Lucas Grace several weeks before, reporters had begun showing up.

She'd had to turn her phones off. She knew better than to answer the door; no one was out there but reporters demanding a statement.

"I wish they would just go away," she burst out, pushing her hands through her hair before glaring back at him. "I hate having all the windows so tightly covered all the time."

"They need their pound of flesh," he told her. "But they'll go away. Eventually."

She stared back at him angrily. "That's easy for you to say. It's not your pound of flesh they're trying to strip off."

Without waiting for another one of his asinine comments, Amelia turned and stalked to the kitchen.

"That's very true," he agreed as he followed her. "But have no fear, sweetheart. Until I've taken what I want of your pretty little body, I promise not to allow anyone else to take what they want."

Amelia was certain she couldn't have heard him correctly.

She turned slowly and stared back at him. "What did you just say to me?"

She hated the *almost* smile he gave her. That tight curve of his lips. There was no softness there, and no mercy.

"You heard me," he told her. "You're mine first. Until I'm finished with you, then no one else can have any part of that lush little body." Leaning against the counter, Crowe crossed his arms over his chest and arched his brows with an arrogance that had her teeth gritting.

"I don't deserve this attitude or your smart-assed remarks." And she didn't think she could bear the hurtful, unemotional quality of them, either.

He laughed, a merciless, hollow sound. "Logan, Rafe, and I didn't deserve to be orphans, disowned and torn from our families. My sister didn't deserve a life of emotional isolation, and every lover any of us had didn't deserve to be raped and murdered. And I'll be damned, but I didn't deserve the nightmares I had nightly that one of us would fuck up, and you'd be next."

Before she could register the fact that he had moved, his hands were gripping her shoulders, his voice rasping furiously, his eyes blazing more brilliantly than ever.

He wasn't cold any longer, but now she felt as if her heart were suddenly in danger from the man standing in front of her.

"Do you think I didn't have nightmares, too?" Her voice broke on a sob, the memories of her haunting fears rushing over her. "But I wasn't afraid for myself, Crowe." She had to fight back the tears that would have fallen. "I was terrified you would disappear as Stoner did. That would have destroyed me."

As quickly as he had grabbed her, Crowe released her at the mention of her ex-husband.

"You think Wayne is the reason Stoner left you?" He turned back to her, his gaze suddenly shuttered, his face brooding.

Did she think Wayne had been behind it?

Amelia would have laughed at the question if the situation had been less nerve racking.

She knew he had been behind it. "After he left, Wayne came to my room and assured me he had taken care of all of it," she remembered bitterly. And she couldn't help but feel the smallest measure of gratitude to the bastard for that. She was certain Wayne hadn't meant to be merciful, but that one time—

Crowe laughed, a hard, bitter sound that had her flinching. "Hell, Amelia. Did you really care that much for him?"

"I hated him." The sharp exclamation surprised him. "He was a bastard who deserved to be castrated and imprisoned—"

"He was a disease that needed to be eradicated. Trust me, Amelia, all he deserved was a bullet to put everyone he knew out of the misery he caused them." Amelia flinched at the rage that seemed to radiate from Crowe.

She'd once thought she knew this man far better than anyone in her life, but she'd never imagined he would condone murder.

Even if he felt it was deserved.

Facing him, her chin lifted, her hands planting on her hips. "He deserved to be punished, not put out of his misery. Killing a man like Stoner Wright is a waste of a damned good sin better used for something a hell of a lot more fun."

And of course, she should have watched what she said around this man.

"Such as?" he growled, moving closer to her again, his head bending to give her the full force of his imperious gaze.

Her eyes widened then narrowed as she all but rose to her tiptoes in confrontation. "I can think of far more interesting sins for you to commit, Crowe," she snapped back at him. "And would have thought you could as well." Her gaze flickered over his face, the savage planes and sharp angles, the brooding, heavy-lashed eyes, and his merciless gaze. "Or have you lost the imagination you once had?"

Then, his lashes swept to half-mast, his expression suddenly turned so blatantly sensual it sent a wave of pure, fiery lust sweeping through her body.

"If it's sinning with you, then I do indeed have a hell of an imagination."

Completely male and erotic, the look on his face, the sound of his voice, and the sudden shocking contact as he pulled her against his very aroused body had a surprised cry falling from her lips.

Her palms flattened against his chest, but whether it was to push him away or to absorb the heat of his body, even she couldn't say for sure.

What she did know for sure was that the air around them heated, growing heavy and saturated with a sexual hunger she hadn't shared with anyone but Crowe in her life. That same intensity burned in his gaze as his eyes glittered with hunger and male dominance.

Her body, betrayer that it was, responded immediately.

Her breasts, already swollen, her nipples already tight with the need for his touch increased their responsiveness. Between her thighs the folds of her pussy swelled, her clit throbbing, pulsing, greedy for the slightest touch as the need to climax began to burn in her womb.

She couldn't handle this.

She knew the danger of it, the risks that came with allowing him to touch her, allowing herself to need his touch.

"What are you doing?" she whispered, hearing the aching need in her voice. "You know this isn't wise."

"When was I ever wise where you're concerned?" One hand moved from her back to clasp her waist before pushing beneath the soft cashmere shell she wore with a black skirt.

Inhaling sharply at the feel of his callused fingertips and palm against her sensitive flesh, Amelia found herself helpless against the wave of erotic pleasure flooding her senses.

"We can't do this." A hard gasp broke the thought as he cupped the curve of her breast, tested the rounded firmness, then investigated her achingly hard nipple.

Pleasure raced from the hard peak to the throbbing bud of her clit, then clenched the delicate tissue of her vagina.

"Why can't we do this, elf?" he asked, his voice a sensually dark croon. "Trust me, I bet both our parts are in fine working order." His strong teeth nipped gently at the full curve of her lower lip. "Just think, we don't have to hurry now. You won't have to smother those wild little moans and I won't have to restrain this completely primitive need I have to leave my mark on your skin where everyone will see it, and know by God that you're claimed, Amelia." Possessive hunger exploded from him with a force she couldn't have prepared herself for.

His lips covered hers, parted them, and turned a meeting of flesh into a stamp of dominance that Amelia found herself helpless against. Found herself luxuriating in her helplessness, in the complete submission of her senses to this one man.

Something primitive and so primally female it seemed to burn in the very depths of her senses surged to life as he held her to him and stoked that flame to a full, hungry blaze.

Each dart of his tongue against hers, each stroke of his thumb over the responsive tip of her nipple, each new press of his erection into her lower stomach fanned the flame higher, brighter.

Her hands caressed his shoulders, the need to touch his flesh growing—but it hadn't yet overcome the need to hold on to his kiss. Instead she fisted her fingers in his hair, heard his muttered groan as she tried to pull his lips tighter to her, to feel that same lash of pleasure-pain she had felt that summer so long ago.

She had ached for this.

She had dreamed of it.

Nothing—oh God, nothing had ever been this good, felt this wild and incredible.

"Ah God, Amelia." His lips left hers, his kisses moving over her jaw, his tongue taking brief tastes, his teeth nipping sensually as the fiery caresses moved to her neck.

Ultrasensitive, completely responsive, the flesh beneath her ear was so tender, so susceptible to the stroke of his lips, his tongue, that the nerve endings seemed directly connected to each sexual center of her body.

His lips covered that bit of flesh just beneath the lobe, tugged it into the heat of his mouth, and began drawing on it with slow, sensual hunger. It sent a rush of sensation stabbing at her nipples before streaking heatedly to her womb, where the sharp clench and burn had a lash of fiery heat striking repeatedly at her clitoris.

Oh God, she was going to come.

"Crowe." The strangled cry was either pleasure or protest—even she wasn't certain which.

Another brilliant pulse of sensation surged through her system, immersing her in such a storm of incredible, sensual hunger that she felt lost.

Pulling back, Crowe gripped the hem of her cashmere shell and dragged it over her lace-covered breasts. His head lowered, his lips burying between the curves, his tongue licking lazily, sensually at the sensitive flesh there.

Amelia's breath caught. His lips were so close to her nipples.

The small latch at the front of her bra released, allowing

him to push the delicate lace cups from her breasts, baring her curves to his gaze.

Amelia stilled as his head lifted. Forcing her eyes to open partway, she stared up at him.

"How fucking pretty," Crowe breathed out roughly, one hand cupping the swollen weight of a breast as he rubbed over the tight, hard peak with his thumb. "Such a pretty pink, like the sweetest candy, and so tight and hard."

The dark croon sent a rush of sensation to tighten spasmodically in her womb.

"I dream about sucking those pretty nipples." His head lowered as he brushed his lips against the violently sensitive little tips.

"Oh God—" A hard, brutal flex of pleasure centered in her womb, pulsing outward and nearly hurtling her over that edge of sensation into release.

Lifting his head, he stared down at her, his brown eyes piercing and hungry.

"How long has it been, fairy-girl, since this hot little body has come from the pleasure it was given?" he whispered, though the demand in his voice was unmistakable.

Heat flooded her face at the explicit question.

"Don't—" Before she could voice more of the protest a strong, male finger lay against her lips.

"Uh-uh," he said firmly. "Answer me, Amelia. Tell me how long it's been."

She couldn't. Oh God, she couldn't tell him. The shame of it was unbearable. Her fingers fell from his hair to his neck.

"I *was* married," she reminded him desperately.

Pure fire erupted in his eyes. Savage, intense, the fury that blazed in the rich amber of that predatory gaze caused her eyes to widen. "Amelia, don't bother lying to me by saying that little bastard made you orgasm," he rasped, his tone grating. "Because I promise you won't like the consequences." His head lowered, his lips brushing over a tight peak again.

Immediately the pleasure returned in fiery spikes of sensation.

"Who was the last man to bring this pretty"—his tongue swiped over the hard tip as she cried out desperately—"pretty little body to its release?"

"Why does it mat—" A cry tore from her throat, her body tightening, sensation striking in a furious burst of heat in her core as he covered her nipple with his lips, sucking it into the heat of his mouth with a blazing, fierce hunger that had him drawing on it with tight, deep pulls of his mouth.

A second later the fiery heat was gone just as quickly, his head turning as his cheek rested against the painful ache of her nipple.

"Tell me," he demanded again, his voice harsh. "Tell me, Amelia. Or I stop now."

Stop? Oh God, she couldn't bear it if he stopped.

"You!" she cried out desperately, twisting against him as she tried to tempt him to pull the throbbing, swollen flesh back into his mouth.

His head lifted, his gaze heavy-lidded, possessive.

"You," she whispered again. "I've only come for you."

CHAPTER 4

It was as though Amelia had been lost, wandering aimlessly in a cold, deserted loneliness until Crowe touched her.

Until his lips possessed her, his dominance warmed her.

Before, she had been helpless in a world of manipulations and a desperate battle to ensure Wayne never destroyed the man who owned her heart, or the secrets it sometimes seemed she had sold her soul to protect.

Now she could be free.

There was the smallest chance Wayne was gone forever.

But even if he wasn't, the world now knew him for the monster he was, and the power he had controlled was snatched from his grasp.

And she was in Crowe's arms again.

"Don't stop," she begged brokenly, certain she couldn't bear taking a breath without the pleasure rippling through her.

His head lifted. "So long," he whispered. She felt him release the little clip of her skirt, then slowly ease the zipper over her hip.

The silk slid down her legs to pool about the four-inch heels of her black pumps.

"Sweet merciful heaven," he breathed, lifting her arms to remove the cashmere shell. When she lowered them again he brushed the straps of her bra over her shoulders; they slid down her arms and to the floor next to her skirt.

Left clad in silk thigh-highs—the lacy band circling her leg just below her thigh—and black silk-and-lace French-cut panties, Amelia felt her nakedness as she never had before.

Her breasts felt heavy, her nipples aching and hot. Her skin was so sensitive, the brush of the air against it was nearly physical.

"Hold on to me," he demanded, gripping her hips as she moved her hands immediately to his shoulders to balance herself.

In the next second he was settling her rear on the kitchen island, parting her legs and moving quickly between them.

"This is crazy."

She moaned, her head tipping back on her shoulders as he cupped the swollen curves of her breasts.

She was helpless. The moment he sucked her nipple into the moist heat of his mouth, the world around her disappeared.

Vivid, pulsing heat struck at her pussy as his tongue lashed at the sensitive peak. Sensation poured through her—brilliantly hot, spilling slick, heavy moisture as her body prepared itself for his possession. Her stomach clenched, stealing her breath before the sensations struck at her clit, swelling it tighter, pushing her closer.

If he would just suck the tender flesh tighter and amplify the rising sensations already burning through her.

"So good," she panted, her voice rough, rasping.

She didn't even recognize the sound of it.

All she recognized was the rising demand for more.

More of his touch, more of his kisses and the wild hunger burning between them.

As she lifted closer to him, his lips released the pleasure-tortured tip long enough to order, "Look at me, fairy-girl."

Her lashes lifted drowsily, her gaze falling to his then to where his tongue peeked out to rub against the velvety point as one hand stroked down her belly, his fingers finding the wet silk between her thighs.

"Hell," he groaned. "This is why you were at the spa last week?"

This was the smooth, curl-free folds between her thighs.

Had she somehow known this night would come?

"Ah hell, Amelia!"

Awe? Regret? What emotion filled his voice as his fingers slipped beneath the leg band of her panties to find the bare folds of her sex.

And the slick layer of her juices covering them.

Should she be ashamed that even as he touched her, more of the slick, heated dampness spilled from her?

Should she be embarrassed as his fingers stroked, caressed, and left her gasping for air?

"Oh baby, you're so hot and wet," he muttered against her nipple.

His touch glanced over her clit. The violent wave of pleasure that suddenly struck at her senses pushed her so close to her release that her breath caught. She was certain the little wave of ecstasy would bury her beneath the explosive sensations her body was so desperate for as he found her other nipple.

A second later the firmness of his touch eased, pulling her back from that edge—only to push her higher once again.

"Crowe, please," she cried out desperately, widening her legs farther, hips arching forward to let his fingers find the clenched, snug entrance of her sex.

Rclcasing hcr nipplc again hc liftcd his head, his gaze meeting hers as the tip of his finger began easing inside.

"Sweet tight little pussy," he crooned. "As tight as you were the first time I had you."

The first time she had been a virgin.

This time she knew what was coming.

His fingers eased deeper inside her.

"Crowe. Yes, God, please . . ."

The violent shaft of sensation rocked her body with fiery bursts of such exquisite pleasure she was certain release was only a second away.

Pulling back, still using a single finger, he penetrated to the farthest depths of her vagina then *rubbed.*

Whimpering brokenly, her nails digging into the shirt covering his shoulders, she fought to fall from the edge of complete rapture he had her poised on.

"Please. Crowe, please," she cried out, hips writhing, ecstasy threatening to overtake her.

"Shh," he murmured, his gaze dark and filled with lust. "I won't leave you hurting, baby. I promise."

But she was hurting now.

She knew she would hurt later.

Her womb clenched again, a hard spasm of pure sensual intensity that once again stole her breath.

"Easy, baby," he breathed as he pulled back the deep thrust of his finger.

"Easy?" she gasped, disbelief filling her for a brief second. "Are you crazy, Crowe? You're killing me."

In the next second her eyes opened wide, lips parting on a breathless, soundless scream as two broad fingers pushed inside her.

They stretched her, opened her.

Her inner flesh rippled, flexing around the intruders, her juices spilling to slicken and heat the delicate muscles as Crowe stroked and rubbed inside her with each firm thrust.

"Do you like that, fairy-girl?" he ground out, his voice a hard, hungry rasp as he worked his fingers inside her again, twisting, stroking sensitive tissue, and violently awakening nerve endings.

Amelia leaned back slowly, desperate for each sensation, locked in a battle to reach that farthest edge of sensation where complete rapture waited.

"Oh God, yes." Strangled, shocked, breathless: The sound of her own voice barely penetrated the haze of pleasure surrounding her, sinking inside her.

"Lie back for me, Amelia."

Leaning over her, he eased her to her back before dropping a kiss on her lips and straightening once again.

With one hand he guided her feet, first one then other, until they rested against the edge of the island, her knees bent, thighs splayed.

Forcing her lashes to lift, she watched him, his golden gaze locked on her pussy as his fingers slid back, releasing his possession of her, despite the tight flex of her muscles tightening around them.

How had she lived all these years without this? How had she lived without *him* for so long?

"Crowe." She would have sobbed his name, but she couldn't find the breath. "Please . . . please . . ."

Bending over her again, his fingers began moving inside her as she worked her pussy against each hard thrust, feeling the pleasure building, her body tensing.

Dressed in nothing but high-cut panties, the leg band straining where he'd simply pushed it aside to possess her, Amelia found herself wishing she'd simply omitted the panties altogether that morning.

"Deeper," she begged, her voice harsh, desperate, burning need searing her vagina as the clenching, steadily rising hunger and pleasure surged higher with each fierce stroke of his fingers inside her.

"Deeper, baby?" he moaned against her breast as he began kissing his way down her torso to the tight clench of her stomach.

Before he moved to the sensitive flesh between her thighs, he held the silk to one side and paused long enough to watch his fingers retreat from her inner flesh, thick juices coating his flesh.

A second later he took her again, the digits pushing in deep, hard, nearly sending her exploding into bliss.

As his fingers thrust inside her, his tongue flicked over the swollen bud of her clit. He tasted her with quick, firm flicks of his tongue and hard, tight suckling kisses along her flesh.

Amelia couldn't hold back her cries.

Pleasure swamped her, infused her. Crowe's lips and the heated interior of his mouth drew on the hard point, sucking it firmly, his tongue rubbing it, rasping against it as he fucked her hard, deep, sending jagged flares of ever-deepening pleasure to pierce her senses.

The hard knot of her clit swelled further, pulsing as the storm shook her body and flares of sensation tore through her.

Sensation exploded inside the tortured depths of her pussy with a violence that dragged a gasp of agonizing pleasure from her lips. Echoing stronger, deeper in her womb, it peaked in her clit in a furious explosion of pleasure. It was both agony and ecstasy.

Cataclysmic. Furious.

The sensations held her in a grip of overwhelming, burning rapture.

She wanted it to last forever. She feared another second of it would destroy her.

Locked in the grip of pure sexual intensity, she wanted

nothing more than to burn in the sensual flames until nothing else existed, until nothing could pull her from it.

Crowe jerked at his belt, the painfully hard erection beneath his jeans demanding Amelia's attention.

He'd learned over the years that no other woman could ease that clawing need locked in his balls.

No other woman had the power. Only Amelia had ever satisfied that need.

A need he'd never known until he touched her, possessed her, seven years ago.

As he slipped the leather belt free, the computerized alarm system gave a harsh beep before announcing, "Basement entrance."

Amelia jerked at the sound, her eyes widening. She came off the island counter, scrambling for her clothes.

Eyes narrowed, he watched her frantic search for her clothes, then the fumbling haste to get them on.

He had no fear, no sense of worry or concern for her safety, but her nervousness definitely had him curious. So curious he crossed his arms over his chest and leaned against the counter to wait.

"Would you not just stand there?" she muttered, moving hurriedly from the family room back to the kitchen.

She was now fully dressed, her hair a little less mussed than it had been, her expression irritated.

His lips parted to ask her exactly what she wanted him to do when she suddenly gasped,

"Oh my God! Crowe, fix your belt. Now!"

His brow lifted.

"Basement stairs." The computerized voice announced before Crowe could say anything.

"Fix it now!" she hissed before quickly turning around in front of him as though to hide the fact that he had been preparing to undress.

"Amelia," he growled, fixing the belt. "What the hell—"

Before he could finish, Amelia's new-found brother, John Caine, stepped in the kitchen, his expression hard, his gray eyes flat and cold.

At the sight of Crowe, he relaxed marginally, though the question in his eyes as he looked between Amelia and Crowe was unmistakable.

Amelia nervously cleared her throat before stepping to open the refrigerator.

"Do you two want a beer, or coffee?" she asked, breathless, her hands shaking.

"Get out of the kitchen." Stepping to her, Crowe pulled her back before closing the appliance. "He doesn't want a beer."

"How do you know?" Pulling her arm from his grip and shooting him a glare, she looked ready to shatter from nerves.

"Because I've known him far too long for either of us to be comfortable."

John only grunted.

"Oh." She turned back to John slowly before frowning at Crowe again. "Then you knew he was investigating Wayne as the Slasher?"

He could see the accusation in her eyes, the fear that he had suspected Wayne and hadn't told her.

"Unfortunately, I didn't," Crowe assured her. "Nor did I know he suspected Wayne was his father. If I had, then I might have figured things out quicker."

"I doubt that." John stepped farther into the room, suspicion filling his eyes as his gaze lingered a second too long on Amelia's neck before he looked at Crowe. "It didn't help me figure things out quicker."

There was a silent warning in the man's eyes, and Crowe knew it was for him. The warning to stay away from

Amelia tempted Crowe to prove that *no one* would keep Amelia from him ever again.

"I wondered why your truck was outside." John at least tried to show a little tact where the question was concerned.

"Why did you think it was out there?" Crowe drawled.

Surprisingly, Amelia was the one who spoke up. "Crowe just stopped by to make certain everything was okay." She cleared her throat as she clasped her hands in front of herself again. "The reporters are still refusing to leave."

"Bastards," John bit out. "They'll give up soon, though, I think. There's not much more to report now that Wayne's dead."

John crossed his arms and leaned against the doorway, giving Crowe a look that promised they would talk later.

Crowe grinned back at him. "I was just curious."

"By the way," John's gaze moved to Amelia, "I left my bags downstairs. Just tell me where you want me to put them."

Crowe stiffened furiously. His bags? Dammit to hell. John moving in with her?

"You can take Wayne's suite. That way you'll have plenty of time to see if the FBI missed anyplace that Wayne could have hidden the rest of his journals or anything else they're still looking for."

"What's missing?" Crowe asked.

"My mother's heirlooms, and all the money he had in savings. He'd been slowly making withdrawals over the past few months, and just before Amory kidnapped me, Wayne withdrew all my savings as well."

The last comment had her voice filling with worry.

"Amelia, I told you, you don't have to worry about the money," John told her. "I'll take care of everything."

John didn't see what Crowe did in the stormy blue-green depths of her eyes or in that stubborn curve of her chin: determination to take care of herself. Over the years, she'd never asked anyone for a damned thing. If he wasn't mistaken, though, a hell of a lot of people in this county hadn't minded asking her for favors.

Especially favors that would get them out of trouble with Wayne Sorenson.

"I appreciate the offer, John, but I told you, I'll take care of it." There was no hiding the firm refusal in her voice. "I won't be a charity case, especially to the brother I've only just found. He would have had to hide the cash here in the house; it's the only place he would have been assured of being able to check on it daily."

"We'll see then." Her brother nodded, his gaze gentling as he stared back at her. "If it's in his rooms, I promise, I'll find it."

Watching Amelia, Crowe found it impossible to understand how a man could be as cold and cruel to his child as Wayne had been to Amelia. She was so delicate that even understanding how she had endured the many "punishments" was an impossible feat.

"I'll show you up to the suite." She glanced at Crowe again before heading to the doorway. "I'll get clean linens if you'll show Crowe the basement entrance." The suggestion was made in a less-than-steady voice as she paused at the doorway and glanced back at him, her eyes dark, wary. "Good night, Crowe, and thank you for checking up on me."

He inclined his head mockingly, letting her see in his gaze the knowledge that he she was running from him.

"I have to go away for a while, Amelia," he told her, watching as she paused, her back still turned to him. "I'll be gone for about six weeks. When I get back, be waiting for me."

The soft, dark strands of her hair brushed below her shoulders as she turned back to him. "I stopped waiting for you a long time ago, Crowe. A very long time ago."

His teeth clenched, grinding furiously at the sudden flash of something filled with pain and bitterness that flashed in her eyes.

"See you soon, fairy-girl," he promised.

Heat flooded her face at the intimate name, and a hint of anger tightened her lips, but she didn't say anything more.

Turning, she all but ran from him like a frightened doe in hunting season.

Crowe restrained his chuckle, well aware of John's scrutiny and the disapproval in his gaze.

"Come on, I'll show you the way out," John growled as he rubbed at the back of his neck. "How the hell did you get past that horde out there if you came in another way?"

It really wouldn't have mattered how he came in; he could have done so without the journalists being aware of it.

"I'm just good like that," he claimed as John led him from the kitchen.

And through the dining room to a narrow hall at the back of the house.

"I just bet you are," John muttered under his breath.

Crowe pretended he didn't hear the comment, though he had a feeling John knew better.

Just as Crowe knew better than to believe that John didn't know about the training Crowe had in the military. And that the training would have ensured his ability to enter the house without being seen.

Opening one of the hall doors, John stepped inside long

enough to flip the light switch and brighten the rough-lumber steps leading to the basement.

This feature was not part of the plans sent to the county after they begin keeping such records, though. Crowe knew it wasn't, because Crowe had gone searching for the house plans during those first weeks, seven years ago, when he'd begun secretly seeing Amelia.

The rough drawing submitted after Wayne's father purchased the house indicated no more than a four-foot crawl space beneath the house.

"Interesting." Crowe gazed around the open, though cluttered basement. "Believed in saving everything, didn't he?"

If the antiques were any indication, more than three generations had been storing their cast-offs down here.

"No kidding," John agreed. "The attic is worse. You can't even walk around up there, let alone figure out where to look for anything in particular."

The basement was far smaller than the house above it and, if he wasn't mistaken, laid out a bit oddly.

"Stay away from her, Crowe."

Well now, hadn't that just been thrown out of the blue, Crowe thought, amused.

Narrowing his eyes, he gazed out at the basement for long seconds before he finally turned back to the other man.

"That's not your decision to make," he reminded the deputy. "And even if it were, it wouldn't do you any good, John. Don't try to stand between me and Amelia, because I promise you, I won't stand for it."

John's lips thinned, his gaze turning cold. "You don't have a choice. You used her to draw Sorenson out of hiding, and I don't appreciate that. I won't let you use her again, no matter the reason. She doesn't deserve it. And by

God, *you* don't deserve *her.* Not anymore. Not the man you've become."

Crowe nodded as though considering the warning before smiling mockingly. "There's where you're fucking wrong," Crowe assured the other man, letting him see the full, blazing determination that filled him. "I do deserve her. I deserve her far more than you even know, John. And if you think I'll let you stand in my way, then you're wrong."

"Dammit, Crowe—"

Crowe turned on him slowly, forcing back the humanity it had taken him years to find again after leaving the military.

The man John saw now was the stone killer he had been then. The killer John knew existed in his past.

"Yeah, I know what you are," John sneered. "I may have not reached your level, Callahan, but that doesn't mean I wasn't invited there."

Crowe let his lips tilt further. The operation he was part of was so much higher than the invitation this man had been given, it was laughable.

"An invitation is one thing," Crowe said softly, "the years of training afterward is another. Don't think you can take me on, John. Your association with my uncle won't save you. He should have warned you of that."

"But has anyone warned my sister about you?" The air around the deputy sizzled with fury. "And isn't she just a little innocent for you? Find a woman with enough experience to handle that ice your heart has become."

"She can handle it just fine," Crowe promised him, wondering how pissed Amelia would get if he punched the bastard in the face. "Now let's end this little pissing contest before one of us says something you may regret."

The hard line of John's jaw tightened furiously as he

let his anger rule him rather than using it to strengthen him. Maybe, Crowe thought, John should have accepted that invitation just for the training that went with it.

"The grudge is what I worry about," John snapped, the gray-blue of his gaze sparking with charged energy. "What will that grudge dictate where Amelia's concerned, Crowe? She's Wayne's daughter. She was raised by him, she worked with him. Try to tell me you'll ever trust her enough to let that ice around your heart melt for her, and I'll call you a liar. The only reason you're here now is because she's that final snub you can give Wayne by actually getting into her bed rather than just letting him believe that was where you were."

"And I'll be there, in her bed," Crowe promised him. "He teased me with her for seven years. Had I suspected for a second who he was, John, just for a second, then I would have taken her and dared him to come after her," he added softly, dangerously. "Now Sorenson is no longer here to hold her from me, or to threaten her. Don't doubt this: I will have her now."

John drew himself stiffly erect as Crowe let a hard, confident smile curl his lips. "You think I won't warn her about how you feel?"

Crowe smiled. "Why bother? You and I both know she just heard every word I said."

Reaching up, Crowe tugged at the digital audio-video line only barely visible in the small gap between the overhead ceiling tiles and the wall.

"Next time, try using less wire. That way it doesn't end up revealing itself," Crowe suggested before tipping two fingers to his forehead and striding past John and leaving the basement.

Crowe ignored the somber regret that filled the deputy's gaze.

He ignored the jagged, unexplained strike of pain deep

in his own chest at the knowledge that Amelia wouldn't have been able to resist listening, watching, any more than he could have resisted if the roles were reversed—and just how angry he would have been.

Amelia stared at the video screen John had wired into her room when he had installed the more advanced security system. When he'd wired in the audio she'd rolled her eyes at him.

He had grinned and told her it would eventually come in handy. It always did.

Now part of her wished she'd never let him do it. At the very least, she wished she hadn't turned it on to see Crowe one last time. Watching him leave, seeing his icy expression, the hardness in his eyes made her wish she'd just seen him out herself instead of giving in to the need to run and hide.

This was what she got for being so hungry for him that she had to see him.

This is what she got for loving him.

But all she was to him was the final snub at the man who had destroyed Crowe's entire family's life.

Wayne had murdered Crowe's grandparents and parents, and had tried to see him and his cousins imprisoned since they were teenagers.

Having her in his bed, and breaking her heart, again, would be the ultimate prize because evidently he didn't consider shattering her soul seven years ago to be enough.

She had six weeks before he would be back, roughly the same amount of time before the DNA results on the body believed to be Wayne's would be in.

And if Wayne was dead, it was six more weeks before Amelia could have her life back.

If.

God, she prayed it was over. Only then could she have

more than just her life back. Only then could she have the one dream that had sustained her after losing Crowe. The only thing that had held her here, that had kept her fighting, breathing, living.

The chance to finally be free . . .

CHAPTER 5

Six weeks later

Crowe stared at his copy of the DNA results, just as his cousins Logan and Rafer stared at theirs—with a sense of pure, unadulterated rage and disbelief.

He was aware of the others in the room as well. His uncle, Ryan Calvert; Archer Tobias; the FBI special agents assigned to the Slasher case, Elliot Weston and Jake Donovan; as well as the forensic experts Nash Callum and Dr. Joseph Edger.

"The clue that tipped us off was the remnants of the latex mask." Nash spoke into the silence as Crowe slowly closed the file and looked up. "It was made with a special polymer that should have disintegrated completely, but they didn't get the mix just right. The amount of latex used allowed just enough of it to adhere to part of the skull for testing. From there, we began running the DNA against all known databases, and we got damned lucky. Jimmy Bowers actually sold DNA samples to a testing facility over twenty years ago and allowed the DNA to be included in a batch shared among government research agencies. From there, we were able to trace his connection to Wayne through John Caine's DNA. But we also ran the samples against Amelia to connect them to Wayne and came up negative."

"Because she's not Wayne's daughter," Crowe stated softly, only barely managing to hold back the satisfaction raging through him.

"No, she's not," Nash agreed, the dark brown of his gaze somber as it met Crowe's.

Son of a bitch, Sorenson was still alive. The bastard had once again managed to escape.

"What is he, fucking Houdini or something?" Rafe muttered, slapping the report on the table before throwing himself back in the chair and pushing his fingers through his hair.

Raw disgust filled Rafe's expression as well as Logan's.

Crowe felt the door he'd managed to open on his humanity slowly begin to close.

"Where is he?" Crowe directed the question to the special agents.

"We don't have a clue." Special Agent Weston breathed out heavily as he leaned forward, his arms crossing on the top of the dark conference table, his gaze gleaming. "But according to the profile we have of him, he's close enough to know exactly what's going on, with whom, and where. And he's just waiting to strike, when you least expect it."

And he would strike at Amelia.

The thought had Crowe's entire body tensing with the need for action. She would never be safe, she would never be free until Sorenson was dead. It was the only way to ensure he never harmed her again.

And there was only one way to draw him out—

"Unless we force him to make a move again," Crowe mused, narrowing his gaze and staring back at the agent coolly.

Weston nodded slowly.

"His daughter," Agent Donovan guessed, his attention now on Crowe as well. "That drew him out before."

"But there was no proof we were lovers, only supposition." Crowe nodded. "If he continues to think we believe he's dead, and Amelia and I begin a very public affair . . ."

"Then he could snap," Donovan agreed. "But I think we keep the truth of her parentage to ourselves. Wayne learns that she's not his daughter, he won't give a damn what happens to her."

The agent was wrong, Crowe knew; Wayne would still care. It was Amelia he'd have to keep that information from, though. If she found out that she wasn't related to Wayne it would give her the out she needed to possibly leave Corbin County, and Crowe couldn't allow her to do that.

She belonged to him.

She might not like it, she might not want to admit it, but he wasn't going to allow her to run from it. They had something to finish. Whatever had eased the ice beginning to overtake him seven years ago, haunted him. He'd been completely frozen inside after he'd left. So frozen that at times he worried himself. He nodded slowly, aware that his cousins stared back at him in disapproval.

"You can't keep that information from her, Crowe." It was Logan who hissed the protest beside him.

He turned to his cousin slowly. Dark blond hair, intense blue eyes with only the faintest shadow of the steel-hard core of determination he possessed.

"You'd do it," he replied coldly. He turned his gaze to Rafe. "As would you in the same situation. Don't try to tell me you wouldn't."

"We would protect her, Crowe," Rafe swore. "Just like you've protected Cami and Sky."

"I know you would," he agreed. "If you could. But trust me—she'll run. The minute she learns Wayne isn't her father, she'll go, because she'll believe he won't care anymore. But we all know he will. We all know he'll kill her, just like he's killed the others. And he'll do it faster because she's not his daughter."

The muttered curse as Rafe sat back once again was all the agreement Crowe needed.

"You're taking a hell of a chance," Archer stated.

The sheriff had stood by them since they were all were little more than boys. Archer had stood against his father, the cousins' powerful grandparents, the men who had run the county for more than forty years, and he'd stood by them as sheriff.

"It's one I have to take," Crowe said.

If she ran, then any chance of catching Wayne might go with her.

"This could have the added benefit of drawing Amory Wyatt back as well," Weston said. "He's only returned to the scene of the kill once, as long we've been tracking him. A similar situation, actually. One of his former partners targeted a young woman he seemed to be fond of while in the area."

Crowe wanted to shake his head, to force that statement to make sense. But he couldn't quite push any logic into it.

Amory Wyatt had gone by a variety of names but the FBI had dubbed him the Master. He took certain serial killers under his wing and aided them, as long as their kills met his criteria, or his warped code of honor.

No one knew who he was, what he really looked like, or where he disappeared to when he was finished. But they did know he would return to an area if a former partner targeted a victim outside his "code." And for some reason Amory Wyatt had decided both Crowe and Amelia were no longer on that list of potential victims. He'd made that clear when he'd left Amelia and another young woman Wayne had kidnapped together on his porch, albeit naked and still drugged, but unharmed.

"Then we could possibly capture not just Wayne, but Amory as well?" Archer mused, his expression harsh.

"If we play our cards right, yes," the agent agreed, his hazel-green gaze calculating as he watched Crowe.

Nothing mattered to Weston but finding Amory Wyatt. The man lived, ate, and slept the search for the serial killer. It was as though it were a personal vendetta for him. Just as the death of Wayne Sorenson had become Crowe's personal vendetta.

"I don't like the means," Archer sighed, agreeing with Logan and Rafer. "And I sure as hell don't like keeping the truth from Amelia, but like Crowe, I can't help but believe she'd run as fast and as hard as possible if she learns she's not Wayne's daughter. It would be her 'get out of jail free' card and we'd lose our shot at getting Wayne once and for all."

"Get real," Weston laughed. "It would be guilt chasing her out of here. You can't convince me she didn't know what he was doing. I just can't prove it. That's all that saved her."

Crowe stared back at the agent with icy disdain, his lips curling in disgust. He leaned back in his chair and watched him for long silent moments. "You don't know Amelia, Weston. Don't presume to understand her or to judge her. Trust me, she's given more to this county in bruises, broken bones, and sheer courage than anyone can imagine. If you even consider attempting to go after her, then you'll deal with me."

"And me," Logan promised.

"And me," Rafe said, leaning forward to glare at the agent.

"Stay away from her," Archer advised him, his voice harsh. "You don't want to take all of us on."

The agent only shook his head slowly, a mocking smile tugging at his lips. "All I want is Wyatt. What the rest of you do with Sorenson and his stepdaughter is up to you." He rose from his chair, motioning to Donovan to follow him before turning and leaving the conference room.

Crowe watched as Weston left, feeling as if there was something was vaguely familiar about him. He just couldn't put his finger on what.

"Amelia finds out you've held this information from her, there will be hell to pay," Logan said, pulling Crowe's attention back to him. "The people in Sweetrock are putting her through hell, Crowe. That would fix all of it."

"Not for much longer, they won't." Rising to his feet and jerking his leather jacket from the back of his chair, he faced the other three men before turning to Nash. "Keep this to yourselves. We draw Sorenson out first. Once he's taken care of, then we'll fix the rest of it."

The nods were reluctant, but he saw their eyes. They would commit themselves until this was finished. Once it was finished, then Crowe would deal with the fallout.

After Amelia was safe.

CHAPTER 6

Amelia hadn't had a migraine in over a year, but oh boy could she feel one coming on now. That building pressure behind her eyes, the heavy throb beginning at her temple.

Yep, migraine.

And its instigator's name was Linda.

Linda Grandor. Well, Linda Justin-Grandor.

The mayor's daughter. And the newly appointed county attorney's wife.

Too bad Linda didn't have the one saving grace her husband had, which was compassion.

Amelia had once believed Linda's mother, Ruth Anne Justin, had that compassion as well, but there Ruth Anne was behind her daughter, obviously backing her. Linda stood on her doorstep now, dressed in a black wool peacoat and stylish leather boots beneath gray wool slacks with expensive black leather gloves on her hands. A mini me of her mother.

At least, outwardly.

Not that Ruth Anne appeared to be pleased with the situation.

"I'm rather busy, Linda. Ruth Anne," she assured them

both as she blocked the doorway and stared back at them firmly. "You should have called first."

Ruth Anne's brows lifted, amusement gleaming in her hazel eyes.

That amusement quickly disappeared when Linda's head snapped around in suspicion as though somehow sensing her mother's defection. Flipping her long, silken blond hair over her shoulder, Linda gave her mother a short, imperious glare before turning back to Amelia.

Amelia had already had enough and moved to close the door in their faces.

"That would be ill advised, Amelia," Linda snapped, pressing a gloved hand flat against the door as Amelia moved to close it.

"I've done a lot of ill-advised things over the years, Linda." Amelia glanced back at Ruth Anne, her expression hardening at the shame and regret that flickered in the mother's gaze.

"And I'm certain once the FBI realizes this then they'll place you in a cell, where you belong."

The accusation had Amelia stilling as the cap on her anger began to loosen.

"My God, Linda, that is enough!" her mother demanded, shocked outrage filling her tone.

"I will not—"

"I will damned well not listen to any more," Amelia decided.

Moving back to slam the door she was caught unaware as Linda suddenly pushed herself inside, her cheeks flushed a harsh red. Anger gleamed in her eyes and curled her fingers into fists.

Hell, she knew Linda, and she knew this wouldn't turn out well. If only she had an ounce of the mercilessness Linda possessed, Amelia thought in resignation as she stood next to Ruth Anne and watched the childish petulance that filled the daughter's face.

"For pity's sake," Ruth Anne muttered, embarrassment filling her expression. "I'm so sorry about this, Amelia."

"Why would you dare to apologize to that killer's little bitch?" Linda suddenly snarled, furious. "Tell her why we're here, Mother. Are you frightened of her? You know her and her family for what they are now, you can stop kowtowing to her."

The moment the words left her lips a dark, heavy shadow shifted, extending from behind Amelia into the foyer as both Linda and Ruth Anne stared behind her in sudden apprehension.

She knew who it was.

"Are you demanding kowtows again, Amelia? And here I thought my kowtows were the only ones you were accepting this week. Shame on you," Crowe chastised her mockingly.

Amelia felt her own fists clench, her back teeth grinding—she just didn't need this.

"Ruth Anne. Linda." Dark, rasping, his voice sent a sexual thrill racing up Amelia's spine as the other two women stared back at him speechless.

Neither of them missed the hand that settled on her shoulder, or the possessiveness in the fingers that gripped her lightly.

"We were just leaving, Crowe," Ruth Anne assured him, the false brightness in her gaze suddenly at odds with the flicker of trepidation in it.

"Mother," Linda hissed, turning on Ruth Anne with just a hint of nervousness. "We have to—"

"Pick up dinner for your father. I know, dear," Ruth Anne broke in seamlessly, firmly, as she gripped her daughter's arm and dragged her ruthlessly through the doorway. "We'll visit with Amelia some other time."

Just what she needed, a later visit.

Amelia made a mental note to ensure her doors remained locked at all times and that Linda and Ruth Anne's names were listed in the do-not-open-for-any-reason file.

"Now, what the hell do you want?" Amelia demanded as she tried to shrug out of Crowe's grip, watching as he gave the door a firm push with a flick of his hand.

The crack of wood against wood seemed overly loud in the entryway as he waited for the door to close before slowly releasing her.

"Does it matter why I'm here?" he asked, a hint of mockery in his voice grating on her already irritated senses.

"Of course it matters. Just as it mattered why they were here." Flinging her hand toward the door, she managed to jerk out of his hold on her to stalk into the family room.

Heavy dark furniture made the room depressing, even with the shades and curtains open and the balcony doors thrown ajar. The only bright spot was the huge, flat-screen television hanging on the wall across the sleek cherrywood of the desk her mother had used for household accounts.

She paused in the center of the room as Crowe moved past her and began pulling the shades closed over the wide windows.

"It's not dark enough in here yet?" she asked incredulously as he moved to the balcony doors and pulled the shades closed there as well.

"There are still a few reporters hanging around town." He shrugged as he turned back to her. "I'd hate to give them something more to speculate on."

It was the look in his eyes.

The amber and brown swirled and shifted, holding her, mesmerizing her as he moved to her, ensnaring her in the brilliant hunger reflected there.

"No." She barely had time to utter the word before she found herself in his arms.

In that single second the years fell away. She was eighteen again, her body hot and eager for his touch, her sensuality an untouched canvas awaiting each stroke of his fingers.

Those fingers threaded through her hair at the back of her head, clenched in the thick strands, and pulled until her face tilted up to him, leaving her vulnerable to his kiss.

There were no preliminaries.

His lips covered her as he ignored the whispered protests, a part of his conscience growling in outrage.

He would just take this kiss, he assured that snarling inner voice. He would take nothing else.

He needed it.

He needed the taste of her, the feel of her. He needed to know she was safe, living, breathing, and still aching for him.

God knew, he ached for her.

The ice surrounding his soul didn't seem as cold or as unending when she was in his life.

His lips moved over hers, his tongue pressing inside. The taste of her, hot and sweet, exploded against his senses as a whimper fell from her lips. A sound more of pleasure than protest as he felt her arms lift, her fingers digging into his hair. Slender and graceful, her delicate little body arched to him, pressing tight against him, tempting the sexual hunger he fought to rein in.

God yes!

The taste of her alone was an aphrodisiac. The feel of her was pure temptation after years of pent-up need.

Her tongue met his as his lips slanted over hers, a little feminine groan of rising need sounding from her. The sound of it ratcheted his hunger higher, harder.

His lips sipped at hers as her hands pulled at his hair.

As though trying to pull him closer, to force his kiss deeper, she tugged the hands full of hair toward her.

She wasn't protesting any longer.

She was demanding more.

She wanted him, needed him with the same hunger he needed her. A hunger raging out of control.

The taste of her sank into his senses like sunlight and a promise. Her tongue twined with his. Lick for lick, touch for touch as their moans met and mingled in the seductively dim light of the room.

Pushing his hand beneath the hem of her sweater, Crowe moved immediately to the front catch of her bra and flicked it open. Pushing the cups back from the rising curves, lust transmitting to a hunger so intense it was all he could to keep his hands from shaking, Crowe fought to rein the hunger in enough to ensure her pleasure, to ensure he didn't hurt her.

A faint little shudder raced up her spine as his hand curved around a swollen breast, his thumb finding and rubbing the tight sensitivity of her nipple.

"Fuck." Tearing his lips from hers, Crowe eased back just to swing her into his arms. "Come here, sugar elf. We need a bed for this."

He had to get her to a fucking bed before he ended up taking her on the floor. He was so hard, so ready to fuck, his balls were throbbing in agony.

It felt as though he had waited forever to touch her.

The stairs were taken two at a time as the heated curves of her lips pressed against the base of his neck. The flick of her tongue seared his flesh with sensation.

She was as ready for him as he was for her. There was no longer any need to allow guilt to flay him, to fear she didn't want him. Hell yes she wanted—she wanted with the same driving desperation that he felt.

Pushing into the bedroom Crowe kicked the door

closed, pausing only long enough to lock the deadbolt before bearing her to the bed.

Somewhere she'd lost a shoe, he thought, as he removed the other and tossed it to the floor before straightening.

"Undress," he said, his fingers going to the buttons of his shirt as his voice rasped with the harsh demand.

Vulnerability shadowed her gaze, but her fingers went to the clasp of her pants as he shed his shirt.

She eased the material over her hips as he tore his boots from his feet. Shedding his jeans, he groaned as the sweater came over her head and fell to the side of the bed a second later, along with the bra he'd unclipped downstairs.

Clad in nothing but black silk panties, the long strands of her hair fanning around her face and shoulders like a dark halo, she seemed surrounded by innocence.

Hard-tipped breasts, swollen and flushed, teased him with the candy-pink promise of her tight nipples. Silken skin sheened with the lightest glimmer of perspiration made her look damned lickable, and there, between her thighs, the black silk of those panties glistened with the evidence of her juices spilling from her sex.

It had been forever since he'd seen her like this, laid out for him, tempting him. Forever since he'd touched her.

His gaze licked over her, from the dampness of her panties to the tight peaks of her nipples.

Then he stared down at the band of her panties again, drawn by a slight shadow peeking out, drawing his interest.

"Take the panties off," he demanded, his gaze moving to her face as she hesitated.

Her eyes flicked to his heavy erection as her fingers clenched in the blankets beneath her. A pink flush of hunger filled her face, washing down her neck and to her already tempting breasts as her gaze lifted to his almost shyly.

Amelia, shy: Even as a virgin she hadn't hesitated to give him whatever he demanded of her. Hell, just six weeks before she had nearly allowed him to have her on that damned counter in the kitchen.

Why hadn't he noticed this then?

His gaze lowered to that shadow again.

Had she actually had her soft flesh inked? And if she had, why was she hesitant to let him see it?

Moving, he stretched out on the bed beside her, his fingers going to the band of her panties. Before he could push the elasticized silk lower, her hand was there to stop him.

She covered the shadow with her fingers as she drew her lower lip between her teeth indecisively.

"You know I'm going to see what it is," he told her softly. "Why are you trying to hide it?"

A frown edged at her brow. "You weren't supposed to pay attention to it."

He had to laugh a bit at that. "Baby, anything that's touched your sweet flesh has great interest to me, especially if it's permanent. I'm a damned jealous man, remember?"

So jealous, it had been all she could do to keep him from revealing their affair each weekend, seven years before.

"Just turn the lights out," she demanded, her brow wrinkling as he pushed at her hand.

Crowe only shook his head before catching her wrist in his hand and pulling it effortlessly over her head, along with the other wrist, and holding them captive.

He didn't glance back up at her, but let his fingers stroke the silken flesh above the band of her panties.

"When did you have it done?" he asked. The thought

of the mark below the material had his dick aching with greater intensity.

"The day before I married—" A hard breath eased from her lips as his fingers touched the dampness of her panties before she could utter that despicable name.

A moan whispered from her lips instead as he gazed from the moisture-soaked crotch of her panties back to the edge of that intriguing little shadow.

God, he was dying to see it, yet a part of him was terrified of what it could be.

She had gotten a tattoo the day before she married. He knew there wasn't a chance the inked brand had any significance to Stoner Wright. What then had been so important to her?

Slowly, his gaze trained on the area, Crowe pulled the band of her panties lower, his breath catching, his jaw locking at the first sight of his wily, impossibly imaginative Amelia.

How long it must have taken to complete that tattoo. But she had done it. There, inked on her delicate flesh, sat a pretty, forlorn little fairy, chin propped on delicate arms that lay across her knees, glaring out at the world. Daring the watcher, determined in her stubborn refusal to relent—

Or daring them to breach the silken material of her panties.

"My fairy-girl," he whispered, brushing his fingers over the colorful little tattoo. "Always mine."

"That wasn't for you," she protested unconvincingly, though the slight moan in her voice as his finger trailed to her thigh spoiled the power of the statement. "I liked fairies before you ever called me that."

And she had. That first time he'd had her had been the night of the county's fantasy-themed social weekend.

"And what a beautiful little fairy you made," he

breathed out, his gaze lifting to her once again as that particular memory only made his cock harder. "You were especially beautiful, spread out in the moonlight, the material of that pretty fairy dress hiked above your hips as I ate your fairy pussy."

The blunt, explicit words had heat washing across her face as he stared back at her, a hint of a smile tugging at his lips.

"Crowe, that's raw," she berated him, breathless now as his fingers stroked closer to the slick, waxed folds of her glistening sex.

"You waxed for me then, too, didn't you, Amelia?" he whispered. "The only curls you left were these right here."

His fingers feathered across the soft fluff on her mound, just above her clit.

"For me," she stated, a moan leaving her lips as her hips jerked upward at the feather-light stroke of his fingers above the swollen, naked inner lips.

"Lie to yourself if you have to, fairy-girl," he teased, then his expression stilled, his gaze caught by that damned, defiant little fairy inked into her flesh. He whispered, "So sweet. So damned pretty."

He wasn't surprised that he'd never found a woman who could compare to her. No other woman had ever made him feel the things Amelia made him feel, or made him burn as she made him burn.

Laying a heated kiss along her thigh he moved between her legs, slowly spreading them before easing himself into position to taste the swollen, lush flesh he'd dreamed of tasting again.

Amelia watched, barely able to breathe. Heat washed through her senses, anticipation flooding her bloodstream.

Finally, oh God, finally—

Her back arched, her feet digging into the bed to lift

herself closer as he laid an erotic, far-too-short kiss on her sensitive flesh.

She needed more.

As his gaze lifted to her and the wicked intent in his expression registered, she barely had time to draw in a hard, deep breath. His tongue licked through the saturated folds, a hum of appreciation vibrating against her flesh. Crowe took instant, hungry advantage of the dampness spilling from her sex.

Amelia's hips jerked, pressing more firmly into the caress as his fingers parted the dewy flesh. With each rasp of his tongue over the entrance of her vagina, she felt more of the damp warmth gathering inside before it spilled to his lips. Pleasure rushed through her senses in waves, flooding every corner of her being. Nothing else mattered in this moment.

Only this.

Clenching her fists in the blanket beneath her, panting in rising excitement, her body burned, pulsed with sensation. Ever-deepening pleasure crashed through her. Radiant heat raced from each inch of flesh his lips and tongue caressed as the fiery ache for more began to build inside the depths of her vagina.

"Crowe!" she gasped moments later as his lips covered her clit in a teasing kiss.

Spikes of imperative ecstasy shot through the sensitive bud, nearly sending her spiraling into chaos.

So close.

A keening wail of pleasure tore from her lips as she felt herself reaching for the sensual peak, only to have him pull back.

"Please, Crowe, please," she begged.

That edge of rapture taunted her, just out of reach.

"Oh, sugar elf, how I intend to please you," he groaned,

laying a gentle kiss on her clit before moving lower, before destroying her senses.

His tongue licked, stroked, rimmed her sensitive entrance. When she was certain she couldn't bear it another second he sent it pushing forcefully into the clenched, gripping tissue in a thrust that nearly pushed her into the flames of rapture.

The first time he had penetrated her with the wicked thrust of his tongue, she had just turned eighteen. The shocking caress, the pure carnality of it had thrown her into her first explosive climax.

Now the erotic kiss had her burning for more, aching, needing a deeper, harder caress. She was no longer content to accept mere carnality. She wanted that erotic pain, that sweet, fiery lush sensation that melded ecstasy and agony into a blinding kaleidoscope of dark, vicious rapture.

She wanted what she had never had.

She wanted that part of him that she knew he held back from her seven years ago.

"You're killing me, Crowe. Please stop teasing . . ." The demand was fueled by a certainty that whatever sensation her body was begging for, Crowe could deliver. His tongue retreated, his hungry lips moved to the throbbing bud of her clit, but still he teased.

Swollen, pulsing with need, the bundle of nerves ached and throbbed with such desperation that the quick, firm little kisses he bestowed on it weren't nearly enough.

Those kisses tormented her.

The hungry licks and quick thrusts only made sensation and the rising pulses of near orgasm radiant with fiery longing. She couldn't bear it. She would never find her release, never explode with all the burning power she could feel building inside her.

Her hips writhed uncontrollably. She fought for a

sensation she had no idea how to attain. A hunger for a pleasure she had no idea how to ask for burned through her senses. She feared she would be burned alive in the flames.

Sensing the roiling need surging through her body, Crowe increased the pressure of the lashing licks against the most sensitive area of her clitoris and almost growled in satisfaction.

It wasn't enough for her.

She needed more, he could feel it. All that trapped carnal hunger he'd sensed burning inside her seven years ago was now clawing to be free.

Her body was silently begging for more. The cries falling from her lips were a demand for more. The heat radiating from her flesh, reaching out for him, assured him she was now ready for more.

Her hips lifted to him, grinding the fiercely swollen bud of her clit harder against his lips and tongue as her body shuddered with the rising demands.

Oh little fairy-girl, just let me show you what you need.

The thought faded beneath the discovery of more of the slick, thick feminine sweetness spilling from her pussy. It coated the swollen, parted inner lips, spilled down the silken cleft, and laid a layer of natural lubrication over the tiny, puckered entrance between her buttocks.

God, he'd dreamed of this.

His hand lifted from one hip, drew back just a bit, then fell to land against the soft, rounded curve of her rear in an erotic, heated caress. A precursor to all he intended to give her.

Her hips jerked. A cry echoed around him as she bucked against him, pushing her clit against the tight heat of his mouth as he suckled it inside.

He'd been dying to give her this. Dreamed of taking

her with all the dark eroticism he'd hesitated to unleash on her seven years ago. Tender and so innocent, he'd been certain he'd terrify her with the hunger tormenting him. She'd been too young. Her senses had been too innocent.

She wasn't eighteen anymore.

She was a woman. His woman. And just as she now ached for the dark sexuality inside him, he'd ached for seven years to give it to her.

The light, heated little slap against her bottom as Crowe's lips sucked her clit into the burning heat of his mouth sent a hard, rolling wave of sensation tearing through her.

That edge of long-awaited, only barely perceived hunger burned brighter now.

The next heavy caress landed harder, stilling the frantic roll of her hips.

"Like that, sugar elf?" he growled. "Or this?"

His lips released her.

"No. Don't stop." She tried to reach for him, her eyes flaring open, the sudden desertion driving spikes of clenched desperate need through her clit and into her womb.

The hand that landed on her buttocks laid a heated caress over the mound of her pussy.

Amelia froze.

Eyes wide, she stared back at him as that firm caress exploded against her slick, wet flesh. A breath later it pierced her clit with enough force to drop her back to the bed, her back bowing, pleasure suddenly exploding through her senses with the force of an erotic tidal wave.

It tore through her. It ravaged her senses and caused her hips to jerk upward as a breathless cry exploded from her lips.

"Fuck."

She barely heard the exclamation as it fell from Crowe's

lips. One second she was shuddering in a peak of such agonizing need she wondered if she'd survive it. In the next a strangled scream parted her lips at the heavy, blunt force parting the intimate entrance and thrusting several inches inside the gripping channel of her vagina.

Amelia forced her eyes open once again in time to direct her gaze between her thighs.

Crowe's hard hands gripped the cheeks of her rear, arching her to him as he drew back, pulling the length of his cock from her. Her juices glistened on the hard flesh that sank inside her. Slick, coating the heavy width, lubricating it for—

The next heavy thrust speared to the depths of her vagina, forcing apart the tight muscles and delicate flesh and throwing her headlong into the dark, erotic pain she'd never realized she needed.

"More." She could barely gasp out the word. "Please. More."

Buried full-length inside her, Crowe fought the need tightening his balls, the release threatening to escape his control, and clenched his teeth to hold back just a little longer.

There was no latex separating them. He was inside her, bare, the snug grip of her pussy rippling around his flesh, milking at the iron-hard shaft of his cock.

He'd forgotten to use a condom only once in his life, that first time he'd taken her. He hadn't forgotten it before, nor since.

Until now.

Until the need to feel her, hot, slick, and naked around his shaft overrode his normal caution.

Drawing back, his gaze trained on the pleasure radiating through her expression, Crowe fought and failed to free himself. Instead he pushed inside her again, her cries echoing around him as the fist-tight grip she had on him drew a hard groan from his chest and obliterated the last ounce of reason he'd possessed.

Hard, driving thrusts pierced her flesh, each forceful thrust inside the depths of her pussy pushing her closer, burning deeper as he came over her. His elbow braced at her shoulder; the other hand slid between her buttocks, his fingers finding the hidden entrance of her rear.

She was holding on to him now, her nails digging into his flesh as a heated pressure began to push against that forbidden entrance.

The blunt pressure of his finger penetrating, stretching her, sent spikes of fiery sensation to rake over nerve endings far too sensitive. It was pleasure. Pain. Agony and ecstasy.

"Yes." Lifting to him, crying out for him, that sharp edge of bliss clawed at her, raking talons of sensation dragging her into chaos.

Pushing inside her, stroking overly sensitive, overly responsive nerve endings, he penetrated the ultra-snug entrance. Each shallow thrust buried his finger deeper, took more of her as his cock stroked hard, deep, into the violently aroused tissue of her pussy.

First one finger stretched her, then a second. Hard, pistoning thrusts of his cock drove her higher through the swirling sensations. Each alternate thrust of his fingers pierced her with a dark excitement, that painful edge of pleasure.

Each piercing, stretching thrust of his erection inside her pussy pushed her relentlessly, mercilessly along that sharp edge of bliss bordering agony.

"That's it, baby," he whispered at her ear as she fought

to take him harder, deeper, her hips writhing beneath him. "Fuck me, little fairy. Sweet, sweet Amelia. God, I love fucking your tight little pussy."

She exploded.

The words, punctuated with the hard thrusts of his fingers inside her anus, and the blinding, stretching thrusts that parted her vagina, overloaded her senses.

Pleasure gathered, tightened, then released inside her in such a wave of blinding, burning sensation that every particle of her body, her mind, her soul, became filled with it.

It radiated. It seared her senses and burned through her soul, jerking her against him, shuddering through her with such chaotic ecstasy she wondered—for a moment—if she had died.

She knew for a fact it changed her.

The question was: How had it changed her, and would she survive it?

CHAPTER 7

What the fuck had happened?

Lying still and silent before dawn began peeking over the mountains, Crowe stared into the moonlit night outside the balcony doors, directly across from Amelia's bed.

It wasn't the first time he'd been here.

The room as well as the bed.

Once, long ago, he'd taken her here, in her bed, after slipping onto her balcony, then into her room.

He'd kissed her awake that night. Covering her lips with his hand as she came in his arms, he'd buried his face in her hair and given himself to the pleasure he'd been certain couldn't have been as destructive as he'd thought it was the first time.

He'd been wrong.

Then as well as now.

Now, because he'd been certain, once again, it couldn't have been as good as he'd remembered. And he was right. It was so much better than he'd remembered that it defied description.

"You're quiet."

The sound of her voice, soft in the darkness, should have surprised him, but hell, he'd known she was awake.

He was aware of her now in a way he hadn't been seven years before. So aware of her that for precious moments as his release met hers, he'd been certain they'd been a part of each other.

"Just thinking," he finally answered. "I thought you were asleep."

Her head lifted from his chest, her hair caressing his flesh like living silk.

Watching, he was struck, not for the first time, just how fae she seemed sometimes. Far too delicate and tiny against him, yet pulsing with some unknown magic he couldn't decipher. A magic that mesmerized him, even as it eluded him.

That was the power she had over him, and it was damned dangerous. Not just for his peace of mind, but also for her safety as well as his family's.

She stared down at him, those pretty turquoise eyes somber and far, far too knowing.

"Just say it," she whispered, resigned pain echoing in her voice.

The soft demand had his eyes narrowing on her, a chill racing up his spine.

"Say what?"

"What you came here to say." Holding the sheet to her breasts, her gaze pierced him clear to his soul. The thought left him feeling a bit off balance.

God, where was that ice that had shielded him for the past seven years? In the space of the time he'd been buried balls-deep inside her, he swore the heat of her hunger had melted it.

"You didn't deserve this life," he sighed.

Her laugh was soft, and filled with such bitterness he wanted to strike out at the world for the pain that had created it.

"No, Crowe," she retorted. "It's you, Logan, and Rafer who didn't deserve it. It was the women you could have loved, the lives you could have had, the happiness and joy that was stolen from all your parents. That was undeserved, yet inflicted anyway. It was so undeserved that I'm wondering how you could bring yourself to be here in his daughter's bed."

The question was there, unvoiced, and for a moment, for one incredibly insane moment, he nearly told her the truth. He wanted to tell her the truth with such strength that the words nearly fell from his lips.

"Why are you here, Crowe?" The question fell from her lips instead, firm, the demand that filled it bringing a heavy breath from his chest.

"DNA tests are in."

Amelia felt the breath still in her chest. She wanted to scream. The need to voice a wail of denial lay unrequited from a lack of air rather than a lack of will.

Instead she fisted her fingers in the sheet to still their trembling while she locked her teeth together, firmed her lips, and promised herself she wouldn't allow them to tremble.

"He's alive," Crowe continued when she said nothing, but only stared into the savage features of his face. "We won't fool him a second time, Amelia. Drawing him out won't be easy. This time it will take more than a suspicion that you belong to me. This time you're going to have to convince him you belong to me—"

Slowly, as though every cell in her body ached, she drew away from him until she sat on the edge of the bed, her fingers gripping the mattress as her head lowered for long minutes. Finally, forcing herself to stand, she turned and faced him.

Gloriously naked, achingly wounded, he thought, as the fury he'd kept buried for so long began to burn in his gut.

"Convince him I belong to you?" she whispered.

"We'll have to convince everyone, Amelia—"

She shook her head, then lowered it again, slowly. "I belonged to you seven years ago," she said, her voice hollow, shredded with such pain he flinched. "Now I don't think there's enough left of me to belong . . ."

He wanted to jump from the bed, pull her into his arms, and show her different. Instead he watched as she pulled her gown and robe on before leaving the bedroom, the door closing softly behind her.

He let her go, not because he wanted to. Not because he needed to.

He let her go until he could find a way to once again control the bitter, overriding rage about everything he'd been forced to walk away from seven years ago. Because staring in her face moments before, he'd realized just what he may have lost.

The cup of coffee sitting on the table in front of Amelia whispered steamy promises in the dim early-dawn light. Soft, foggy wisps of heat rose from the dark liquid, drawing her gaze and holding it for long moments before a long, slow breath parted her lips and once again her gaze turned to the winter wonderland the world had become overnight.

The snow that had fallen the night before covered the backyard in a thick, heavy veil of white. It covered trees, brush, plants that lay dormant for the winter, and the cement and polymer figurines that filled the back garden.

The weeping cherry tree, barely six feet in height, looked like a heavy mound of white fluff. The half-grown fir trees held the snow with an air of strain, while the very air swirled with the remnants of the flakes that had blown in overnight.

The ugliness of the cold autumn months was covered with a jewel-bright white cape of frigid beauty. As cold and perfect as the heart of the man lying in her bed upstairs.

His heart might be cold, but his touch and his hunger had been anything but. He had been burning hot, incredibly sexual and wicked. And he had been everything, every part of him she had missed in the past seven years.

And she was just as weak as she had been all those years ago as well.

Weak and incredibly stupid, because she wanted to believe his heart wasn't frozen. And she knew better.

She'd known better as he held her after that final, explosive climax, her head cushioned on his chest, the sound of his heartbeat against her ear. With his hands buried in her hair, his fingertips rubbing against her scalp, he'd sent her racing from complete peace and relaxation into a hell she'd prayed she'd never know again.

He's alive. This time it will take more than a suspicion that you belong to me. This time you're going to have to convince him you belong to me—

Amelia looked down at her hands. They were still trembling so fiercely she was actually hesitant to lift her coffee cup again. She'd already singed her fingers carrying the damned thing to the table.

Wayne was alive.

Drawing in a shaking breath, she fought back her tears and a lifetime of memories. Memories she'd hoped she could put behind her, yet it seemed they would forever haunt her.

"You shouldn't sit in front of open windows," Crowe informed her quietly as he stepped into the room.

Moving to the side of the window he pulled the shades

closed, effectively blocking the view of the outside as he blocked the view inside as well.

"There seems to be a lot of things I can't do," she said softly. "But fucking you now isn't one of them, right?"

Sitting across from her, Crowe watched her silently. Still, she could feel his look like a physical caress. As though the air itself were determined to remind her of what it felt like to be touched by him.

"Don't kill the messenger, fairy-girl," he murmured, the look in his eyes too calculating to suit her. "I just delivered the news, I didn't make it."

"Neither do you seem too concerned by it," she stated, crossing her arms on the table as she stared back at him painfully. "And perhaps, Crowe, that's the part that really worries me. You act as though it's nothing more to be worried about than walking across the street, and I think you know better than that."

Watching her, Crowe was reminded of a time, years before, when he'd acknowledged just how slick his Amelia was.

That girl's smart as a whip. Watch out for her, boy. Once she sets herself on a goal, or a man, she won't let go.

That was Clyde Ramsey's warning the summer Crowe had made her his lover. And Clyde had been right. She was smart as hell, intuitive, and with a heart far too tender for the world she lived in and the people who ended up using her.

And that included himself.

He wondered when she had woken up and realized she'd been all used up.

"Why should it worry you, Amelia?" he asked, shaking his head as he stared around the room, remembering the stories he'd heard over the years, the suspicious bruises she'd carried, the quiet air of sadness that had always surrounded her.

"Why shouldn't it worry me, Crowe?" The blue-green of her eyes darkened, an emotion akin to betrayal gleaming in the rich color. "He's a serial killer with how many decades of murder attached to his name? Do you think he's just going to step out and wave his hands with a cheery little *Here I am*?"

"Not if he's smart," Crowe decided, reaching out to catch her hand as it formed a fist on the table. "And I think he's smart, Amelia. Smart enough to know I'm waiting on him. But he's not smart enough to completely lose sight of everything I'm doing. Or that you're doing. Trust me, he's close. Close enough that this time he'll make sure we're sleeping together, and when he's certain, when he's convinced we've gone on without him, *then* he'll give us that cheery little *Here I am*."

Enclosing her small fist with his much larger one, Crowe tasted the bitterness of the deception he was practicing. He hadn't expected that. He'd been protecting Amelia in one form or another for years, and until now, he hadn't realized how often he'd deceived her to do it.

"You're waiting for him," she repeated softly, pulling her fist from beneath his hand. "Perhaps that's the part that frightens me, Crowe—knowing that you're waiting for him, and knowing the lengths you'll go to catch him. It makes me wonder what, or who, you're willing to sacrifice for your own revenge."

"I'll sacrifice whatever it takes, Amelia." Reaching across the table, his hand was around the back of her neck, pulling her forward before she could evade him and glaring back at her, his lips nearly touching hers. "I'll sacrifice whatever the fuck it takes. Even us."

Slowly, she shook her head. "You can't sacrifice what never was. And there never was an us."

He released her then, sat back and let his lips tilt with a mocking curl. "There's always been an us, Amelia. There always has been, and whether you like it or not, in one form or another there always will be."

When had he grown so hard? Amelia wondered.

Seven years ago his amber-brown gaze had been softer, warmer. For a few precious weeks she had been certain he was a man on the verge of falling in love.

With her.

Rising from the table, unable to sit still beneath his steady regard any longer, Amelia paced to the end of the counter that separated the breakfast nook from the kitchen.

The news that the body that had burned in that car wasn't Wayne only reaffirmed her suspicions and destroyed that small kernel of hope she had held in her heart.

She was still Wayne's prisoner, and Crowe's sacrifice. It wouldn't matter if she stayed in Corbin County or if she ran. As long as he was alive he was a threat not just to her, but to the one thing she'd sworn to protect above all else.

"You need to leave, Crowe." Pushing her hands into the pockets of her robe she faced him squarely, knowing her soul couldn't survive this man or the threat he represented to her.

He laughed.

The strong-boned, savagely hewn features of his face filled with genuine amusement while the sensually full curves of his lips curled with a hint of mockery.

"Ah, Amelia, there's not a chance in hell that you're kicking me out of your bed, or your life, now." Making that announcement he rose from his seat, turned to her, and stared back at her knowingly. "I warned you six weeks ago I was coming back for you. Now, until Wayne's in custody, or until he's dead, baby, we're fucking joined at the hip."

"Joined at the hip? No, Crowe, we're not joined anywhere. I'm just the tool you think you need to draw him out again by proving to him that you've one-upped him by fucking his daughter." She couldn't help but stare back at him in amazement. "That's not going to happen again. I let you use me to draw him out six weeks ago and all he did was find another way to fool all of us. I can't do it again. And you're very, very wrong about whether or not we're finished," she said, hardening her soul to the pull this man had on it. "You and I were finished when I walked into my bedroom seven years ago and found the note you left me. Sorry, but in this case there are no second chances. I'm not strong enough for it."

She couldn't afford a second chance with him. Because if by chance Wayne was ever arrested or killed, then just as quickly as Crowe had joined her at the hip he would rip himself from her, as he had done so long ago. And when it happened, it would destroy her to the point that she would never be able to stay in Corbin County. She'd have no choice but to leave. Sooner or later, no matter what happened or how it happened, this would never be her home again.

And now he was asking her not just to allow it, but to cooperate with it.

Watching as his eyes narrowed on her, his expression losing all amusement, Amelia steeled herself for the coming battle.

Crowe leaned against the kitchen counter, his eyes gleaming in the dim light of the room, and crossed his arms over his powerful chest. The unconscious posturing of male intimidation. She knew all the moves by now.

"And you think it's going to be just that easy?" he asked her as though genuinely curious.

She knew Crowe. The calculation in his eyes, the

assessing nature of the beast lurking beneath the calm exterior. Yeah, she knew him far too well.

"I won't be your pawn or a handy lover until Wayne's captured or dead," she informed him, fighting to hide the hurt and anger growing inside her. "I have no doubt you want to believe I'm the only tool to catch Wayne, but I think we both know he was finished with that the day he faked his death. But knowing he's alive changes the rules for you, doesn't it? It changes the rules for any lover you would have as well. Do you think I'm the only safe fuck around, Crowe? If he comes after me, then it's something you expected. If he doesn't, then at least you've had a ready fuck for a while?" Bitterness fed the disillusionment rising inside her.

She could feel her nails biting into her palms as her fists tightened in the pockets of her robe. Anger surged through her.

"The last thing I ever considered you was a safe fuck." Dropping his arms from his chest he straightened from the counter, his gaze licking over her with the heated promise of a lust that would destroy her. "That doesn't mean I'll let you go now that I can have you, either. The identity of the Slasher was all that was holding me back from you, fairy-girl. I know who he is now. I know who to search for, and I'll be damned if I'll let him stand between us any longer."

"There is no us, Crowe!" Desperation filled her cry. "You make it sound as though we had more than a few one-night stands. You don't have to lie to me now any more than you were willing to lie to me seven years ago."

She had told him she loved him. She had sworn she wouldn't demand anything from him, and she hadn't. Three nights later she had found that damned letter on her bed.

"Do you think leaving you that summer was easy?" he asked, his gaze shuttered.

Amelia pushed her fingers through her hair wearily before shaking her head, her arms falling limply to her sides.

"I just don't think it matters anymore if it was easy or not," she whispered. "What matters is the fact that I finally gave up, Crowe. On you. On us. And I think we both know you gave up before you even left that note on my bed. Hell, I was never more to you than a few gratuity fucks to begin with for the information I provided you. And it's a little late to pretend otherwise." She inhaled harshly. "Better yet, it's far too late. Find someone else. Someone just as hard and cold as you've become."

"And you forget who made me just that hard, and just that cold."

Before she could evade him he jerked her against him. A second later she didn't have a clue where her robe had been thrown or how he'd managed to get her out of it so fast. What she did know was that she found herself with her back to him, his hard, powerful body covering her as he bent her over the kitchen table.

"What are you doing?" she gasped, but she knew what he was doing.

Thick, fully erect, the head of his cock butted against the still-slick, still-ready-for-him flesh between her thighs.

"Feel that?" he snarled at her ear, as she felt him shove his jeans to his thighs, pressing the wide crest of his erection farther between the swollen, intimate lips. "My dick doesn't get this hard for a gratuity fuck, nor does it get this fucking hard in exchange for information, no matter how much I appreciate it."

The clenched entrance of her vagina began spreading apart beneath the blunt head as he began pushing slowly inside her.

"Tell me, Amelia, do you get this wet for just anyone you help? Does your pussy clench and try to milk just any man's cock inside it like it's dying for a taste of his cum?"

One hard thrust and several inches spread inside her.

He paused then, his hands hard on her hips as she fought to breathe through the pleasure that bordered agony.

"Feel that, fairy-girl?" he groaned at her ear. "Your pretty pussy sucking at my dick, flexing and milking it like it's begging me to fill it with my release?"

Oh yes, she could feel it.

Nails digging into the table beneath her, she could only gasp out in surprise as he pushed her legs farther apart, spreading her thighs before gripping one and lifting it until her foot rested on the seat of the chair next to them.

The position allowed her to feel him more fully, allowed his flesh to stretch her with increasingly devastating results.

The next thrust took him deeper, stretched her wider, stroked already sensitive flesh, and built a need inside her she couldn't control.

She shouldn't allow this, but she couldn't tell him to stop, either. She was too busy trying to breathe through the pleasure.

"So sweet and wet."

Drawing back, his heavy flesh tugging at the inner tissue and stroking nerve endings rioting with sensation; Crowe teased her, holding no more than the head of his erection inside her.

"Do you feel my cock throbbing?" he growled at her ear, nipping at it.

A second later his lips caught the lobe, played with it. The caress of his lips sent electric surges of weakening pleasure tearing through her.

"Crowe, please—"

She couldn't keep her vagina from clenching desperately, attempting to pull him deeper, to suck at the hot, thick crest as it did indeed throb inside her.

"I've been hard for you every time I've seen you for the past two years," he growled.

A breath after he spoke he thrust inside her again, filling her to the hilt and drawing a hard, harsh cry from her lips.

The next thrust had her crying out, her flesh melting around his cock as he began moving, deep, fierce thrusts, penetrating her, destroying her.

Lying across the table, his bigger, harder body holding her in place as he impaled her in steadily building thrusts of his cock, Amelia felt the loss of control along with a complete unwillingness to find it again as pleasure burned inside her.

Tension began to tighten through her, her vagina clenching desperately on each thrust, fighting to hold him in place each time he withdrew.

"Damn you, I love fucking you," he bit out, his arm moving beneath her cheek, cushioning it as her hands gripped it, holding on to him fiercely as the strokes inside her increased.

Each penetration stroked across increasingly sensitized nerve endings. Her womb clenched, her hips moving against him, pushing against him, driving him deeper, harder.

"Ah, sweet baby," he groaned. "That's it, tighten on my cock. So fucking tight. Clenching like a fist."

His cock throbbed, pulsed, and seemed to thicken further inside her tender flesh as rapid-fire bursts of sensation began to tighten at her clit.

"Crowe . . . oh God, it's so good . . ." It was too good.

The feel of him behind her, his voice at her ear, pleasure thickening it, deepening it, was another caress against her senses.

"Did you dream of me, baby?" His lips brushed against her neck as he whispered the words. "Did you feel me inside you when you slept? My dick filling you, fucking you until you didn't think you could live if you didn't come for me?"

"Did you?" Amelia could hear her own hunger for it, to know she had been more than a gratuity fuck. "Did you dream . . ."

His thrusts increased, driving inside her powerfully, the race to release stealing her breath for precious seconds.

"Crowe . . ."

It was there. That tightening of her body as the pleasure became too much to bear. Heat seared her, burned through her as her muscles locked in place, her clit pulsing. Her pussy rippling, milking—

Light and color exploded behind her eyes as a keening cry fell from her lips at the sudden, white-hot detonation of sensation erupting through her.

Her fingers tightened on his arm, sobs tearing from her lips as she lifted to her toes, trying to take him deeper. His thrusts increased, slamming into her, driving her higher, amplifying her release and a second later filling her with the white-hot lash of his semen.

The harsh, guttural groan that tore from his lips at the first burning ejaculation inside her tore another sob from her throat. Shuddering, crying out mindlessly, she felt another internal explosion, a heavy, unexpected orgasm as the heat of his release filled her.

Jet after heated jet escaped his cock and marked her, owning her, reminding her of things she knew it was far too dangerous to be reminded of.

"I dreamed . . ." he groaned at her, the sound almost too soft, too rough, to understand. "I dreamed . . ."

Too dangerous for her peace of mind, her heart, and her sanity.

Holding on to his arm as the storm of exquisite ecstasy tore through them both, Amelia knew, deep inside her heart, inside her woman's soul, that she was helpless against him.

Helpless against his touch, helpless against his lust, and helpless to do anything but follow him into hell.

A hell she had prayed they could both avoid.

CHAPTER 8

Walking into the nearly completed addition to the Community Center—a huge, four-section meeting wing—Amelia eyed the folding walls that separated the room the Ladies' Auxiliary and Social Planning Committee had reserved for their weekly meetings.

The detailed murals on the folding walls weren't finished, but the sketch of the early, historic Corbin County scene was precisely drawn and awaiting the painting phase. Painting would begin after Thanksgiving, with the murals in each of the four rooms scheduled for completion the week before the kickoff of the social season.

The Corbin County socials were a historic event all their own.

They had begun when Sweetrock was no more than a freight wagon stop for ranching supplies and had fewer than a dozen families supporting it. Those families had supplies brought in over the mountains and then sold them to the ranches and small farms that sprang up around the four large spreads the Irish Barons had secured land for.

Each weekend, the ranching families supplied the beef, the cowboys' families and those in Sweetrock supplied the additional dishes, and guitar-playing cowboys supplied the music.

The first socials were just about getting together. The ranching families and their employees rarely had any other chance to socialize or meet their outlying neighbors. The summer weekend festivities had changed that.

Each of the eight murals scheduled to go on the back and front of the four false walls depicted scenes from those early social events.

The meeting wing of the Community Center had originally been proposed by Amelia's mother just before her disappearance and suspected death. The year Amelia was voted into the position of event coordinator, she had proposed overseeing the project herself to revive it. She'd been shocked when the planning commission had accepted her suggestion and gave her the go-ahead to secure quotes.

Wide and roomy, the first and smallest of the four rooms easily accommodated two dozen women plus several tables of snacks and treats, with plenty of space for the officers' podium to face the rest of the room. By the podium were two covered tables, each with three chairs on a three-foot-high stage.

Thankfully, a social and event coordinator wasn't considered an officer.

The meeting rooms were proving to be not just useful, but also marginally profitable: their schedule after completion was already filling up.

Amelia wondered, though, if she would be here for the ribbon-cutting ceremony.

She had a feeling she wouldn't be.

With the little visit Crowe had interrupted two days before from Linda and her mother Ruth Anne, she might not make it past this particular meeting.

Smothering a sigh, Amelia placed her oversized briefcase

on the chair beside her, watching as her friend and most vocal ally in the past weeks strode into the room and headed toward her.

For once, Anna wasn't dressed in jeans, either. The Ladies' Auxiliary and Social Planning Committee had a strict dress code. Denim was not considered acceptable, Amelia thought in amusement.

Anna's smartly tailored black skirt and white cashmere sweater were paired with three-inch heels and minimal makeup. She'd pulled her shoulder-length hair haphazardly to the back of her head, with long heavy waves falling here and there along her nape and the sides of her face. She looked chic and comfortable.

Business-y with a side of sex kitten, Anna's fiancé, Archer Tobias, had commented when she showed him the outfit the week before. Amelia had no doubt Archer had taken advantage of the sex-kitten part before Anna left the house.

"I can't believe I let you talk me into this," Anna muttered in irritation as she dropped her purse on top of the round table Amelia had chosen.

"Talked you into what?" Amelia questioned with the utmost innocence. "Becoming part of Archer's life? I thought he talked you into that."

Anna's green eyes narrowed back at her as she propped her hands on her slender hips, cocking one boldly. "Funny, Amelia, real funny. But, strangely enough—" She looked around curiously. "—I don't see Archer here."

Turning back to Amelia, she lifted her brows with questioning mockery as though she had somehow misplaced her fiancé.

Amelia rolled her eyes. "Do you go on investigations with Archer? Would he take you to a shootout with him?"

"Only in my dreams," Anna snorted before blowing out a hard breath at Amelia's chastising look. "Fine. Fine.

I know. Sheriff is a political position and any wife of Archer's has to be part of the community," she said, repeating her grandmother's warning. "I get it, I really do." She looked around again, pouting. "But the Ladies' Auxiliary and Social Planning Committee? Geez, Amelia."

"You'll survive," Amelia promised. "Just be yourself and remember, every woman here is one of the most strong-willed, influential women in the county. Don't let them browbeat you. Never cower or back down. They see it as a weakness. And always, always be as certain of your information as possible before stating it or someone else will find a way to make you appear weak."

As she spoke, Anna's eyes widened with a look of distaste. "Sounds more like a pack of coyotes than a ladies' auxiliary," she murmured, looking around again. "Come to think of it, I see a few resemblances."

Amelia bumped against her hurriedly to silence the observation as she tried to muffle her laughter.

"Just tell me when to wake up then," Anna suggested. "Because I've met all these women at one time or another and I find them all completely boring. Several of them have actually crossed the line to irritating."

Amelia had a feeling she knew the two her friend was talking about.

Amelia had never found the group boring, though. She had so loved her position—the planning of each event she chose for the socials and all her interactions with the vendors and entertainers—that boredom had never been a consideration. There was no part of the job she hadn't loved.

Even dealing with the ladies in the auxiliary.

She was going to miss it.

"What's wrong?" Anna's question pulled her back, forcing her to focus on the present rather than the past and what she knew was coming.

"Ladies, if I could have your attention." Linda stepped

to the narrow podium behind the tables and addressed the group as the officers took their seats. "If I could have your attention," she repeated as the other officers appeared less than comfortable.

The tension in the air increased.

"Is this a funeral or a meeting?" Anna muttered as she and Amelia sat down. "And why isn't anyone sitting with us?"

Amelia would have answered but her gaze caught Linda's at that moment. The determination she read in the other woman's eyes had her stomach sinking.

"Before we begin discussing our normal week's business we have a situation that must be addressed," Linda announced, her gaze moving around the room.

Linda stood stiffly erect, her plumpening figure dressed in black slacks and a dark gray, loose sweater that hid her curvy hips. Her blond hair was pulled into a tight ponytail today, her makeup applied with a heavy hand.

"What is her problem?" Anna questioned under her breath.

"Ladies," Linda repeated as everyone's attention turned to her. "As president of the Ladies Auxiliary and Social Planning Committee, I never imagined the day would come when it would be my unfortunate duty to ask an officer or coordinator of our organization to step down or to rescind her position."

Anna came sharply to attention beside Amelia with an angry, hissed, "Oh hell no, she isn't."

Placing her hand on Anna's arm, Amelia kept her attention on Linda.

"Because of the very unique position that we, as the auxiliary's officers, find ourselves in, as well as the position our very good friend and social planning coordinator finds herself in, I sent an email ballot out for a vote to determine whether we should keep Amelia in her position or let her go."

A low hum of whispered discussion raced around the room. Amelia kept her gaze on Linda despite the heat of humiliation that suffused her face.

"The vote that came back was, unfortunately, to release Amelia as social planning coordinator, effective immediately."

Effective immediately.

The sense of loss threatened to strangle her.

"Excuse me," Marianne Collins, the widow of a former commissioner, requested firmly, waiting until all eyes turned to her and Linda gave her the floor with a hesitant nod. "I did not receive a ballot by email or otherwise. My understanding of the auxiliary guidelines is that it requires a unanimous vote to rescind an officer or position."

"I didn't receive a ballot, either," Anna said, ignoring Amelia's silent look of warning.

Tightening her lips momentarily, Linda bent her head to her mother, listening as Ruth Anne spoke. Linda finally gave a quick, hard shake of her head before straightening once again.

"Marianne, Anna." She nodded to both women. "Unfortunately, we as an organization, and Amelia personally, are facing a rather unique position." Linda stepped from behind the podium as she pushed her hands into the pockets of her slacks and looked down momentarily before lifting her head, her expression one of regret. "This situation threatens the integrity of the auxiliary as well as the participation of the residents, vendors, and performers that are required to ensure the success of each event, as well as the season."

"Linda?" Timid-voiced, steel-willed Kate Hardy, the daughter of the city commissioner, spoke up. "Why weren't we all asked to vote? As Marianne stated, the guidelines require a unanimous vote."

"Where's the fairness in that? Or in the members you chose to send the ballot to?" Anna stood to her feet mutinously, her arms crossing defiantly over her breasts. "Who received this email? Only those you could convince to vote your way? Strange, I thought the auxiliary was a democratic organization, Linda, not your personal little sandbox."

A wave of protests as well as agreements swept the room as Amelia grabbed her friend's arm and jerked her back to her chair. "Enough," she demanded, her voice low. "Don't make enemies here, Anna. Not over this."

Anna glared back at her. "Your words," she reminded Amelia. "Don't cower or back down. This isn't right—"

"Anna," Linda stated from the podium. "Regardless of the fairness of it, or the guidelines, unfortunately, the original creators of the auxiliary simply never foresaw this particular situation." She grimaced in distaste. "I'm very sorry about this, Amelia, but despite my own personal feelings, we need you to turn over all materials, plans, and contacts to the committee, as required by the by-laws you signed when you accepted the position as the auxiliary social planning director."

Oh, she just bet they did, Amelia thought painfully as she shook her head. "I didn't sign the by-laws, Linda." That single piece of advice Wayne had given her five years before made more sense as she continued. "You'll find instead my own notarized addition at the end of the packet stating that I only be required to turn over any plans, contacts, or information received from the coordinator I replaced. I received nothing. I understand your fears and your position as president of the auxiliary. But what you're asking me to do is turn over what amounts to untold hours of personal time and effort as well as forgoing the use of my own experience and contacts I've made for future employment once I've turned over my materials. I can't do that. I won't do that."

Livid anger filled Linda's expression as the auxiliary secretary showed her the back of a packet Amelia assumed was her own.

"This vote and the demand that she step down, *after nearly completing plans for not just this year's social, but next year's as well,* is completely unconscionable and so lacking in fairness as to be laughable," Anna protested strenuously as she rose again, flattening her hands against the table in front of her as she glared at Linda.

Closing the packet and moving once again behind the podium, Linda stared back at Anna, anger burning in her face and gaze.

"Tell me, Miss Corbin," she asked heavily. "What do we do when residents refuse to attend because the daughter of the man who murdered his way through this county is still planning the socials? How do we explain that? How do we, in all good conscience, force the citizens of this county to face his daughter or face the subtle ways this county punishes its residents for not attending or not supporting the events?"

Shame lashed at Amelia, just as Linda intended. Whether it was fair or not, as she stated, Amelia had no doubt the auxiliary committee had already received phone calls stating just that.

The position it left both her and Linda in was less than deserved or wanted. But here they were.

"I would have, and still would, do anything if I could change what Wayne had done," Amelia stated, her voice heavy with regret. "No one could feel more shame or regret over a family member's actions than I do." She fought back her tears, but she couldn't stop the thickening of her voice. "I'm not protesting the fact that I've been asked to leave; it was no more than I expected. What I find unfair is the timing. As Anna stated, this has come after the completion of plans and contracts of the next two years' events. I'll leave, but I will not turn over all copies of the plans, materials, and contacts to the board or anyone else. Nor will I sign away my right to use them at a future date in any employment situation. I will not allow you to steal what amounts to seven years of my life and simply hand it over to someone who has no idea of the untold hours of networking it took to complete each event."

The position and the work she put into the planning of events and coordinating each phase of the county's social calendar had been her life. She had had no family, no lovers. She'd had her events, and she had loved each phase of it.

"That's bullshit," Anna argued at her side, brushing Amelia's hand aside as she tried to shush her friend. "If the victims' families actually requested your resignation, then I could understand it," she continued fiercely. "But I know those families. Amelia knows them, well. We stood at their funerals together and held their loved ones more than once as they cried. And I know for a fact they all distrusted and disliked Wayne Sorenson and considered Amelia one of their dearest friends. No one but those families has the right to ask for her resignation. Certainly, Linda, you don't have that right."

Amelia shook her head. Anna could only think of the loss of time and cherished projects Amelia would lose if forced to walk away. She wasn't considering the position the auxiliary would be in with the rest of the public.

It wasn't Linda who addressed the argument this time, though. Her mother, Ruth Anne, rose to her feet instead.

"How effective will any of that effort be, Anna, no matter the work or the love that's gone into it, if the residents—whether of the victims' families or not—can't tolerate the daughter of the man that all but destroyed this county? Or that his daughter is allowed to continue to build her reputation and her name because of this position?" Ruth Anne asked gently. "I may not approve of Linda's handling of this situation, but I must say I agree with her arguments for it. Just as those who were asked to vote understand it, as well as the committee. And it's a committee Amelia must work with. One that must approve each phase of her plans. How can we do that effectively when there's resentment or even fear for our personal safety should we question or disapprove those plans?" She held up a hand as Anna moved to protest, but it was Amelia's gaze she met with compassion and regret. "My dear, you are a cherished friend who has, I know, suffered the consequences of standing between Wayne and the petty injustices he often used to strike out at many of our families. We kept the vote secretive in an attempt to protect those we asked to vote as well as ourselves, because Amory Wyatt was and now—along with Wayne—still is free and a possible threat. Only this evening did we learn Wayne wasn't in that explosion as we all first believed. And he has by the very fact that he murdered each woman suspected to have been in a Callahan's bed, with the exception of you, shown his preference for you. Who's to say he wouldn't return and kill again should one of the auxiliary officers, members, or the group as a whole do something that displeases him? No, it isn't fair," she sighed. "To any of us. But it's an issue we can't ignore."

Amelia covered her mouth, her fingers shaking nearly as fiercely as her lips as she fought to hold back her tears. Beside her, Anna plopped back into her seat, her arms crossing over her breasts as she glared back at the officers on stage mutinously.

Looking around the room, Amelia didn't miss the members' unwillingness to meet her gaze. This was a battle she couldn't have won, no matter the argument used. She would have warned her friend of that, if she had known Anna would argue so fiercely in her defense.

"The auxiliary by-laws demand that all work done in its name and all contacts or efforts made under the committee's direction belong to it," Linda stated, her voice soft, the earlier aggression lost beneath a saddened weariness. "The officers of the committee are willing to sign an addendum that should you turn over this year's plans and notes and do what you can to aid a seamless transition; then we'll acknowledge your right to use the knowledge you've built over the years should it be required to employ yourself. We never wanted to hurt you, Amelia. And I personally never felt any animosity toward you, though I admit I have a great and overriding animosity for the situation itself." Her expression firmed then. "But neither do any of us want to be hurt because of you."

Amelia glanced around the room once again before lowering her head for long moments.

Each woman in this room had, at one time or another, come to her for help because of Wayne. None of them was stupid; they had known the price she would pay each time they asked for her help. But they had asked anyway.

The bruises, broken bones, and years of humiliations inflicted by Wayne meant little in the face of their personal safety. She couldn't blame them for that.

She'd told herself that should she ever need any of them, then they would stand behind her. That Wayne had been wrong when he'd called her a fool for standing against him to help them.

"You'll regret putting your neck in the noose every time they come whining to you," Wayne stated somberly, regret threading his voice as she lay on the floor, fighting to breathe after he'd slammed his fist into her abdomen. He'd caught her off-guard and she'd sworn he had to

have cracked a rib. "When will you learn, Amelia?" He hunched beside her to brush the hair back from her face as he stared down at her, his tone incredibly gentle. "They could be standing here, knowing the pain you're feeling, and they'd still use you up. They would still ask you to risk yourself because they're such fucking cowards that they can't risk themselves or accept the reprisals for the choices they've made."

Each one of these women owed her.

But they couldn't do anything if the reverend whose daughter had been murdered by Wayne protested Amelia's involvement in the socials by asking his congregation to ignore the county's varied ways of rewarding participation or punishing absence.

They couldn't stop the newspaper articles that mentioned her involvement with the county's events, and they couldn't stop the protests by citizens or residents unaware of how often or how hard Amelia had worked for them in her position as Wayne's assistant.

"Don't you dare give in to them, Amelia," Anna hissed at her side. "They knew they could play your conscience."

But they were right. Amelia hated acknowledging it, but it stared her in the face through the eyes of the women who accidentally met her gaze.

She nodded slowly, ignoring Anna's muttered curse beside her.

"Get the release prepared," she told Linda wearily as she gripped the hand of the case she'd brought with her. "Once it's prepared you can email me the agreement for my lawyer to go over before I sign it."

Turning, she moved around Anna's chair, preparing to leave.

"Amelia." Ruth Anne's gentle voice had Amelia shaking her head fiercely as she hurried from the meeting room, all but running in her haste to get away from them.

She had to get out of there before she lost control of the tears gathering in her eyes and the sobs tightening her chest.

She couldn't allow herself to cry in front of them. She wouldn't allow herself to do it.

Once she reached her car, the tears and the sobs escaped.

Locking the doors, Amelia laid her head against the steering wheel. As alone as she had ever been, she lost control of the agony ripping through her heart.

Even as her tears fell, the sobs jerking through her body, she knew none of it would help. It would never matter how many tears she shed; it could never replace everything Wayne's evil had cost her.

It could never replace her soul.

The meeting with the project developers and directors for the proposed Avalanche Resort was running far longer than Crowe had anticipated. So much so that when Ivan Resnova's cell phone interrupted the latest project report, he was actually thankful and a bit curious.

"One moment, gentlemen," Ivan requested as he glanced at the caller ID before accepting the call with a brief, "Yes?"

A heavy frown pulled at Ivan's brow as he listened for long moments.

"Were there protests?" he asked, piquing Crowe's curiosity further before amplifying it long moments later with the order, "Make a list of those names, please, and I'll ensure the matter is looked into."

Ivan paused again.

"No worries," he said after listening several more seconds. "It will be taken care of."

The call was disconnected before Ivan turned slowly toward the project developers.

"Gentlemen," he requested. "I need a moment alone with the sheriff and Crowe. If you don't mind?"

It took only moments to clear the room. As the conference room door closed, Ivan's gaze met Archer's, then Crowe's.

"I have a friend on the ladies' auxiliary," he informed them. "It would seem a secretive vote went through to remove Amelia as social coordinator. Amelia was, it appears, rather guilted into agreeing to follow the vote and step down." He turned to Archer. "Anna bullied six very disapproving officers, demanded the position herself, then forced an immediate vote and walked away with the position herself. As she left, she informed the committee she was actually too busy planning a wedding to deal with such details, but would ensure she chose a co-coordinator, as the auxiliary guidelines allow, with enough experience to handle the job."

Crowe rose slowly from his chair, the memory of Linda and Ruth Anne's visit two days before suddenly making sense.

"Where's Amelia?" he growled, anger building at the thought of what had been taken from her.

"She returned home, I was told," Ivan sighed. "My contact attempted to call her, but it appears she's not answering her phone."

Crowe didn't wait to hear more. Snarling an obscenity, he turned and stalked from the room, then strode past the gathered project directors without a word.

Son of a bitch. He was growing sick of strikes against Amelia. And he was fucking sick and tired of watching her pay for crimes she had no part in.

It was time to put a stop to it.

CHAPTER 9

Taken.

She was no longer Amelia Sorenson, social and event planning coordinator. She was just Amelia Sorenson, Wayne Sorenson-slash-the-Slasher's daughter.

The first title had been taken from her. Too bad the second couldn't be. She would have gladly let them have that one.

She had depended on that position to keep herself busy, to ensure she had a life. To be able to enjoy what was left of her life.

She stared around the room she had taken as her office, her gaze touching on the sketches she'd made for the various themed weekends, suggestions for costumes sketched in various degrees of detail.

Then there were the sketches for decorations in the city square. The lights and themed entertainments and activities carefully detailed. Moving to the large whiteboard she'd placed on a stand in the center of the room, Amelia gazed at the intricately detailed schedule of events, entertainments, and performers for the season.

Beside the whiteboard were the colored sketches for each weekend with the entire square represented first. Behind the main sketch were several others of each grotto's decoration, the band gazebos, as well as the dance square.

Brightly colored lights surrounded the music gazebo and surrounding bricked dance area. The gardens, trees, and flowering bushes that grew around the dance area would be decorated with multihued lights and gossamer wings peeking from the leaves.

Wings also flared from the backs of two white horses drawing a white carriage decorated with flickering candlelight and sheer veils draped around a pure white upholstered bench seat.

The Fairy Ball.

The summer she turned eighteen, an attempt at a fairy-themed weekend had been made. Amelia had watched from her father's office as the decorations had been put up that week, and she had filed away her own ideas, determined that one day she would coordinate the socials—and once she did, she would have her own fairy theme.

This year she had planned her fairy theme.

Reaching out, she traced the gossamer wings of the fairy maiden moving onto the dance floor to accept the hand of the dark fairy prince who awaited her.

Delicate and bold, the fairy maiden looked up at the dark prince from the corner of her eyes as though considering the hand he held out to her.

The fairy was dressed in golds, russets, and soft browns. The sheer chiffon and tulle of the flowing dress made the maiden appear more delicate, while the wings rising from her back gave her the appearance of floating above the bricks she would have stepped to.

The dress Amelia had nearly completed for herself, wings and all, waited in one of the spare bedrooms in the downstairs guest wing of the house. The dress she wouldn't have a chance to wear now. Breathing out wearily, she lifted the whiteboard from its stand before storing it in the closet across the room. Returning and gathering the various theme boards from the larger easel, she carried them to the closet as well and closed the door on the sight of them.

There were notebooks of carefully detailed plans, sketches, and proposed themes. Contracts with various bands, a comic, three children's entertainment agencies, and even a fairy clown were already signed.

There were volunteer lists, notes made from years of planning and scheduling, and more notebooks of even more detailed lists that her mother had left from the years she had coordinated the social weekends.

There were lists of those who most enjoyed working with the younger children. Lists of the best cooks and their best dishes. Observations of the entertainment best suited and preferred by the children, the bands that drew the largest crowds, the themes most asked for, most preferred, and those that were the best value with accompanying prices broken down to the last penny.

She was stacking the notebooks in the totes she had taken them from when the office door opened slowly.

Stilling, Amelia drew in a deep, hard breath before turning hesitantly to face the man she'd drawn as the dark prince.

Savage.

He was the descendant of that first Irish Baron and a Native American princess, the only daughter of a great chief and dearly loved by not just her father, but all her people.

His hard features reflected the proud, independent, strong-willed ancestors he'd sprung from. A throwback, Amelia's mother had called him, even more so than his father.

So strong he had survived a lifetime of evil perpetuated by the man that claimed to be her father.

"You once told me any relationship with me would never work because my father so hated you," she now stated bitterly, remembering the letter she had found on her bed the night he had destroyed her life. "Tell me, Crowe, what will you tell everyone who questions why you're screwing a serial killer's daughter? Especially the daughter of the serial killer who murdered every member of your family except your sister and first cousins? How will you excuse that betrayal to every Callahan he murdered?"

That question had tormented her in the six weeks he'd been gone. Lying in the dark, staring into dim light of the moon outside her balcony doors, she'd tried to imagine an excuse that would work.

She hadn't found one.

"I stopped paying attention to demands a hell of a long time ago, Amelia." Broad shoulders shrugged negligently as he hooked his thumbs in his belt loops and watched her somberly. "And if I were to decide to answer such an asinine question I guess I'd just have to tell the truth."

The truth? That he was using her to draw out that killer? Or that he was determined to punish the only person he could link to that killer?

"The truth," she murmured. "That answer could get interesting."

"Hell, we're having sex, not making babies. Right?" he growled before adding, "I doesn't matter who contributed his sperm to your creation, or whose DNA may be part of you. All that matters is the woman you are. And that woman bears no resemblance in any way, shape, or form to a killer."

Her lips curled mockingly. "That really doesn't matter to most people, Crowe. What does matter to them, though? That every appearance of disassociating themselves be maintained. The child might be innocent, but the parent isn't, so of course the child must be guilty as well. Right?"

She wasn't going to confront the first part of that question.

"You know better than that." He breathed out roughly, standing still, almost motionless as he watched her with a hint of wariness. "Come on, Amelia, I don't give a damn what they think. Neither should you."

Should she know better than that? What they thought had just taken away all the joy her life had contained in the past seven years.

"Evidently I don't know anything," The retort sounded much angrier than she felt. She was simply too damned tired to work up the amount of rage it would take to match her voice. "Why are you even here? Haven't you figured out yet that Wayne doesn't care what we're doing as long as one of us is being punished?"

When Crowe had left that summer, seven years before, she remembered the dark silence that had seemed to fill Wayne until he'd learned of Amelia's interest in Crowe a year later. Thank God he'd never learned the full truth of their relationship. She'd been punished enough just for that "interest."

God, Amelia should have known. How had she not suspected what he was or the evil he possessed?

"Then we stop allowing the punishments," he decided.

She stared back at him, bemused. She knew Crowe, and she knew he didn't buy into such naive psychobabble.

"And you propose to stop it, how?" she asked, mocking the statement as she crossed her arms over her breasts defensively. "Let's see, perhaps I should just inform the auxiliary they can vote me out every day of the week if they want, but I'm tired of being punished so I'm just going to ignore it. When they call Archer to force me out of the meetings, I'll just ignore him as well: But tell me." Tilting her head to the side questioningly, she gave him a hard, bitter look. "How do I ignore that tiny cell he'll lock me in?"

A dark chuckle rasped from his chest. The sound of it was far too sexy for her peace of mind.

And why the hell did she even care how sexy it sounded?

"The imagery is amusing, fairy-girl, but hardly what I meant and I think you know it."

This time she was the one who shrugged as though she simply didn't give a damn.

"There's no way I can ignore the facts of life at the moment, either, Crowe." Dropping her arms, she stared around her office as regret beat at her soul with bruising force. "Wayne's not here to punish; neither is Amory Wyatt. That just leaves me. And they'll make sure there's no escaping the fact that I'm being punished."

And she was sick of it.

Fury lashed at her senses as she fought to beat it back, fought to do as she had always done in the past when faced with the unfairness of the choices she'd had to make.

"So you're just going to lie down and accept their blows like you were forced to accept Wayne's?"

Amelia stared back at him silently as the question hung in the air between them, the implications racing through her mind. He smiled knowingly.

She clasped her hands before her, patiently linking her fingers together as she considered the best way to answer.

He chuckled in amusement, shaking his head. "Considering which lie to tell me?" An arrogant brow arched with mocking emphasis.

"Or trying to figure out what the hell you're talking about," she scoffed, watching him warily.

There was really no way he could know or even

suspect the truth where Wayne's abuse was concerned, was there?

"Lying, little sugar elf? When did you pick up that nasty little habit?"

She'd picked up that nasty little habit to protect his sexy tight ass, she thought in exasperation. After that, it had become her means of survival.

"Lying about what?" Just what she needed, Crowe possibly knowing more than he should.

He shook his head slowly, a low sound leaving his lips. "Now, Amelia, let's be honest here. Do you think I've not heard all the nasty little rumors running around since we identified Wayne as the Slasher?"

How had, or could, anyone have known to gossip about it? Surely he was just trying to bait her, to force the truth from her some way.

"What sort of rumors?" she asked hesitantly, uncertain whether or not she wanted to know.

His lips pursed thoughtfully for a moment before they curled into a mocking smile.

"The day Wayne brought you home from college he took you to old Doc James to have your wrist set," he stated. "Doc's notes were pretty concise, sweetheart. The break, he observed, wasn't consistent with the reason he was given for it."

The look on his face said he demanded an explanation.

"I fell." She pushed the lie from between her teeth. "I told him that."

"What caused the fall?" The studied innocence in his expression warned her he had a trump card just waiting for her.

The problem was, Amelia couldn't really remember what reason Wayne had given for the fall.

She excused herself with the fact she had been in an incredible amount of pain at the time.

"You didn't answer me, Amelia." He advanced on her slowly, his narrowed gaze locked with hers. "Exactly how did you fall?"

"I don't exactly remember how I fell, Crowe. What does it matter how it happened?"

"Wayne broke your wrist, didn't he, baby?" His voice deepened. The incredible gentleness in his tone—shadowing the anger toward Wayne in his gaze—had her aching to tell him the truth, to tell him—oh God, to tell him everything. And she knew that wasn't possible.

Tightening the hold she had on her fingers, Amelia forced herself to stand her ground and glare back at him.

"Why would you ask me such a thing?" She hated lying, but God he was pushing her. She didn't want to lie to him but neither did she want to answer his questions.

Unlike Wayne, if he became suspicious that Amelia was hiding something, Crowe would know what questions to ask.

The low rasp of another chuckle had her heart racing faster. He knew something. Something more than what he may have found in Doc James's records.

The question was, exactly what did he know?

"Shall I make it easy for you?" he suggested, moving toward her, the lean-hipped, powerful stride bringing him to her in just a few steps until he was preventing her from placing any distance between them.

"Oh, why don't you," she invited mockingly, wondering at what point pressure against the fingers would result in a break.

No doubt Wayne could have answered that silent question for her.

She only barely controlled a flinch as Crowe reach out and brushed her hair back from her cheek.

"Cami told me about the journal, Amelia," he murmured as she felt the blood leach from her face. "The same day he forced you to leave school, and when you arrived back in Sweetrock, your wrist was broken. Now, how did your wrist end up broken?"

"I fell," she lied, coldly.

If Cami had told Crowe about the journal and Wayne's reaction to it, then only God knew the questions Crowe would ask. Especially if he ever learned of Amelia's visit to Clyde Ramsey's ranch or the months before Wayne arrived at the school that Cami had been unable to find her.

She couldn't afford those questions. Not yet.

Crowe could see how tightly her fingers were clenched, the pressure against them turning them white.

She was lying. Pride and willful determination gleamed in her gaze, her control over her responses so great that only her fingers betrayed her.

"Hmm," he murmured. "Where did you break it?"

He was learning. Amelia was great at the surface lie, and she made it damned good. Until you looked beneath the surface.

"You know, Crowe, it's been so long and it's of so little concern to me that I don't remember much beyond the fact that it really hurt. So can we be done with the questions and answers already? I have things to do, and arguing with you is not on tonight's itinerary."

The sarcasm fell off her tongue as though it had been created for sass. Her posture, tone, expression—hell, he bet at the moment every cell in her body was poised for another smart-assed comment.

It made him hard. It made his balls ache with the need to come, his cock throb with the need to fuck. And the need, the hunger wasn't for just any woman. Hell no, it couldn't be that easy.

It never was when it came to Amelia.

His sweet, never-argued-with-him sugar elf was definitely beginning to surprise him.

"So pencil me in, fairy-girl," he growled, reaching out for her, his hands gripping her hips before she could jerk away from him, pulling her quickly against the hard length of his denim-covered cock.

Damn her, what did she do to him? The feel of her against him, the warmth of her body, the sound of her breath catching, only increased his hunger for her.

"Let me go, Crowe." Small hands pressed against his broad chest as though to push away from him and escape the hold he had on her.

"You want to be free, sugar elf?" Lowering his head, he pressed a kiss just below her ear. "Letting you go means I won't be able to taste that sweet little pussy like I've been dying to do."

Her eyes darkened, the flush mounting her cheekbones, which turned from the bright red of anger to a fierce pink, indicating the arousal building in her body.

"I don't care—" she tried to protest.

"But I do care," he promised, nipping the lobe of her ear. "Because when I finished I was hoping I could convince you to return the favor."

The thought of her mouth, heated silk, and damp hunger had his cock flexing in a hard, hungry pulse of need. Damn, she made him crazy to fuck her.

"Come on, fairy-girl," he teased her as his senses burned to take her. "If you won't tell me the truth about all those little accidents you've had, then at least play with me for a little while."

Before she could stop him he managed to release the catch at the side of her skirt, slide the little zipper down, and push the skirt from her hips and over her thighs.

"Dammit, Crowe," she gasped, trying to jerk out of his arms again.

"Come back here." Wrapping one arm around her back to jerk her against him, Crowe stared down at the mutinous flare of anger in her eyes as it vied with the arousal darkening the gray-blue orbs. "Tell me you don't want me, Amelia, and don't you fucking lie to me, either, damn you. Tell me you don't want me and I'll let you go."

"This has nothing to do with what I want." She jerked against his hold again, struggling to pull away as she glared up at him. "I won't let you bully me."

"Bully you?" He narrowed his eyes on her, watching the sharp flare of her delicate little nose and the curl of anger at her lips. "I'm not trying to bully you baby, I'm trying to get into your pants. There's a difference."

"Maybe I don't want you in my pants," she retorted, her breathing rough, the blood pounding in the vein up the side of her neck.

She was just as turned on as he was and he knew it.

"Tell me your pussy's not wet," he dared her. "Tell me those pretty pink nipples aren't hard and sensitive, begging you to let me suck them until you swear you're ready to come from nothing else. Go ahead, Amelia, lie to me some more. Tell me you're not dying to ride my dick until the world explodes around you." His lips were nearly touching hers now, his gaze locked with the shocked, aroused depths of hers. "Because I promise you, baby, I'm so damned ready and aching to ride that hot little pussy that it's all I can do not to take you standing here."

Her eyes darkened further, lips parting as her eyes widened just that little bit.

"Do you want that, too, sugar elf? My cock buried in your tight little pussy as we stand here?"

He lifted her against him, ignoring her gasp as he pulled her up his body until his denim-covered shaft pressed between her thighs and her knees gripped his hips naturally.

"Yeah, that's the way you do it," he growled, reaching

between them to loosen his belt and jeans before drawing the painfully hard length of his penis from inside his pants.

He wasn't about to let her go long enough to pull her panties down her legs.

"I'll eat that pretty pussy later," he promised as he tore the silk and elastic from her body, then dropped the ruined material to the floor at his feet. "Now lift that sweater and let me have those hot little nipples."

To convince her, he tucked the wide crest of his erection just inside the swollen, incredibly slick folds of her heated cunt.

He stopped there, watching as her hips pressed lower, her knees tightening at his hips to hold herself in position for the penetration he was teasing her with.

"Give me those pretty breasts," he ordered her again, wondering if the top of his head would blow off from the pressure he was putting on his aching cock. "Let me suck one of those pretty nipples while you ride me, sweetheart," he groaned. "Come on now, take that fucking sweater off."

A whimper left her lips, but her hands moved from his shoulders, gripped the hem of the sweater, and pulled it slowly up her torso before lifting it over her head.

The bra was no obstacle. Thin, delicate lace covered the tight tips, making it impossible to wait for her to remove it. His head lowered. Pushing the low-cut lace aside with the fingers of his free hand, he latched on to one hard tip, drawing it into his mouth and pressing his cock deeper between the swollen lips of her sex.

Amelia heard her whimpers with a distant sort of shock that wasn't nearly enough to pull her out of the grip of pleasure so incredible, she was helpless against it.

His mouth drew on the overly sensitive peak of her

breast as he wrapped his arm around her hips, holding her firmly against him. He pressed the thick erection against the entrance to her vagina; the wide crest stretched her flesh, demanding entrance and igniting her senses.

She could feel too much, too many sensations, too much pleasure.

She ached for him with a soul-deep hunger she couldn't rid herself of. A hunger that weakened her, that held her mesmerized as pure, white-hot pleasure began to whip over her flesh.

Between her thighs, the mushroom-shaped crest of his erection parted her further, dragging an agonized moan from her lips. More of her juices fell from the inner depths of her vagina. The excess slid past the slight penetration to slicken her folds further.

"Crowe, more," she whispered, a part of her shocked at the demand.

He eased farther inside her, slowly, so slowly until the full width of the blunted tip was buried inside her, stretching her with a heat she was still shocked she could actually take.

"Damn, that's it baby, suck my dick inside," he groaned, the explicit words shocking her as much now as they had the first time he had uttered them seven years before.

Even more shocking was the realization that the uncontrolled flex and ripple of her internal muscles felt as though she was indeed trying to suck him inside her, to milk the engorged flesh and draw it deeper inside her body.

Pulling the lace of her bra over the curve of her other breast, Crowe covered the unattended little bud with his mouth. Sucking it deep in his mouth, he used his tongue to lash at the sensitized nerve endings as his erection surged deeper inside the tender depths of her body.

Crying out at the stretch and burn of her flesh, she was

only dimly aware of him moving, turning her, his body tensing as he pressed her back against the wall.

In the next breath a hard thrust sent the heavy shaft surging fully inside her, burying to the hilt as her vagina clenched and spilled its damp heat along the invading flesh. His lips abandoned her breast; his head lifting, he stared down at her with a fierce, predatory hunger.

Amelia couldn't stay still, despite the grip he had on her hips or the tight press of her body into the wall. Her knees tightened on his hips, her hips shifting, lifting and moving against him as sensation struck at the responsive flesh stretched around him.

"That's it, baby. Ride me. Show me how hungry you are for me," he growled, his lips moving to her neck in hot, hard little kisses that heated her flesh and sent hot surges of electrified pleasure racing from the contact.

Show him how hungry she was for him? She had thought, for a while, that she wouldn't survive after he'd left seven years before. The world had been a bleak, gray existence filled with pain and hunger. Then with a fear that drove such deep, nightmarish spikes of terror through her senses, it had nearly broken her.

As overriding as the pain without him had been, the pleasure now was a hundredfold in the opposite direction. So good, so hot and addictive it was almost agonizing.

When his lips covered hers, his hips drew back. His tongue pressed between her lips as he thrust his cock inside her again, suddenly moving, his hips pounding against hers. Pleasure whipped through her body in steadily increasing waves of searing tension.

Her nails dug into the cotton of his shirt as her knees tightened further at his hips, clenching on them, lifting herself against him and pressing down hard as he thrust inside her. She drove him deeper into the sensitive depths of her vagina, her flesh rippling, tightening on each heavy thrust.

His kiss was a hungry mating of lips and tongues, stroking the need and driving the lust building in their bodies. Striking need and burning lust began tightening in her pussy, pulsing in the sensitive bud of her clit as his pelvis raked it with each inward stroke.

The sensations grew stronger each time he took her.

Amelia whimpered at each hard, flaring pulse of sizzling pleasure as he shafted harder, faster inside her. Each inward thrust and quick withdrawal tightened the pleasure and pushed her deeper in the maelstrom of ecstasy.

"Look at me, Amelia," he growled, jerking his head back as his thrusts became shorter, the friction against tender nerve endings increasing. She forced her eyes open, her gaze meeting his.

Heavy, drunk with pleasure, hammered gold gleaming against the deep brown depths of his eyes, Crowe held her gaze.

"God, yes," he whispered. "Let me see your eyes, baby. Let me watch you come for me."

She couldn't bear it.

Staring into his eyes was like being hot-wired into a sudden, deepening electric pulse. It drew the pleasure into ever-tightening waves of destruction.

The pressure was beating at her clit, in the clenched tissue of her vagina. Each thrust forged past the spasming muscles that struggled to hold on to the shuttling thickness of his cock.

Agonizing pleasure struck at the tender bud, at her womb. It sent forks of sharp, rasping sensation tearing through her vagina, clenched it, tightened around her clit. It suddenly imploded inside her with spirals of ecstasy so blistering, they ignited a harder, sharper explosion.

Her senses ruptured. Flying into a blinding, white-hot

vortex of erupting sensation and clashing ecstasy, she feared she'd never survive it.

It shouldn't be like this.

She sobbed with the exquisite near agony of the ecstasy overtaking her, possessing her, marking her spirit.

As her pussy spasmed and milked at his cock, her release spilling around it, Crowe surged inside her in a final thrust that triggered his own orgasm and filled her with jet after jet of hot semen. A harsh, low male groan vibrated from his chest.

She could feel everything. The smallest touch, the stroke of air against her flesh, each cell of his body that met with hers amplified through her senses. The dampness of his perspiration stroking against her flesh, the heated warmth of hers as it met his already damp flesh.

Nothing escaped her senses. Not the pulse of his release, the rasp of his shirt against her nipples, or the breath that carried her name from his lips to stroke against the flesh of her neck where he'd buried them.

What also didn't escape her notice were those few precious seconds when she swore she could feel him so clear, so close that they must be a part of each other. That sense of unity, of completeness, brought her the first, fragile moments of peace in far more years than she could remember.

CHAPTER 10

It was days later before Crowe actually realized that Amelia had never really answered his question about Wayne's abuse.

He was immersed in reports from the Brute Force agents, the personal security team from the agency he co-owned with his cousins and the Resnova family.

Based in Sweetrock, the agency had garnered attention even before the Resnovas had invested in it. Now Crowe had every available agent not currently on assignment searching for Wayne Sorenson.

They were cutting off every venue of aid Wayne could possibly turn to. All his contacts were under investigation, or had an agent in place should Wayne attempt to contact them. Phones were tapped and the better part of the agency's considerable electronic strengths were aimed at detecting any and every sign of the murdering bastard.

Bank security cameras had spotted him walking into one of the larger banks in Aspen. The disguise he had worn was enough to fool the naked eye, but not the facial recognition software Ivan Resnova had contracted from the far-flung Resnova family member who had created it.

They'd almost had him.

They had a single agent in town. He'd slipped inside the bank to catch sight of Wayne, who had obviously spotted the agent first. He'd rushed from the bank before the team could reach it and disappeared in a throng of shoppers in the outdoor bazaar several streets away.

They had managed to find out why he was there, though, and they'd uncovered yet another of Wayne's identities. Under the assumed identity he'd rented a safe-deposit box years before. A court order was pushed through with the governor's influence, and the box was opened to reveal a handgun, ammunition, close to a million dollars' worth of high-grade, uncut diamonds, and several hundred thousand dollars in cash.

The assets were turned over to an account set up to eventually split them among the law enforcement agencies that had chased the Slasher for over fourteen years, as well as the family members of the victims Wayne and his partners had murdered.

So far, they'd found three safe-deposit boxes, two mountain cabins, as well as a home in Aspen. There were three vehicles, stashes of cash in each of the cabins, and a safe in the home that held more cash, stocks, and bonds in yet another assumed identity.

Wayne had been busy, Crowe reflected bitterly as he tossed the reports to the table before him and stared around the small room he'd taken to locate the multiple monitors and computers running the security programs and assessing national and state as well as private and business security systems throughout Colorado and several other surrounding states.

The little electronic bot programs Ivan sent out through the Internet to attach to the public security systems damned well beat any Crowe had seen outside the intelligence community. They sifted through millions of faces that passed thousands of cameras across Colorado, especially the counties closest to Corbin County.

Some days, Wayne was a busy little beaver.

A week before in Boulder, two days before that in Montrose. He hadn't yet ventured into Corbin County as far as the cameras had detected.

Crowe had a feeling Wayne was closer than any of them could guess, though. He wouldn't have left Corbin County, and—unlike the FBI agents—Crowe was sure he hadn't left the state or the country.

Wayne had no intentions of escaping. Nothing in the world mattered as much to the man as destroying the Callahans' lives before they had a chance to get used to the happiness they were finding.

And the news stations were flashing stories of the Callahans' happiness daily. Crowe made certain they were. They were especially focusing on Crowe and his new lover, Amelia Sorenson, the daughter of the man the world was coming to revile. The daughter the public was seeing as strong, compassionate, and a leading figure in past battles with the Slasher, the uncaring county attorney who had attempted to destroy the Callahans.

Stories were beginning to filter in about the many and varied citizens she'd helped escape the vengeful wrath of the man who wielded enough power to falsify evidence or have it planted against those he considered his enemies.

The young man whose family home was saved after Amelia had managed to slip the family's lawyer proof that the owner couldn't have been involved in the large excavation of marijuana found growing in his basement, because he had been out following his hobby. A camping and rock climbing enthusiast, he had been perched on a cliff somewhere in Asia about the time the crop had been planted, and he'd been recovering from a fall in Budapest when the authorities had harvested it.

He'd returned home in time to face several DEA agents and Wayne Sorenson as he'd unlocked his front door. Wayne had proof the owner couldn't have been involved. He'd attempted to destroy it, knowing the guide who'd dropped him off at the bottom of the cliff was on an extended trip somewhere in the Congo and unreachable. The doctor and nurse who had treated him and sent the original documents had then contracted a case of sudden forgetfulness after the file they'd sent Wayne "disappeared."

Wayne thought he'd shredded all proof. Amelia had been terrified he was right until she checked the memory card she'd programmed the fax machine to store all information in. It was still there, within hours of being overwritten by the time she'd managed to get to the office ahead of Wayne and send it to the homeowner's attorney.

There were families who had nearly lost their homes after having their receipts for cash payments of land taxes mysteriously disappear. Records in the county attorney's office would show nonpayment with the county taking possession immediately to pay the delinquent bills. Just as mysteriously, those receipts would be found. Under a doormat, in a vehicle's seat; one had been found stuck in the collar of the family dog after it came in from a trip outside.

Hell, Crowe had known who had been behind it the minute he heard the stories, just as each victim had learned who had saved their lands or family members framed for crimes. Or even auxiliary members, it was rumored, whose husbands had been framed or sons targeted.

That story had been particularly satisfying to hear, Crowe thought. Watching it hours before, he'd smiled smugly at his own ingenuity in digging up the information. Because it sure as hell hadn't been easy. It wasn't as though Amelia had been wise enough to give him even a particle of the information he'd come up with. Hell no, his agents had dug it up by following this thread of information, then that one, then digging like sons of bitches to get enough to threaten to fill in the gaps themselves.

Only then had the auxiliary members—such as the mayor's wife, Ruth Anne Justin, and her daughter, Linda, the wife of the current Corbin County attorney, Jason Grandor—spilled their reluctant, less-than-pleased little guts.

Giving the security monitors that viewed the estate a final glance, he gestured to the tech to keep watch before leaving the room and going in search of Amelia. He knew she had an appointment scheduled that afternoon with several entertainers scheduled for the spring social season. Why she had elected to keep the meeting, he wasn't certain. He'd be damned if he would have given that damned auxiliary the satisfaction of doing any damned thing.

The fact that his sister had fought for and won the title of social planning director didn't affect his feelings on it whatsoever.

Hell, Anna should have known better that to take the position. She and Amelia both should have left that damned committee hanging in the wind. Just as they had intended to leave Amelia hanging.

Grimacing at the thought of their reactions should he voice his opinion, he stepped into the kitchen in time to watch Amelia finish her coffee next to the sink.

"You sure we're going to that meeting?" he asked her, bracing his hand against the door frame as he glared at her.

"Stop staring at me like that," she ordered.

He narrowed his gaze. "Like what?" Like he wanted to fuck her? She should be used to that by now.

"Like you believe I should be locked away for my own

safety or something," she drawled, that slightest edge of amusement a hell of a lot better than the stoicism she'd carried in the past days.

"Or something," he agreed with a disgusted little grunt. "Those women don't deserve your damned help."

"Anna does," she refuted.

"Anna only demanded the position to give it back to you," he argued. "Only this time you have to drag Anna along with you, bitching every breath."

Amelia couldn't help but grin at that comment, because it was the truth.

"She threatened to neuter the fairy clown yesterday." She gave a muffled laugh at the memory as she moved away from the sink toward him. "Are you ready to leave?"

"What time's the damned meeting?" he asked.

She glanced quickly at the watch on her wrist. "Fifteen minutes."

"Five minutes per block." He grinned. "That works for me. It would give me time to talk some sense into you."

Amelia rolled her eyes. "It never takes me five minutes to walk a block, Crowe. If it takes you that long then I'm going to wonder how you keep all those tight, manly muscles."

"Wal-Mart," he stated somberly. "They were on special one weekend."

Wal-Mart, her ass. If Wal-Mart was selling muscles like that, on special or not, then they'd stay packed.

"I'll be sure to post that information on Facebook," she grinned as he helped her put on the heavy, faux-fur-lined coat over her shoulders. "I can think of a lot of interested parties."

"I bought all they had," he assured her as he opened the front door to face a black jacket wall of Brute Force agents. "Come on then, fairy-girl, let's take your little walk."

"My little walk," she murmured. "Who can enjoy it with a wall of bodyguards surrounding them?"

Stepping into the clear mountain air she inhaled slowly, filling her lungs with the crisp, cold wintry air as they moved down the steps of the portico to the cement walk that led around the driveway to the black metal gates.

Gates that were free of reporters hanging off them for a change. They'd disappeared with Crowe's arrival at the house, and hadn't returned.

At least, not yet.

"How did you get rid of the leeches?" she asked as the small sidewalk gate was opened by one of the security agents.

Standing back, the two agents watched the area carefully as two moved in before them and two behind them.

"Feed the beasts and they'll go on their way," he grunted.

"Until it's time for them to eat again," she pointed out. "Then they'll be right back."

"In that case, I may have a few meals prepared for their consumption," he stated in satisfaction. "Let's just say we have them taken care of for a bit."

Frowning, she tried to get a good look at the street across from them to get ideas for decorations should the Fairy Carriage use the street as one of its routes. She found her way blocked by a black wall.

"This is ridiculous, Crowe," she muttered.

"Yeah, reporters tend to carry that title." He spoke as though he believed they were still on the subject of journalists.

Glowering back at him, Amelia tightened her lips and came to a quick stop.

The agent behind her nearly tripped over her.

Crowe seemed unsurprised. Pausing, he looked down

at her, one black brow arching arrogantly over those predatory eyes. "Problem, sweetheart?"

"Make them move," she ordered, her tone completely reasonable and logical, she was certain. "I can't see where I'm going, nor can I get an idea of what's needed if I can't see the street as we walk."

"Perhaps," he agreed. "But neither can anyone get a clear line of sight, either."

Drawing on what little remaining patience she possessed, Amelia shoved her hands into the pockets of her coat and glared up at him from beneath her lashes.

"Move them, Crowe, or I promise you I'll find a way to do what has to be done without you."

His head lowered, his gaze hardening. "I'll take pictures for you. Hell, I'll have video taken for you, but I will not have them move and risk Wayne or some dumb bastard he's hired attempting to put a bullet in your head."

Amelia curled her fingers into fists.

She liked to think she wasn't an ignorant person. She didn't get into public confrontations, no matter who the conflict was with. She didn't give others a reason to gossip about her if at all possible.

She had no intentions of starting now.

"I'm ready to return to the house." Turning, she began walking the short distance back. "I'll have Anna bring the entertainers there."

She wasn't going to argue with him. She definitely wasn't going to attempt to knock any sense into him while the agents were watching and listening so curiously.

"Amelia, you don't have to return to the house," he stated reasonably.

"Will you have them get out of my way then?" She didn't bother to glance at him as she continued to walk. She had a feeling she knew his answer.

"I can't do that," he sighed. "But I know you wanted to see a few of the grottoes—"

"Don't worry about it," she suggested briskly, increasing her stride as they neared the iron fence surrounding Wayne's property.

"I won't let you risk yourself like that." His voice was tighter now.

The gate was opened as it had been before. Two security guards moved to each side as the other four surrounded them instead.

Pulling her cell phone from her coat pocket, she quickly texted Anna that she wouldn't be able to come to the meeting, but Anna could bring the entertainers to the house instead.

Really? Anna texted back with a frownie face icon. *Suggested this 2 Crowe 2day. He said NO! Archer says Crowe has to call first.*

Amelia texted back. *Tell Archer you get to take care of this then.*

Amelia stopped in the middle of the walk, glaring at the phone before slowly turning her gaze up to Crowe as she ignored the now frantic pinging of the text messages Anna was rapidly sending.

He stared back at her coolly, his gaze implacable as it lifted from the screen of the phone to meet hers.

"Making decisions for me, Crowe?" she asked him softly.

"Protecting you," he amended, his voice low as he gripped her upper arm firmly and began moving toward the house once again.

"Protecting me," she repeated with a bitter little laugh. "Yeah, that's what Wayne said when he locked me in the basement for two days and nights when you returned two years ago. He was just protecting me."

Jerking her arm out of his grip, she stalked up the steps

to the door, entering the house and quickly stripping her coat. She hung it neatly in the closet, refusing to look at him. She could feel him staring at her, silently searing her as she ignored him.

"Leave," he ordered the guards, his voice dangerously quiet as Amelia strode from the foyer.

She didn't hear their response. She rather expected they hadn't given him one.

People tended to just obey Crowe without argument.

"Don't fucking turn your back on me and act as though I don't exist." The harsh growl rasped from his throat as Amelia found herself suddenly swung around to face him.

She simply wasn't in the mood to be pulled around or manhandled. Even gently.

Rising to her tiptoes, getting as close to the glitter of amber in his gaze as possible, she let loose.

"Don't imagine, for even a moment, Crowe Callahan, that I'm one of your employees or one of your damned starstruck flunkies, because I'm not. You may get your orders obeyed, but trust me, it's only because you're stronger, not because I agree with you by any stretch of the imagination." Her finger poked into his chest with a quick, imperious little jab as she snarled the declaration out at him.

"My what?" Incredulity filled his tone.

"You heard me. Don't make me repeat myself." Turning on her heel, she headed for the desk on the far side of the room. "You can leave now to do whatever skulking around it is that you do and leave me the hell alone. As far as I'm concerned, I'm finished with you for the moment."

Finished with him.

She was finished with him?

"Oh baby, I thought you knew me better than that," he

drawled, allowing his lashes to drift partially over his gaze to hide the full effect of his intentions.

"I know you as well as I need to know you." She tossed her head like a feisty little mare.

Well hell, that was okay, because he was just the stud for her.

He smiled. A slow, easy curve of his lips as he turned and walked back to the wide double doors leading to the foyer.

And closed them before deliberately sliding the lock in place.

"Ya know, sugar elf," he breathed out with deliberate relish as he turned back to her. "You're getting ready to know me a whole lot better."

Wariness had filled her gaze, darkening the turquoise color and giving it a faintly green cast. Like the ocean just before dusk.

"I'm not in the mood for this."

Oh yeah, he was just that easy to turn off—or not.

Amelia cursed her own unruly tongue and her untamed body.

Son of a bitch, she knew better than to dare him.

It was common knowledge: *Don't dare a Callahan, you'll regret it.*

But what had she done? She'd gone and dared the most stubborn, most determined, and definitely the most darkly sexual Callahan known to draw a breath.

"Crowe, trust me, this isn't the time." She narrowed her eyes on him and hardened her tone.

As though that was going to work, she thought with a spurt of sarcasm.

"Oh baby, trust me, when it comes to you, it's always the time."

He paused several feet from her and pulled off the

leather jacket he wore before tossing it over the back of a couch.

Her eyes widened at the shoulder holster and lethal handgun he wore. The same one he unclipped and laid over the jacket a moment later.

"You're falling behind, sugar elf," he warned her, taking a seat on the large wingback chair next to the couch and unlacing his boots.

"In what way? Undressing?" she snorted. "It's the middle of the day, and I'm sure Anna will be here any moment . . ."

He shook his head as he spoke. "No, she won't be."

"Why not?" He seemed entirely too confident. That wasn't good.

"Archer texted. Told me to send a message if he needed to bring Anna over here. I didn't text him back."

Great, they were conspiring together. Just what she needed, her best friend's lover conspiring with her own. That simply wasn't fair.

"I'll be certain to tell Anna the two of you have your own little codes," she suggested sweetly.

She acknowledged she could possibly be in just a bit of trouble here. Trouble she had been counting on Anna to bail her out from with a speedy little arrival and several social entertainers.

It appeared that wasn't going to happen.

"I'm sure Anna's already figured that one out, darlin'," he promised her. "And now, you're really behind."

His boots were off and lying carelessly beneath the chair as she watched him with an edge of caution.

Rising to his feet, he stared back at her with that knowing little smile that was guaranteed to spell trouble.

"I'm not having sex with you." Sometimes, that worked, to just take a stand with him immediately and let him know how it was going to be.

In this case, that dark chuckle that left his lips definitely spelled trouble.

"Works for me," he informed her with a sexy smile. "I'll just have sex with you. All you have to do is lie there, sugar elf."

Her mouth almost dropped open in incredulity. "You are so not serious."

"I am so very damned serious," he informed her, all amusement easing from his expression. "Done with me, are you, baby? Let me show you just how done with you I am not."

CHAPTER 11

"Crowe, this is not the best idea you've had in a while," she informed him nervously as he took a step toward her. "Actually, it's going to end up being one of your worst."

"Really?" His expression appeared curious; his gaze told another story. "In what way, sweetheart?"

In what way?

"Son of a bitch," she muttered, irritation getting the best of her. "Is that all you can do—question every damned thing?"

"Isn't that the only way to get answers?" he asked with a smug smile. "So, are you in the mood yet, baby, or do I get to have fun with that pretty little body of yours all by myself?"

"It's my body, too, Crowe." She tried for that no-nonsense voice she had heard her mother use.

"Hmm, before I'm finished, that inquisitive little brain of yours is going to realize just who commands it."

Before Amelia could blink in outrage he'd moved. Pulling her into his arms and lifting her against his body just enough that only the tips of her toes brushed against the hardwood floor.

"Crowe. No." The surprised gasp came as he gripped the band of her skirt, his fingers tightening on it.

His gaze narrowed further on her.

"I don't have that many clothes, Crowe." Admitting to that sent humiliation sweeping through her. "You have to stop destroying what I do have."

What flashed in his gaze she wasn't certain. Something wild and primitive. Something possessive.

His fingers relaxed just enough to flick open the tiny metal clasp and ease down the zipper securing the band. A second later, the silk-and-wool material slid down her legs to the floor.

"Crowe . . ."

"No more protests, Amelia," he warned her, the dark gentleness of his tone sending a tingling sizzle up her spine as his palm shaped the sensitive curve of her rear.

The callused tips of his fingers stroked against her flesh, dipping between her thighs to test the damp silk of her panties.

"How long have your panties been wet, baby?" Those diabolical fingers slid beneath the elastic leg to find the swollen, silken folds beyond.

Gasping at the pleasure streaking through sensitive nerve endings, Amelia smothered the moan threatening to follow it.

"Answer me, sugar elf," he demanded as he swung her in his arms and moved to the couch, laying her back on the thick cushions gently.

He made her feel delicate and fragile rather than clumsy and lacking in grace, as she knew she often was.

Following her, Crowe came over her, one hard thigh pressing between hers as his head lowered, his lips feathering over hers.

"Crowe, you have to stop this." He was weakening her, stealing her pride and her will with his touch.

The feather-light caress of his lips changed instantly. The moment the protest escaped he sealed them in a kiss that didn't just steal her protest. It stole her senses.

As his lips and tongue dragged a needy moan from her throat, his hands stroked, caressed, and pleasured.

Experienced fingers quickly unbuttoned her blouse, pushing it back from her shoulders as his lips moved from hers to the rise of her breasts above the delicate lace cups of her bra.

He was undressing her. Lifting her against him as he quickly removed the blouse and her bra, leaving her clad in nothing but her silk panties.

"This has to stop," she whimpered, the sound anything but convincing.

And it wasn't as though he was actually listening to her.

His lips moved to the rise of her breasts, stroking over them with heated kisses as her breath caught with pleasure.

She couldn't think when he touched her. When she lay beneath him, her senses clouded with the building ecstasy, then she didn't have the will to think. She sure as hell didn't have the will to protest.

Her hands smoothed over his shoulders, loving the feel of his skin, stretched over tightly bunched muscles and rippling beneath her touch.

After licking a nipple with heated male hunger, he must have decided that wasn't nearly enough. A second later his mouth covered the hard tip, sucking it in.

Once it was captured, he still wasn't content. His tongue lashed at it, sending hard, clenching strikes of sensation to attack her womb.

Moving with hungry purpose to the other breast, he nipped and kissed his way to her tight nipple before drawing it into his mouth and suckling the sensitive peak with male hunger.

Her back bowed, the pleasure was so intense. Panting, blood rushing furiously through her veins as feverish need burned beneath her flesh, Amelia knew the battle had been lost before it even began.

Her nails raked against his hard shoulders. Clenching her thighs around the heavy male thigh between hers, her hips rose and feel, the bud of her clit pulsing with painful pleasure as the erotic need rose furious inside her.

The silk of her panties needed to go. They were between her and Crowe. His pants needed to go.

His clothes needed to go.

"Undress, damn you," she cried out furiously, pulling at the shirt covering his shoulders, trying to drag the material up his back and over his head.

He moved, his hands no longer stroking her flesh, his hard body no longer covering hers. Jumping to his feet, he needed only a matter of seconds to undress. His shirt was tossed to the floor, his pants discarded quickly, the boxer briefs quickly pushed over his hips and tossed aside before he returned to her.

The panties he simply ripped from her with a rasped, "I'll buy you more."

She didn't give a damn. She could do without panties if it meant he would touch her faster.

He didn't stretch out over her this time.

Oh, hell no.

Anticipation raced through her entire system as he dragged her hips to the side, pushed her legs apart, and knelt between them.

"Oh hell yeah," he growled, shoving one of the small couch pillows beneath her hips to lift them closer then lowering his head to the saturated folds of her sex.

His tongue swiped through the dew-drenched slit. Licking, stroking, he caressed and tasted her, licking from the snug entrance of her vagina up and around the swollen bud of her clit.

The rasp of each caress sent spirals of increasingly tightening sensation wrapping around and through her clitoris. Her inner muscles clenched and ached, the emptiness inside her becoming increasingly painful as her hips writhed beneath his caresses.

He was torturing her. Teasing her.

His tongue flicked over the hard bud with quick little swipes, the pressure just firm enough to give her a taste of the explosion waiting beyond the edge of pleasure he had her poised on.

Her fingers fisted in his hair, clenched, then eased to grip his head as she begged for release.

Extreme, erotically intense, each lick of his tongue, each suckling kiss sent such a rush of sensation tearing through her that she wondered if she would survive the coming climax.

She was certain she couldn't bear more sensation. Certain that the least bit more pressure would throw her into release. Instead, when his lips covered the violently sensitive bud of her clit, it wasn't release he threw her into.

It amplified the pleasure to a near-painful level. When she was certain she couldn't bear more, two long, experienced fingers began working past the snug, ultrasensitive entrance to her vagina.

The pinching heat of the penetration had her inner muscles rippling, milking at the slow, widening penetration of the clenched tissue.

Her hips arched, trying to force him deeper. Her feet dug into the cushions of the couch to lift her closer, ragged cries escaping her lips as the suction around her clit eased and his tongue began torturing her again.

Licking, stroking. His fingers pushed in slow, shallow

thrusts, working inside her in slow degrees as he filled her senses with nothing but him.

His lips and tongue drove her clit insane. His fingers teasing, taunting her with the steady stretch and burn that never increased at a fast enough rate to throw her over the edge.

Stroking inside her, then easing free of the snug grip of her pussy, he ignored the shattered cry that fell from her lips. His tongue danced over and between the swollen, parted lips of her pussy, slipped to the clenched entrance, then sent flames reaching out over her body as his tongue plunged inside the spasming depths.

Amelia was thrown into a sensual, chaotic storm as he fucked her with slow, lazy thrusts and licking tastes of her inner flesh. His moan vibrated against the entrance, filled with male hunger and rising erotic purpose.

Her hips jerked and writhed against each plunging stroke. Her fingers fisted in his hair, clenched in the strands, desperate to drag him closer. She had to get him closer.

"Please, Crowe," she cried out, growing more desperate with each plunging stroke of his tongue.

Experienced fingertips moved to her clit, stroking it, rubbing.

Panting, fighting to breathe past the incredible pleasure whipping through her, Amelia whimpered as his tongue eased from her inner grip and his fingers replaced it. His lips moved back to the hard, throbbing bud of her clit, enclosed it, and destroyed her senses.

The first, hard suckling pressure and firm rub of his tongue against the side of the overly sensitive bundle of nerves was destructive. Her senses exploded in such a furious series of ecstatic bursts that she lost her breath, as well as the tenuous hold she had on her emotions.

Waves of violent pleasure were tearing through her, shuddering through her body as she dimly realized he was moving. Rising between her thighs, coming over her—

"Crowe!" Her eyes widened, the shudders racing through her deepening, extending as the wide, heated length of his cock began tunneling quickly through the hard clench and release of her vagina.

His groan was more a growl of extreme pleasure as her hips jerked into the hard impalement. Hammering inside her, shallow thrusts, then deeper, as though even in the grip of his own racing pleasure he had to torture her with the ecstasy exploding in her, only to build and explode again.

His lips surrounded a hard nipple, tonguing it, sucking it deep inside his mouth as his cock shafted inside her with furious, driving thrusts.

Pushing her higher, his hand slid beneath her rear, his fingers sliding through the narrow cleft until he found the puckered entrance hidden between them.

Already slick from the excess of the liquid warmth escaping her pussy, his fingers needed no extra lubrication. Gathering the essence over the tight entrance, his fingertip penetrated her.

Easing back, he gathered more of the natural lubrication, pushed inside her again, then repeated the motion several times until his finger was impaling her with each hard, deep thrust that his cock took her pussy with.

One finger eased the tight tissue, then two. Working inside the tender depths, stretching until he was fucking her with controlled thrusts of his fingers as his cock burrowed deep and hard inside the tightening muscles of her vagina.

Whimpers fell from her lips, gasping cries as the internal spasms of yet another destructive climax approached.

It was right there, so close.

Each hard, rapid thrust of his shaft slamming inside

her, the slap of their bodies, the sheen of perspiration that only aided his thrusts and did nothing to cool her body, increased the pleasure.

She wanted to scream, but couldn't find the breath.

Pumping harder inside her, his cock throbbing, swelling impossibly thicker inside the swollen depths, Crowe buried deep, paused, thrust again almost uncontrollably, before she felt that first fiery pulse of semen releasing inside her.

The feeling of Crowe's release spilling to the greedy depths of her body was an unexpected trigger.

Amelia heard the wail that escaped her lips. She was only dimly aware of her body bowing, her head slamming back against the cushions of the couch. All she was frantically, totally aware of were the catastrophic, soul-deep explosions of such brilliant pleasure detonating inside her that it wasn't possible to stay alive.

It swelled inside her, pushing past inhibitions and past hurts; it tore aside any shyness and ripped through distrust as though it had never existed. It exploded with a rush of fiery pleasure that detonated another deeper, violent explosion of pure, fiery rapture.

Racing fingers of electric heat overtook her senses. Like brilliant imps of sensation they buried inside her soul; just as he'd swore, her body would now know who commanded it.

Her soul knew the other half of her, and it grieved.

Because she knew, to the very depths of her spirit, that nothing, no matter how she might try, would ever fill that part of her spirit once Crowe walked from her life. And she knew, no matter how close he held her now, no matter the words he whispered against her breast, she knew—

She knew there was no holding the man who owned her heart. No holding on to the pleasure past the completion of his quest for vengeance.

She would pay, but not by Wayne's hand, for committing the ultimate sin of loving Crowe Callahan.

She would pay by Crowe's hand, when he learned her secrets and took from her the only dream she'd had to hold on to for seven long, lonely years.

She would pay—

As the final harsh shudders eased and exhaustion overtook her, she realized his head had lifted from her breasts. Moving slowly, no doubt aware of the catch of her breath as echoes of raptures clenched her muscles, he eased the still-firm length of his cock from the involuntary tightening of her inner flesh.

She could feel him staring down at her as her body released him, her breath catching at that last wave of pleasure washed gently now through her senses.

Lifting her lashes and staring up at him, the knowledge of everything she would soon lose weighing on her soul, she stared up at him, fighting to hide the lonely ache growing inside her, to hold back the tears that would have filled her eyes.

"Don't forget," he said. "This isn't over, Amelia. And you may want to be finished with me. You believe that you can just decide when this is over." His head lowered until their noses nearly touched. "And you just might even be able to convince yourself of it. But hear me now, fairy-girl, you're mine. And this will not be over until I decide it's over."

There was no stopping the bitterness that escaped her or the painful tightening of her chest. Ribbons of pain stretched from the very depths of her heart, wound around it and tightened to a clenching fist she feared she'd never escape.

"I always knew that," she whispered, fighting to breathe from the pain and the realization that the cap she'd forced over her emotions seven years before had been hopelessly shredded. "But just because you control my body, my pleasure, doesn't mean you'll ever control me. Your chance at that died a hard, cold death seven years ago. And you'll never have a chance at it again."

It was a bluff. The greatest bluff of her life, but she'd be damned if she'd give him the last of the ammunition he needed to completely destroy her.

His lips tilted in a mocking grin. "Don't dare me, fairy-girl, you may force me to prove otherwise to you. I don't think either of us wants to see the results that could have, do you?"

"I think right now, all I want is to get up, get dressed, and go shower," she told him quietly.

She pushed herself to a sitting position, looking around before grimacing and picking up the shreds of her black silk panties as she restrained a sigh.

"I told you, I'll buy you more," he reminded her, his voice harsh and tight.

Amelia only shook her head. "Don't worry about it, I have more panties."

She just didn't have more silk panties. She enjoyed wearing them the most, and he'd just ripped her last pair from her body.

"Dammit, Amelia," he said as she buttoned her blouse before rising to her feet, collecting her skirt, stepping into it, and pulling it over her hips.

"And damn you," she stated without bothering to look at him. "The next time you decide I can't keep a meeting, or a schedule I've put together, why don't you allow me the same knowledge." Securing her skirt, she looked up at him then, and hated Wayne even more for the knowledge that she was losing far more than she had ever imagined when Crowe decided to walk away.

"I wasn't trying to keep you from the damned meeting," he growled as he dressed as well. "I was taking you to the damned thing, Amelia. You were the one who decided to turn back."

"I couldn't walk without tripping over your damned goons," she yelled, too many emotions, too much pain swirling through her senses now. "I couldn't even see the damned street for their shoulders."

"Which means Wayne couldn't get a bead on you with a gun sight," he snapped back, his expression creasing with frustration. "For God's sake, Amelia."

Raking his fingers through his hair, Crowe stared back at her in frustrated anger, wondering why the hell she would imagine he would deliberately try to hurt her—just to what?

Embarrass her? For what reason?

What would he gain from hurting her other than another mark against his soul? God didn't look kindly on men who damaged innocent little fairies with such deliberate cruelty.

"I'm going upstairs, Crowe," she breathed out, that heavy dark thread of an emotion he couldn't quite decipher causing the frustrated anger to grow inside him.

Lowering his brows he watched her silently for long moments as she tucked her bra in the pocket of her skirt, picked up the overly large sketchbook she normally kept on the desk in the corner, then picked up the low-heeled shoes that had fallen from her feet as he swung her in his arms earlier.

She kept her head down, her expression hidden as he watched her. But when she passed him and headed for the door, it didn't lift. Her shoulders weren't exactly drooping, but there was something weary and saddened in their less-than-straight line.

Snarling silently, he watched as she opened the door, stepped through it, then closed it softly behind her.

Hell, he'd have fucking felt better if she had just slammed the door. She wouldn't have had to slam it hard. Just a little bit. Just enough to indicate whatever it was she was feeling that clouded her turquoise eyes and hinted at the shadows filling her.

What the hell had Wayne done to her over the years? How had he managed to take the feisty, too-willing-to-fight little fairy-girl that had stolen Crowe's heart and dim the glitter of life that filled her?

She was more sensual, more heated, and filled with a hunger he couldn't always identify. She was all woman, and responded to his touch like no other woman ever had. As though she waited, every moment of every day, for him to just touch her.

But there was something else in her gaze, too. A loss, a hunger he simply couldn't determine the cause of.

A secret.

Rubbing at his jaw and narrowing his gaze on the door, the answer came to him slowly. Those were secrets shadowing her eyes. Emotions, yes. A pain and loneliness that went soul-deep. But there were also secrets that added to that pain and loneliness. Secrets he obviously hadn't yet uncovered.

Just as he had yet to get her to admit to the abuse Wayne had inflicted on her. Years of bruises, broken bones, unexplained "falls," and uncounted days missed in her job as Wayne's personal assistant.

Added to that were four months she'd all but disappeared from the face of the earth after he'd left seven years ago. She'd remained in Corbin County nearly six months, quieter, less impulsive and daring than she'd been before they had become lovers.

Several women who worked in the courthouse with her had told the investigators Crowe had sent out that they had come upon her several times, certain they'd caught her crying. She would recover quickly, though, they'd reported, leaving them uncertain if it had been quiet sobs they had heard or not.

Then one day, she just hadn't come into work.

Even Wayne had been confused, then—several days later when she hadn't returned—concerned. For weeks, he'd been furious, it was reported. The young woman who had filled in for Amelia in those months had often heard Wayne arguing with her furiously on the phone, demanding she return.

She hadn't returned until days before she was scheduled to leave for college that next summer, nearly a year after Crowe had left.

Drawn, more delicate than normal, shadows hollowing her eyes, she had walked into the dorm room she and Cami Flannigan shared and explained to her friend that she'd just needed time to think. Too many things were out of her control, she'd told Cami, and her relationship with Wayne, she had explained, had become too confrontational. She'd needed to escape and had known that if Wayne found her, he'd drag her back before she had figured anything out.

The instances of bruises and "accidents" had been adding up at the time. Crowe had guessed she had disappeared in an attempt to escape Wayne, only to have him find her and do just that, drag her back.

Cami had agreed, even thought that Amelia had returned of her own volition, determined to finish college and reluctant to leave Corbin County for some reason.

Now Crowe wondered exactly what had been going on. Even his security investigators had been unable to figure out where she had been and what she had been doing at the time. And they were the best in the business. If they couldn't learn the truth, then there was no truth to learn in most cases.

Amelia had them stumped. And now she had him stumped as well.

If there was one thing Crowe couldn't abide, it was being in the dark where information was concerned.

Information was power, and it was protection wrapped into one neat, tidy little package that could never betray a man. Something had happened in the four months she was gone, something that had changed her even more completely than Crowe's desertion had.

He needed to know what that something was, he decided. This feeling he had that she was hiding something, that something stood between them, was driving him insane. And it was concerning him. If Amelia had secrets, that meant there was something more out there that he wasn't prepared for if she needed protection from it.

And that he wouldn't abide.

Protecting Amelia was all that had ever mattered.

CHAPTER 12

The next day dawned bright and sunny, though wicked cold, without a cloud in the sky. A rare enough sight for Corbin County as they headed into the beginning of November.

Locking herself into the family room with a querulous demand that she not be bothered, Amelia even went so far as to drag out the brightly colored sketches and plans for the social events and waited.

An hour passed by before the first security guard checked in on her. Twenty minutes later Crowe peeked in and quickly exited as a sharpened color pencil flew unerringly in his direction. She waited another hour and a half before Crowe quickly checked on her again before ducking to avoid yet another pencil as he slammed the door closed.

She had, at the very least, an hour.

Sliding the metal plate she'd found earlier from the pocket of her jeans and hurriedly pulling a hip-length insulated leather coat from inside the cushioned stool in front of the easy chair, she moved to the wide double doors and made good her escape.

She slid the thin metal plate in against the door alarm

box Crowe's men had installed to alert them to the doors opening, quickly opened the door, stepped out, then closed it quietly. A grin tugged at her lips when the alarm remained silent. Pulling on chocolate-colored leather gloves, she kept close to the house until she reached the corner, then slid quickly across the twelve-foot span between the house and small garden shed.

The gate to the iron fence surrounding the property was there, the alarm box on it causing her to grimace in irritation, but it didn't stop her. It hadn't stopped her when she was younger and Wayne had installed alarms around the perimeter; it wasn't going to stop her now.

She reached the gate, mentally patting herself on the back for having dressed in jeans and low hiking boots.

The snow was still deeper here. The storm that had rolled in several nights before had dumped more than a foot and a half of snow in Sweetrock, and triple that amount in the higher mountains where Crowe's cabin was located.

The resort the Callahans planned on Crowe Mountain would definitely get enough snow for its projected ski slopes.

Stepping up on the old woodpile against the iron fence, she managed to get her foot on the upper rail before pulling herself up, balancing for a moment before dropping to the snow-packed ground on the other side.

She landed with legs bent, one hand catching her as she tilted forward. A smothered giggle escaped as she glanced back to the house and stuck her tongue out at the balcony doors she'd slipped from.

She straightened quickly, but remained crouched enough that the five-foot evergreen hedge in the neighboring yard hid her presence. Not that the neighbors would have cared if they saw her. Old man Hershaw actually used to keep an old wooden box on the other side of the woodpile Amelia used, seven years before.

He'd caught sight of her one night when she'd slipped from the house, after wrenching her ankle on the jump from the top of the fence. The next evening a long, wide box had been set against the fence, making it far easier to get back and forth. Until then, the climb back over the fence had been hell.

She would have thought Crowe was smart enough to consider the fact that she was beginning to feel like a damned prisoner. He was the one who'd taught her how to trick the little alarm boxes back then, and how to avoid the cameras Wayne had placed outside.

Stepping from the Hershaw property to the front walk, she drew in a deep, freedom-drunk breath and started down the sidewalk quickly.

The house was only four blocks from the center of town. A good little walk, she'd always called it. She could walk to work in the summer in heels if she wanted to without limping as she reached the courthouse.

She wasn't wearing heels now, and her stride was deliberately quick as she moved for the center square, a near acre of grass, grottoes, small ponds, a large corner band gazebo, and a bricked dance square.

Wayne had actually petitioned once to use half the square for what he claimed was desperately needed county offices and businesses. He'd also petitioned to hold the socials two weekends a month and only during the summer months rather than spring, summer, and fall as had been the case since their inception.

Each time the vote had come up, his proposal had been soundly voted down, despite the hours of debate and veiled threats he'd made against the city council. The truth had been that the socials had no doubt cramped the fair-weather weekends he used to practice killing innocent women.

The bastard.

Her fists clenched as she shoved them in the pockets of her coat and tipped the lower part of her face into the wide collar to take advantage of the remnants of body heat.

The temperatures were already dipping in the valleys, and the snow was piling up quickly. Sweetrock was located in a sheltered valley, protected by the mountains rising all around it, so snow didn't melt as quickly as it did in the larger cities. Corbin County's population might be growing by the year, but the city council tended to ensure that Sweetrock itself didn't grow as quickly. It retained its small town size and charm, while still growing enough to keep it from becoming a modern-day fiefdom that would eventually end up a ghost town.

She loved the county and the small town she'd been raised in. She might have hated the necessity of dealing with Wayne, and the frustration of being unable to prove he believed he had murdered her mother, but it hadn't been Wayne that had really concerned her. At least, she hadn't known it was Wayne.

Every waking moment, every breath she took, and every dream she had centered on trying to figure out who the Slasher was and how to catch him. She had her own secrets to protect, secrets the Slasher could have destroyed her with rather than just killing her.

Crossing over to Main Street and striding up the brick walk to the west side entrance, Amelia didn't pay much attention to the three men stepping from the bar across the paved street. They were paying attention to her, though, and they were determined to show her they were paying attention.

* * *

Crowe opened the door into the family room only ten minutes after the last pencil had been launched in his direction and only barely restrained the furious curse that would have sizzled the air.

"Malone!" He barked out the team commander's name into the ear set he wore, throwing open the door with such a vicious push that it bounced.

"Malone," the answer came less than a second later, the deep baritone of Rory's voice alert and in command.

"She's gone," Crowe snapped. "Son of a bitch, she's either been taken or escaped herself, but she's gone."

"Mike, run cameras," Rory commanded, obviously having sprinted for the small room housing the cameras and other security hardware they used. "Zoom in on the family room balcony doors. Team One, foyer," he barked into the link, "ASAP. Armed and ready for off-property search. Crowe, she slipped from the patio doors to behind that garden shed and the pile of wood I told you we should move," Rory continued him, his tone cool. "She made her way to the front walk along that line of hedges on the neighboring property and then the cameras lost sight of her approximately five minutes ago."

Rory was obviously on the move if the slamming of the security door was any indication as he muttered. "Mike was fucking sleeping."

Crowe checked the clip of his weapon quickly as he stepped back into the foyer to face the five hard-eyed agents of Team One. Lifting his gaze, he watched as Rory came down the stairs two at a time.

As though his presence was a signal, the other five moved quickly for the door as the black Brute Force Denali came to a quick stop at the front of the house.

The driver rushed from his seat, leaving the door open before quickly moving into the backseat. The remaining four agents rushed along the front walk, spreading out and heading toward the town square at a running pace.

Taking the driver's-side seat, Rory had the vehicle in gear before Crowe had the passenger-side door closed.

"How did she bypass the doors?" Rory's voice was calm, controlled.

The younger man had come into his own in the past year. Leadership and control had settled on his shoulders like a second skin.

"I'm not sure, but I have a pretty good idea." Crowe grimaced. "I just never expected her to try to escape. I taught her how to bypass the door alarms from the inside when she was sneaking out of the house seven years ago to meet me. I suspect that if I check the alarm box on the doors, I'll find a thin metal plate between them, tricking the system into believing the door was closed as she opened it."

"Mike should have caught her slipping from the house to the garden shed," Rory stated, his tone calm—but Crowe could hear the furious undertones. "I want him off my team, Crowe. Immediately."

Crowe gave a short, firm nod. "Contact Ivan once we find Amelia and have it taken care of."

Pausing at the first intersection leading into the square, Crowe and Rory both cursed viciously. The vehicle was thrown into park and they were running up the street at a brief glimpse of honey-streaked brown hair and pale skin amid three large male bodies.

The worst was about to happen.

The moment she actually paid attention to the three brothers exiting the pub, Amelia knew she wouldn't be able to evade the coming confrontation.

Dwight, David, and Dillon Carter had been a pain in the ass since the day she'd caught Dwight cheating off one of her tests in high school and reported it to the teacher.

She hadn't studied her ass off for a month to ace that end-of-semester exam so Dwight's lazy ass could steal the answers from her and pass a class he didn't deserve to.

"Well, if it ain't little Miss Sorenson." Dwight's sneer was the first indication of trouble.

The second was the three male bodies suddenly surrounding her and blocking the view from the tavern they had exited.

"Dwight, don't make me tattle on you again," she warned him wearily. "You know Crowe Callahan will make mincemeat of you and both your brothers."

"Crowe ain't dumb enough to fuck you, bitch." Dillon slurred the words, obviously having had too many drinks at the pub to remember that she had never, not even once, been caught lying.

Sober, all three of them would have been smart enough to know that accosting her would get them in a world of hurt if she was telling the truth. They would have backed off at that point.

Drunk, though, they didn't possess so much as a single brain cell among them capable of thought.

It didn't make them necessarily dangerous, but it did make them unpredictable. And that was nerve-racking for Amelia, even though she'd never heard of any of them actually hurting anyone. Certainly in the eight years since that test she'd ratted Dwight out on, they had never hurt her.

Of course, that was before any of them had known who and what Wayne was.

"He could be." David, normally the smartest of the three, proved this wasn't a good day for him. "I would."

They all laughed uproariously.

"David." Amelia addressed him rather than the other

two, hoping that itty-bitty spark of good humor he usually had would come into effect if she treated him as though he were sober. "You don't want to make Crowe hurt you, do you?"

Staring back at her, David struggled to focus bleary, alcohol-dazed eyes.

"Why would Crowe hurt me?" he asked, rubbing at his jaw in confusion as he looked at his brothers. "Did we do something to Crowe?"

"She says Crowe's fuckin' her. She thinks he's gonna get mad if we bother her," Dillon answered, weaving a bit as he looked at his brother with a smile wide enough to show the missing tooth Crowe had knocked out of his head ten years before.

"Naw, Crowe won't fuck her." David shook his head with all seriousness. "He don't like it when his fucks get killed by her daddy. He wouldn't fuck her 'cause her daddy might kill her."

"Yeah, he wouldn't fuck you." Dwight's dirty finger poked at her shoulder, nearly knocking off her feet and no doubt leaving a bruise.

"That hurt, Dwight," she said sharply, wondering how three men who were so damned laid-back and serious when they were sober could get so ignorant when they were drunk.

"Oh, I'm sorry." Dwight jumped back, his expression at first contrite before it creased in sudden thought and turned belligerent. "Who cares it hurt? That dumb-ass daddy of yours killed our aunt. I think you owe us."

Great, just what she needed, for a brain cell to actually spark and attempt to work as it drowned in booze.

"Yeah, you owe us," Dillon informed her, stumbling just a bit as they began moving in on her. "He killed our aunt. Raped her and cut her heart out. I think we gotta rape you now, and cut out your heart."

The heart in question began racing in fear as she stared at them, backing up as they moved in closer. They were too drunk to be predictable. The fact that they wouldn't mean to hurt would be zero comfort if they actually managed to do so.

"Yeah, get us some of that." David grinned with drunkenness. "And then get her heart. We'll split her heart, too."

"David, I would never hurt you." She focused on the brother considered to be the easiest of the three to get along with. "And I didn't hurt your aunt. Why would you hurt me?"

" 'Cause your daddy hurt us," David answered her somberly, so intently Amelia found herself suddenly, horribly afraid they could indeed carry out their threats. "He killed our aunt, Amelia, and you know we loved her."

Their aunt had indeed loved them. She had helped raise them, spoiled them, and mothered them when their own parents had taken very little time for them.

The three brothers moved for her as one then, reaching for her, trapping her as she attempted to turn and run. They surrounded her, the scent of alcohol, old sweat, and anger overwhelming her senses. The people she had once fought to protect now longer cared if she was protected.

Amelia parted her lips to scream, praying someone heard her.

The sound came out as a squeak.

Between one breath and the next the three men were suddenly thrown back, tossed like mannequins in a demon's grip as Crowe's snarl rumbled in his chest like some damn animal.

Thick black lashes surrounded eyes that were now more amber than brown as rage contorted the savage features of his face, made the hard planes and angles sharper, more defined.

And Rory wasn't exactly standing still.

The security agent didn't just throw the largest of the three brothers back, but caught him before he fell and shook him like a helpless pup.

Of course, Dwight was whimpering like a helpless pup, which rather helped the image along a bit.

Nothing was private in Sweetrock, either. Customers were pouring out of the pub like rats from a sinking ship. Where no one had so much as poked their heads out of the door as the three brothers surrounded Amelia, now the sight of Crowe and Rory tossing them around like oversized toys had the entire bar emptying out to observe the confrontation.

Some were cheering at Crowe and Rory to "Do it again," while others were encouraging the Carter brothers to get up and fight like men.

Amelia wondered if it were possible to find a rock to hide under as the bar patrons hooted and hollered, no doubt hoping to see bloodshed.

"What the hell is going on?" It was Archer, stepping from the entrance to the town square, no doubt drawn by the brothers' drunken cries as Crowe and Rory advanced on them now. His fiancée, Anna, stood behind him in confusion, her gaze catching Amelia's as she quickly gave a hissed, "What the hell happened?"

"You don't want to know," Amelia sighed, the answer more or less working for both of them.

"The hell he doesn't," Crowe refuted, her hope that he would ignore the question shot to hell as he glowered at her with pure male outrage.

Moving from the Carters, he reached her in two long strides, glaring down at her with such anger that she couldn't help but wince as he turned to Archer. "Let me guess. The two of you were meeting here with her and those fucking entertainers she was so desperate to see yesterday?"

Archer frowned before glancing at Amelia, then Anna. "I was under the impression we were meeting both of you. Anna?"

Crowe and Archer both turned to Anna just as Amelia tried to shoot her friend a warning look.

Anna was no one's dummy.

Her eyes widened innocently. "I honestly didn't think to ask."

Bullshit. Amelia almost smiled.

Anna had been suspicious. She had actually asked, and Amelia had stated that she was certain she wouldn't be alone. It wasn't as though Crowe ever gave her five minutes of peace. If she couldn't have slipped from the house then she would have brought him along. Him and the hulking-shouldered agents who refused to give her so much as a sliver of an opening between them to see the streets she had yet to plan the decorations for.

Crowe grunted at the answer.

"Look, I'm already here, just let me finish this so I can—"

"Forget it." Crowe gripped her arm as she turned toward Anna. "I'll be damned . . ." He stared at his empty hand in surprise as Amelia suddenly ducked, twisted, and managed to escape his grip in a move it had taken John less than three days to teach her when he'd first moved into Wayne's house with her.

"Amelia." Growling her name, he stared back at her in warning now. "I'll be damned if you're going to be rewarded for scaring the shit out of me. Those entertainers can go to hell for all I care, and you can get your ass back to the house."

In what tiny particle of his mind had he decided that

he could make decisions for her? That he could order her around like a ten-year-old?

She stared at him in complete amazement as the realization dawned that Crowe didn't see her as an adult so much as the eighteen-year-old she had been seven years before, looking for adventure despite the danger it represented.

"I'm not your damned kid and I'm sure as hell no teenager you can drag back to the damned house for not keeping curfew." She was shaking with fury. "How dare you, Crowe Callahan. How fucking dare you decide what I can and cannot do, and what the hell makes you think you can tell me what I will and will not do?" She turned on Archer, outraged as he frowned back at both of them. "You are not to allow him to drag me out of here, *Sheriff* Tobias," she ordered him, determined to regain at least a measure of her independence. "If he does, then you better do something about it."

More than two dozen of the bar's customers were suddenly silent, their gazes trained on her, drunk, sober, and in between, soaking up every word and no doubt making mental lists of who they would call first. She was certain several were taking videos with their smartphones.

Just what she needed, her own little page of notoriety on Facebook.

"I warned you," Rory muttered behind her, obviously to Crowe.

"What did you do to her?" Anna hissed at her brother.

Archer lifted his gaze heavenward as he tilted the dun-colored hat back on his head. "I say my prayers," Archer sighed. "I go to church when I can and I even take old women to the grocery store when they need me to. And this is the thanks I get."

"And I voted for you," Amelia snapped back. "Now make him leave me alone while I do the job I came here to do, or next time I'll vote for old Charlie Weaver if he runs again."

Archer frowned down at her. "Charlie Weaver's in the rest home now, Amelia. You can't vote for him."

Crossing her arms over her breasts, she could feel her teeth grinding as frustration threatened to overwhelm her.

"I swear, Archer, I'll campaign so hard for your competition that you'll think I'm related to them if you don't get me to that meeting and get me to it now."

"I'm going to paddle your ass," Crowe muttered as though dazed, or astounded, behind her.

"Just listen to him." She stepped closer to Archer, throwing her hand back at Crowe as the crowd began to press closer around them. "He's threatening bodily harm now, Archer. I'm about to demand police protection."

"Police protection?" Archer questioned softly before his gaze suddenly sliced up and over her shoulder toward the crowd.

"Police protection," she repeated, her tone low despite the determination filling her. "I'm certain you heard him threaten me. Shouldn't you be arresting him or something?"

It was all Archer could to do to keep from laughing in her face. Amelia found herself having to fight her own smug smile as she propped her hands on her hips and faced him with a forced glare.

Okay, so she wasn't as pissed as she had been moments earlier. No doubt the dazed astonishment in Crowe's voice as he threatened to paddle her had something to do with that.

"Police protection," Archer sighed, staring out behind her as he slowly shook his head. "Some days, I wish I could *give* this job to old man Weaver." He stared back down at her. "This is one of those days."

"Nice little fantasy," she commiserated in a less-than-sympathetic tone. "Now, if you don't mind, I believe I have several entertainers waiting for me in the conference wing of the Community Center, and you and Anna promised to help re-measure those two grottoes before I leave." She glanced over at Crowe, a shiver working up her spine at the focused glare he directed at her.

"We *will* discuss this later," he promised her as the crowd behind them, no doubt bored at this point, began breaking up and turning back toward the bar.

A careless shrug was her only answer as she directed a speaking look back to the sheriff. She didn't dare let herself do more than glimpse Anna from the corner of her eyes. Her friend, and Crowe's sister, was obviously fighting giggles as well as the urge to agitate the situation further.

"Fine." Archer rubbed at the back of his neck as he glanced at Crowe, then behind her—likely at Rory, she thought—before turning his gaze back to her, a grin tugging at his lips. "And you used to be such a quiet little thing, Amelia."

The amusement evaporated instantly. "Yeah, and that did me a lot of good, too, didn't it, Archer?"

The situation itself might have amused her for a moment, but the underlying reason for her escape from her own home still stood. She wasn't a child, and she wasn't going to allow Crowe to treat her like one any longer just because she was his ticket to catching Wayne and making him pay for the hell he'd put the Callahans through.

She understood his need for vengeance. She understood his belief that only through her would he find the chance he needed to capture Wayne. But keeping her locked out of sight wasn't going to help his cause.

She wasn't in danger of Wayne aiming a rifle in her direction, lining her up in a set of rifle sights. The man believed he was her father and had no intention of shooting her, and he was a lousy shot to boot. No, Wayne wouldn't take such an easy route. He wanted to punish her and, through her, punish Crowe.

Before he ever killed her, Wayne would make sure she wished she'd never been born.

CHAPTER 13

Crowe was dangerously silent.

Shadowing her through the meetings with the entertainers and the subsequent walk around the band gazebo and dance square, he didn't say a word other than to speak into the earbud link he wore to direct Rory Malone once they left the Community Center and walked to the square.

The comedian Amelia had signed for the late-summer act was one of the more popular national figures in the field. His handsome face, fit body, and deliberately outrageous one-liners had her and Anna in gales of laughter more than once; Archer chuckled and shook his head at the entertainer's ability to find a joke in damned near everything.

He was even brave enough to poke fun at Crowe's silence and dangerously intent expression as Amelia explained a few of the themes that would be carried into the grottoes surrounding the square.

"Strong silent type, is he?" he murmured at Amelia's ear as she pulled a small notebook from her leather jacket to make a list of not just the comedian's requirements but also new ideas for decorations to coordinate with his acts.

"Strong definitely," Amelia admitted, glancing at Crowe

from beneath her lashes as his expression tightened, his lips a tight, hard line as the comedian leaned close to speak to her.

"Jealous type?" he asked.

"I'm sure he could be," Amelia admitted as she refrained from smiling in amusement at the deliberate questions.

"Ah. So, does the strong jealous type guard you, or . . ." He trailed off before grinning wickedly. "Does he guard your body?"

Her brow lifted slowly. "I and my body are pretty much one and the same," she informed him.

"And here I had so hoped I could run away with your mind," he snorted.

Amelia couldn't help but laugh.

"Seriously, are you lovers?" he asked her, the deliberate jokes and amusing asides absent as he glanced between them.

"Would it matter either way to your show?" she asked curiously, wondering why he cared.

"Well, if you're not, then I could petition for the position myself," he admitted with a slow grin. "If he is, then I may reconsider . . ."

"That might be a very good idea."

The sound of Crowe's voice behind them had them both jumping and turning to face him.

Shooting him a disapproving glance, Amelia turned away from him deliberately.

"I think I've listed everything you mentioned needing for your opening act, as well the shorter shows during the band's breaks on Saturday night," she told him. "Is there anything else I need to know?"

She refused to allow Crowe to intimidate her, and despite his wariness the performer evidently wasn't above teasing wild animals as well.

He shot her a deliberately teasing look. "Is there is anything else you want to know?"

"There's something you want to know." Crowe spoke behind him, the dangerous rasp of his voice causing Amelia to still as the entertainer turned slowly to face him.

"And that is?"

"I won't just kill for her, I'll kill over her. So while you're deciding if you're brave enough to try to poach what's mine, think about that."

A rakish smile curved the comic's lips. "Hell, son, if I hadn't already considered that, I wouldn't be standing here. I just decided to be nice and let the lady make the choice."

Crowe snorted. "Shows how smart you are." Turning to Amelia, he arched one brow with sardonic emphasis. "Anna and Archer have to leave and she wanted to talk to you a minute first, but—" He slid a look at the entertainer beside her. "—she didn't want to interrupt." His smile was all teeth. "I didn't have that problem."

The comedian beside her chuckled, almost causing Amelia to wince as she shot him a warning look. He was pushing at the wrong time. Crowe wasn't predictable in the least, and he was decidedly dangerous as well.

"I think we're finished then?" She glanced to the man at her side.

"For the moment." He let a smug little smile tip his lips. "If I can think of anything else I'll be sure to let you know."

Amelia gave a brief nod before turning to Crowe. "Is Anna still in the conference room?"

"With Archer." He nodded before giving the other man a deliberately mocking look. "The sheriff is even more possessive, my friend, so I'd be careful were I you."

The comedian glanced back at Amelia, his brows arching as his gaze twinkled merrily. "Must be something in the water," he drawled, directing a subtle wink to her as Crowe's glare deepened.

"There is. Usually the body of the last moron that pissed me off."

"And that is my cue to roll," the other man announced with a laugh. "See you soon, Amelia."

A quick nod and a smile and he was striding off quickly, heading to the Community Center and Archer's patience. Amelia turned to Crowe with a disapproving frown.

"You weren't nice," she berated him, deliberately spacing her words.

"He's still alive, right?" he growled. "I didn't shoot him. And trust me, I wanted to. Bad."

"You're being deliberately provoking," she accused him.

Amber fire gleamed in his narrowed eyes, making the thick, long black lashes appear lusher than ever.

"I have yet to provoke," he promised her. "Trust me, baby, once I get started provoking, there will be no doubt in your mind whatsoever."

"The trouble with you, Crowe," she pointed out, "is that you're always provoking. Unfortunately, you haven't seemed satisfied with what you've provoked."

Striding quickly past him, ignoring the tight-lipped, less-than-pleased look he gave her, Amelia hurried back to the Community Center where Archer, Anna, and the flirtatious comic were obviously still talking.

She'd managed to slip out of the house, and she'd completed the chores she'd had scheduled, but, like Crowe, she was less than pleased with the results.

What now?

Brooding anger built inside him as he escorted Amelia back into the house, all too aware of her lowered head and the quiet discontent in her gaze.

Why the discontent?

And what the hell had she meant, he wasn't satisfied with what he had provoked? If she meant he'd provoked her into slipping from his protection and now wasn't satisfied with it, then hell no, he wasn't satisfied.

Dusk was already edging over the mountains, shadowing the back gardens as they stepped into the family room. Amelia moved to the wide desk on the other side of the room, where she laid the small notebook she had slipped out with.

She kept her head lowered for long moments as he watched her.

"I won't be bullied," she stated softly, lifting her head to stare back at him, her turquoise gaze holding a stubbornness he hadn't realized she possessed. "Slipping out was wrong of me, and I realized that even before I did so. But I have a job to do, and I can't do that job with security personnel standing shoulder-to-shoulder around me so you can force me to give into your demands."

He wanted to grimace at the quiet words and the realization that what she had done today could have resulted in her death. He hadn't been with her because he had been determined to force her to remain in the house rather than going to the town square and Community Center to keep the appointment that Anna could have easily handled.

The comedian, Phillip Cannedy, had set his teeth on edge. The flirtatious demeanor and arrogant certainty that he could have any woman he wanted grated on Crowe's possessive instincts. Something had just kept telling him to kick the shit out of the man for daring to approach Amelia with such familiarity.

But he hadn't known yesterday who she was meeting, or that the man was a man-whore wannabe. All he'd been able to think was that she insisted on endangering herself for that damned social committee that had just thrown her out and taken away the position and the work she so enjoyed.

"Do you have any idea what it would do to me if something happened to you, Amelia?" he asked her, rather than agreeing or disagreeing with her.

She nodded somberly. "I know how important it is, Crowe, to catch Wayne. But you're not going to draw him out if you keep me locked up."

No, she did not just say that. Surely to God, she didn't believe that was the only reason she was important to him?

"You think the only reason it would affect me is because of Wayne?"

Frustration flashed in her gaze as her hands lifted helplessly. She tucked them into the pockets of her jeans as though she had no idea what to do with them.

Her shoulders lifted in uncertainty but the somber regret in her gaze told another story.

"I'm sure you don't want to see me hurt," she answered him. "And I'm certain that should I be hurt, you'd regret it. I don't believe you're unfeeling at all, Crowe."

"But you believe the only reason I'm in your bed is because of who you are and how you could help draw Wayne out?"

"I don't believe you find me unattractive at all," she sighed. "But I also don't believe I'm any more or any less than the means to an end. Having someone to fuck in the bargain without worrying about how or when the Slasher will strike is an added benefit."

"Son of a bitch." A short, harsh laugh left his lips as he stared back at her in disbelief. "Amelia, what have I ever done to you to make you think you're no more than a fringe benefit to me?"

She pulled her hands from the pockets of her jeans before she crossed her arms over her breasts and stared back at him, her gaze darkening with wary stubbornness.

"What am I to you, then?" The question was posed in a tone that suggested she was doing no more than patronizing. "You walked away seven years ago without so much as a good-bye. You spent six weeks slipping into my bedroom to have sex with me. You slipped in that last night to leave that excuse for a note behind, but you couldn't even tell me good-bye? And now you expect me to believe I might be more to you than a means to an end?" Incredulity touched her voice. "If I mean more, Crowe, then perhaps you should have let me know when I was willing to believe it."

Perhaps he should have, Crowe admitted, perhaps he would, once he could untangle the knots tightening in his chest and in his gut. The second he could work through those and make sense of the emotions that kept him walking a tightrope where Amelia was concerned, then he would tell her. Until then—

"What the fuck do you want me to say, Amelia?" he growled, grimacing at the quick flash of pain that suddenly flashed in her gaze.

Just as quick as it had been there, it was gone. She stared back at him, her expression calm and somber as she slowly dropped her arms and drew in a deep breath.

"I won't slip out of the house again," she told him. "The Carter boys aren't dangerous, but they did drive home the fact that had it been anyone else, I could have been in trouble."

"Not dangerous?" he snapped, amazed that she would say anything so asinine. "Amelia, did you forget what happened today?"

"I didn't forget anything." Sharp, concise, her tone was nothing if not confident. "You forget, Crowe, I know the people of this county a hell of a lot better than you do, and I know the Carter boys better than most for the simple fact that I've spent a hell of a lot of years working to keep those boys out of jail just because Wayne didn't like them. They wouldn't have hurt me. They just like to piss me off."

He stared at her for long, silent seconds as he tried to work that one out in his head.

He couldn't do it.

"Are you fucking crazy?" he finally asked her conversationally. "Or just delusional? At the very least, you're on some damned good drugs and I want to know who the hell's supplying you so I can shoot their fucking asses for endangering your concept of reality," he bit out. "For God's sake, Amelia."

He'd been saying that a lot lately, Amelia noticed as she stared back at Crowe's astounded expression.

Whether she was crazy or not, she knew Dwight, David, and Dillon. Despite the fact that for a second, they'd scared the shit out of her, she knew they wouldn't have hurt her.

Her lips parted.

"Don't you fucking dare ask me to call Archer and have them released from jail," he suddenly snarled, pointing his finger back at her imperiously. "Don't you even consider it."

"Crowe, it's not right to lock them up," she sighed wearily. God, she didn't want to fight about this. "Their aunt was Deanna Lopez. She was the first victim found fourteen years ago. Deanna was the only security those boys had. After she died, their mother gave them up to child services and the foster homes they were shuttled out to were some of the worst. Once they sober up, they'll find me and they'll apologize, and it will never happen again. That's what they do. Wayne has tortured those boys since Deanna's death. I won't add to the hell they've had to live through."

"Bullshit." Anger filled his face now. "What happened

to Deanna was bad enough, Amelia, but those boys are grown fucking men. They weren't the only ones to lose someone who stabilized their lives. And they sure as hell aren't the only men in this county who lost someone they loved to the Slasher."

"No, they weren't, and it's damned obvious you don't give a damn about anyone else Wayne tormented but you, your cousins, and the actual victims," she yelled back at him. "But you had stability after your parents' deaths, Clyde made sure of it, and he damned sure didn't lock you in the basement with the rats, Crowe, and starve you while he made you live in your own waste. That's what happened to Dwight, and he had it the easiest. David was left for weeks sometimes without food in the foster home he was sent to. He went to school so he could eat and see his brothers. Dillon was beaten so often that just going to school was hell, and everyone ignored the fact that he was being abused until the night his foster father force-fed him cocaine. He would have died if he hadn't stumbled from the house and into the street where Archer nearly ran him down. You don't have to remind me they weren't the only ones who suffered, but just like everyone else, those boys deserved a break. They were just three of the ones who didn't get one."

She was furious by time she finished. Her fists were clenched, heat creating a layer of moisture on her forehead that had her wishing she could turn the furnace down or shed the sweater she wore. And every muscle in her body was tight, demanding action.

"That doesn't mean I'm going to have Archer release the men who nearly raped you and threatened to cut your heart out to share among themselves," he yelled back at her, surprising her.

Shocking her, really.

She'd never seen Crowe yell at anyone.

"Son of a bitch." Turning away from her, he stalked to the other side of the room before turning again with such military precision that the sight of it had her gaze widening just slightly.

She knew he'd been in the military, she'd just never glimpsed him moving as though he had been in the military. Crowe appeared to move with seamless, gliding grace rather than precision.

"I've never heard you yell at anyone," she breathed out, shaking her head as she watched him warily. "I've never heard of it."

"Oh, I yell often," he informed her, the angry snap of his tone matching the amber blaze of fury in his gaze. "Especially when I'm forced to deal with someone who can't protect themselves for all the effort they're using to protect others."

She wanted to roll her eyes at him, but the look on his face was one she had never glimpsed before. She had no idea what he was capable of now.

"Stop trying to make me feel stupid, Crowe," she demanded, not in the least afraid of him, but wary.

"If the shoe fits."

"Then it fits you just as comfortably." She confronted him, her hands going to her hips as she stared back at him in angry disbelief. "What happened to the compassion I saw in you seven years ago? What happened to the man who understood and even sympathized with the kids in the Community Center whose parents didn't care where they were or who they were with? The man who slipped and gave one of those children a teddy bear when she cried for her mother at night?"

"That wasn't compassion you were seeing," he snarled back at her. "It was lust. I would have done anything that summer to get into your pants and it was obvious those kids were a soft point."

"And you're a liar." She was the one yelling now.

Pointing a finger at him furiously, she was only barely aware of the fact that her hand, hell her entire body, was shaking with her anger.

"And you're living in a fucking dream world if you think I'm going to have Archer release those men."

He was in her face now, his head lowered, his nose almost touching hers as he gripped her shoulders firmly and glared down at her.

"I will not do it," he enunciated clearly, concisely. "Get it out of your damned head."

"Then I will," she stated softly, so furious at him that she didn't even bother yelling. "I wanted you to understand, but it's obvious you have no intentions of even trying to."

"When three sons of bitches attack my woman and attempt to rape and murder her, then hell fucking no." His hands tightened on her shoulders as his voice rose. "No, Amelia. Don't you think I've lost enough? Don't you think I fucking get tired of having my lovers tortured and fucking murdered? Do you think for even one minute that I'll allow it to happen again, Amelia? Especially to you!"

He froze as he said the words, his gaze narrowing on her, his lips clamping so tight they were a straight line rather than the sensual, eatable curves she loved to kiss.

Just as quickly as he had been in her face, his hands gripping her shoulders, he released her. Turning on his heel he stalked to the double doors he had closed as they stepped into the family room and threw them open before stalking out.

Thank God he didn't see the tears that fell from her eyes before she could turn and dash them away, or hear the sob that escaped her lips. For a moment, she wished she had never pushed him. She wished she could go back and just keep her mouth shut. She should have just called

Archer herself rather than trying to talk to him. Archer knew the Carters; he would have at least understood why she didn't want to prosecute three men who had suffered far more than she had over the years.

She had always liked them, despite the fact that Dwight stole her work to cheat on their exams. The day she had reported him to the teacher, she had been dealing with a shock she couldn't process and a pain she had no idea what to do with. She'd looked over and caught Dwight stealing her answers and before she could stop the words she had ordered him to stop.

She hadn't meant to say it so loudly. She hadn't meant to get him into trouble. But even now, she remembered the wounded look in his eyes. Three days later, she remembered the bruised eye that was nearly swollen shut when he returned to school.

And Amelia had known it was her fault. The school had called his foster parents and told on him, and the father in the household had beaten him until he could barely walk for days.

After that, the Carters had begun targeting her. She rarely said anything about it. She had never reported it, and she had never done anything else, ever, to get them in trouble. Especially after Dillon had nearly died of that cocaine overdose, and she'd seen how the weeks he had lain in a coma had affected his brothers.

She still saw the hurt and fear in Dwight's eyes. And she knew that as bad as things had been for her, at least she'd had hope.

That next summer, after Crowe's desertion of her had nearly destroyed her, she'd found another reason to keep fighting. She'd found another reason to hold on to the mercy and compassion Wayne had sneered at her over.

The Carter brothers hadn't had hope, and that was a lesson she had never forgotten. It was one she reminded herself of often and held so deep in her soul that no one, not the man she hated above all others, or the man she loved above all others, could ever guess it existed.

Shaking her head, she moved to the desk and the laptop she kept there. Opening it and powering it on, she waited until the programs loaded and opened her email.

The inbox was loaded with messages. She didn't even glance at them.

Pulling up a new mail, she typed in Archer's address then began the letter.

This would be more official anyway, she told herself. Proof that she had no intention of changing her mind.

The Carter men wouldn't get another chance after this, she promised herself. This would be their last one, and she would make that plain to them. She would even make it easy on Crowe and have Archer pick her up tomorrow to take her to the jail where she would be certain they understood every word she said to them.

She wasn't going to allow them to risk their safety. They weren't thieves. They didn't do drugs. They had never so much as spoken sharply to a child or any woman besides herself. And to her only when they were drunk.

They deserved this one last chance, whether Crowe wanted them to have it or not.

CHAPTER 14

Crowe forced himself to go to the security room after leaving Amelia. He had to cool down and think before he headed to the spare bedroom where he stored his rifle. The need to take it apart, clean it, ensure it was ready to perform the second the Carter boys left that damned jail, was almost overwhelming.

He'd heard of the three men who never failed to take out their anger on Amelia if they happened to catch sight of her when they were drunk. The same three men who helped her carry her groceries from the market to her car when they were sober. Or who changed her flat tire one stormy night after she left work.

The contradiction in the men had appeased his worry for her at the time. Of course, he hadn't heard of it happening in the two years since his return. If he had, he would have ensured it never happened again.

Nodding to Cameron, who didn't appear in the least inclined to sleep, he moved to one of the computers set up to play back feed from the security cameras around the property.

The tall, hard-muscled tech hadn't been his idea of an

electronic security expert when he applied to Brute five years before, but he'd proven himself over the years.

Rough talking, when you could get him to speak, a brutal martial arts gutter fighter, and a damned sap when it came to women and babies, he never failed to keep whatever team he worked with laughing over his protective nature when it came to his computers and the women or children involved in any of their assignments.

"We had a few shadows on camera four while Ms. Sorenson was out of the house," the tech, Cameron Fitzgerald, told him quietly, toggling between monitors and zooming in and out to check current shadows. "I'm damned sure it was someone fucking with my cameras, but I couldn't get a clear picture. I marked it on the log and sent it to the gurus at home."

The *gurus at home* were Ivan's top electronic wizards in Manhattan. The security programmers Ivan had pulled in from the vast network of contacts he'd made over the years could do things with security devices and programs that Crowe had sworn couldn't be done.

Pulling up the recording the other man had marked, he narrowed his eyes on the shadows the cameras had recorded, wondering what the hell was moving in the heavy growth of pine, naked oak, and brush that grew on the perimeter of the yard at the back and sides of the house.

The stone and wrought-iron fence that surrounded the block-size estate did nothing to protect the inner yard, and hampered the cameras set up to watch it.

Seven years ago Crowe had sneered at Wayne's attempt to ensure no one invaded his property. He'd used the very weaknesses he was now cursing to slip through the trees and make his way to Amelia's balcony and then into her bedroom and her bed.

He'd invaded not just Wayne's property, but also Wayne's daughter, he thought in satisfaction. The bastard had played the Callahans' friend for years. He'd had dinner at Clyde's ranch with them, bringing his quiet, somber daughter with him. He'd commiserated with them, assured them he'd do everything he could to help them, then used whatever information he could find during those visits to attempt to frame them.

Watching the video recorded earlier that day, Crowe watched the shadows that kept eluding the cameras' attempts to zoom in. He could hear Cameron cursing on the audio feed, then five minutes later an order to the remaining security personnel to check it out.

All of them.

"You left the house unsecured?" he asked the tech.

Cameron turned to him, his serious, intent blue eyes almost electric in color. "I only had two fucking men here, Mr. Callahan, the rest were out with you. I did a full electronic lockdown on the house while they were out, with all indoor cameras set to detect not just movement, but also temperature change. I had to make a decision, and identifying what was screwing with our cameras was too important. That's our first defense."

"And this was Wayne's test against them," Crowe murmured as the program on his laptop began detecting the subtle evidence of electronic interference. "Did Mike patch the cameras into the new anti-jamming hardware Ivan set up?"

"I still have to check the integrity of equipment and software." Cameron turned to him. "Mike was a sloppy bastard. I've spent about every minute I've had spare just trying to decipher why the stupid son of a bitch plugged what into where. No sooner did I walk in here than shit started happening. But that one's next on my list, after the diagnostic test I'm running is finished." He tapped the monitor he was watching. "I'm showing temperature changes in this room, and in the kitchen. It's confusing the hell out of me. The temperature modules on the cameras and the security boxes attached to the doors are all working fine. The glitch has to be in the computer."

"How long before you can track it down?" Crowe questioned, staring at the diagnostics showing on the screen.

"I'm hoping soon," Cameron sighed. "Otherwise, I'm going to have to track Mike down and beat the fuck out of him for being stupid."

Crowe moved back to the laptop, his gaze checking the status of the program to detect the interference used to confuse the cameras. He still had several hours left to go.

The time in the control room had allowed him to settle down, though.

"Ms. Sorenson is sending out email at the moment," the tech noted absently. "To Sheriff Tobias. Should I intercept it?"

"Let it go." Crowe shook his head. "Anna's still getting email through Archer, just in case Wayne gets stupid enough to email her. It'll make it easier to track from his official address."

"Fuck yeah," Cameron answered, his voice distracted now as he keyed commands on the holographic keyboard in front of him.

Crowe almost grinned at the sight of the hard-core marine with his tattooed biceps, savage expression, and intent, odd-as-hell eyes playing that holo-board like a master pianist.

"Give me a call if the audio notification on this program sounds," he told the other man as he rose to his feet, his gaze moving to the foyer camera, which picked up Amelia leaving the room, entering the foyer, then heading up the stairs.

"Will do." Cameron's voice was still absent, distracted, but Crowe knew he'd heard every word.

Leaving the control room and moving through the hall, he reached the main wing of the house as Amelia entered the bedroom.

He paused for a moment to draw in a hard breath, still seeing the shattered guilt in her eyes as she talked about the Carter brothers.

He'd read their file. He hadn't wanted to think about it as she spoke, nor while he'd been in the control room. Wayne's vendetta against the Carters hadn't run as deep as it had against the Callahans, but for some reason he'd been determined to destroy them in other ways.

As he continued to Amelia's bedroom, he made a mental note to ask Ivan if he'd run across their names in Wayne's journals, which Amory Wyatt had ensured they received. He needed more information and he was going to need it before Amelia took matters into her own hands and made certain no charges were filed against the little bastards.

Entering the bedroom, he wasn't happy to see she was just changing from the jeans and sweater she had worn into a pair of girlie pajamas. The white leggings and long shirt all but hid her figure and assured him that his little sugar elf didn't have sex on her mind.

She usually came to bed in one of those silky, sexy-as-hell nightgowns he loved rather than this nonsexual body armor, he thought in amusement.

"Am I in the doghouse?" he asked, unable to hold back the hint of a smile that tugged at his lips.

"Do I have a doghouse?" she asked, her expression far too somber.

God, he hated seeing the hurt in her eyes.

"Yeah, you do." He nodded. "The word *no.*"

Her shoulders lifted as though uncertain before she turned away from him and moved to the bed to turn it down.

"I haven't said no," she finally said. "But I am tired tonight, Crowe."

Oh, he just bet she was.

Intercepting her, Crowe tucked his fingers beneath her chin and silently urged her to look up at him.

He wanted to see whatever emotion it was that baffled him.

"I can't help needing to protect you, Amelia." He addressed the problem the only way he knew how. "I might go about it in a way that offends you sometimes, and sometimes we're going to go head-to-head over it. But I'm not trying to hurt you, or anyone else."

Her lips tightened as emotions raged in her darkened eyes. He could see, and he could feel, something building inside her, between them, but he was damned if he could figure out what it was.

"Don't worry about it," she finally gritted out.

"Amelia," he whispered gently. "You have to talk to me."

"About what, Crowe?" Pulling from his grip she paced across the room before turning back to him, her hands lifting to rub at her arms as though some chill had settled on them. "What do you think we need to talk about? How you can make me come around to your way of doing things?" Mockery filled the tight little smile she gave him. "See, I'm not real good at that. I tend to get myself in more trouble than necessary because I can't seem to understand the concept of protection that everyone else seems to believe I need or deserve."

"I didn't ask you not to voice your opinion, Amelia," he objected, realizing the power she had to strip aside his control over emotions he didn't even know he possessed.

The frustration, hunger, and fears for her that roiled inside him never failed to create a combustible mix that took less than nothing to set off.

"That's exactly what you want," she scoffed in disgust, those pouty lips he was dying to feel again tightening in anger. "You want me to just put my head down and accept whatever dictates you deem necessary."

"Bullshit," he growled. "The only time I want you to put your head down to accept anything is when I when I'm shoving my dick between your lips."

Her eyes widened, then narrowed as anger suffused her face.

It was more than anger, though. Hell, he realized in that second, it was always more than anger. In the fierce gleam of those exceptional turquoise eyes there was far more than anger. There was the pain he'd put there seven years ago. A wound that had never healed, just as the wound he'd inflicted on his own heart when he was forced to walk away from her hadn't healed. A wound that had deepened with her marriage and the knowledge of her abuse.

He had been the one to strip the innocence from his fairy-girl's eyes, no one else. He had been the reason she had stayed beneath Wayne's thumb, the reason she had remained in this house with his abuse rather than finding a way to escape it.

"Why don't you just say what's on your mind, Amelia?" he suggested, the raging emotions filling her eyes reaching out to smack him with every look.

"I don't have the time," she lashed out, her tone caustic. "I don't think I'll even live long enough to give you a full list."

"Yet I'd bet my entire fortune on the fact that you're wet right now. Wet and willing and just waiting for me to touch that hungry little body of yours."

Something snapped in her eyes then. The pain that seared her emotions exploded in bright, rich color for the briefest second.

"You just walk in here as though it's your right." Her fingers plowed through shoulder-length strands of hair as her teeth gritted furiously. "As though you didn't walk out of my life with no more than some fucking letter filled with lies," she cried out. "Leaving me didn't have a damned thing to do with whether my father loved or hated you. It had to do with your own fucking cowardice."

"My cowardice?" Just because she was right didn't mean he wanted, or intended, to accept it, he thought with bitter humor.

"You were too damned scared of loving anyone—"

"I was too damned scared of losing another lover, you mean?" he reminded her, watching each pain-filled flash that filled her eyes, despite his own building emotions.

What he felt was full-fledged torment at the realization, then and now, of what he had lost.

"No one knew about us. I didn't tell a soul until after you left. No, Crowe, it wasn't losing another lover you were so damned scared of, it was having that block of ice around your heart melt and desert you. And we both know it." Tears glittered in her eyes. "How many women did you have after me? How little did I even matter . . ."

He couldn't listen to more. God help him, if he let her keep pushing him he might end up revealing far more than he could risk her knowing.

He'd only meant to stop the pain-filled, tear-thickened words with a quick kiss. What it turned into was anything but quick. The second his lips settled on hers, they parted, accepting him, taking more of him. The essence of her filled his senses, immediately overwhelming him with need as he shoved his tongue past her lips and took total possession of her kiss.

This was what she did to him. She overwhelmed him with his own hungers, with a sexual intensity he had no desire to control.

She was a switch and every time he touched her, the need to fuck her surged through his body with tidal force.

He'd believed he could handle one simple kiss.

He'd been so damned wrong.

Jerking his head back—he was amazed at his ability to break the contact—Crowe stared down at her, his breath dragging in his throat. They were both panting for air as he watched arousal darken her eyes and flush her dazed expression.

"How the hell did I stay away from you for seven fucking years?" he growled, realizing he was still holding her neck, keeping her in place as he stared down at her. "By fooling myself into believing there wasn't a chance in hell that a kiss could do this to me."

He grabbed her hand, dragging it to the desperately stiff erection beneath his jeans.

"I missed you, Crowe." The whisper of sound sent piercing lust arrowing straight to his dick. And it sent pain exploding in his chest as her voice hitched in a whispered sound of agony. "I needed you."

Leaning forward again, he brushed his lips over hers rather than saying anything more. Feeling them part for him, he caught the lower curve between his teeth in a sensual little bite. Unable to help himself, unable to control the need for it, Crowe returned to her lips, parted them with his own, then took another slow, lip-rubbing, tongue-tasting kiss from her.

As he kissed her, his hands pushed beneath the loose top she wore. There he found silken, heated flesh. Swollen, hard-tipped breasts filled his hands once he released the front catch of her bra. They fit his hands perfectly, just the right size to cup and caress.

Slowly, he drew her closer to him, the need to feel her body against his overwhelming any objections or common sense.

So overwhelming.

The sexual, sensual hunger that tormented him grew, becoming hotter, brighter than ever before. It was like this with her—only with her—each time. Always better than the time before. Always the greatest pleasure he'd ever known.

And it always made him hungrier for more of her.

"Damn you!" He was furious with himself.

Furious with her.

And so fucking horny as he sat down in the chair next to the balcony doors that he forgot about the program running downstairs, shadows on the cameras, or anything else that could have possibly delayed his possession of her.

He was going to fuck her.

Just as soon as he could.

"Damn me?" Dazed, but more than eager, she straddled his thighs as he pulled her down to him, feeling the feminine softness and heat of her pussy, even through their clothes.

"Oh my God, Crowe. Yes," she cried out as he held her to him, holding her hips in place while he flexed his own, the steel wedge of his cock rubbing against that soft pad of her pussy.

Gripping the hem of her shirt and quickly drawing it up, Crowe had to stifle a groan as her arms lifted languidly, sensually. Before the material cleared her upraised arms his head was lowering. Before it could fall to the floor his lips covered one hard, flushed peak, sucking it into his mouth.

Amelia felt her head tip back weakly, exquisite pleasure singing through the almost painfully swollen nipple he was sucking at.

Damp heat surrounded the throbbing tip as he pulled

it tight and hard into his mouth. His tongue rasped against it, rubbing it and throwing her into such a firestorm of sensation she couldn't have fought it, even if she wanted to.

She didn't want to.

Drawing on the tormented bead as his hands roved to her hips, Crowe pushed the soft, elastic waistband of her leggings over her rear.

Spearing her hands into the thick, course warmth of his hair, Amelia held on tight as her hips moved, grinding her pussy against the bulge beneath his jeans.

Each hard draw of his mouth around her nipple built a hunger inside her that she couldn't—didn't want to—combat.

Pressing her feet flat against the floor, her fingers kneading his scalp as his mouth devoured her nipple, Amelia worked her hips against him. The mewling whimpers falling from her lips echoed with need. She could feel the hunger rising hard and fast—always there, always rising.

It was beating at her senses, ravaging her body, and creating a hunger that was rapidly—no, not rapidly—the hunger for him had already ravaged her heart.

Because she had always loved him.

Panting, gasping for air, Amelia cried out as Crowe lifted his lips from the nipple he was tormenting only to move to the other and draw it inside his mouth instead.

Sucking at the matching little bud, flicking his tongue, then capturing it between his teeth, he tugged at the ripe tip, devouring it. Each fiery draw increased her hunger and had it building, escalating, creating a tension deep inside her pussy that seared her senses.

Riding the denim-covered bulge of his cock, Amelia felt the grinding pressure against her swollen clit in hard pulses of sensation that lanced her with exquisite pleasure.

A sizzling and intense hunger clenched her vagina with such need she felt poised on a sharp, aching edge of intensity.

Each draw of his lips pierced her nipple with static, electric pleasure. It surged forcefully to the depths of her womb, clenched it, stealing her breath with its power.

"Crowe. Oh God. I swear you're killing me."

"We'll die together then," he muttered as his lips freed her swollen nipple. "Damn. It looks like a ripe little berry."

He drew her attention to the peaks of her breasts.

The once light-pink tips were tightly swollen and blushing a rich raspberry red.

Amelia caught her breath as his hands, pushing into her sleep pants, curved around the cheeks of her ass and squeezed the flesh erotically.

"Stand up," he rasped, the order issued in a tone so rough and filled with lust that she shuddered.

Even if she wanted to, she couldn't have disobeyed him. And God knew, she didn't want to.

But standing up meant no more grinding against his cock. No more of the incredible pleasure—

"Now!"

Her eyes widened in shock as she instantly straightened then stepped back from him. His fingers clenched in the band of her pants then in one smooth move had the material at her ankles as he fell to one knee in front of her.

Amelia stepped out of the leggings as Crowe dropped them carelessly to the floor before rising in front of her.

Between one breath and the next they were tearing at his clothes. Desperate, crying out in frustration, she felt the need to get him naked tear through her. She finally managed to release his belt as he tossed his shirt aside.

"Your boots," she gasped as his zipper rasped open,

the material parting as he pulled the length of his cock free.

"No time," he groaned. "Come here, elf."

Lifting her against him, Crowe took the few steps to the dark dresser before she even realized they were moving. The cool wood brought a gasp from her lips as it met the flushed warmth of her rear.

"I can't wait," he groaned, moving instantly between her thighs.

"Then don't wait. Don't wait. And don't let me think," she cried out, the ragged emotions, the guilt, and the price of her silence easing as their hunger rose, met, and exploded out of control.

She gripped his shoulders with desperate fingers as he lifted her legs, pushing them apart and watching as the broad head of his cock pressed between the swollen lips of her pussy.

"Now. Now." Her knees pressed against his hold as he began working the wide, throbbing flesh inside her.

Watching, desperate to breathe, but unable to draw in a full breath, she watched as the dew-slick folds parted, encasing the heavy width of his cockhead as it began pressing inside the entrance.

At the first, heavy pressure a wave of sensation tore through her, taking her breath.

Her vagina clenched in a spasming wave of such painful pleasure that she cried out at the renewed shock of it. The intense sensations were so erotic, so exquisitely sensual that a shock wave of impending ecstasy struck at her womb, her body jerking with it.

The throb of her clit, the erotic ache in her pussy all combined to send a rush of heated moisture to meet the crest now capping the entrance.

"Crowe." The first, fiery stretch, the protesting muscles of her entrance parting for him, the feel of his cock throbbing as it wedged her open, pulsing, teasing her with the impending impalement, filled her senses with a hunger that bordered addictive.

"Yes," she hissed, then cried out in protest as he retreated, stealing the fiery pleasure-pain.

Only to repeat the process.

Continually working his cock inside her, no more than an inch at a time, he impaled her over and over, rocking in and out, causing her vagina to milk at his flesh as the physical ache, the clenching, throbbing waves of pure sensation stealing her breath, grew to an unbearable intensity.

The slow, internal stroking, the pinch of each stretching, shallow impalement pushed her to the brink of sanity as he leaned her back against the mirror.

His hands cupped her breasts, thumbs and forefingers gripping the peaks and milking them erotically as he thrust inside her. Watching each impalement, grimacing each time he pulled back from her.

"Oh yes." Back arching, fingers curling over the edge of the dresser, Amelia twisted her hips against him, thrusting back as her breath came in short, rough gasps.

"Like that, don't you, elf?" he suggested, still keeping his thrusts slow, a little deeper, then shallow, then deeper, his cock stroking, stretching, delving into her pussy to create such incredible pleasure she could scream from it if she could find the breath.

"Yes." She could barely speak.

The word was more a hiss of pure desperate ecstasy.

Sizzling, electric sensation surged from the tightly swollen peaks of her breasts to the throbbing bud of her clitoris in wave after wave of building, tightening, agonizing—

And he was fucking her too slow—

"Damn you!" Lifting herself to him, thrusting back in

rolling lifts of her hips, Amelia was ready to sob from the agony of need.

She couldn't stand it.

Agony and ecstasy.

"Damn me?" A hard grimace pulled at his face, drawing his lips tight as a bead of sweat rolled down the side of his temple and another tracked down the hard, corded planes of his stomach. "Ah, elf, why damn me?"

"Fuck me, damn you!" Breathless, caught in hard, ever-sharpening spirals of agonizing pleasure.

Each razor-thin, erotic blade of sensation bit into her senses. They tightened her muscles, her pussy, until she thought she couldn't stand any more.

Only to be forced to take more. The pending climactic implosion was held back, just out of reach.

Staring up at her tormentor, her lover—God help her—her heart, she was poised to fly straight into rapture and forced to stay tethered within the most ecstatic torture she could have imagined.

"Tell me, Amelia," he crooned in an erotic, exotically roughening tone. "Don't you love it, baby? Because God help me, I'm loving every sucking clench of your tight, sweet—" He grimaced again, a groan rasping from his throat. "—tight little pussy."

As though helpless in the grip of his own tormented need, he suddenly penetrated her with a single, hard, to-the-hilt thrust—oh sweet God, so deep inside her—

Her eyes jerked open, staring up at him as he held still. The heavy throb of the flared crest buried inside her impossibly stroking nerve endings she hadn't known she possessed.

"I love it. Love having you inside me." Broken, breathless, the cry tore from her as her pussy fluttered around the heavy shaft buried inside her.

"Fuck!" The harsh exclamation seemed torn from him

as another of the twisting waves of sensation tore through her sex, tightening the muscles around the heavy girth invading her.

"Ah baby. My sweet, sweet Amelia. Never knew anything this damned good."

Watching his eyes, the raptor brown and mixed fiery gold as it flared, his pupils dilating as his hips shifted, tilted just enough—

The flared edge of the heavy cock head buried deeper, higher, suddenly raking against a once hidden bundle of nerves in a shallow indent high in her cunt. Just a small dip, but Crowe knew exactly where it was and exactly how to find it.

"Yes." Another hiss of near rapture escaped her.

Holding his gaze, Amelia tightened her muscles on him again, milking at his cock, stroking it—sucking at it erotically. "Fuck me. I can't bear it. Fuck me, Crowe. Deep. Please."

His expression tightened, a grimace contorting his face as sweat beaded his forehead and shoulders, his hip jerking—hard.

Amelia stared up at him, barely able to hold her eyes open. Needing to see him, to watch him. Needing to pleasure him, she used the muscles of her vagina to do what she had never done before. To stroke and suck his cock deliberately. Erotically.

She jerked, shuddering as his hips clenched and he thrust against her involuntarily, the hard throb of his flesh so intense it was like a caress inside her.

"Oh—good. So good," she gasped, still holding his gaze. "So empty without you." Her hands gripped his powerful forearms as his fingers plucked at her nipples again.

"Always so empty." Her back arched, the constantly twisting, erotically sharpened waves of intense pleasure building, multiplying, tightening. "Oh God, Crowe. I love this. Love your cock so tight and hard, opening me, taking me—"

His shattered, broken snarl of disintegrating control was like another trigger. It set off slashing internal contractions that were so close to an orgasm—yet not quite there—she knew that when it came, it was going to control her.

A broken sob parted her lips.

She loved him. Loved him so much. Oh God—oh God.

He was suddenly moving, impaling, his cock shuttling through the slick, saturated depths with destructive, torturous results.

Fucking her with ever-quickening thrusts Crowe lowered one hand, caught one of hers, and lifted it from his arm before bringing her fingers to the engorged bud of her clit.

"Touch yourself," he groaned. "Let me see, baby. Let me see you pleasure your pretty clit, elf."

Amelia found the painfully engorged bud as he watched. His hand returned to her hips, holding them tight, watching her fingers as she stroked, caressed, pushed herself closer to the peak of pure rapture.

Sweat ran in rivulets down his flexing abs. His expression turned savage, as relentless as his strokes. The chaos suddenly surged, nearly taking her, building, reaching out to her.

"Yes. Yes." Her hips churned beneath him in short, shallow thrusts. "God yes. Fuck me, Crowe. Fuck me. Fuck me until I never forget how hard you feel inside me."

His head tipped back. A snarl tightened his lips as he buried deep, hips twisting, maneuvering the thick flesh to stroke that high, inner spot, the hooded crest tucking in, raking against those erotically raw nerve endings.

Cataclysmic.

Waves of exploding, body-wrenching, ecstatic chaos.

She tried to scream his name as he fucked inside the rapidly flexing, clenching depths of her pussy until he was buried to the hilt.

His cock throbbed, thickened further, then fiery pulses of his release began flooding her. Each jetting ejaculation of semen sent another bolt of lightning-swift, razor-edged sensation tearing deeper inside her.

The force of the explosions raked through her senses with such pleasure she knew she would never be free of the need to experience it again and again.

Her legs tightened around his hips, her pussy flexing and milking his cock with such internal spasms and ever deepening rapture that reality simply receded.

She was crying out, but she didn't care what she was saying.

She was begging, pleading, but she didn't know why, or for what.

Life itself was flooding her in a release so primal, so erotically violent there was simply no way to survive it.

Distantly, fearfully, Amelia knew when she could think again—when she could breathe again—it would only be to find that who and what she was before tonight would never exist again.

Crowe had somehow changed her.

To the very depths of her being he had changed something so intrinsic that she feared she may not even know the person who eventually rose from the ashes of a pleasure this perfect, this radiant.

"I have you, baby," he swore, his voice strained, hoarse as he held on to her hips, holding her to him, refusing to release her. "I have you."

The most perfect pleasure given by the man who completely owned her heart. The man who completely owned every part of her that she had to give.

This was why she had never been able to bear the thought of another lover. Crowe had touched her first. She had loved him first. And she'd never been able to convince herself that she wasn't supposed to belong to him forever.

Because that woman's soul he held, that part of her refused to allow her to do anything else.

"I love you. I love you so much, Crowe. Oh God—Oh God—Crowe," she cried, her hoarse voice broken, filled with pleasure, with pain, with a longing there was no hiding from. "I died without you—"

The memory of her cries echoing around him still had the same power they'd had at the moment they first fell from her lips.

The power to rock him to his very soul.

She had never told him she loved him. Not even that night, seven years before, when he'd taken her innocence on her father's office couch. Or the night she found his note then hid in the corner of her balcony, sobs ravaging her slight body as he had fought to contain his rage.

What would he have done, he wondered, if she had told him then that she loved him?

Holding her tucked against him hours later, watching as the first fragile beams of dawn began lighting the edges of the curtains and shades beneath them, he knew the words she had cried out to him had opened a door he couldn't close now.

Crowe closed his eyes, desperate to escape what he had seen in the depths of her gaze for the briefest time. There, unlocked, shining so pure, so fucking innocent, had been her woman's soul.

It had glowed in her face, transforming her expression with such love, such perfect, soul-deep, tenacious love that the sudden realization of this woman's strength and courage had terrified the hell out of him.

Because he'd felt it. As though she had somehow found a break in the walls protecting his soul, he'd felt a part of her invading him before he could stop her.

Before he could pull back, pull his ejaculating cock from the fist-tight grip she'd had on him, he'd come so hard, so brutally deep his balls still ached. So explosively that somehow, his defenses had dropped, and she had slipped in.

And that chink Amelia had found in his soul was like a raw, open wound he couldn't force closed now.

His parents had loved in just that way. As Amelia's love had glowed from the depths of her being, so had the love of his parents, and his cousins' parents. They had loved with such ferocity that it had bound them—even past death, he often suspected.

Opening his eyes once more, he stared down at her pale, slumbering features and felt his heart twist at the open, naked vulnerability she possessed. And he hadn't even realized it. He'd never let himself really see or accept how much she loved him.

How much he—

Crowe quickly slammed the door on that thought.

He couldn't let himself think it. He wouldn't admit it even to himself. Because if he failed as his father had, as his uncles and his grandfather had failed, and Wayne actually managed to steal the life that gleamed so bright and pure inside her, then he'd never survive it.

The pain would lacerate his soul until there was nothing left but to follow her into death. He would leave Rafer and Logan to protect themselves—and that was just never a good idea. Those two could get into trouble faster than two Christmas pups. But he'd also be leaving Cami and Sky without the added protection of their lovers. And leaving Logan and Sky to raise their twins alone. And he knew there wasn't a chance in hell his cousins and cousin-in-law could keep after two little Callahan hellions.

He'd sworn he'd never allow anything to weaken the promise he'd made his cousins the night their parents were killed. The solemn vow that he'd look after his younger cousins, always. That he'd never allow anyone or anything to threaten his protection of them.

He'd sworn it on all their parents' graves as they were buried. And now, there was his sister Anna as well. The sister he'd believed was killed so long ago. He had sworn it again when they returned here two years ago, only to realize that the death that stalked them before they left had returned as well.

Or it had never left.

And now he was dangerously close to betraying his promise.

Because he may have closed the door on that one thought, but he didn't know if he could repair the damage to the protective shield around his heart and soul.

As he finally allowed sleep to gather inside him, Crowe admitted he may have just lost it to this courageous, enduring woman.

Hell, he had lost it long before this night. He may just have lost it the night he watched a pretty little autumn fairy peek from the summer foliage and motion him to her with a slow, teasing curve of her finger.

Yeah, he decided, that was when he'd lost his heart.

CHAPTER 15

The shadows programmed into the wireless and wired cameras Crowe had installed outside the house finally revealed themselves the next afternoon. Staring at the screen thoughtfully as he rubbed his finger against his upper lip, Crowe wondered where the hell Wayne had managed to get his hands on a military jammer armed with the ability to reprogram the monitor setups.

That was one hellaciously expensive piece of equipment.

"Son of a bitch," Cameron muttered behind him as the new tech, Jase Grogan, watched as the shadowed images slowly cleared to reveal the recognizable figure of Wayne Sorenson.

"How the hell did he do that?" Jase breathed out, leaning in close to examine the reprogramming details.

"What I want to know is how the fuck that mad dog got into my system." Cameron's Texas drawl was now a deep rasp of anger.

"Shit!" Jase exclaimed, his tone still low as they all leaned in closer.

Crowe hit rewind, scrolled back mere seconds, and watched again as Wayne smiled up at the camera before just disappearing.

"What the hell just happened?" he demanded, sitting back in the less-than-comfortable chair before leaning forward again and typing several commands into the program that had managed to pull the image in.

Nothing worked. One second Wayne was there, the next he was gone. Just that fast and just that impossible.

"Oh hell no, we got a problem here," Cameron muttered.

At six foot four of heavy marine muscle, he shouldn't have been able to work himself beneath the makeshift counter that ran the length of the small room, but that was exactly what he did.

Crowe and Jase looked at each other in bafflement before staring down at the long, jean-encased legs stretched out along the floor.

"Come on, boys and girls, stop admiring my damned legs and help me trace these cables. I want to know where each damned one is going and how it's hooked up."

He tugged at the first cable.

Jumping to chase it to its entry point in the system, Jase was damned careful to stay away from those legs. The last man to step on them, it was said, spent the next six months sitting at a computer. Though Crowe was certain it was either a gross understatement or an exaggeration. He hadn't decided which.

It took over an hour of chasing cables before Crowe and Jase managed to track down the problem. The cable running from the camera's WiFi base to the security router had been left unplugged. That one cable, an additional layer of security, had allowed Wayne to infiltrate their system.

Crowe stared at it as Cameron pushed himself to his feet then moved quickly to where the cable appeared plugged in. Then they looked closer at the gap between the cable's end and the plug it went into.

"Man, that bastard Mike is gonna be wearing my shoe

straight up his stupid ass once I catch sight of him. Dumb motherfucker. I should just shoot him."

"Good luck finding him," Jase grunted as he moved to reset all the hardware after the cable was pushed firmly into place. "He went AWOL after Rory sent him back to the office yesterday. Said he was damned sick of dark rooms and rolling commands. Though he didn't mention where he was going." The tech rolled his shoulders in a lazy shrug.

"Oh, he'll be back," Cameron assured them. "That overconfident little prick won't be able to help himself."

And Crowe had to agree with this estimation. Mike would be back simply because he wouldn't be able to bear his curiosity. Once everything was over, he would just show up again, demand a job, and go to work.

His cousins had warned him about the man's lack of dedication on the job, but Crowe had excused it. Mike had been a good friend, and until now his often irresponsible behavior had never threatened a mission.

As the monitors and computers came back online, Cameron stretched out his arm and tapped one of the upper monitors' touch screens, displaying the temperatures. Both Jase and Crowe then winced at his subsequent curses on every paternal and maternal line Mike may have possessed.

"Damned sensors," he finished as he moved to one of the keyboards. "I've changed every security box on each door and every window myself through the night." He rubbed at the overnight growth of beard on his unshaven jaw. "I don't get it."

"What's going on?" Jase moved from his chair to stand behind the other man.

"What's going on?" Cameron snorted. "Either the thermostat on the heater has shot up to a hundred and fifty degrees in the library, or one or all of the internal thermostats on those security boxes is filled with gremlins. Because I damned well know they're not all malfunctioning."

"Jase, go check the library. Take one of the inside security agents with you. Don't go alone. And be sure to get one of the new earbuds before going down. Stay in direct contact with Cameron while you're checking them."

"Got it." Jase moved to the biometric cabinet, let the camera scan his eye, then punched in his security code. When the door opened, he pulled free the small communication device before setting the frequency to the one Cameron used at all times.

Jase left the room. Crowe watched the cameras as he moved through the house, making sure they were all picking up the tech's image and body temperature—as well as scanning for weapons—as he passed each camera.

"Something's wonky here, Crowe," Cameron informed him. "And when I find out who's responsible, they might not survive it."

"You'll have to beat me to them," Crowe growled, interrupted by the ring of the cell phone he wore at his hip.

Pulling the smartphone free of the holster, he let the biometrics on the door scan his identity, then pushed in his digital code and stepped out to the hall as the request for videoconferencing came through.

"What can I do for you, Sheriff?" he asked. "Things are kind of busy here."

"Make time," Archer demanded, his expression somber as he stared back at him through the phone's small display.

"I'll give you what I can," Crowe promised. "So get started."

"I received an email from Amelia last night. Did you know it went out?"

Crowe nodded. "I knew it went out, I don't know what was in it."

Surprise gleamed in the sheriff's gaze, causing Crowe to snort. "I'm not her warden, Archer. Besides, I figured if there was a problem you'd get hold of me."

" 'Archer,' " the sheriff began, quoting Amelia's message. " 'It's my decision after hours of consideration that I will not be pressing charges against Dwight, David, and Dillon Carter. To be honest, I don't even remember the exact nature of the altercation with them, but knowing them as I do, I know no harm was meant. The agents of Brute Force acted on the appearance of a threat, though none was intended by the suspected assailants. It is my wish that you would escort me to the jail at some point in the coming day and allow me to speak to them before officially making known that I will not be pressing charges. I ask this as a friend, knowing you're under no obligation to grant me this wish, and likely under great pressure not to. I would hope, though, that the friendship we've had over the years has meant as much to you as it has to me, because it is a request I would gladly grant you were the positions reversed. Sincerely, Amelia.' " Lifting his gaze from the printed email, Archer glared back at Crowe. "What the hell have you done to her?"

"Sheriff, I'm well aware of your history with Amelia." Crowe drew the word out suggestively, reminding Archer of the fact that he and Amelia had been considered an item a year or so before the Callahan cousins returned to Corbin County.

"Cut it out, Crowe," Anna's voice snapped from somewhere on the line, causing Crowe to grin.

His sister had a habit of using the exact tone their mother had once used whenever Crowe was trying to maneuver her into letting him do something he shouldn't be.

Archer continued to wait.

"We argued over the *alleged* altercation," he growled. "She wants to show them mercy. I want to boil them in pig fat, peel the hide from their flesh, then de-bone them like fucking chickens."

Archer groaned.

"Geez, Crowe, tell us how you really feel." Anna's disgusted exclamation had him shaking his head at her.

"Did that argument include the information that this isn't the first *alleged altercation*," Archer mocked.

"It did," he agreed. "What does that have to do with anything?"

"Crowe." Anna moved behind Archer's shoulder, her expression concerned. "Listen, you are not going to make her press charges."

"As much as I love you, baby sister, butt out," he growled.

"Then let me say it." Archer sighed, his raptor gaze piercing as he stared back at Crowe. "Listen to her, Crowe. Let her talk to them, let her get this out of her system. Those boys might have scared her this time, but there's more behind this than you know . . ."

"Yeah, they had bad lives. They were beaten and deserted," he snapped. "So join the fucking club. The rest of us don't get drunk and threaten to rape and cut out the heart of an innocent person."

The hell she was going to drop those charges.

"I'll be there this evening around six to pick her up," Archer stated, his voice suddenly hard, alerting Crowe to the fact that he wouldn't be swayed easily. "And I will be bringing her to the jail to talk to them, and I will heed her wishes unless a damned good reason to do otherwise comes up."

Crowe narrowed his eyes on his friend. "You're speaking to me, Archer, as though I'm not a reasonable man," he drawled, knowing he was getting ready to be damn unreasonable.

"No, I'm talking to you like a man who has no idea of the depths of mercy and compassion his lover possesses,"

Archer stated coolly. “I do. I’ve worked with her, Crowe. I’ve worked with the people she helped and the people she took more than one fucking beating for, and I’ll be damned if I’ll see her sacrifices wasted because you’re unaware of the nature of the people you’re dealing with or the men she’s protected, agreeably, for far too long. Come to the jail with her, let her talk to them. Then talk to her yourself.”

Gritting his teeth, Crowe held back the snarl that threatened to erupt. “I’m sick and tired of being told how I don’t know people—”

“Not people, Crowe,” Archer sighed. “The people of Corbin County. It’s different here and you know it. The very fact that the socials are still so successful should tell you that. I’ll see you this evening.”

The call ended before Crowe could tell the man to go to hell. Or question him about the beatings Amelia had yet to tell him about.

An oversight he intended to correct. Quickly.

Letting himself back into the control room, he had no more than begun reading the diagnostics on the video and audio systems when the system itself sounded an alert.

Unauthorized attempted access, main gate. Alert, unauthorized attempted access, main gate. The computer’s mechanical voice repeated the warning as both Cameron and Crowe moved quickly to the monitor displaying the front gate.

“Holy Mother of God,” Cameron hissed through his teeth. “Is that who I think it is?”

Reaching up to pinch the bridge of his nose, Crowe let a grimace tighten his face before breathing out his own curse.

“Yeah, it’s him,” he snapped.

“Do I let him in?” Cameron asked doubtfully. “He’s gonna be as pissed and mean as a rattler in August.”

“That’s his normal disposition,” Crowe sighed as he

stared at the glare the attempted intruder was directing at the screen.

Fuck you, Crowe, John Caine mouthed at the camera. *Let me the fuck in. Now.*

"Let him the fuck in," Crowe breathed out. "I'll go downstairs and see if I can distract him long enough to get him back out the door."

"Yeah, good luck," Cameron muttered. "Didn't someone tell me old Sorenson's main suite was his now?"

Crowe slammed the control room door on the question and stomped down the hall to the curved staircase and the brother he wished he could send packing for just a little while longer.

CHAPTER 16

Sweetrock's spring-summer social season always began on the last weekend of April. The opening event, the Corbin County Winter Ball, was an event every young girl, teen, and female adult looked forward to all winter. It was considered more exciting than the senior prom because everyone could attend. Old, young, and in between, everyone had the chance to dress up and dance the night away.

Beneath the walkways of the dance square, pipes had been laid decades ago that carried heated air and kept the bricks free of snow and ice.

Nothing short of a blizzard or ice storm ever stopped an event during the social season. And not even that stopped the Winter Ball.

One of the most important phases of planning the ball was ensuring that every woman, teenager, and preteen girl who wanted a gown for the highly popular event was able to acquire one.

Donations of gowns and cash to the fund that sponsored it were always given diligent attention. Sponsors often attended yard sales, estate sales, and buyouts in search of gowns to add to the collection.

Volunteers helped with alterations, while accessories were gathered and made available by the same means.

Each gown had to be returned in the same shape it went out, with the exception of any normal cleaning requirements. Other rules governed the gown transactions as well. For the most part, those rules were adhered to. After all, most parents and adult recipients had no desire to have their name printed in the local paper, listed on the courthouse wall, or announced over local radio as owing the Social Planning Fund anything, whether it be a dress or the required volunteer hours.

This was the reason the socials were so successful, with such a high rate of resident participation and donations, in an age when few small-town yearly traditions were surviving.

The upcoming Winter Ball was the first of the events that Amelia had worked toward for seven years. The theme was Fantasy Winter Wonderland, and each grotto would be decorated accordingly. One had winged fairies, figures volunteers were still working on, that would seem to flutter above the ground in welcome. Another was decorated as Pegasus's stall; a large white horse figure had been completed the year before. There was a grotto with a large looking-glass screen that projected the image of a magical advisor.

Gargoyles filled another grotto. Three-foot elves held a tea party in yet another.

Volunteers would be costumed with tiny wings and pointed ears and would play the Old World–style hosts.

For Amelia, knowing that the plans she'd initiated were progressing—even though someone else now carried the title of coordinator—was bittersweet. That Anna had demanded the position only to inform the committee she would of course find a reliable co-coordinator was incredibly amusing.

There were only six months to the Winter Ball and only eleven months to the Fairy Ball. Dozens upon dozens of wings were waiting in auxiliary storage, and still more were being made or fitted. Some guests were making or purchasing their own, and still others had volunteered to serve as non-fairy hosts.

Standing in front of one of the twelve grotto easels, studying the design layout she'd created, Amelia leaned close and carefully sketched in the winged foal that a group of high school design students had created for an end-of-semester project.

They had contacted Anna that morning to inform her of the creation, which had been completed the week Wayne had been identified as the Slasher, to add to the county's social fairy ball weekend. It had proven Ruth Anne's declaration that participation would suffer for the ill will held toward Amelia thanks to Wayne Sorenson and Amory Wyatt. And it had reminded Amelia that no sacrifice she had made in the past would change that.

She couldn't even blame town residents for their fear. Wayne had shed blood for generations. He had murdered his victims unhindered and unsuspected no matter the law enforcement agencies or private investigation firms hired to track down the Slasher's identity.

"What the hell is going on here?"

Amelia's eyes widened as she jerked back from the drawing and swung around to meet the furious gaze of the man everyone believed was her brother. If she could have chosen someone to be her brother, she had to admit, John would have been on the short list of possible choices.

Staring into his stormy gray eyes as three of Crowe's bodyguards flanked him in the foyer, she shrugged as though weary of battling the reality of her position any longer.

"Ask Crowe," she suggested with a tight smile, still

less than pleased with the fact that Crowe had not supported her concerning the Carter brothers. "They're his flunkies, not mine."

Poor Rory Malone. Amelia hid her amusement as he directed a chastising glare her way. He really didn't deserve that, but he was one of the black-clad shoulders she couldn't see over whenever she wanted to leave the house. And he was also one of the men pounding on the Carter brothers the day before.

"Amelia, I told you, I don't hire flunkies," Crowe growled as he entered the room from the dining room.

He wore snug, low-slung jeans and a black shirt, the sleeves of which were rolled to just below his elbows, the tail tucked into the belted band of his pants. The dark colors called attention to his hard abs and powerful thighs.

He'd exchanged the boots from yesterday for a pair of more traditional cowboy boots, though he'd opted against a Stetson.

She only smiled. A tight, mirthless curve of her lips that held not so much as an ounce of amusement. She ignored his glare, just as she had been ignoring it all day.

"Call off the damned flunkies, Crowe," John snapped. "I do live here with my sister when I'm in town whether you like it or not."

Crowe grunted at that, though he did give the security personnel a tight nod to dismiss them.

Amelia shook her head as Rory turned and left the room. "As long as you remember that's the relationship," Crowe drawled.

Anger flashed in John's gaze.

"Screw you," he muttered, the anger hardening his tone as Crowe leaned against Amelia's mother's antique wood cabinet, his arms crossed over the broad width of his chest.

Crowe only chuckled at the suggestion as Amelia turned back to the colored drawing she'd been working on.

"How long will you be in town this time?" Crowe asked him.

"Until I leave." Lazy disregard filled John's expression. "Do you mind if I talk to my sister for a few minutes or is she under some damned house arrest I wasn't aware of?"

Crowe straightened slowly. "Since when do you have a problem with your sister's protection, John?"

The latent warning in his tone had Amelia turning back to the two men with a frown.

"Since I walked into this house to a tension thick enough to cut with a knife and the knowledge that you're playing into this fucking county's attempts to ostracize her by keeping her locked in here."

Crowe turned back to her mockingly. "Have I locked you in, Amelia?"

She took her time tucking her pencil behind her ear before breathing out heavily. "I'm allowed out of the house as long as the living wall of muscle you hired is shuffling in place around me."

John's stormy gaze narrowed. "Meaning?"

Amelia rolled her eyes. "You know, six of his flunkies surrounding me, shoulder-to-shoulder, and taking every step I take? A living wall."

Crowe slid a long, lazy look her way. The amber gleam in his gaze held a promise of retribution.

She would have been worried where that look was concerned, but it wasn't as though he would actually hurt her. At least not physically.

"Big mistake, Crowe." John shook his head as a rumble of laughter vibrated in his chest. "But the original question stands. Can I talk to my sister alone?"

Crowe shrugged. "Just do yourself a favor and don't let her talk you into letting her leave the house without protection the way she managed yesterday and again this morning." Crowe shook his head at her. "And how she had the gall to lie to a friend like Rory, I haven't figured out yet."

"Are your tightie whities still in a twist over that?" She acted surprised. "Really, Crowe, I just wanted to check the mail."

Crowe turned to John. "Rory assumed she meant the mailbox at the end of the driveway, not the post office in town. She'd managed two of the six blocks before the rest of us caught up with her. And that was after assuming she would never do anything so stupid again after several drunks caught sight of her yesterday when she slipped out of the house and made it to town. They were dragging her into the town square after deciding she made a handy tool to punish Wayne for his crimes."

Amelia sniffed indelicately. "I told you, Crowe, that wasn't a serious threat."

"Threatening to take turns raping you before they sliced your heart out is definitely what I call a damned serious threat. Dammit, you just told me last night you understood that you shouldn't have left the house alone." He turned on her incredulously. "For God's sake, Amelia."

"He uses that phrase far too often." Crossing her arms over her breasts and cocking her hip challengingly, she chanced a glance at John. "It was the Carter brothers. And until he allows me to go to the jail where he had them thrown and discuss this with them, then yes, he and I are at odds and all bets are off when it comes to obeying his trifling little dictates."

"For God's sake," he muttered again.

"Uh huh," John agreed as he caught her look before turning to Crowe. "She's not going to listen to you where those three are concerned. Give it up."

The exasperation in his tone had a smug smile tugging at Amelia's lips, all but enraging him. Watching her, Crowe couldn't believe the rebelliousness and sheer determination she possessed.

"You'd make a mule question your damned stubbornness," he bit out, gritting his teeth.

"They're bozos and they were just drunk," she reminded him. "Last year they threatened to sell me to white slavers after raping me. Crowe, I told you, they can't be taken seriously."

The look on Crowe's face wasn't comforting in the least. It was downright dangerous. John watched the argument with far too much curiosity.

"Amelia, do you really think I'm going to continue to allow that?" Crowe asked, his voice strangely gentle considering the savage gleam in his eyes.

"Why bother." Pulling the pencil from behind her ear and tossing it carelessly to her desk, she shot him a furious look. "It's not as though you'll even be here to make it stick if you do try to stop it. So why not just stop with the damned threats already."

Amelia was tired of dealing with this.

She'd thought, after the past night and the hunger she'd felt in him, the emotions she could have sworn she saw in his gaze as he took her, that he would soften at least marginally. But he'd refused to even discuss the Carter brothers with her, or allow her to call Archer after he hadn't answered her email.

"Dammit, Amelia, since when have you even given me a chance to take care of anything today?" he accused her, his voice a hard rasp now. "I've been so fucking busy chasing the damned glitches on that computer I haven't had time to do anything else."

"All I needed was a yes or a no," she reminded him furiously.

"All you need is a damned spanking for being so fucking stubborn."

She saw it in his face then. He had no intention of taking her to the jail. No intention of allowing her to see the three brothers.

Swallowing tightly she squared her shoulders, blinking back the tears of betrayal and turning to John, resolving to herself that if Crowe could cut her out of a decision so crucial to her own peace of mind, then she could at least give the appearance of cutting him out of her heart.

"How long will you be home?" she asked, ignoring the rasp of pain in her voice. "I know the house seems a little full at the moment, but the security agency that stepped in and took control of my life is rather large."

"Amelia," Crowe growled dangerously.

She didn't so much as flick him a glance. "And I'd fix dinner, but there are a lot of mouths to feed and currently, no cook. I'm not exactly safe around the stove."

"Sounds like another pizza night," John offered with somber gentleness.

"Pizza it is." She nodded. "Though as with all things, you have to check with the warden before ordering. He tends to be a very cautious man. Let me know what he says."

Turning on her heel she moved back to the desk, picked up her pencil, and turned back to the drawing.

Crowe felt like punching something. He had a feeling if he hit the wall, though, all he'd gain from it would be sore knuckles.

"Might as well give in," John sighed. "When it comes to those three, from what I understand, even Wayne gave up protesting."

"Because he knew they'd kill her eventually," Crowe grunted.

"If that's what I thought, then I would have already taken care of it." John shrugged, his voice lowering. "Or called you. I understand you take care of dirty little projects like that free of charge, without so much as a request."

Of course, the bastard worked with Ryan Calvert so he no doubt knew of Stoner Wright's demise.

Crowe stared back at him icily, daring him to go farther, well aware that despite the lowering of his tone, Amelia could hear every word her brother uttered.

"What are you after, John?" Crowe said.

"The truth." John shrugged. "Just the truth. Rather like these tabloids I'd say."

From the pack at his feet, John bent and pulled a handful of newspapers from inside before tossing them to the floor. Uppermost and center was a picture of Amelia at the news conference she'd given, Crowe standing behind her.

The caption read, *Is Amelia Sorenson Crowe Callahan's baby mama?* Beneath the caption, in smaller letters, *Sources close to the Callahan family hint that Crowe Callahan and Amelia Sorenson may be announcing an addition to the family soon.*

From his periphery he watched as Amelia's hand lifted, pressing to her chest as the whispery sound of a sharply inhaled breath was heard.

"Crowe?" His head lifted, his chest tightening at the somber fear in her expression. "Did you do this?"

"I didn't refute it," he told her coolly.

No, he hadn't done it, but he also hadn't bothered to deny it. Wayne would draw his own conclusions and as long as Crowe kept Amelia protected, then it wouldn't harm her.

"That's the reason for the shoulder-to-shoulder living wall, little sister," John stated mockingly. "He's terrified Wayne will slip out of reality and just take a shot at you."

"But why not just tell me?" She didn't take her eyes from him.

Amelia couldn't believe he would do something like this—endangering her deliberately.

Crowe's expression wasn't giving away anything but his anger as he shrugged. "Once the article was on the stands, Wayne would believe whatever he wanted. Refuting it wouldn't have done any good."

"Wouldn't have done any good?" John snarled, moving between Crowe and Amelia as he glared back at Crowe. "You're fucking playing with her life, Crowe, and I don't like it."

"Back down, soldier," Crowe barked.

Amelia wondered who was more surprised—her or John—when her brother did just that.

The knowledge that he had reacted out of instinct twisted John's expression with morbid amusement.

"Don't get in my way, John," Crowe warned him then, the dark warning sending a chill racing up Amelia's spine as she watched the confrontation. "You'll regret it."

"What will you do, Crowe? Put a bullet in my head like you did Stoner's? The body count is going to start adding up and you haven't even taken out the Carters yet. Tell me, Crowe, is my sister aware you killed her husband, or is that a secret you only shared with your uncle?"

Amelia turned slowly, shock shuddering through her as her gaze pivoted between and Crowe and her brother. She could feel herself shaking from the inside out and heard Wayne once again telling her not to worry about Stoner, he'd taken care of everything. He wouldn't be back.

She'd been certain Wayne had killed him, hadn't she?

She remembered staring at him the first time he said it, an icy chill invading her at the look of smug satisfaction in his gaze. But, she admitted, she hadn't been able to make herself believe he could actually kill Stoner. Stoner wouldn't have just stood idly by as Wayne took a shot at him, or used the Slasher's knife against him.

But had she known Crowe had . . . No. She refused to

even think it. Just as she had always refused to put Crowe's name on Stoner's disappearance. Because doing so would only make her soul bleed harder. It would only make her heart ache more. If he would do such a thing to protect her, then wouldn't it have to mean he loved her? But if he loved her, how could he stay away from her?

Crowe could see the glazed disbelief in her eyes slowly being overshadowed by a shadow of belief. Hell, she had known all along that Wayne was too damned weak, physically, to do anything about Stoner Wright. Just as, Crowe suspected, a part of her had always known that if he ever learned of the abuse she was suffering, then Stoner would die.

"She is now," he told John as Amelia's gaze turned to her brother then back to Crowe.

"Wayne said he took care of Stoner," she whispered, her voice tight, her breathing erratic.

Crowe gave a short, tight nod. "Yeah, he did. He made damned sure I knew about the abuse, and when I confronted Stoner he didn't have a second's hesitation in admitting to it. But there's even more, Amelia," he snarled. "The night he left you, no more than two hours later he was in Aspen attempting to rape a sixteen-year-old. Any reluctance I may have had evaporated when I saw him hit that kid."

But his mind had already been made up, Crowe knew. He'd followed Stoner from Corbin County to Aspen, the pieces of his specially made rifle tucked securely in the backpack he carried in his truck.

Amelia shook her head. "The body would have been found. Investigators have tracked him. He uses his credit card."

Crowe snorted at that. "How Wayne pulled that one off, I really didn't care. But trust me, that's a body that will never be found. And don't bother reporting it to Archer or anyone else. Because not so much as a sliver of a tooth exists. And in this case, I promise you, you'll need a body to prove it. Now, you have about three hours before Archer arrives to take you to that fucking jail. I suggest you be ready. Because I'll be damned if I'll take you."

"We're not finished," John drawled as Crowe turned to leave the living room.

"We're finished," Crowe assured him, raking him with a furious glance. "And I'm sure the source that you stole this information from won't be pleased with you."

"Stole it?" John's brows arched in question as Crowe felt his guts tighten. "I didn't have to steal it, Crowe, it was given to me."

Which meant John was now a fully integrated member of Ryan's team. Possibly the second-in-command his uncle had mentioned looking for.

"Crowe." Amelia stepped forward as he turned to leave.

Turning back to her, Crowe forced back his rage that she should have even had to know.

"Why?" she asked, her hand lifting as though to reach out to him before falling helplessly to her side. "Why would you do that?"

"Why do you think I did it, Amelia?" He turned away and stalked from the room.

CHAPTER 17

The bedroom was dark, the lights turned out completely, the drapes drawn over the balcony doors as Crowe sat in the wingback chair across from the bed and stared at it silently.

One elbow was propped on the arm of the chair as he slowly rubbed his finger against his upper lip, his thoughts taking him back to a place he hadn't visited in years. To a time when the darkness inside him had been lit by only one thing.

Amelia.

The contact was still in the military reserve. Crowe held the paperwork that could send him to military prison or exonerate him based on Crowe's word that he'd been working for an upper-level, top-secret black ops group at the time he'd made a very stupid decision.

Crowe's report could be held indefinitely. Or it could go in the next morning, and Joey Fields knew it. That was the reason he was in Sweetrock working for Wayne Sorenson as a gofer and handyman. To keep an eye on Amelia and get to the bottom of the whispers Crowe had heard that she was being abused.

Staring at the contact now, Crowe wondered if he'd

put him in place to find a reason to kill, or because Crowe knew there was a reason.

"Wayne's furious," Joey continued to report. "The bastard keeps hitting her in the face. It's getting bad. Nothing Wayne threatens him with works." The other man looked away, and Crowe knew he was hiding more.

"Whatever you're not saying, I suggest you spit it out. You're not in military prison for a reason, Joey."

The other man snorted mockingly. "Whatever."

"Just tell me," Crowe snapped.

"He rapes her," Joey breathed out roughly. "At first, all I heard was a maid discussing it with the gardener. A few weeks later I was starting to believe it was just talk, so I hid in that tree outside her room and started watching. She came in her room and he was waiting for her. She didn't scream or cry—" He broke off, swallowing tight.

"Finish it!"

Joey flinched.

"She begged him," he whispered hoarsely then. "He threw her on the bed on her stomach and he raped her. At least the bastard used a condom. Then he left, went to the bar for a while, then drove out to that cabin he owns in Aspen."

Joey knew death when he saw it, and Crowe knew the other man had seen it in his eyes that night.

"I can take him out easy . . ." Joey offered.

"Pack and leave," Crowe ordered him. "Return to base, my report will be on your commander's desk within the hour. You'll be sent out to Europe in twelve hours."

"Crowe." Joey stopped him as he turned to leave. "Wayne's supposed to follow him to the bar tonight. He says he's going to make Stoner leave. You might want to be there."

"What time?" Crowe asked him.

"Ten, about the time he leaves. Wayne's going to try to do it private, so no one knows what Stoner's doing to her."

Crowe nodded. The meeting would be in less than two hours.

"Get out of here and get to base now," he ordered Joey again. "And I was never here, Joey. Remember that."

"Remember?" Joey snorted. "Why don't I just forget this whole year of my life, man? I think that would be safer all the way around for me."

"I think I agree with you."

From the cabin he'd met the soldier in, Crowe drove to Sweetrock, keeping to the back roads and hiking through the dense forest the last few miles into town.

At the time, it had been easy to access the tavern without passing too many houses. The small stream behind it that swelled with yearly snowmelt hadn't yet been tamed to stay within its banks. The wilderness grew to within feet of the small block on one side, making it easy for Crowe to slip to the back of the bar where Stoner had just stepped outside.

Wayne was waiting for him just as Joey had reported, with two of the heavily muscled bruisers Wayne hired from time to time.

Grabbing Stoner as he stepped from the bar, Wayne threw him against the wall of the bar.

"Pack your shit and get out before I kill you!" Wayne rasped in the other man's face. "I'll make damned sure Amelia divorces you before you leave."

"We have a deal, old man," Stoner reminded him, his smug tone drifting clearly to Crowe.

"That deal didn't include using my daughter as your personal punching bag."

"Well now, aren't you a fine one to talk," Stoner sneered.

Before the younger man could go any farther Wayne buried his fist in his gut.

"Tonight, Stoner," Wayne reminded him. "Or you'll wish you had."

Leaving the younger man where he sank to the ground, gasping for air, Wayne and the other two slipped around the edge of the bar and left. Only then did Crowe move to Stoner, silently, deadly.

"Crazy old bastard." Stoner moaned as he rose to his feet and stumbled toward the shadowed parking lot. "I'm not going any damned place."

A second later a gasp left Stoner's lips as a force pinned him to the side of the pickup. A razor-sharp knife pressed cold and threateningly against his throat.

"You'll leave," Crowe whispered at his ear, not caring if Stoner knew who he was or not.

"What?" Stoner's heart rate increased, fear echoing in his voice.

"You will leave tonight," Crowe repeated. "If you don't, you'll face me. Wayne will just kill you, maybe. But Stoner, I'll make you suffer. Are we clear?"

"Clear," Stoner wheezed. "We're clear."

"And I'll be watching to make sure you do," he promised, pulling back as quickly as he'd come upon the other man and disappearing into the shadows.

He watched as Stoner rubbed at his neck before rushing to his car, sliding in, and racing the few blocks to Wayne's house.

Crowe was just moving into place in the tree outside Amelia's bedroom balcony when Stoner slammed in.

Amelia had been sitting at the small writing desk and jumped to her feet. Before she could move more than a few feet, Stoner backhanded her across her face.

Crowe felt the growl that tore from his lips, drawing them into a snarl as he lifted the rifle he'd carried with him. He flipped on the laser sight just as Stoner gripped her neck and threw her against the wall.

The fear on her face horrified him. The tears that filled her eyes gave birth to a monster inside Crowe that he never wanted to feel again.

"Crowe Callahan visited me, bitch." Crowe could hear him clearly through the opened balcony doors. "I hope he enjoys you while I'm gone. When I get back, I'll see how fast the Slasher returns once I start telling everyone how protective that bastard is over you. How long do you think it will take before I'm a widower?"

Centering his rifle, Crowe let the little red bead center first on Amelia's forehead, right between her eyes, just to be sure Stoner could see it. Then he moved it to the hand wrapped around her throat as he keyed Stoner's number into his cell phone.

The other man activated the Bluetooth he wore on the first ring, though he didn't release Amelia's neck from his grip.

"Do you really want to die?" Crowe questioned him silkily. "Have no doubt, Stoner, I really want to kill you."

"I'm packing," Stoner whispered, though his hold never loosened as Amelia began to claw at his fingers, her eyes widening helplessly.

"That bead on your hand means I can see you, you fucking bastard. Get your hands the fuck off her."

Stoner released her immediately, paling as he turned, moving quickly to the closet and grabbing a bag he obviously kept packed.

Crowe could hear every word as Stoner cursed and raged.

"He has to leave sometime, bitch. When he does, you'll pay for tonight."

"What are you talking about?" she demanded, her voice raw and thread.

"What or who do you think I'm talking about? Crowe Callahan, that's who."

Amelia gave a bitter, pain-filled laugh that tightened Crowe's chest with regret.

"You're crazy, Stoner. Crowe couldn't give a damn whether you're here. Why don't you just go ahead and leave and stop making excuses. I didn't want you here to begin with."

"Oh, I'm leaving, you little fucking Callahan whore. But I will be back. And when I get back, I'm going to make certain every man, woman, and child in this damned county knows you for the Callahan-fucker you are. How much do you want to bet the Slasher comes out of retirement just to make certain he gets a piece of you?"

Resignation vied with fear in Amelia's expression at the threat. "Better now than later," she said tonelessly. "It beats the constant threats, Stoner. Between you and Wayne, I've really grown tired of them."

In that moment Crowe knew Stoner would never live to see the morning light. Watching the other man slam from the room, he leaned back against the tree trunk and turned off the laser sight before sliding the rifle into the scabbard he'd slung over his back.

He'd wait just a bit, he decided. Just watch her for a few moments before he went after Stoner.

Moving shakily to the mirror hanging over her dresser, Amelia stared at the bruises that ringed her neck—livid red, already darkening to blue. Touching the marks, she let a strangled sob part her lips as her head bent, her fingers now gripping the edge of the dresser. God, how he needed to be there with her. To hold her rather than hiding and watching her hurt like this. The need was so brutal he had taken that first step on the heavy limb when her bedroom door opened again.

Crowe froze, watching, listening as Wayne stepped

slowly into his daughter's bedroom. Dressed in his familiar black slacks and white shirt, he'd removed his tie, but had only pushed his glasses to the top of his thinning gray hair.

Amelia's expressive face was so completely expressionless now that Crowe could feel the fine hairs at the back of his neck lift warningly.

He had known she didn't trust her father, and he'd sensed she was frightened of him. This reaction had him tensing in preparation for danger, though.

"I'm sorry, Amelia," Wayne sighed, shaking his head as she stared back him through the mirror. "I'll take care of this, I promise."

She only nodded slightly.

What the fuck was going on here?

"You hate me," Wayne said then, a grimace contorting his face. "I didn't know he was like this. I swear I didn't."

"Would it have made a difference if you had?" she asked him. Crowe could hear what Wayne obviously didn't recognize.

Pure hatred. And he saw something else.

Amelia had clasped her hands in front of her, twining her fingers together. It was a sure sign she was preparing her entire body to lie. Her expression, her stance, her muscle tone, right to her eyes. Every part of her body followed the lies her lips spilled. Every part of her except her hands. And it amazed him that no one else realized it. No one else even noticed it.

"I would have done anything to keep you safe, Amelia." The sincerity in his tone would have caused Crowe to pause if it weren't for the fact that Amelia so distrusted him.

She did not distrust without good reason.

She drew in a deep breath, giving a smile that sent a

chill racing up Crowe's spine. That smile was so soft, so forgiving . . . and her fingers were twisted together so tightly they were white.

"I understand," she told him. "I understand."

She was lying through her teeth.

What the fuck was going on here and what did Wayne think he was saving her from?

"Good then," Wayne nodded, his hands lifting to her shoulders, his head bending to place a kiss at the top of her head. "Good night, sweetheart, and I promise you, Stoner will not be back."

Releasing his hold on her shoulders, Wayne turned and left the room, closing the door quietly behind him.

Suddenly Amelia's shoulders heaved. Her hand clapped over her mouth and she rushed for the connecting bathroom.

Crowe could hear her retching from the bathroom, the violence of the sounds causing him to clench his fists to hold himself back from going to her. He knew his training and he knew the woman who filled his heart. And both were telling him something was very wrong.

And it wasn't just Stoner.

He forced himself to leave. Forced himself to track Stoner instead.

Pulling his truck into the back of the diner Stoner had stopped at, just a few miles from the cabin he owned, Crowe knew what he was going to do.

Crowe rarely killed without orders. Hell, until now, he'd never done so. He'd left Amelia's with the intent to kill, but each time he began preparing for it, he'd pictured the disappointment and fear he'd invariably meet in her eyes if she ever learned of it.

Pulling the rifle case from beneath the front seat of the truck, Crowe opened it and snapped the weapon together efficiently. Pulling on a black ski mask and gloves, he left the truck and headed around the back of the small diner, keeping close to the shadows.

It wasn't that he intended to kill Stoner there; he was more curious as to why the bastard had parked in the back.

It didn't take him long to figure it out.

The sight of young, hungry runaways wasn't uncommon at that particular diner. The night cook was known to sneak them small portions of food from the hot servers in the back. In his fifties with half a dozen grandchildren, he'd pay for the food himself out of his own pocket before seeing a kid go hungry.

But some kids, it took them a while to actually ask for the food. Those kids, especially young girls, often found themselves at the mercy of men like Stoner. That particular young girl hadn't been willing, though.

He'd gotten her out of the diner somehow—or perhaps he'd caught her coming in, Crowe didn't ask which. But when Stoner used his fist to disorient her and began tearing at her clothes, Crowe had hád enough.

Acting quickly, he moved to the corner of the diner, called out the name he'd heard Stoner call her as though concerned, and made enough noise to wake the dead as though searching for her. It had been enough to get Stoner moving.

Tossing the kid aside with a curse, he'd rushed to his car and within seconds was speeding back up the road toward the cabin he owned. Exactly where Crowe wanted him.

Crowe took care of the girl first. Calling into the diner, he told the old cook there was a kid in the back lot, probably hurt and frightened, who could use a good meal and a friendly shoulder. Then he'd headed farther into the mountains.

Stoner didn't have much longer to live.

Once Stoner had nearly raped that kid, Crowe hadn't had a conscience left.

The stone-cold, merciless hunter the military had trained kicked into place, and Stoner was no longer a man. He was prey. A rabid, senseless waste of life that no longer deserved to breathe.

Pulling into a hidden spot below the cabin, Crowe pulled the black ski mask over his face, donned specially made leather gloves certain to leave not so much as an identifying smudge, and grabbed the rifle from the seat next to him. Leaving the vehicle, Crowe hiked the extra mile to the cabin, certain Stoner had beat him there until the sound of his vehicle pulling into the drive assured him Stoner was only just arriving.

Slipping behind the stacked firewood next to the driveway, Crowe watched as the vehicle came to a stop in front of the cabin. A second later his gaze narrowed as the passenger-side door opened and a young girl fell from the car.

"Come here, you little bitch," Stoner snarled as he jumped from the driver's side and moved quickly to the girl as she tried to back away from him fearfully.

"Please don't do this," the girl cried out desperately. "I'm only sixteen. Please."

"That's okay, bitch, the younger the pussy the tighter the hold, ya know?" Stoner laughed drunkenly, obviously determined to victimize young, defenseless girls that night.

Dimming the light on the smartphone he carried, Crowe called Stoner's number again.

"What the fuck do you want?" Stoner screamed through the link as UNVERIFIED *came up on his phone's screen, obviously alerting him to who was calling.*

Crowe laughed lightly, his gaze narrowed as the girl took advantage of Stoner's momentary distraction to race from the drive and hopefully off the mountain.

"What do you want? I left already. Go fuck the little bitch and get your own case of frostbite. I don't care in the least."

Stoner was looking around, obviously hoping to catch sight of his third victim of the night and cursing at the realization she was gone.

Silently disconnecting the call, Crowe felt his entire system sliding into killing mode. Stoner had made his final mistake as Crowe realized that letting him live meant the rape of a kid. Stoner wouldn't stop until he found a victim to hurt. Possibly to kill.

"You bastard. Hang up on me will you? Just wait till I get back to that bitch wife of mine. Fucking Callahan whore. The next time you kiss her all you'll taste is my fucking cum filling her mouth. You can have some real sloppy seconds. Then I'll be nice and let the Slasher know what a Callahan-fucker she is so he can take her off both our hands."

Crowe stepped back as Stoner slammed into the cabin. Crowe went after the girl. He'd make sure she got home, or back to her parents, then he'd return for Stoner.

Less than two hours before dawn Crowe slid into place in a stand of evergreens at the back of the cabin. Through the kitchen window he could clearly see into the well-lit room as Stoner stood at the back door. He was silent, staring into the night as he finished what appeared to be another in a long line of beers.

Pulling the rifle to his shoulder Crowe knew he didn't have long to wait. He could smell a hint of urine where Stoner had relieved himself off the porch, obviously more than once. And it was obvious the lazy bastard was considering it again rather than walking to the bathroom at the front of the cabin.

Yep, here he came. Crowe waited until he was fully in

view, caressing the trigger. Then as Stoner reached down to loosen his pants Crowe took the shot.

The bullet tore through Stoner's heart, dropping him to the porch in less than a second.

No hesitation.

Stoner had signed his own kill order the moment he'd wrapped his fingers around Amelia's neck. Trying to rape not just one, but two young girls had removed Crowe's last hesitation.

Amelia was his. He'd forced himself to leave her to protect her, and he'd be damned if he'd allow some bastard with a heavy hand to abuse her.

The hike back to the truck was made quickly, and the drive to the cabin made with no one to witness the black shadow of a vehicle easing up the mountain at that hour of the morning. Stepping into the cabin once again, Crowe moved to the back porch, gathered up Stoner's body, zipped it in a body bag, and placed it in the covered back of his truck.

Sliding back into the vehicle, he reversed from the drive and sped down the mountain the same way he'd gone up it, then returned to the hidden spot he'd found to park the truck in. Using the secured sat phone he kept on him at all times, he then keyed in the number to a controlled line.

Base Control answered immediately. "Texas-Tahoe-Base. You're a go. We have sat lock and awaiting identification and instruction."

"California-Baker-Charlie," Crowe confirmed before continuing. "Sterilization required. Marker in place. Request cleanup ASAP with direction to authorized processing needed."

"Sterilization and immediate cleanup approved at marker, California-Baker-Charlie-Two," Base approved.

"Direction ordered to Tahoe-Alpha-Three, coordinates incoming. Authorized processing confirmed and approved. Proceed immediately to coordinates. Texas-Tahoe-Base, out."

"Coordinates confirmed Texas-Tahoe-Base. California-Baker-Charlie, out."

Disconnecting the link, Crowe activated the satellite map on his phone, put the vehicle in gear, and headed down the mountain once again.

Moments later his lips curled in a smile of satisfaction. The low hum of a stealth drone overhead drew his attention. Seconds later the mountain trembled as the cabin exploded into a ball of fire that Crowe knew would burn the building to next to nothing.

And once he reached Tahoe-Alpha-Three, Stoner Wright would be burned until even the ash was ashes.

Wiping his hand over his face, Crowe remembered thinking how he would just pray Amelia never suspected, let alone learned what he had done.

And what the hell had happened?

John-fucking-Caine had happened, and he and Ryan's high-flying ideal that Crowe shouldn't step into a relationship with Amelia without telling her the truth was biting him in the ass. *There shouldn't be secrets between the two of you, son,* Ryan had advised him when he first learned what Crowe had planned.

No doubt, his uncle had sent John in just to tell Amelia the truth.

But why?

And why now?

CHAPTER 18

What now?

There were too many secrets, too many lives ruined because of Wayne Sorenson, and still he was out there. Nothing they had done so far had pushed him into making a mistake.

Amelia stared at the pictures she'd pulled from the loose board in her bedroom floor after Wayne had supposedly died. Pictures of her and Crowe from seven years ago. One picture alone had sustained her. One she'd shot of them together by lifting her phone above them as they lay on her bed.

She hadn't warned him first as she usually had. She had just snapped the picture. Later that night she'd printed it and hidden it with the rest. She hadn't pulled it out until months later when she'd been so torn, desperate, and uncertain what to do.

That picture had dug talons of agony straight to her soul because the expression on his face was one she had never seen on another man's, at any time in her life. Especially Crowe's.

She had never seen gentleness, need, and something akin to desperation mixed and merged to create a look so similar to what she would have described as devotion; she'd convinced herself for years that that was exactly what the emotion was.

Then life had happened. Crowe had returned and of course he'd had lovers. Those lovers and his experiences with them were drawn out in detail by friends of those victims once the Slasher murdered them.

He'd had lovers. He'd touched other women and allowed them to touch him. A part of her hadn't blamed him. She couldn't have him, not as long as the Slasher lived—those stories proved it. But she needed him. She ached for him until a part of her had felt as raw and agonized as an open wound.

She looked at the picture again.

She would have killed for him. If she had known Wayne was the killer, she would have killed him in his sleep and gladly gone to prison for it if it meant Crowe would find peace or happiness.

Coming to that realization wasn't hard. She had hated Stoner. She had hated him even more than she had hated Wayne at the time. Hated the few times he touched her with such strength that she had been physically ill each time he forced her beneath him.

Thankfully, those times had been few and far between.

"Amelia?" John stepped into the family room, his expression drawn and saddened. "You okay?"

"Did he love me?" she whispered, looking at that picture again.

Moving to her, John looked down at the image she held and breathed out roughly. "Never seen that look on Crowe's face before I saw him with you. And only when you're not looking. If he loved you then, he loves you now."

Covering her lips with her hands, she tried to force back her tears as she nodded slowly then looked up at him. "Do you trust me, John?"

He stared down at her for long moments before finally nodding. "I trust you, Amelia."

"Enough to let me use your phone?"

The secured line he used couldn't be detected or traced. She needed that. To make the call she had to make, she needed a line no one would even know was in use.

Somber, silent for long moments, he finally nodded, drawing the device from the pocket of his jeans.

It was tiny. A sort of flip phone unlike any she had ever seen.

"How do I key in a number?" she asked.

John talked her through the process quickly before turning and moving to the doorway as though keeping watch for her.

She quickly dialed the number, another secured line she knew couldn't be hacked or traced.

"Who is this?" With a voice as dark and cool as Crowe's could be and just as suspicious, Ethan Roberts answered the call.

"It's me," she said quietly. "It's Amelia."

Silence filled the line for just a second.

"Amelia, baby, are you okay?" Her mother's voice was hoarse as though crying, and definitely worried.

Thea and Ethan Roberts had lived a hell most parents could never imagine.

"I'm fine," she promised. "Is Dad still on the line?"

"You're on speaker, honey," her father assured her. "Jack and the team are here as well. He was heading out in a few hours to your location."

She drew in a hard, deep breath. "Do you remember, just after we realized Wayne was alive, what you said?"

"What I told you was the only way to draw him out?" His voice became icier than ever. "I remember."

"I think you were right. I think it's time." Her heart

was beating sluggishly now, terror striking at her as tears filled her eyes. "I think it's time to do it."

"Are you sure, Amelia?" he asked her. "Be damned sure, baby."

"I'm sure," she promised him. "How soon—" Swallowing tightly, she had to force herself to finish the question. "How soon before all of you can be here?"

"Give us three hours and we'll be there. If not sooner," he promised. "Are you going to tell Crowe before we arrive?"

"Would he believe it without seeing it?" she asked.

He sighed heavily. "Hell, I didn't believe it until I saw you," he admitted.

She nodded slowly then asked the question she knew would torment her if she left it unasked. "Did you hear the rumor that Crowe killed Stoner?"

Her father and his team collected rumors, favors, and other related information with surprising regularity. She had always wanted to ask if he'd heard any rumors regarding Crowe, and hadn't had the nerve.

She could hear the curse her uncle, Jack Roberts, bit off.

"I heard a very faint rumor," he admitted. "A body that was disposed of through military means by a black ops member resembling Crowe. I guess that's what happened?"

"A rumor," she verified.

"You okay?" he asked.

Her chest clenched, pain knifing her senses at the realization that there was so much more to Crowe than she had ever known. She knew the man he was with her, but without her he'd been cold, silent, a military machine that did the government's dirty work without pause to protect those he loved from the government's enemies.

"I'm fine," she promised. "I'll be better, perhaps, once you get here."

"We're on our way then," he repeated. "Leave the lights on, baby girl, we'll be there soon."

Leave the lights on.

She disconnected the call and walked slowly to John as he turned back to her. The fondness in his expression was something she hated to lose.

"Tell me, John, would you have liked me much if you hadn't thought I was your sister?" she asked him, keeping her voice low.

He smiled at that, leaned close, and whispered, "I have a feeling we both know—"

Tears filled her eyes again as he stared into her eyes.

"I wish you were." Her voice broke on a sob. "You would have made an incredible brother."

"Are we telling anyone yet?" He grinned at the conspiracy they'd both believed no one else knew about.

"Just for now, for a few more hours, will you be my brother?"

He nodded slowly, opened his arms, and drew her into his embrace. "Then come here, baby sister, let me give you a hug. I have a feeling once Crowe finds out, the hugs will be over."

Would he be jealous? Not jealous, she thought. He was too confident for jealousy. No, Crowe would be territorial. There was a difference. Jealous implied the belief that he somehow might not be able to hold her. Territorial didn't just imply that something belonged to him, it verified it.

John's hug was filled with fondness and affection. Just as she had always thought a brother's hug would be.

"Okay, little rebel, let's see what you've got." He grinned as she pulled back. "And let's see if I'm right about the secret you've been hiding for seven years."

Her gaze narrowed on him. "How do you know there's a secret?"

His lips twitched. "Crowe's had his uncle investigating why you disappeared for four months before starting college, and where you go every couple of months that had Wayne so pissed off that he actually called the state police several times to try to track you down. We haven't found proof of anything yet, though," he admitted. "We just have our suspicions."

"And your suspicions?" she asked, terrified that somehow Wayne had his suspicions as well.

"Wayne had no clue, sis," he promised, evidently reading the concern on her face. "He thought you were seeing Crowe for a while until he tracked Crowe down several times while you were gone. He was certain you had a lover, but had no idea who and decided to wait and see."

"There was no lover." She shook her head, stepping back from him and glancing to the stairs. "I lost my heart before that, John. I couldn't bear the thought of it."

He nodded somberly. "Yeah, you have that way about you. All loyalty and dedication."

She had to grin at the forced patience of his tone. "Let's just hope it pays off."

Reaching out, he pushed back the hair that had fallen over the curve of her cheek, tucking it behind her ear as though he wanted to see more of her face.

"If it doesn't," he told her, "then he's a raging fool and deserves to be shot for his stupidity alone."

Not shot, but kicked perhaps, she thought as she moved away from the man she wished could have been her brother, if he'd had another father, and headed up the stairs.

Watching her walk away, John crossed his arms over his chest before wiping a hand down his face and staring toward the ceiling, praying God was listening to prayers that night. Because he knew it would take a miracle to save them both.

CHAPTER 19

Amelia was silent as both Crowe and John escorted her into Archer's office that evening, along with six security agents.

She'd deliberately dressed in old jeans, a sweatshirt, and hiking boots. The jacket she wore was denim lined with fleece, and she'd left her leather gloves in the SUV.

Archer sat silently at his desk, Anna behind him as they entered the large room and the goon squad stepped back to allow her to face them.

She'd known Archer all her life. He was a friend; once she'd almost made him her confidant before drawing back out of fear of jeopardizing his standing in the community should Wayne ever learn the other man knew his true nature.

Archer's gaze moved to Crowe coolly before settling on her once again. Giving a heavy sigh he rose slowly to his feet, his gaze compassionate.

"How are we doing this, Amelia?" he asked her.

He asked her, not Crowe, and his voice as well as his expression let everyone know it was her decision this time.

"Just the two of us, Archer," she informed him.

"Dammit it, Amelia," Crowe growled warningly. "Don't do this . . ."

"You can watch the monitors, Crowe." Archer hit a key at the computer, bringing the six wall-mounted monitors alive on the wall next to his desk. Next, he turned on the speaker next to them. "Audio included."

"Amelia," Crowe's voice was lower now, darker. "At least let me go in with you."

She shook her head slowly, not daring to look at him as she moved her gaze to her friend.

Anna knew her history with the Carter brothers, and Amelia knew she understood why this had to be done. Still, she'd warned Amelia that Crowe's anger could cause him to strike out at the boys himself.

It was a chance she had to take. Amelia prayed the man that once existed would see what she saw in the brothers' sobriety, and if he didn't, then she would have to deal with it when the time came.

"Let's go then." Archer moved around the desk to the security door on the other side of the room. "John, you have security."

Her brother moved into place behind the desk opposite Archer's where the doors' locks and the cells' security features were controlled.

The snick of the main lock seconds later indicated the door was unlocked.

Pulling it open Archer stepped inside before looking back at her. Amelia moved past him slowly, her hands pushed into the pockets of her jacket as the main door closed and locked behind them.

It took a minute to get into the main detention area. Eight cells, four to each wall were contained in the jail. At the end of the hall the Carter brothers were in one cell together for this meeting.

Amelia moved to the front of the iron bars, staring at

the three men somberly as they stared back at her, their expressions heavy and filled with repentance.

The oldest brother, David, sat forward on the cot slowly, his face drawn, his gaze filled with self-disgust and sorrow.

It was the youngest, Dillion, sitting on the floor, his back against the cement wall, who spoke first though.

"I wouldn't hurt you, Amelia." His voice was scratchy and hoarse. "I couldn't hurt you. You know that."

"We're real sorry, Amelia," Dwight whispered tearfully as he sat at the other end of the cot from David. "You know, all the years we've been drunk and said things to you, we've never hurt you."

Amelia glanced away from them for long moments, fighting the tears that wanted to fill her eyes and the guilt that had followed her for so many years. But, when she turned back to them, her eyes were dry, her expression firm.

"That day in school," she cleared her throat before going on. "When I called Dwight out for cheating off me, I didn't mean to say it so loudly. I really didn't mean to say anything at all," she told them firmly. "I had just buried my mother the day before. That same night, Wayne locked me in a small, dark cellar in the basement for crying."

She had to breathe for a moment to continue as each man watched her closely, their expressions tightening painfully. "Each time," she continued, "that I ensured the three of you were shielded from whatever harm Wayne meant to you, I was punished by him. What he did to your aunt, he should die for. What he did to everyone he struck against, he should be punished in the same manner for." She straightened her shoulders then, forcing herself to harden, her gaze to meet each of the Carter brothers' in resolution. "But I will never again be punished for what he's done, especially by the three of you. The next time you take that first drink, think about that. Because the next time you attack me, pretend to attack me, or insult me in the ways you have in the past, I will press charges against each and every one of you. Are we clear?"

Dwight and Dillion nodded slowly, a tear easing from their eyes before their heads lowered, regret and years of pain reflected in their eyes.

"Amelia." David drew her attention then, his voice filled with sorrow. "You should have had us jailed years ago. We didn't deserve your mercy then, or now." He seemed to sit taller though, his gaze meeting hers with a determination she had never seen in it before. "What happened outside the bar was inexcusable. It was unforgivable. But, for Dwight and Dillion's sakes, I'm grateful, and I swear to you, it will never happen again." He swallowed tightly then. "For myself, all I can say is that if I ever take another drink, if I ever allow myself to lose my senses in such a way again, then I hope you do press charges. Because we've always known, sober, what a good woman you are. And drunk, we always knew that compassion in you understood our hurt and anger. But you didn't deserve to be the focus of that. And I'm sorry."

Amelia nodded slowly. "I hope you mean that, David." She looked at his brothers for a second. "And I hope all of you manage to find a way to put the past behind you. That's all any of us can do at this point, until Wayne's caught, or proven dead. Your rage is at him. If you need an outlet for it, focus on him, not on me. Because I will never allow it again."

She didn't give them a chance to say anything more.

"Archer." Turning to the other man she met his gaze and saw the understanding in it. "I won't be pressing charges against them. What happened was a misunderstanding, nothing more."

"I understand," he said softly. "I'll take care of their release. And I'll make sure they understand just how damned lucky they are."

Amelia inhaled slowly, then turned and moved back to the exit. The door unlocked immediately. Stepping through it she waited at the primary exit until Archer joined her, then as the door unlocked, stepped back into his office.

Crowe stood silently, his eyes boiling with fury, with the knowledge that she had all but admitted to the punishments Wayne had inflicted on her, the abuse she had suffered over the years for the many times she'd aided so many in the county.

"Crowe," Archer's voice held a warning. "Don't say anything I may have to lie about under oath. I won't appreciate it."

Crowe's lips thinned.

"Are you ready now?" he asked Amelia.

"I'm ready," she stated, her fingers still curled into fists as she moved past him, aching for his arms around her and immeasurably grateful that they weren't.

The Carter brothers were taken care of, she thought as she left Archer's office, with Crowe, John, and the security agents surrounding her as they led her to the SUV waiting outside. There was only one battle, one secret left to reveal. The most important of them all.

As Amelia entered the house with Crowe and the others, she watched silently as he moved up the stairs, the sound of her bedroom door closing quietly, causing her to flinch.

She had to tell him.

Her parents would be here soon. Too soon. She didn't have much time left.

"Rory?" she whispered to the agent still standing behind her.

"Yeah?" Soft, shadowed with suspicion and wariness on a normal day, his tone now held a sense of dangerous watchfulness.

"What would you do to protect those you love?" she asked.

Rory blew out a hard breath. "Whatever it took."

She nodded slowly and took the first step up the stairs.

"Amelia?" His question had her pausing. "What would you do to protect those you love?"

"Die," she whispered.

"Dying's easy," he warned her. "It's the living that gets hard. And sometimes, that's the only way to save not just those you love, but yourself as well. Can you live again, Amelia?"

Could she live again?

She was about to find out.

CHAPTER 20

The bedroom door opened slowly, spilling light into the room for brief seconds before Amelia closed the door behind her. Her delicate silhouette appeared tinier and more fragile than ever as the light caught her from the side and spread around her.

Watching as she moved toward him, Crowe was once again reminded of the young woman she had been seven years before and how easily she had touched a part of him he'd believed dead for years.

"When I find Wayne," he told her, his voice guttural, so rough he barely recognized it himself. "Every blow, every moment of fear you felt. For every goddamned second he hurt you, I'll torture him."

She stared back at him, the aching sadness and pain he glimpsed inside her tearing at his guts, ripping his soul apart.

"Are you angry with me?" he asked as she moved before him. What he wouldn't give to be able to decipher the expression on her face now.

"No. Should I be?" she asked.

"If the question has to be asked," she had once said,

"then no doubt I should wonder if there's something you're guilty of."

"There's no anger," she sighed then, her voice drawing a frown to his face before her next question had him tensing. "Would you hold me, Crowe?"

Hold her? She had to ask him if he would hold her?

"You don't have to ask, fairy-girl," he assured her, opening his arms and drawing her to him. "I'd hold you anytime."

Her slight weight settled across his thighs as she tucked herself against his heart. Her head rested against his shoulder as he held her close to him and waited.

He'd been forced to take her to the jail such a short time after John's revelations to her concerning her ex-husband that Crowe hadn't had a chance to discuss them with her. To allow her to rage, to hate, to do whatever she had to do.

That thing with the Carters was over, he'd known that the minute they left Archer's office. But her silence, the heavy burden her shoulders seemed to carry, hadn't eased. It hadn't gone away. The sight of it assured him that the darkness he could feel moving through her, around her, would have to escape sooner rather than later.

"It was a shock to hear about Stoncr," she finally admitted. "For seven years I've had to convince myself you didn't love me, or I couldn't have survived, Crowe. When you did come back into my life then I had to convince myself it was to capture Wayne, because you never told me any differently."

No, he hadn't, he admitted. He'd made mistakes he should have never made where she was concerned. Hadn't said things he should have said. Had said things he damned well shouldn't have.

"Do you remember when I came to you after you tried

to leave to meet Cami that night, after she and Rafer were together?" he asked her.

She'd dropped the note at her former friend's feet, asking her to meet with her as they had met with her during their teenage years. For a while Wayne and Mark Flannigan had decided Amelia was a bad influence on Cami, in some way. They had kept the girls separated for more than two years during their early teens.

Her head lay against his chest, fingers splaying as though to absorb his heat.

"I knew who you were the moment you covered my mouth with your hand that night," she whispered. "It was like having my midnight fantasies suddenly come to life."

"When I realized you were still risking yourself for us after Wayne had learned what happened that summer, I nearly had a stroke," he admitted, running his hand over the ultrafine material of her blouse sleeve. "Nothing was worth the risks you were taking for us," he went on roughly. "Nothing. Because if I lost you, Amelia, then my family would lose me as well. You were always my first priority. The knowledge of that put talons of guilt into my soul at times, but I couldn't change it. Protecting you was important, if not more so, than protecting the last of the family I possessed."

Tipping his head to stare down at her, he found himself trapped in the gleam of her gaze even as darkness shielded the color.

"Wayne forced me to marry Stoner." She admitted what he already knew. "Had I not married him, Wayne would have had Cami arrested as well as you and me. He said it was the only way he could be certain I stayed away from you. But I think it was because he believed you would come for me."

He touched her head, stroked her hair. Touching her

brought him pleasure. Just touch, it didn't matter where. The feel of her skin, the silk of her hair, the warmth of her against him. He couldn't find the words—he couldn't describe what she made him feel.

"Why didn't you tell me that summer that Wayne was beating you?" Would she answer him this time or find another way to distract him?

"There was nothing you could have done, Crowe," she said, surprising him. The answer was given with gentle acceptance and a knowledge that the past could never be changed. "I couldn't leave with you at the time because you were constantly moving, according to Clyde. Besides, even if I could have left with you, you would have had to return, according to your parents' will. And the Slasher was waiting." She looked up at him then. "I understand why you went after Stoner. It wasn't something I could have understood then. No matter who it was. The teenagers he attempted to rape—he deserved to die for that. They're children. You don't hurt children. But it can't be about me. Killing someone for hurting another person who has the option of walking away is still murder. Killing Wayne at that time, just because he hit me, would have stained everything we felt for each other with blood."

But he would have done it.

Had he known for a fact Wayne was abusing her as severely as he now realized, it would have pushed him over the edge.

Cupping her face with his hand and tilting it up so he could stare into her incredible eyes, he let his thumb brush over her lips before flipping on the radio.

Cupping her cheek once again, Crowe allowed all his furious, hungry possessiveness to rise to the surface as his head lowered, his lips a mere breath from her ear.

"You are mine! Mine by God, and no one but no one

will hurt, abuse, or dare to fucking harm what's mine, ever again."

Fury, hunger, possessiveness.

Territorial.

Her thoughts of earlier suddenly flared in her mind.

The primal staking of claim couldn't have been more obvious if he'd branded her.

"Yesterday, tomorrow, and by God forever. You. Are. Mine."

He nipped the lobe of her ear as her entire body flushed with a sudden, sensual heat and melting sexual submission she had no idea how to combat.

She didn't want to combat it.

"We need to talk," she whimpered as his lips brushed against hers, rubbing over them with heated friction.

"The night I came to you, after you left Cami that note, it was like coming out of the cold, Amelia. Suddenly I was too warm, too sensitive. Everything was rushing back to life and I had no idea how to handle it."

Her lips parted and a shocked breath rushed past them. And he took complete advantage of it.

Covering her lips fully with his, he let his tongue lick past her lips, taking quick, erotic tastes of her as her arms curled around his neck and she began taking, just as she had been giving.

Shifting on his lap, holding his kiss as she struggled against his restraining grip, she gave a satisfied little murmur as she broke contact, slowly straightening to her feet.

The dim glimmer of light from the radio case was just enough glow for Crowe to see that escape wasn't her objective.

Slender, graceful hands moved to the closure of her jeans, easing the little metal buttons free as Crowe quickly went to work on the buttons of his shirt. He was shrugging the material from his shoulders and tossing it to the floor as she wiggled from the snug jeans.

Tugging his boots off, he dropped the last one to the side of the chair, never taking his eyes off her as she released the last buttons of her blouse and pushed it from her shoulders, letting it flutter to the floor.

"We need to talk." Her voice was breathless, that little catch of lust in her tone hotter than hell.

The sound of it hardened his dick further, causing the blood to pound through the heavy veins in quick, hard pulses of excitement.

As she released the catch of her bra, he quickly released his jeans and shoved them off his hips and down his legs. She dropped her bra to the floor. Clad only in a pair of incredibly tiny boy shorts, the mound of her pussy barely hidden, she caused a rough, barely muffled groan to pass his lips.

Kicking the jeans and boxer briefs free of his legs, Crowe gripped the painfully hard shaft of his cock, his fingers tightening on it as need for her began to beat at his brain.

"Are you going to take those sexy-as-hell panties off?" he asked suggestively. "As pretty as they are, I'd rather see all that pale pink, pretty flesh it covers."

"This?" Her fingers caressed the material covering her pussy. "Like this, do you?"

His gaze slid from the pretty white boy shorts over the rounded flesh of her tummy. He was momentarily distracted by the hard tips of her nipples but finally managed to drag his eyes to the sensual depths of hers.

A small smile titled his lips as sensual promises gleamed in her gaze.

Oh hell yes. His fairy-girl, his sugar elf—the temptress he'd always known she harbored in that lush little body was finally making herself known.

He lowered his gaze again, drawn helplessly to the

sight of those graceful fingers pressing beneath the band of her panties.

Hidden, silken fingers met what he knew had to be dew-saturated, slick and swollen, aching-to-be-tasted-by-him folds.

"Let me see." He'd been pushing her to this, certain that behind her shy demeanor Amelia was hiding the sexual wildcat he'd sensed lurking.

"Do you deserve to see?" The husky, teasing whisper of her voice had his balls drawing tight to the base of his cock.

"Fuck no," he groaned. "No man deserves to see that sweet, pretty pussy. But I'd die for it."

He'd die for *her.*

He'd killed for her and he would do it again.

In a fucking heartbeat.

"So I saved myself for an undeserving lover?" She had him on thc cdgc of his scat, his fingcrs stroking ovcr his dick as need for her throbbed beneath the swollen stiffness.

His lips parted as he fought to draw in air, her fingers delving deeper. Pushing inside the silky, wet flames of her swollen inner heat.

"So undeserving," he agreed. "But dying for just one sweet taste."

Her fingers slid free. Stepping to him she laid two fingers, the fingers that had possessed the tight depths of her pussy, against his lips.

"Just a taste?" she suggested as his lips parted to taste her slender fingers. "Is a taste enough?" Her fingers paused as they tucked just inside the low band of the material hiding her intimate flesh from his gaze. Crowe licked his lower lips, the taste of her lingering against his tongue.

"I said I didn't deserve it, not that I wouldn't gorge myself once I shoved my tongue in your sugar, elf."

Her eyes widened, then narrowed, her fingers still resting beneath the band of her panties.

Yeah, he grinned back at her; that was where the nickname originated.

Then slowly, temptingly, she pushed the material of the boy shorts over her thighs, the dim light of the clock not nearly enough to fully appreciate the treasure she was revealing.

Reaching out, Crowe flicked on the low lamp next to the chair. The light wasn't bright enough to shock her senses, but fully illuminated that stubborn little fairy tattooed beneath her hipbone.

The golden glow spilling across her creamy flesh painted her a tempting, exotic treat he was dying to experience.

"Sugar elf, huh?" she murmured, stepping between his spread thighs.

"And I have a hell of a sweet tooth." He couldn't take his eyes from the swollen, glistening folds of her pussy, the tempting, sweet dew lying along the swollen folds, heavy and slick, gathering in small droplets ready to spill to his tongue.

"So taste me," she whispered, her breathing growing rougher, faster as she lifted her shapely leg and placed her small foot on the arm of the chair.

Crowe needed no further invitation.

Sliding from the chair, he did a quick turn, gripped her hips, and twirled her around, quickly setting her shapely rear on the chair cushion. Kneeling now between her thighs, he was entranced.

Rather than being thrown off balance or attempting shyness or confusion, she smiled that Lolita smile of hers, her thighs parting farther as her fingers slid over her thigh to stroke over the narrow, delicately pink slit revealed by the swollen folds that flared open at his touch.

He didn't give her a chance to change her mind. Leaning forward, his tongue distending, he tasted in a long, slow lick that had the sweet feminine taste of silky heat exploding his taste buds.

She slid lower in the chair as he lifted her leg, bending it at the knee to set her delicate foot on the edge of the cushion she sat on.

Parting the folds farther with his thumbs he watched the glistening slide of her juices easing from the plump, clenched entrance of her pussy.

"Don't tease me," she demanded, staring back at him with gleaming sex-hungry eyes. "Let me feel your tongue tasting me, Crowe. Give me what you promised. Shove your tongue inside me."

The words were barely past her lips when his head lowered and his tongue was suddenly tunneling inside the dew-rich, heated depths of her cunt.

Pushing her foot into the cushion, Amelia lifted her hips to the hungry penetration, her hands clenching on the chair arms as he set his hands beneath her hips to allow his tongue to penetrate her farther.

"Sweet heaven, Crowe," she moaned. Her head dug into the back of the chair as she thrust against his teasing tongue, her cries deepening while lust, hunger, and need rocked her senses. He pushed her, drove her, his tongue fucking inside the sensitive depths of her flexing inner flesh as she lifted to each ravenous lick.

"I dreamed of this." The words were torn from her desperation. "Oh God, Crowe. Oh God, don't let me be dreaming." She had a sudden, horrifying fear that this was just a dream. She would wake up and he would be gone. Just as he had been gone so many nights before.

"Look at me." The naked escalating fear overwhelmed her. Just as it had in her dreams. Until she let her gaze lock with his. Until she felt his lips surround the swollen, aching bud of her clit as his fingers thrust, hard and deep, rocking her, surging through her with sharp sizzling jolts of electric current.

"Oh God, yes," she cried out, poised on release and aching to fly into the brilliant display of heat and light she could feel building inside her.

Turning his hand, he twisted his fingers inside her, reaching deep and high, filling her, rubbing—

His lips tightened on the savagely sensitive bundle of nerve endings, his tongue licking, stroking, rasping over and against the delicate nub until stars exploded, brilliant, filled with color and blazing heat as her orgasm rushed through her with such pleasure that there was no way this was a dream.

Rising fully to his knees, Crowe gripped the heavy weight of his cock, anticipation racing through his senses at the nearness of the snug heated flesh that brought so such pleasure.

"Wait!" Her palm flattened against the perspiration-damp flesh of his abs.

"Wait?" For what? Interruptions? Explosions?

Fuck, he'd kill the son of a bitch stupid enough to wake *him.* Stupid enough to disturb him. He'd kill.

"I want you." Honest-to-God chill bumps raced up his fucking spine at the huskily whispered words.

"Then let me give you, me," he groaned, the fully engorged crest of his cock throbbing furiously as she held him back.

A siren's smile curled her lips.

His heart picked up speed, racing furiously as she slid slowly from the chair, sitting before him as he knelt in front of her staring into his eyes. She brushed his fingers aside.

He'd never asked this of her though God knew, he'd dreamed of it.

"The stupid fucker who wakes me up is going to regret it." He groaned his earlier thought as she gripped the base in both hands, her eyes still on his as her lips parted, her head leaning forward. Her tongue peeked from between her lips, the damp warmth of it washing over the engorged head as he reached out, gripping the arms of the chair desperately.

Control. Ah fuck . . .

Her lips slid over the thick head, taking it slowly, enclosing it in the liquid warmth of her mouth, holding it captive with the exquisite, rubbing, ball-drawing licks of that wicked little tongue.

Her hands on the iron-hard shaft, her mouth worked over it, sucking it deep only to release him, lick, make him crazy with the way she tucked her tongue against the underside and rubbed. Enjoyed it. Hell, she was licking around the head of his cock, drawing it in, sucking him deep like she loved having him in her mouth. Like she loved the hard pulse of his dick at the back of her throat and loved the hint of the taste of his pre-cum against her tongue.

And all the while she looked up at him through her lashes, her turquoise eyes dark, more green than blue as her suckling mouth sent ribbons of sharp-edged sensation tightening around his balls.

God help him, a blow job had never been his fucking good.

This intimate.

The way her gaze stayed locked with his, the way the colors shifted, the love he could see—feel—to his fucking soul as she sucked his cock.

There was no walking away from her again. He'd known that the moment he'd touched her the first time. He'd known the day would come when walking away from her ever again wouldn't be possible.

Until tonight he might have possessed enough of his own heart and soul should the unthinkable happen.

Ah hell—her lips were bearing down on the thick width, taking the crest deeper, her tongue rubbing and stroking that oversensitive little spot just beneath the head as she sucked him tighter.

Incredible. "Amelia, baby, so good," he groaned.

His hands tightened on the chair arm, his head bent as he stared down at her and her drunk-on-him gaze that grew more dazed with pleasure by the second. "Ah yeah, that sweet, hot mouth."

He was becoming drunker by the moment himself, more addicted to the fiery, soul-deep pleasure she gave him.

With each deep stroke of her mouth over his cockhead his control disintegrated further. Pleasure whipped through his system, erotic and sizzling with heat. Then he felt the first uncontrollable flex of the engorged crest as his release tightened his balls.

"Fuck, I'm gonna come—" He couldn't hold back much longer. "Amelia, baby." Moving one hand, forcing himself to release his grip on the chair arm, he sank his fingers in the warmth of her hair, intending to pull her head back before he found his release in the snug, heated confines of her suckling mouth.

"Amelia, dammit." He grimaced, realizing by the hunger in her eyes that she had no intentions of releasing him.

His cock throbbed, his balls tightening further as he began moving against her, fucking the reddened, cock-swollen lips surrounding him. His hand tightened in her hair, holding her in place. Electricity sizzled up his spine then back down, struck his balls, and sent his senses careening with pure, male ecstasy.

His dick pulsed violently, shooting a hard, heavy pulse of semen to her suckling mouth. Spasms of aching pleasure racked his balls, sent another wild surge of release spilling to her mouth, another as a shattered groan rasped from his throat and the final blinding pulse of release shot furiously between her tight, shuttling lips.

The grip of sexual intensity held him prisoner for long moments, racking his body as her lips slowed, easing him along the climactic ride until, with a final shudder, he pulled back, watching as she released him slowly.

Cupping her cheek, he used his thumb to wipe a creamy bead of semen from the corner of her mouth, grimacing in pleasure as she licked the final taste of him free of the pad of his thumb.

"What you do to me," he whispered.

Easing back from her, he helped her slowly to her feet before pulling her into his arms for long moments.

Finally, it was Amelia that moved.

"We need to get dressed," she whispered, her expression far too somber for his comfort. "We have to talk."

She had just given him more pleasure than he'd had from any woman in his life. Crowe watched her for a long silent moment before doing as she asked, the warning tingle across his shoulder blades assuring him trouble was coming.

He pulled his boots up then lifted his brow questioningly.

Her lips parted.

"Unauthorized entrance requested," the computerized voice announced as he watched Amelia's lips tremble.

"It's too late," she breathed out roughly. She closed her eyes for a moment before rising and moving to the door.

Pausing, she waited until he caught up with her.

"What the hell's going on?" he growled.

She opened the door as the computer announced the presence once again.

"Have your men let them in, Crowe. Two vehicles and

eight occupants. I promise you, they're not here to hurt anyone.

"Then you can tell me who it is first." Command and an overwhelming gut instinct of perhaps not danger, but definitely a sense of chaos was arriving, gripped him.

She swallowed tightly. "My parents," she said faintly. "My real parents. Please let them in."

CHAPTER 21

Her parents?

Staring back at her, Crowe could see the pure fear in her eyes. A fear that went far beyond simply revealing her real parents.

"Is this a threat, Amelia?" he asked her softly.

She blinked back at him, at first confused, then her expression filling with wounded hurt. "You think I would threaten you? How could I threaten you, Crowe?"

He shook his head before raking his fingers through his hair.

"I don't believe you're threatening me. I need to know if the occupants of those vehicles are a threat to you?"

"I would have told you if they were." The whisper was filled with hurt, uncertainty, and a shadow of betrayal.

Why would she feel betrayed?

He shook his head before raking his fingers through his hair. Yes, she would have told him; he'd been overwhelmed by his determination to protect her, his fear for her. He'd needed to know she was certain there was no danger in that vehicle. Before he could vocalize his fears his earbud communications set pinged, drawing his gaze to the table where he'd laid it.

Grimacing, he stalked to the table, flipped off the radio, and picked up the earbud, setting it in place before activating the link.

"Crowe here."

"I hate to bother you, my friend." Ivan's voice came over the line. "But we have visitors demanding entrance, and you will not believe who they have been identified as."

"Tell me," Crowe demanded, his gaze going to where Amelia stood watching him, her expression forlorn, her gaze shadowed with hurt and fear.

"None other than Commander Ethan Roberts, his brother, Jack, and the four men of Ready Team One. They are refusing to identify the two smaller heat sources though."

Ethan and Jack Roberts, owners and co-commanders of the independent military response team Ready Team One. There were four permanent members of their team, all accounted for. One of the smaller heat sources might be Amelia's mother.

"I believe the smallest heat source could be a child," Ivan mused.

A child?

Amelia's mother, Thea, had been rather young when she supposedly died, Crowe admitted. But he could have sworn he'd heard she hadn't been able to have any more children after Amelia.

"What would you have us do, Crowe?" Ivan continued.

"Patch me through to the gate," he ordered, his gaze still locked on Amelia's when he saw her flash of uncertainty and the strengthening of the shadowed fear.

She wasn't showing any sign of lying, though. Rather than gripping her hands in front of her, signaling evasiveness or deception, she stood with her arms relaxed at her sides.

The comm device clicked several times as the link was routed to the gate.

"Ethan," Crowe greeted the other man, thinking of the past years and the jobs that had brought them into contact with each other.

What did he have to do with Amelia?

The eyes. Amelia's were turquoise; Ethan's were the same color.

The color of her hair. The same as Ethan's.

Surely God's sense of humor couldn't be so cruel?

"Hello, Crowe," Ethan answered. "May I see my daughter?"

Realization was slashing through Crowe even as Ethan spoke.

"Identify the two heat signatures you're hiding first," he demanded of the Ready Team One commander. "And I'll consider it."

He wasn't prepared for Amelia's response.

"No!" Terror filled her expression as well as her voice. Tears flooded her eyes and she rushed to him, her fingers gripping his arm desperately as a sob jerked from her chest.

Amelia was crying?

Sobbing? Amelia never sobbed.

"Please, Crowe, I'm begging you." The tears were running down her face in heavy rivulcts now as she began trembling so hard she was almost shuddering, pulling at his arm, her breathing harsh. "Plcase don't. Let them come in. Anyone can pick up the conversation from the gate. I'm begging you not to let that happen."

"Crowe." Ethan's voice was heavy and somber. "Do as she asks. I swear to you, there's no danger coming to your door from either heat signature."

Crowe's gaze remained locked with Amelia's as a ghostly air of warning skated across his shoulders.

"Ivan, let them in," he answered, still watching Amelia's eyes, his chest tightening painfully as she laid her head against his arm, silent sobs still shaking her shoulders for several seconds.

"Are you certain?" the other man questioned, obviously having heard Amelia's pleas through the link.

"Let them in," he repeated. "Come to the front door and have John, Rory, and three other agents with you."

"Coming now." The link disconnected.

Amelia's head lifted from his arm, her face wet with the tears she had shed, her breathing still erratic.

"I can't risk Wayne hearing . . ." A sob jerked through her before she could control it. "I'm so sorry, Crowe," she cried, lifting her hand to cover her lips as more tears began falling down her face. "I'm so sorry. I should have told you . . . I should have told you . . ."

He wouldn't let himself think. He couldn't.

There was too much rushing through his head, too many suspicions and too many implications. Her reaction, the sobs, and the terror that Wayne would hear something. The times Amelia had gone missing over the years, a few days here, a few days there. Clyde's call, three months after Crowe had left her, to tell him Amelia had come to the ranch, begging to get in touch with him. But she wouldn't tell Clyde what she wanted. She just wanted to talk to him.

She had needed to talk to him.

She hadn't said it was important. She hadn't said life or death was involved. Just that she *had* to talk to him.

Reaching out, he touched her face, using his thumb to brush a lingering tear from her cheek.

"What have you done, Amelia?" he asked her quietly, knowing and refusing to admit to what he knew.

"The only thing I could do," she answered, her voice tear-thick as she drew away from him. "The only thing I could do."

Turning away and wiping her eyes, she drew in a hard breath. Her fingers were still shaking as she straightened the top she wore, then stiffened her shoulders and moved for the door.

Explanations. She had come up to their room to talk to him, he remembered. His hunger for her had been too great to wait, though.

Crowe was beginning to wonder if perhaps he should have waited.

Amelia could feel Crowe moving behind her as she descended the stairs, aware of Ivan Resnova, several of his men, as well as Rory, John, and Ivan's uncle, Gregori Resnova, waiting in the foyer.

John caught her gaze, and what she read there had her shaking harder than ever.

Understanding.

John knew what, who, was coming.

She could feel it racing through her.

Ivan Resnova stepped forward as well as the four cousins he'd hired as security agents for the company he and Crowe co-owned with the other Callahan cousins.

"The vehicles are parked just outside, Crowe," Ivan stated, his cool gaze sliding over Amelia before returning to Crowe. "Are we certain this is safe?"

"It's safe," Crowe growled, but she could hear a thread of some emotion in his voice. An awareness perhaps. He didn't know exactly who was in the car, but did he suspect?

"Very well." Turning to Rory and another agent by the door, he nodded.

The front door was opened, four agents moving quickly outside it as Crowe brought Amelia to a stop at the bottom of the staircase.

She couldn't breathe. She couldn't swallow. Panic was

pushing at the edge of her mind, tempting her to just spill the truth before her parents walked in the door.

She heard the first curse.

Ivan had moved to the front door, and now his gaze turned to her in accusation.

Stepping aside he allowed her uncle, Jack Roberts, into the house. Behind him her mother rushed in, and then her father, Ethan, and the burden he carried. They were all surrounded by the four men who made up the independent Ready Team One.

It was Amelia's father's burden that held everyone's attention as her head lifted from Ethan's chest.

Brown and gold swirled together, creating an oddly penetrating gaze. Long, thick black hair was pulled back from a delicate, fragile little face with a stubborn chin and high, Callahan cheekbones.

She was dressed in jeans that practically hung on her tiny frame, while the sweater and jacket she wore couldn't shield the fact that she was far too small for her age.

Was Crowe holding his breath?

Those eyes locked on her as her grandfather set her on the floor and helped her out of the heavy jacket. A bright smile curled her lips and joy lit her face as she looked from Amelia then to Crowe, then back to Crowe again.

Finally, Kimberly Crowe Callahan Roberts gave a muted little cry and threw herself into her mother's arms.

"Mommy, I missed you so much," her baby cried as Amelia caught her, lifted her up, and held her as tightly as she dared.

Burying her face in the heavy silk of Kimmy's hair she tried to force her tears back, hating the thought of sobbing again, here, in front of so many.

"Hello, Crowe," Amelia's mother, Thea, greeted softly. "I'm sorry we had to do it this way."

"We had to protect her, Crowe," Ethan stated as Amelia tried to reassure herself it was going to be okay.

Kimmy lifted her head then, her gaze spearing to her father's as Amelia fought the need to scream at everyone for staring at them as though they couldn't believe what they were seeing.

Blinking, Kimmy watched him as Amelia turned to him. He was staring at their daughter as though dazed, disbelieving.

"Crowe, I'd like you to meet Kimberly Crowe Callahan Roberts. You wanted to know where I disappeared to four and a half months after you left?" She stared back at her daughter as Kimmy watched her father somberly. "Kimmy was born three and a half months early."

"But I was strong, wasn't I, Mommy?" Kimmy smiled at her, though Amelia could see the uncertainty in her eyes.

"You were, baby." Amelia agreed.

Kimmy looked around the room then. Rory first. She gave him a little smile as he winked at her. Then John. She almost giggled when John blew her a kiss.

Ivan simply stared at her, causing Kimmy to glance back at her mother, once again uncertain before looking back at Crowe.

Amelia's heart broke as Kimmy's eyes filled with tears and she turned back to her mother. "Daddy doesn't like me?"

Heartbroken, her breath hitching with the tears filling her eyes, Kimmy laid her head against Amelia's shoulder, rejection slumping her too-small shoulders as Amelia stared back Crowe and fought more tears.

"What have you done, Amelia?" Crowe whispered then, his voice strangled, his gaze still locked on his daughter. "What have you done?"

Kimmy's head jerked up. The look she gave her father had him flinching. "She made sure that bad man couldn't get me," Kimmy informed him fiercely. "And she made sure that mean old Wayne couldn't hurt you. And you should like me just because I'm your daughter and because I'm a very good girl. I'm a good girl, my grandpa and my grandma and my mommy and my uncles all say I'm a good girl and that if you don't like me then it's because you've got a mean heart."

"Kimmy," Amelia exclaimed, shocked at her daughter's outburst.

"Mommy, I'm a good girl." Kimmy's lips trembled. As she turned back to her mother, her first tear fell. "Tell him. I'm the best daughter."

"Baby, he just met you." She couldn't breathe. Amelia fought the pain raging through her as she stroked her fingers down the back of her daughter's thick hair. "He didn't know about you."

Kimmy's chin jutted out, and the look she gave Crowe should have cut him off at his knees. "He should have known he was a daddy," she accused him tearfully. "'Cause I always pray, and I'm a good girl, and I asked God all the time to make my daddy find us and make you safe." Kimmy turned back to her, too somber, too serious. "I cry when you're not home, Mommy. That bad man might hurt you, and daddies are supposed to take care of their mommies and their good girls. They're supposed to, Mommy. And I begged God and I know God heard my prayers. I know he did."

Crowe stared at his daughter as the words fell from her lips. He was strangling. The band around his heart and his throat was tightening as years of memories surged to the forefront of his brain.

She had prayed.

I bet you have a good girl, too, the daughter of a friend

he'd had several years before said when he'd told her she was good girl.

Crowe had told her he didn't have any children.

The little girl stared back at him for long minutes, frowning before saying, "I bet you do."

And he had laughed, but all he could see in that second was Amelia, a child in her arms. A daughter that looked like him, yet was as delicate and fragile as the woman he couldn't forget.

"I couldn't tell you," Amelia whispered as he felt everyone's stare on him, condemning him, accusing him. "I couldn't, Crowe. I couldn't risk our baby . . ."

Because of the Slasher. Because she hadn't known Wayne was a killer, but she knew he would have done anything to get his hands on her and Crowe's daughter.

The thoughts whipped through his mind, tearing at him as he stared back at the delicate, hurt-filled expressions of both mother and daughter.

"Why don't you like me?" Kimmy asked, causing Amelia's gaze to whip back to her.

"Kimmy, no . . ."

"I could never not like you," Crowe whispered over the protest Amelia would made.

Kimmy looked confused now. "You don't want me?"

"Kimmy, stop," Amelia ordered the little girl gently. "Stop, baby."

"I do want you," Crowe promised her, feeling that possessiveness rising inside him now like a fever he couldn't control. "Yes, Kimmy, I do want you."

"Then why do you look so mad at me and Mommy?"

"I'm not mad at you," he promised. "I'm not mad at you in any way."

"You're mad at Mommy?" she asked softly.

His lips quirked. "I'm not mad at Mommy."

"Come here, squirt." It was Ethan who rescued them all as he took the girl from her mother's arms.

Crowe's fingers fisted at his sides as he fought to hold back the urge to jerk his daughter from the mercenary's arms. Ethan had obviously been with his daughter from the beginning, just as Amelia's mother, Thea, had been.

"Mr. Roberts, Rory will show you and Amelia's mother to your rooms." Ivan stepped forward then, his expression cold and hard as he glanced at Amelia. "Once you've settled in, we can make arrangements for your men. For the moment, the spare house that was once Amelia's has been housing the agents on duty here. They can stay there."

"Jack stays here," Ethan informed the other man, his tone firm as he turned back to the others. "The rest of you go ahead to the spare house. I'll contact you once I've settled things here."

Four battle-hardened, scarred, icy-eyed men of war. None of them were married or had families, but before they left, each of them took Kimmy in his arms and accepted a hug and a kiss as though it was some fucking ritual, Crowe thought.

He recognized the jealousy crawling through him as well. They had been there as his daughter grew, as she turned into the fiery, outspoken little minx she so obviously was.

Other men had raised and protected his child.

His child.

He should have been protecting her. His cousins should have been her uncles. He shouldn't have been introduced to his daughter after she was old enough to realize he hadn't protected her and her mother.

Finally, Kimmy gave her mother a kiss and tightened her arms around her neck.

"I can live with you now, Mommy?" she asked, obviously determined that she wasn't going to be separated from her again. "I'm always scared the bad man's hurt you when you're not home at night."

"I know, baby." Amelia held her with a desperation Crowe couldn't have missed if he'd wanted to. "And I promise, I'm trying to make sure you get to stay with me every night."

She couldn't promise her daughter they'd be together.

She couldn't even promise her daughter that the bad man wouldn't hurt either one of them anymore.

Ethan took Kimmy from her arms, kissed Amelia's cheek gently, then followed Rory up the stairs while Thea hugged her daughter tightly before following.

Her uncle, Jack Roberts, moved forward. He didn't hug Amelia. He faced Crowe instead. "I think of the sacrifices my niece has had to make because she loved you," he said, his voice soft. "We could have taken her from here." He looked around the house. "We could have taken her anywhere in the world and she could have lived safely with her daughter . . ."

"Jack, stop, please," Amelia begged him, her hands catching his lower arm in supplication. "Please don't do this."

He didn't even glance at her. "She deserved a life that didn't include hanging around here to protect you until that damned Slasher could be caught. A life that didn't include lying to her family about the son of the bitch she had to claim for a father that was abusing her." Anger filled Jack's voice.

"Uncle Jack, please. Please don't do this."

Crowe turned his gaze to her, his fists so tight he swore his knuckles were going to pop from the flesh. "Enough, Amelia," he growled. "You couldn't tell me the truth. At least let someone else do it."

"No," she protested, glaring at her uncle. "Stop this now, Jack. It wasn't his fault."

"It wasn't then," he agreed, his expression scathing as he turned back to Crowe. "But the second he decided to accuse and judge you for whatever the hell it is he has in his mind, then it becomes his fault."

"For God's sake, Jack," she whispered, pain filling her voice as Crowe saw the aching regret in her eyes. "He didn't know and I won't have this. Not now. Not like this. Let it go. Now." Her voice hardened. Jack grimaced before staring down at her like a damned teenager wondering if he could get away with some prank.

"Amelia . . ."

"Now, Jack," she demanded. "Let it go."

The look Crowe was given would have worried a lesser man. A man who didn't know his own strengths, his own abilities.

"We'll talk later," Jack promised him.

"I'll be waiting for you," Crowe assured him, inclining his head in acceptance of the upcoming confrontation.

"Chill out, badass." Jack grinned, his head dipping to kiss the top of Amelia's head gently. "We're going to make everything work out, just you wait and see."

They were going to *make* everything work out?

Unclenching his fists long enough to rake his fingers through his hair, Crowe turned and stalked from the foyer and from Amelia.

He couldn't trust himself, couldn't trust his own response to her or the self-disgust raging through him.

Because he should have known, he told himself. The day Clyde had called, weeks after Crowe had left, to tell him Amelia had been at the ranch looking for him, he should have known.

He had known.

Striding through the kitchen and out the back door.

The shock of icy wind slicing through his clothes barely registered. The snow swirling through the air, the hint of the blizzard moving in—none of it registered.

His daughter.

All he could see was his daughter, her soft little voice asking him why he didn't like her. Telling him her mother had protected her, that was what she did.

"You fucker!" The words tore from him as he glared into the darkness. "Come on out, Wayne. Come on, you son of a bitch, because I'm going to cut your fucking heart out. Wherever you're hiding, however you're hiding, enjoy it tonight. Enjoy it, because I'm coming for you."

He stared out at the cold, the snow, the moonless night wrapping around him.

"I'm finished playing, Wayne. You're dead."

CHAPTER 22

"Crowe?" Thea Roberts stepped into the darkened kitchen as Crowe refilled the coffee cup he'd brought down from the security center. "How have you been?"

He was sucked back into the past just that fast.

Thea Teague Sorenson and Kimberly Corbin had been the best of friends, even before marriage. Thea had been a regular part of Crowe's life until his parents' death. And then for several years later, until her own supposed death.

Turning from the counter and staring back at her through the dim light, he realized she looked different. Not just physically, though she retained enough of her former looks that he could identify who she was. She looked stressed, but there was an inner contentment in her gaze. The look of a woman well satisfied by not just her lover, but also her relationship with him and the life he provided her.

"What happened, Thea?" he asked her, leaning back against the counter to watch curiously as she pulled a stool from beneath the center island bar and lifted herself to it. "Why did you desert Amelia?"

"Desert her?" Thea shook her head, her once naturally dark hair a soft, dark blond, her green-and-gray-toned hazel eyes enhanced by contacts and appearing more green than they had before her disappearance. "I would have never deserted her. She was my baby. But, just as Amelia was forced to do, I had to make a choice to let her live safely where she was, or force her to live with the same danger Ethan and I believed we faced."

He propped his hands on the counter behind him and watched her intently. "I thought Wayne was the danger you faced?"

"But we didn't know that then." She sighed, brushing her hair back from her forehead as her lips twisted wryly. "Wayne learned Ethan had returned from the navy. He was having us watched, though we were unaware of it. We were heading to Aspen to see a divorce lawyer, then we were going to return to Sweetrock and pick Amelia up from school before leaving Colorado and moving to California. We were nearly to Aspen when the brakes went out on the car. Ethan had nearly managed to get us to the bottom of that last mountain on the old route into Aspen, along the river, when the car exploded and we went through the guardrail into the water."

He frowned. The old route had been closed several years before because of the number of vehicles crashing through the guardrails and catapulting into the churning rapids below.

Lowering her head and obviously fighting to keep her emotions under control, Thea dragged in a deep, hard breath. When she looked back at him, tears glittered in her gaze. "I was six weeks' pregnant with Ethan's child. Our second child." Her lips twisted with bitterness. "Neither Ethan nor I was aware I was pregnant when I married Wayne. Ethan had left the night after our first time together, several weeks before I was due to marry Wayne. Ethan had no idea I was preparing to break off my engagement with Wayne; he believed I was marrying Wayne despite the fact that I was a virgin when he took me to his bed."

"What made him believe you were going to continue with the engagement?" Crowe asked, wondering at the countless lives Wayne had destroyed.

"Wayne," she admitted painfully, staring at the bar where she traced a faint scratch with her nail. "Ethan and I were, and still are, fiery together." Lifting her head, her hand stilling, she made the admission softly. "But Ethan was a hothead in those days. Wayne suspected we had begun seeing each other again, the manipulating bastard. The day after Ethan and I were together, he made certain Ethan overhead him telling a friend that I had gone with him to pick out a ring that morning and how excited I was now that the wedding was drawing closer. Then he pretended to confide in that friend that I had shared his bed in the house we had chosen. He even claimed that I wasn't a virgin, but it didn't matter to him because he knew I'd make a loving, proper wife," she sneered. "Ethan knew I was a virgin when we were together, but we had argued that night and I cruelly told him I'd marry Wayne regardless. He believed me, I guess." She shrugged. "When he disappeared I stupidly went ahead and gave in to parental pressure and married Wayne, not realizing until too late that I was pregnant with Ethan's child. Ten years later Ethan was in Sweetrock visiting friends when he saw Amelia and realized she was nearly identical in looks to his younger sister, who happened to be nearly Amelia's age."

Crowe watched her closely, carefully, well aware that she had adeptly sidetracked from the originally explanation.

"What happened after the explosion?" he asked her, firmly enough that she realized he had no intentions of letting the subject go.

"Ethan was terribly hurt," she sighed. "But I nearly died. The car was carried miles down the river before he was able to get us out of it. By then I was unconscious, losing blood and of no help at all. He managed to get us out and onto dry land, but my purse and his cell phone were in the car, leaving him no way to contact his team. It took Jack and his men nearly thirty-six hours to find us. Ethan managed to keep me alive, but he couldn't prevent the loss of our child. The majority of the explosion had been on the passenger side of the car as well. The windshield blew out, the force propelling the glass into the car and striking my face." When she brushed her fingers against her left cheek self-consciously, he realized where the few changes were concentrated now. "By time Jack had us transported out of the canyon in a way that ensured no one realized what was going on, I'd developed an infection. I spent years fully recovering. The plastic surgeries were horrible enough, but the injuries from the explosion had ensured I could never have more children. Ethan would have sent Jack and the others after Amelia immediately, but he had no idea who had attempted to kill us. He believed for years that it had happened because of the nature of his work. It simply never occurred to us that Wayne was behind it until he was revealed as the Slasher and Ethan's contacts in the forensics division of the FBI told him that the explosion that killed Wayne's cousin was identical in design to the one that nearly killed us. What was more, the unusual compound used in it was, to the last test, the exact same compound used in Ethan's car. All this time we hadn't taken Amelia with us, terrified that his enemies would target her if they were aware we weren't dead." Her voice broke on the statement while tears escaped her eyes and for a moment she fought the sobs that would have escaped as well. "We would have gotten her out of here, just as we took Kimmy as she begged us to, to protect her from the Slasher. We begged her to go with us as she prepared to leave the baby. It was destroying her, to leave Kimmy to be raised by us while she made plans to return to a life that was destroying her. A life no one else knew she was living. She wouldn't leave with us, though." Thea sniffed tearfully. "She was afraid the Slasher would become suspicious, or that Stoner would return and do as he'd threatened by gossiping about the two of you until the Slasher came looking for her, and managed to find Kimmy as well." Her gaze was tormented. "And she was certain if she didn't return, then Wayne would do as he threatened and have you and Cami arrested for the file she had helped you steal from his office the summer before."

"He couldn't have—" Crowe began.

"He would have." A slender, shaking finger was suddenly pointing toward him as her voice hardened, her expression filled with remembered pain and a glimmer of fury. "Not even I or Ethan learned the full truth of this until recently, Crowe. Kimmy was, and is, her heart, and it killed Amelia to leave her baby. But she returned because she knew Wayne was preparing to have Cami arrested, and had already completed the paperwork that would have forced the army to return you to Corbin County for trial. Just as he had threatened her he would do if she tried to leave."

Crowe felt his fingers turning into fists. The need to strike out at Wayne burned through his senses.

"The army wouldn't have let me go at that point." He shook his head, remembering the black ops training he had been inducted into about the time Amelia would have given birth to Kimmy. "Trust me, Thea. I was far too important to them by then."

Thea sat back in her seat slowly. "Even Ethan was unaware until only recently of your acceptance into whatever group you were a part of." She wiped her hands over her face wearily. "Your secrets ran just as deep as hers. And were just as dark and filled with pain." The anger in her gaze receded as he continued to watch her, crossing his arms over his chest and meeting her stare steadily.

"Did you know when she learned she was pregnant, she went to Clyde to try to contact you?" Thea asked then.

He blinked slowly. "She didn't tell him why she was searching for me."

"Wayne and Clyde were old friends. She had no idea how deep Clyde's loyalty to your cousins went. No one did. His rough attitude and weekend desertions of the three of you when you were younger had many of your parents' former friends suspecting Clyde had no more love for you than your mothers' families appeared to have."

And that was no more than the truth, Crowe knew.

"It was deliberate," he told her, realizing now that he should have told Amelia of the many and varied subtleties and progressions of lies Clyde had used to protect his charges. "Clyde was investigating the deaths of our parents until the day he was killed. He never trusted Wayne again, though, after the night I showed him that file Amelia led me to."

But he had never told Clyde who had helped him steal the file, or that he had been seeing Amelia secretly.

"And neither Wayne nor Amelia knew Clyde believed you over him," Thea revealed. "Amelia overheard Wayne's meeting with Clyde when he learned she had given you that information. He told Clyde he'd only just learned that Amelia had given you a file she'd changed the names on, changed the information on, to convince him she was helping him, to get her into your bed. He made Amelia appear to be a sort of secret groupie. Clyde gruffed and growled and told Wayne he'd not seen the file, but he'd be certain to ensure Wayne was given a copy of it if he did. To Amelia, Clyde's loyalty to you was a lie. She couldn't trust him."

Who had Amelia been able to trust? he wondered. From the sound of it, there had been no one to turn to, no one to help her shoulder the burden she carried. Watching Thea, he remembered how his mother had loved her like a sister. Just as, he knew, his mother's death had devastated Thea.

"There's so much anger in you, Crowe," she said, her expression saddened. "And so much pain and fear in Amelia now. She didn't want you and Kimmy to meet this way. And she didn't want Wayne to ever learn of the child she's hidden from him. But Ethan is just as stubborn as you can be, and he knows Wayne will never show himself unless he's pushed."

The control Crowe had been holding on to broke.

"My daughter and my woman are not Ethan Roberts's fucking bait!" The words were torn from him before he could stop them, dragged from the depths of his soul and rasping with burning rage as they shot toward Amelia's mother like verbal bullets.

Grimacing, he pushed away from the counter. The anger he was fighting to pull back only surged higher as Ethan himself stepping into the kitchen, no doubt listening from the doorway—just as Crowe would have been had his woman been confronting another man's anger in such a way.

"But my daughter was your bait." Moving to Thea, Ethan laid his broad hands on her shoulders, standing over her protectively, his eyes blazing with paternal anger. "When I would have convinced her to leave and return to Europe with Kimmy, you walked back into her life and made your demand that she weave that little illusion of being your lover to draw Wayne out," he sneered. "How did that work out for you, asshole?"

"Ethan, don't." Thea touched his hand, turning her head to stare back at him. "Amelia's been hurt enough. Don't add a confrontation with the man she loves to her heartache."

"She could have told me," Crowe snapped furiously. "She could have discussed this with me before bringing our child into this."

"And Wayne would have learned of her child at a time when she didn't have that child with her. And no matter her trust in her parents, her uncle, and the men they fight with, still, she would have been terrified for Kimmy. And Wayne would have found a way to use that fear against her."

Crowe froze, staring at the other man, his jaw clenched to the point that his back teeth were in danger of cracking.

"Are you suggesting I would have allowed that secret out?"

Ethan's smirk only tempted the rage that years of training barely held in check.

"Crowe." The gentleness in Thea's voice hardly registered. "Would you have told your cousins? Or Ivan? Would you have trusted any of your men?"

He narrowed his gaze on her with a deliberately icy look. "I would have seen to her protection, so what's your point?"

"Wayne's managed to stay one step ahead of you from the moment he was revealed as the Slasher," Ethan pointed out. "I'm really fucking surprised you haven't suspected what Amelia has known for weeks. You have a break in your security. Somehow, somewhere, someone is giving Wayne your secrets."

Oh, Crowe didn't suspect a damned thing. He knew. Just as Ivan knew.

"Son of a bitch," Ethan cursed softly. "You were aware of it."

Crossing his arms over his chest and staring back at the couple, Crowe didn't so much as bat an eyelash. He didn't owe Ethan Roberts shit and he sure as hell didn't owe Thea Roberts—or Sorenson—or whoever the hell she was—a damned thing.

Especially not explanations.

"Do you have a suspect?" Ethan growled.

"Go to hell," Crowe suggested mockingly.

"My daughter has stayed here when she could have run from Sorenson's cruelties years ago," Ethan pointed out furiously. "She could have raised that kid of hers, herself, rather than sobbing in grief each time she's had to watch her baby fly away after the secretive visits she was terrified would result in the Slasher or Wayne following her. And you blame her for not telling you those secrets, even knowing the leak you have in your organization? You blame her, even knowing how desperately she's always loved you? Well, aren't you just a fucking fine piece of work, Callahan."

Crowe watched him with scathing fury. "No, Roberts, I blame you and that accident-waiting-to-happen brother of yours for convincing her to place our child in danger rather than keeping her so safely hidden that even Ivan, with all his contacts, couldn't find so much as a whisper of suspicion that Amelia had given birth to that child, no matter his suspicions. I blame the two of you because your fucking adrenaline addiction meant far more to you than the child Amelia has risked her life to protect every day of her life, for nearly seven years. That's who I fucking blame."

"Resnova couldn't have suspected a damned thing." Roberts glared at him through narrowed eyes, his hands flexing on Thea's shoulders as she glanced back at him warily.

Crowe gave a bitter, cynical laugh. "If she'd had a lover there would have been time spent in motels, or a little love nest with DNA of some sort present. There would have been evidence of calls to an unknown party on her cell phone or home line. Or there would have been a burn phone hidden somehow that would have activated long enough for his men to get an unknown signal from her vicinity. There were none of those signs of a lover. What there was, was Amelia leaving for Aspen—and once she reached it she simply disappeared." Crowe stated. "She would return within a week, eyes reddened, her demeanor almost grief-stricken and obviously attempting to hide it. Ivan's been trying to track where she goes and who she leaves with ever since he forced himself into this little game with the Callahans and the Slasher and learned there was a single, living past lover I was determined to hide. His notes reveal he's suspected she had my child for the better part of a year now. Especially since she has refused to see her gynecologist since I left over seven years ago."

It galled Crowe that even he had believed, for a time, that she'd had a lover.

"She was already six weeks' pregnant when you left," Thea whispered, her voice still thick with unshed tears. "We showed up a few weeks after she learned of her pregnancy, and she learned then I hadn't died or just run away. We begged her to leave with us until we learned who had attempted to kill us. To hide with us. Ethan was certain he was getting closer when he learned who had sold the military-grade explosive used in the bomb placed in the car. She refused to leave. Four months later she called, hysterical. She was in some damned nasty hotel room, six months' pregnant and certain she was in labor. She'd run from Wayne's the second she'd begun having pains, terrified she wouldn't be able to hide her baby, trying to reach the clinic she'd had the pregnancy confirmed in, and returned to monthly for checkups because they didn't require an ID. The clinic was an underground medical facility, though, and had moved for whatever reason. She was terrified of losing her baby, and just as terrified that the Slasher would take her infant if she checked into a hospital. It was a miracle we were even in the States."

Crowe felt horror twist in his guts then.

God, he didn't want to hear this. Those underground fucking clinics were often butcher shops. For all the good they did, there were the instances of agonizing deaths and botched attempted surgeries that made his guts twist in terror for Amelia.

"By time we reached her, Kimmy was in distress. She wasn't in the proper position in the birth canal and Amelia was half out of her senses with pain and blood loss." Remembered grief twisted Ethan's and Thea's expressions. "She was screaming for you, Crowe, as some old Navajo medicine woman chanted between her thighs and tried to coax Kimmy into the proper position." Ethan wiped his face, his jaw working fiercely. "It took about a second for our medic to figure out what to do. He shot her full of painkillers as the medicine woman was pulled away from her. By the grace of God he managed to turn Kimmy and I watched as this tiny, whimpering little form was delivered into his hands an hour after we arrived."

"Less than a minute after Kimmy was laid against her chest, Amelia died." Thea delivered the bombshell as a sob shook her entire body.

"What the fuck—" Crowe all but wheezed, icy chills of terror racing through him. "What the hell are you saying. She's alive—"

Ethan breathed out roughly, " 'Save my baby, Daddy,' she whispered as Thea kept trying to bring her fever down with the ice the medicine woman had ready, and a bottle of alcohol. 'Please, Daddy, don't let the Slasher take my baby. Crowe's baby.' Then she just closed her eyes and let go." Ethan was fighting his own tears. "If the team and Jack hadn't been with us, we would have lost her. Our medic always carries his gear with him. He managed to shock her back while I contacted a nearby military base and had a medical support chopper sent out. She was airlifted to the base and hospital and recovered there while Kimmy was stabilized after being born three months early. Amelia had been sick, and none of us knew it." Ethan swallowed tightly. "She didn't know that she'd developed a very rare, very deadly infection caused by the pregnancy itself."

"The same infection your mother fought in the last months of her pregnancy with Sarah." Thea was crying now. "I nearly lost her, Crowe, because she loved your child and you, more than she cared for her own safety and well-being."

He needed to fucking sit down. Every bone and muscle in his body was locked tight, pain radiating through his heart, striking at his soul and leaving bleeding gouges in his spirit as Ethan and Thea revealed the hell his too delicate little fairy-girl had gone through after he'd left her.

"Don't you ever stand before me again and blame my daughter for a single decision she's made where you or Kimmy is concerned." Ethan's tone was filled with a dark promise of death now. "If you care an iota for Amelia or even think you might want to be involved in your daughter's life, then by God, you'd better fix the pain you're causing both of them. Because so help me, Crowe, if you don't convince Kimmy you love her better than a kid loves ice cream then I'm going to make it a priority to ensure you never fucking see either of them again. And you had better go ahead and eat one of your own bullets if you ever cause one of them to cry again, let alone both.

Because if you do, then I'll by God force-feed you one of mine."

The promise of violence didn't even register with Crowe. All he could see was Amelia, her pretty turquoise eyes closed in death as the too tiny form of his premature child whimpered for her mother.

For warmth and safety.

His Amelia had died without him. If only for seconds, she'd still passed from life without him to hold her, to force her to hold on to him, to hold on to every chance they could have together.

Shaking his head, his fury lost in the realization of all Amelia had gone through, Crowe could only stare back at them in stark agony.

"Not care for them?" he whispered, barely able to speak past the emotions threatening to choke him to death. "God help me, Ethan, I've loved her until my soul felt like a dark, dying husk without her. And that child I met tonight was already such a part of my heart that all I can think about is eating that fucking bullet myself if the evil shadowing us manages to touch her or her mother, for even a breath of a second."

He stared at the couple, in equal parts furious and jealous that they had raised his child rather than himself and Amelia, and overwhelmed with a thankfulness that acknowledging it ripped from his heart. Those emotions battled side by side with the blank horror of knowing he'd nearly lost both of them and the overriding fact that he still could.

"Crowe—" Thea moved as if to touch him.

He stepped back with a quick shake of his head. "I have to think . . ." His throat worked convulsively as he fought against the emotions overwhelming him. "I have to finish some things."

Turning, Crowe strode quickly from the kitchen, back through the foyer and up the stairs to the second floor.

It was late. Damned late, he realized, and he knew Amelia hadn't left their daughter's room, which was connected to Ethan and Thea's room.

He had to see her.

He had to reassure himself she was still alive, that she had survived, as illogical as it sounded, even to himself. He had to make certain he hadn't lost her forever.

CHAPTER 23

She had died, and he hadn't been with her.

She had suffered. He had nearly lost not just the child he hadn't known existed, but also the woman.

She had kept him from freezing entirely, Crowe thought as he sat in the small chair at the end of the bed and watched them sleep. To become the man, the agent he'd been, he'd cut himself off from all emotion. Only the most basic loyalties had remained. Those to his cousins, and to the safety of the woman who had risked so much to help them.

It wasn't loyalty that had kept that small corner of his humanity alive, though. It had been the memory of her touch, of the pure emotion in her eyes each time they met his, and the broken agony he'd heard in her voice the night she had read the letter he'd left her.

Amelia had kept him human. She had kept him from becoming a very different sort of monster, but a monster all the same.

Sprawled in the chair, still, silent, he simply watched them sleep, telling himself he couldn't wake them. How many nights had Amelia ached to hold her child against her in such a way? How many nights had she cried for the newborn she'd been forced to let go? How many times had Kimmy cried for her mother?

What justice had there been over the years for them?

What consolation had there been for them?

He knew there had been none for him. He'd existed in a void he'd created himself just to survive. A void of emotionless deception that barely held back the raging fury pounding just beneath the surface.

He let his gaze caress Amelia's profile. The gentle arch of her brow, the little pert nose that could lift to the air with such disdain when she was irritated. Her lips. God, what her lips could do to him. Just the touch of them was more pleasure than he'd ever known in his life.

The delicate line of her graceful throat, so sensitive to his kisses, to the rake of his teeth against the tender flesh.

Tucked beneath the quilt with Kimmy's arms wrapped around her like clinging vines, she held the girl with a tenderness that had his throat tightening.

As he watched, her lashes flickered restlessly, then seconds later opened, focusing on him immediately.

"Crowe?" she whispered, her voice filled with concern.

Crowe shook his head slowly. "Everything's okay."

The world around them was still turning. So far, no one else had suffered at Wayne's hands, but his own world had changed with such a force that he wondered how he would recoup quickly enough to find his balance.

Kissing their daughter gently on the forehead, she disengaged from the snugly wrapped arms and slid from the bed.

Crowe straightened, moving to the door as Amelia tucked the blankets around their child before following him.

"I didn't mean to awaken you," he said softly, closing the door behind them as they stepped into the hall.

"She's not easy to sleep with," she said nervously,

tucking the long strands of hair that fell over her shoulder behind her ear as they moved to their room. "I usually move in a few hours out of self-preservation. She has sharp elbows and no scruples about using them."

He remembered his father saying that about him once, Crowe realized. Laughing, his voice would fill with love as he stated that letting the seven-year-old Crowe sleep with him and his wife was like taking his life in his own hands.

He closed the bedroom door behind them moments later, watching as Amelia moved across the room before turning to face him.

She didn't clasp her hands before her. She stood carefully as though ready to move at any moment, tension radiating through her body.

"I know you're angry . . ."

Shaking his head, he turned away from her to pace to the bathroom door, raking his fingers through his hair as he fought to sort out the emotions he did feel.

He wasn't angry. Not at Amelia.

What he was, was fighting that ice. Fighting the need to go hunting for Wayne by himself, even knowing the risks.

And that he couldn't do. He couldn't go back into the cold again without destroying himself in the process.

Watching Crowe warily, Amelia fought the tears that wanted to fill her eyes, fought the need to sob at the agony resonating through him.

"You talked to Mom and Dad, didn't you?" she whispered then, knowing her father.

Ethan Roberts hadn't agreed with Amelia over the years in her refusal to contact Crowe. After a few years, he'd seemed to blame Crowe for it, though, rather than her. As though he had begun to believe that she doubted Crowe would come to her and Kimmy's sides. No amount of arguing had changed his mind, and no amount of it had changed hers.

"Logan returned for a week the month after I left," he said quietly as he turned back to her, his gaze predatory, sharp with the anger he held back. "I know he saw you in town. Why didn't you contact him? Why didn't you tell him? You went to see Clyde, but you wouldn't talk to Logan?"

"When I went to see Clyde, I was nearly desperate," she whispered, remembering that week with a vivid slash of pain. "Before I left he looked at me with that stare he had." A way of warning a person to say no more than they had to. "As I got into my car he leaned in close and asked me if I cared for you." Her breath hitched on a sob as Crowe's gaze sharpened. "I nodded. That look . . ."

"You didn't speak, you listened when you saw it," he finished for her roughly.

"He said if you came back, blood would spill." She lifted her hand to hide the shaking of her lips for a moment. "Then he said we'd definitely see you in prison, along with your cousins, if you had to kill for me." The sob she was fighting escaped. "He asked if that was what I wanted. And I knew he wasn't talking about the Slasher."

"Because he knew Wayne was abusing you," he snarled. It wasn't a question so much as an indication of knowledge.

"If you came back for me, for our baby, then blood would have spilled," she whispered. "I knew you'd kill for me, Crowe. If you did, you could have gone to prison. I couldn't let that happen. I wouldn't let that happen."

"You died! Damn you, Amelia, what would have happened to me if you hadn't been revived?" He didn't yell, but that rasp of fury in his voice caused her to flinch. She began trembling with not just the memory of it, but the awareness that Crowe was angrier than she'd suspected.

"Ethan would have contacted you then," she swore, frowning in confusion. "He would have offered to keep Kimmy until the Slasher was taken care of." Her heart rate picked up as the glow of gold in his eyes seemed to spark like flames. Her own anger rose then, racing through her senses as she remembered those agonizing weeks after Kimmy's birth. "What do you want me to say, Crowe?" she cried, reaching out to him before pulling her hands back and wrapping her arms across her breasts defensively. "If I had told you about Kimmy none of us would have been safe and you know it. You were in the military; they wouldn't have just let you leave. We didn't know who the Slasher was, or the lengths he would go to. I was terrified for you and Kimmy. Terrified I'd cause you to lose more than you already had."

"You didn't trust me to protect you and our child," he rasped dangerously. "Is that it, Amelia?"

"You know, Crowe, I didn't trust my father, my uncle, and their team to protect my daughter if anyone learned of her, before we discovered who the Slasher was," she reminded him painfully. "It had nothing to do with trust and everything to do with the fact that I was terrified for both of you." She dashed at the tears that escaped her eyes. "I wouldn't have been able to live if anything happened to either of you, because of me. I wouldn't have survived it."

She couldn't have drawn another breath had it happened.

Turning away from him, she fought the sobs rising inside her.

"I did my best, Crowe," she whispered. "I did my best."

"You died!" he snarled again as he swung her around to face him, the savagely hewn lines of his face filled with such fury, such pain, she lost the battle with the tears.

"And if saving you and our daughter meant never drawing another breath in this life then that was the price I'd pay," she cried out, her hands fisting in his shirt, jerking at the cloth, desperate to make him understand. "That was all that mattered to me, Crowe. Nothing else. I couldn't bear losing either of you. I couldn't live with it."

Sobs tore from her chest, the desperation that filled her that night a bleak, haunting memory.

"I would have been there." Naked, burning, the fury that filled him whipped in the air like a brutal wave. "I would have been with you, Amelia. I would have been there for you and you took that choice away from me."

"And I knew you'd be furious," she sobbed. "I knew the chance I was taking that you would hate me forever, Crowe, that you would never forgive the choices I had to make. Is that your prerogative only? Is no one but you allowed to make the hard choices to protect those that mean the most to them?"

"I will kill a thousand times over for you. That choice is far different . . ." His hands tightened at her shoulders, the hold firm. He didn't hurt her; he would never mark her skin and she knew it. But the brutality of his pain was killing her.

"Crowe, I would die a thousand times over for you," she whispered. "For you and Kimmy. I'd give my last breath just as easily as you would have given up your freedom if you were caught."

Except he wouldn't have been caught.

Crowe knew he wouldn't have been, but it was a knowledge he knew Amelia didn't have.

Releasing her slowly, he stepped back.

Distance. He had to find a distance, he thought, forcing back the emotion for the brutal objectivity that had ensured his survival over the years.

"Crowe . . ." Her tear-filled voice was breaking him.

"I'm not angry with you." Keeping his voice calm now, pushing back the rage, he moved slowly, tiredly to the door.

"Crowe . . ." She whispered his name again.

"I have to stop this." He forced the words past his throat then. "Until Wayne's dead, neither of you is safe. Until he's dead, neither of you really belongs to me, do you, Amelia?" He turned back to her then, hating the tears that fell down her face. "Because I won't let you or our daughter live in this fucking nightmare one second longer than I have to."

He forced himself from the bedroom and went to the security room, all the while feeling his soul howling.

She had died. And he hadn't even been there.

CHAPTER 24

It was the sound of Kimmy's screams, high-pitched and echoing shrilly through the house, that woke Amelia from a sound sleep, two days later.

Before her eyes were fully open she was out of the bed and racing across her bedroom to the door. Throwing it open and running along the hall, she was only dimly aware of the sun spilling weakly through the tall foyer windows to the middle of the curving staircase.

Another full-throated scream was followed by a muted, male growling sound that made very little sense.

It was after noon. Wayne never attacked during the day, it was always at night, she thought hysterically as she began running for the stairs, terror pumping through her senses. Any sense of safety she had felt over the past two days evaporated as though it had never existed.

Pure terror raced through her, blinding and filled with the agonizing certainty that somehow, some way, Wayne had gotten to her baby.

The sound of her daughter's screams ripped through the silence of the house again.

"God no. Kimmy."

Gripping the banister desperately, her fingers locked

on the heavy wood, Amelia felt her heart pounding from her chest as she paused only a few feet down the stairs to get her bearings. Listening desperately, that muffled male growl rasping across her senses, Amelia searched the foyer as she fought to figure out which direction to run in.

"Where are you, baby?" she whimpered, fighting to remain quiet, to figure out where her daughter was before wasting time by rushing in the wrong direction.

A deep-throated male roar suddenly erupted in the silence, followed immediately by—girlish giggles?

Kimmy tore across the foyer from the family room, running hell for leather into the formal living room as she laughed uproariously in joy. Behind her, shrouded by one of the checkered blankets Amelia kept thrown over the couch, the tall, broad form of an obviously chuckling male followed her.

Amelia sank quickly to the stairs, sitting on one of the wide steps as weakness flooded her limbs. Tears fell from her eyes as relief rushed through her. She felt suddenly dizzy with the realization that Kimmy wasn't in danger after all.

Another of those deep "dying bear" growls rasped from the living room—was it Crowe shrouded in that blanket, playing with their daughter? Was he the one causing those high girlish giggles that were music to her ears as he pretended to growl at her? The thought of it had a smile beginning to tremble on her lips.

At that moment Kimmy tore from the living room again, releasing another laughing scream and racing into the foyer. Rounding the wide, curving steps, her giggles echoed through the high-ceilinged foyer and traveled through the house.

"Dammit, Logan, how many times do I have to tell you that Amelia's still sleeping?" Crowe's voice snapped from the library doorway as both Kimmy and Logan came to a hard stop.

Looking through the narrow gap between the wide spindles Amelia could see her daughter's expression instantly transform from childish joy to wariness.

Kimmy stood perfectly still, just staring at her father's expression for long moments, her gaze narrowed on him.

That wasn't a good sign.

Oh God, please don't let her—

"That's a bad word."

Amelia winced at the disapproval in Kimmy's voice and the narrow-eyed glare the little girl was directing at the man standing in front of her.

Then her stance shifted. Placing her little hand on her hip, she stuck out her chin stubbornly as her lips drew into a thin line.

The stance and her expression were identical to Crowe's. The only difference, Amelia noticed, was the way Kimmy lifted that little chin into the air. Though Amelia feared that had more to do with the fact that Crowe was looking down at his daughter rather than head-on.

The two faced off, father and daughter, each sizing the other up like two boxers would before beginning to dance around each other.

"I'll be sure to watch out for that in the future." His jaw clenched as he obviously fought against some tightly held emotion.

Or anger.

"But, as I said," he continued, "your mother is sleeping—"

"You just don't like me!" Kimmy's skinny little arms crossed over her chest as her sweet voice held an unfamiliar note of anger. "I thought you just didn't like kids, but you spent all morning playing with Logan's little baby instead and wouldn't play with me at all."

Her anger was fierce. An indication of how deep that anger glowed.

"Now you don't even want me to play with my uncle Logan?" Outraged incredulity filled her voice.

Crowe wiped a hand over his face before reaching back to rub at the back of his neck, staring beseechingly at Logan.

"You made your bed, sleep in it." It was more than obvious that his cousin was upset with him, and now Crowe knew it as well.

He breathed out wearily, the look he directed to Logan hinting at retribution.

"Kimmy." He spoke with the air of man forced to push the words past his lips. "I do not dislike you—"

"You are not my daddy." A small finger jabbed in his direction before Kimmy placed both hands on her hips, obviously out of patience where her father was concerned.

Amelia's eyes widened with shock even as pride began to fill her broken heart.

"The hell I'm not, little girl." Crossing his arms over his chest, he glared back at her. "Sucks to be you, but you look just like me."

For the briefest second he seemed to have surprised himself with the response.

"You said a bad word again. Don't you know daddies don't do that in front of their little girls?" Her tone was scathing, her little face flushing with hurt and anger. "I know you're not my daddy because my mommy says my daddy is a hero and everyone knows heroes do not say bad words in front of their little girls."

Sweet heaven, where had Kimmy heard that? Were her parents allowing her to watch too much television again?

"Kimberly." Crowe's tone indicated his intent to berate her.

"My name is Kimmy, just like my grandma who went

to heaven to be my guardian angel after that bad man killed her," she informed him imperiously as Crowe's expression reflected his shock. "My mommy said my daddy fights bad men and wins. She says he likes to fish and he knows how to play really cool games." Her chin lifted a notch in a surfeit of pride. "She said my daddy will love me more than a kid loves ice cream. My mommy doesn't lie to me, so you lied to her when you told her you were my daddy. You are not my daddy!" She screamed the final declaration to him, dry-eyed and filled with childish fury.

Turning, Kimmy raced back to the family room, passing Logan and ignoring his attempt to stop her.

Amelia watched, filled with anger for her daughter's sake and a pain-ridden sense of loss as she watched Crowe's expression change the minute Kimmy was no longer facing him.

"Geez, Crowe." Logan stared back at his cousin in complete astonishment. "Until now, I never believed you were actually stupid. Too much pride maybe, but not stupid."

"Shut up, Logan," Crowe snapped, glaring at the doorway his daughter had disappeared through.

"Fuck that," Logan muttered, causing Crowe's gaze to swing to him, narrowing.

"Logan . . ."

"Just shut up," Logan ordered, his voice low now. "I know you, Crowe. You're dying to wrap that kid in cotton and hold her tight enough to smother her with your love. Yet you won't even play with her? You don't even try to talk to her." Logan shook his head in confusion as his hands went to his hips and his expression turned caustic. "Asshole. Remind me when young Beauregard Logan gets a little older that you're grounded from playing with him until you learn how to be a daddy."

Turning away from his cousin, Logan headed to the

family room where the sounds of Kimmy's favorite cartoon began to play. "I'd rather watch SpongeBob with Kimmy than talk to you. At least that stupid yellow sponge tries to make sense."

He disappeared into the room as Amelia slowly rose to her feet, staring down at Crowe for long, silent moments.

Fuck!

Crowe would have muttered the word aloud, but he really was trying to clean up his language.

The confrontation brought a memory from his youth that he hadn't realized he'd had, though. A memory he couldn't force back into that dark little void where he usually kept them.

The girl Crowe was playing with threw sand at him, the fine grains filling Crowe's thick hair and tickling his scalp. He used one of the words he'd heard his father use once.

Hearing the word, his father, who never seemed to be far enough away when he was being bad, came to the sandbox and pulled eight-year-old Crowe from it firmly.

His father was disappointed. That knowledge had Crowe hanging his head and scuffing his shoe in the dirt as his father sat back down on the park bench, watching him for long moments.

"Sorry, Dad," Crowe muttered.

David Callahan sighed wearily as he leaned forward, his elbows resting on his knees.

"Look at me, Crowe." Firm but gentle, his father's tone still wasn't one Crowe could ignore.

"Men don't use vulgar language or curse in front of women or children, son," his father berated him.

"You cuss around Mom," Crowe, in all his childish wisdom, felt the need to point out. "I heard you while me and Logan were playing out back."

"Hiding out back you mean?" his father suggested knowingly as he gave Crowe "that" look. The one that assured Crowe he'd done something else he shouldn't have done.

Crowe sighed gustily. "Dad, I promise, I didn't know you and Mom was in the yard," he said. "We was playing hide and seek with Rafe and he hadn't got to the backyard yet."

His father's expression gentled as he reached out and ruffled Crowe's hair gently.

He was forgiven for overhearing his dad cuss in front of his mom, but not for cussing in front of the sand-throwing little girl.

"Listen to me." His father gave him a look that made Crowe feel like he was being trusted with an important secret. "Your mom is my wife, so if I mess up and forget while we're talking, then it's different."

Crowe listened and watched his father's expression carefully as he nodded as though he knew what his father meant.

A small smile touched his father's lips. "But you don't cuss in front of women, and you definitely don't cuss in front of little girls. When mommies give daddies their children, then the rules change. Things you could do before, you can't do anymore, because you realize those children learn from you. And it's a daddy's job to teach their sons that they shouldn't do it. Would you like it if another boy said bad things to the baby Mommy's going to have, if it's a girl?"

Crowe thought about that seriously. He'd been awful mad at that little girl, but maybe she hadn't known the sand tickled his head. His dad had told him before that no one could read his mind, so they didn't always know why he was mad if he didn't tell them.

Finally, he shook his head. "No, I wouldn't like that."

"Think about it then." He nodded seriously. "Don't do anything in front of those little girls that you don't want someone to do to your sister. And remember, curse words are bad words, no matter when or where you say them."

Crowe nodded again. "I'll tell her I was sorry," he breathed out, because it was sure going to be a chore.

"That's a fine thing to do." His father sat back and watched him approvingly now. "I'm proud of you, Crowe," he announced before Crowe turned away from him. "Very proud of you."

And Crowe felt he'd grown two feet the second his father nodded at him as though he just completed a tremendous feat.

Turning, Crowe ran back to the sandbox.

The memory hadn't just been one of learning why little boys didn't cuss in front of little girls; it had been about his father's love. Not once, for even a second, had he doubted his father's love. And he couldn't see David Callahan giving one of his children a reason to ever doubt he was their father.

A part of him wanted to stride into that family room, send Logan's ass packing, and explain to his daughter that he wasn't rejecting her. He could never reject her. He was trying to protect her. He was trying to make a monster realize that striking out at her, before Crowe could kill him, wouldn't hurt Crowe.

The truth was, it would destroy him. It would dig a wound so deep inside him, Crowe knew he would never recover from it. And he'd known since hours before his daughter had shown up that somehow, some way, Wayne was getting information from inside the house. Knowing that, and knowing Wayne would strike before he was prepared if he didn't handle things just right, terrified the hell out of him.

As he stood there, staring at the door Kimmy had disappeared through, Crowe realized he was being watched.

And he knew who was watching.

Grimacing, he lifted his gaze to where Amelia stood, staring down at him, tears dampening her cheeks.

Slowly, she shook her head. "What next, Crowe?" she whispered. "When is anyone going to matter as much to you as killing Wayne?"

Turning, she moved back up the stairs, her shoulders slumping.

"You're wrong, Amelia." He forced himself to move to the bottom of the stairs as she paused, looking back at him.

"No, I'm not." Her gaze flicked to the family room where Logan's and Kimmy's laughter could be heard. "She's your child, not Logan's." She blinked back more tears. "She hasn't had you in all these years, though, and she's survived. I'm sure she'll survive without you now. I'll make sure of it."

She hurried up the stairs then, almost running as she went quickly back to her room.

Running wasn't going to help.

Gripping the banister he moved up the stairs, his gaze narrowed, determination setting inside him. Damn her, she should have known why, he thought furiously. She should have known to the bottom of her soul that he would never turn his own child away.

And if she didn't know, then he was about to inform her.

And while he was at it, he'd make damned sure she never turned her back on him again.

Stalking up the stairs and down the hall, he jerked his cell phone from the holder on his belt and quickly texted

Logan, Rafe, and Ivan that he wasn't to be disturbed unless necessary. And neither was Amelia.

Let them make of that whatever the hell they wanted to.

Hell, even Logan knew him better than that. He knew Crowe was dying to hold his daughter, dying to play with her, watch cartoons with her, and send her running through the house in gales of laughter—but now he suddenly couldn't figure out why Crowe wasn't doing any of that?

It must have been too long since he'd beaten some sense into that little shit.

Pushing open the door to Amelia's room, he closed it loudly, watching as she swung around to face him in surprise.

"You don't turn your back on me, Amelia," he told her softly, warningly.

"Fuck you, Crowe." She glared back at him.

He locked the door. "Why, Amelia, I don't care a bit if you do."

He moved to her as her lips parted in shock at his deliberate misunderstanding. Then, before she could stop him, he had his hands on her. Pulling her to him, one arm going around her back, the other catching her head to hold her in place, he lowered his head and caught her parted lips in a kiss that he swore sent pleasure surging all the way to his fucking toenails.

When they were both breathless, when her hands buried in his hair to hold him to her, rather than pushing at his chest to get away from him, his head lifted.

"You know me, Amelia." He spoke slowly, clearly as he stared down at her, still holding her to him. "And you know damned well I would never count anyone more important than my child and her mother."

Doubt filled her gaze, along with anger.

"Don't speak to me as though I'm a moron, Crowe," she warned him with feminine ire.

"Why not, when you're acting like one?" he charged with a deliberate calm he sure as hell didn't feel. "But I'll give you the benefit of a doubt here. Maybe you're just not really awake yet? Still sleeping, baby, and dreaming about the days when you could get away with such a blatant statement of confrontation?"

He released her slowly as he began unbuttoning the dark-gray shirt he wore.

"Oh, just don't even." Her fingers knotted at the front edges of her robe as though to secure the material to her. "We are so not having sex."

"Aren't we?" Shrugging the shirt from his shoulders, he considered her with hungry irritation. "Tell me you're not wet. Tell me the honey's not just about to drip down your pretty thighs?"

Her eyes widened at the deliberately provoking question or the bareness of his chest, he wasn't certain. It had been over two days since he'd had her, since he'd tasted her hunger and her his. Perhaps it wasn't incredulity as much as the need to touch.

Yeah, right, he thought as she narrowed her gaze on him, her lips tightening with the same derisive mockery their daughter used so effectively.

"Hell no I'm not," she retorted a second later as her fingers were suddenly gripping each other as well as the robe.

"Little liar," he accused her, his gaze licking over her, his mouth watering at the thought of tasting one of the swollen breasts rising above her arms as she tightened her hold on the robe. "You're hot enough to burn me alive, despite your anger. And baby," he drawled, smiling back at her with slow, deliberate anticipation. "I'm spike fucking hard and damned sure intent on putting all those slick, hot juices dripping from your pussy to proper use."

The thought of touching her again, tasting her, sinking

inside the tight, velvety heat of her sex had every cell in his body sensitizing.

"You're crazy." Shock widened her eyes, but he did notice how tight and hard his words made her nipples as they tried to poke through the material of her robe.

"I'm not crazy, I'm horny." Bending, he jerked one boot off, then the next, dropping them to the floor the second they cleared his feet.

He was more than horny. He was hungry. Desperate. He'd missed her in their bed so much the past two nights that sleep had been almost impossible.

He'd wanted her to have time with their daughter, to comfort their child, to make up, at least for a night or two, for all the time they'd been forced to spend apart.

But that time had given her a chance to doubt him, a chance to forget that the danger they faced changed all the rules.

Releasing the button and zipper of his jeans, he pushed them, along with the boxer briefs he wore, over his thighs before stepping out of them. As he straightened, his dick clenched with painful pleasure at the slow, hungry lick of her tongue over her lips while she stared at the wide, heavy girth.

Damn her, what she did to him.

There were no words to explain to her what she made him feel. At least, no words he could come up with to express how she made his heart beat harder. How she made him actually feel his soul aching for her, aching for her pain and everything he couldn't protect her from over the past years.

There were damned sure no words to explain that the thought of touching her, giving her pleasure, bringing her satisfaction, made him feel ten feet tall and invincible. Or how it increased the already strong sex drive he possessed.

Just the thought of her had the power to make him

iron-hard, iron-hot, and ready to fuck her at any given moment.

"What the hell do you think you're doing?" she gasped when he wrapped his fingers around the base of his erection to hold back the warning pulse of cum throbbing in his balls as she stroked it with her gaze.

"I'm getting ready to put all that hot female honey to use," he assured her. "It's going to wrap around my cock, and I'll make damned sure you love the feel of it pumping up that tight little pussy."

Deliberately explicit because he knew it made her wetter, made her pretty little tummy get as tight as her snug pussy clenched. He knew it, because he paid attention to the slightest little detail whenever he was with her.

"The hell you are." Hunger vied with anger and filled her expression with an edge of desperation. "We need to talk first."

Crowe smiled when she faced him. A slow, anticipatory smile that assured her he was definitely going to have her.

"No, we don't." He shook his head slowly, his gaze moving once again to those tight little nipples beneath her silky robe. "I'm going to undress you, lay you down on that bed, and make you beg me to fuck you. Then I'm going to fuck you again." His voice lowered. "And I'll keep fucking you, Amelia. I'll keep making you scream out each orgasm like you're going to die if you have to come again. Again and again until you by God figure out what you know, or I end up killing both of us with pleasure."

Amelia watched the smile that curled Crowe's lips and knew she was in trouble. Because she didn't have the will to tell him no if he actually touched her again.

Her gaze flicked to his erection. The sight of the jutting, heavily veined shaft had her thighs tightening in reflexive need to feel it stretching, stroking her sensitive inner flesh.

The wide, hooded crest damp with pre-cum, blunt and thick, forced the memory of the pleasure he gave with it, despite her attempts to still it.

"Crowe, that's enough," she ordered, trying to inject a sense of determination in her tone.

Determination in the face of his sensuality was damned hard, though, especially when it meant actually telling him no. Because she knew the pleasure she was denying herself, and that pleasure was something she found she was becoming addicted to.

"We're not even close to *enough* yet," he promised her. "Enough is when I'm buried balls-deep inside you and spilling the last drop of my cum into your fist-tight little pussy."

Oh God.

Her stomach clenched, her womb rippling in response to the sexually explicit warning.

And damn him, she could feel her juices all but dripping from her vagina. The outer lips of her pussy were so wet, so slick, that the excess would be dampening her thighs soon.

"Do you really think I intend to sleep with you after what you've done to my daughter?" she demanded.

"Our daughter," he reminded her, his gazc locked on her breasts as she backed away from him.

"Oh, so you remember that she's *our* daughter now? And just what brought on that illuminating discovery, Crowe?" she asked, incredulous.

Well, she tried to sound incredulous anyway. The truth was, even as she had watched the confrontation between daughter and father, she had seen the agony in Crowe's eyes. She had seen it, and even though she didn't know why he was putting distance between himself and Kimmy, she knew it wasn't because he didn't care.

What pissed her off was the fact that he wasn't willing to discuss it with her or anyone else. And he hadn't done anything to ease Kimmy's pain until he *could* explain it.

And she wanted that explanation.

"Crowe, this is not going to solve anything." Other than relieving her ever-present need for him for a while. Long enough to actually sleep perhaps?

Was she really standing there talking herself into having sex with him rather than walking away as she should until he trusted her with whatever was going on between him and their daughter?

"Oh, I think it will, sugar elf." He smiled back at her again.

That smile. Good Lord. It made her entire body ache to touch of him.

How was she supposed to be strong? She loved him until it hurt. Until everything inside her had screamed out for him during the years he had been gone. Her heart, her soul, her body—she ached for him, even now. She was furious with him, knowing he was holding too much back where their safety was concerned. Still, she wanted nothing more than his kiss, his touch, his possession of her—

"Stop right there, Crowe Callahan," she demanded as she felt her back meet the wall, and he kept moving forward. "We are not doing this minutes after you made my daughter cry."

He snorted at that. "Our daughter wasn't crying," he informed her. "Hell no. Just like her mother she's going to wait until I get desperate enough to come begging for her forgiveness so she can bust my chops for being an asshole." He smiled back at her then. "Unfortunately for you, sugar elf, that's not one of your options."

"What? Busting your chops?" She narrowed her gaze at him. "I'd bust something much lower."

* * *

Crowe grinned back at her, joy lighting his heart for the first time in days. Damn, what she did to him.

He was ready to come, just looking at her. He was so damned hard for her, so desperate to touch her, his fingers tingled with the need.

When her arms crossed beneath her breasts, plumping them even more, he swore he was going to end up taking her right there against the wall.

He'd just lift her. When he did, those pretty legs would wrap around his back and he'd just lower her on his cock, feel the engorged length of it stretching her, filling her, until he was buried inside her to the hilt.

Yeah, he could do that.

Or on the bed. On her knees, her shoulders pressed to the blankets as he watched himself take her. Pushing in, pulling back, and watching the sweet juices as they clung to his cock.

Or—his breathing grew rougher. He could take her in a far different way as she had her ass lifted to him. He could part the soft rounded globes, tease and stroke that hidden entrance, and hear her scream with pleasure as he pressed inside her.

Narrowing her eyes on him, Amelia watched as the gold in his cyes seemed to leap and hurn the longer he watched her. Beneath the glow of the small light next to the bed, she could see the pre-cum bead at the head of his cock, the heavy veins throbbing harder, pounding, her pussy clenching at the thought of feeling it inside her.

Her breathing accelerated.

And he was breathing just as hard as she was.

Her mouth watered to taste him; her pussy wept with a hunger to milk the heavy length inside her again. To feel the solid strength of him as he thrust in the thick stalk, his body braced above hers, protective and yet unable to do anything but share the adventure with her.

He couldn't have sex with her without her participation, yet, he could refuse to allow her to participate in other parts of her own life.

"Why do you keep doing this to me?" she moaned weakly as he touched her then, his hands uncurling her fingers from her robe before he pushed the fabric slowly over her shoulders.

"Doing what, sugar elf?" he whispered, his lips going to her shoulders as her robe fluttered to the floor, his fingers moving to the slender straps of her gown. "Giving you pleasure? Keeping you hot and satisfied? Didn't we both go long enough aching for it?"

He pushed the straps of her gown over her shoulders, his fingers stroking down her arms as he tugged it over the swollen, sensitive flesh of her breasts. She trembled at the pleasure she knew he would give her.

"Not talking to me?" she moaned, her hands lifting to his forearms, her fingers touching his flesh, stroking it as she ran them up his arms to his shoulders. "Not explaining . . ."

A shudder raced through her as his teeth raked over her neck.

"I'm going to explain all kinds of things to you tonight, baby," he promised. "How hard I am. How hungry you make me. How sweet your pussy is. How snug and hot it gets as I fuck you. And I might even explain . . ." His hands caressed up her side, stroking her, heating her. ". . . just how much I'd love fucking that pretty, curvy little ass of yours."

Every muscle in her body seemed to clench as pleasure rippled from her womb, surging to her clit then washing through the rest of her body like a sensual tidal wave.

She lost her breath, for a second.

"You're not serious," she gasped, the words tearing from her lips in a breathless little sound that came far too close to anticipation.

One hand moved to her rear, his fingers cupping a rounded curve as he palmed it, parting the narrow cleft that separated it from its mate and causing a forbidden little pinch of sensation in the tiny opening there.

"Feel that, baby?" he whispered, his lips moving to her ear. "I'd take you there. And I'd make it so good."

His fingers slid into the narrow cleft, stroking, probing until they found the tiny rosebud hidden below. Pressing the pad of his finger against it, he caressed it, stroked it, as Amelia felt the tiny entrance clenching in response to his touch.

"You're crazy." Her voice was a helpless, needy moan.

"For you," he whispered, his kisses moving over her cheek to her parted lips. "Always for you, sugar elf."

His lips moved over hers then, rubbing against them, parting them farther. He wanted the sweet, lush taste of her, the pleasure of her tongue dancing with his, and the electricity that sang through his nerve endings as she began to give herself over to him.

As her lips parted, her tongue peeking out to meet his, a hard, desperate groan escaped his chest. He hadn't expected the sound, just as he hadn't known how much he needed her until she gave to him. Until she accepted his kiss, accepted him.

Lips moving together, melding, tongues tasting, Crowe moved one hand from her rear to her shapely waist as the other stroked to the curve of her breast. Swollen and firm, the tender flesh pressed into his hand as she arched to him. A mewling sound of pleasure and need worked through their kiss, clenching his balls at the throaty little demand of it.

Shaping the plump flesh of her breast, his thumb found the hardened tip of her nipple, stroked it, loving the velvety texture as he felt sharp little nails digging into his shoulder.

Oh yeah, baby, hold on tight. Dig those little claws in because you're about to get a hell of a ride.

When morning came she may not know why he was keeping a distance between himself and his daughter, between him and his sugar elf whenever they were outside this bedroom, but she would know it didn't have the first damned thing to do with not wanting her. Or not loving his child.

When morning came, she would know he'd claimed her. That they were branded into each other's souls. Hell, they'd done that seven years ago.

Tomorrow morning Amelia wouldn't consider anything that would jeopardize the loss of his touch, he promised himself. She wouldn't doubt his hunger for her, his need for her. Or his dedication to her.

And she would know to the bottom of her soul that no matter how it may appear, nothing, no one would matter more than her and their child.

Just as she would know he would do whatever it took to keep her safe.

CHAPTER 25

Nipping at her plump, kiss-swollen lips, Crowe let his kisses move along her chin, her cheek, then begin a slow, sensual glide to the uplifted peaks of her breasts.

Her head tilted back against the wall, her breath rushing hard and heavy from her lips as he scraped his teeth over the sensitive column then tasted it with flicks of his tongue. Every kiss, every taste of her flesh intoxicated him further, just as it pulled her deeper within the sensual fog he could feel overtaking her.

Amelia could feel it. Those dazed, body-humming sensations that rose from the pit of her womb, swept through her belly, then began radiating outward and overtaking her. It was like fingers of electricity traveling beneath her flesh, flicking against her nipples, her clitoris, and overriding any sense of self-preservation she may have actually possessed.

Nothing mattered but this.

Weakened by the surge of sensual lassitude filling her, her knees began to buckle, but she didn't have to worry about that. Crowe swept her into his arms, cradled her against his chest, and moved for the bed.

Laying her in the middle of the mattress, he didn't give her time to think, or time to consider. He wasn't about to give her a chance to protest.

Not that protesting even entered her mind once he'd touched her.

Watching through passion-heavy lashes Amelia licked her lips, her fingers curling in the sheets beneath her as she glanced once again at the hard, heavy length of his cock.

Engorged and dark, the mushroomed crest throbbed, a bead of warmth shimmering at the centered slit before he gripped the flesh and stroked his hand down it.

She knew the taste of him. She knew the bruising hardness of his shaft as it filled her mouth, stroking in and out in shallow thrusts, just as she knew the fierce, penetrating force of it between her thighs.

She knew it, and she ached for it.

And damn his hide, he was teasing her with it.

Stroking the hard flesh again, his gaze narrowed on her, those oddly colored eyes burning with lust, but holding the faintest gleam in their depths that revealed he was assessing her responses, gauging them, and probably mentally noting which touch, which bit of flesh to kiss, to achieve maximum pleasure and leave her willing to do whatever he wanted.

She knew him.

All her life it seemed, she had watched him, studied him, and now she was curious, very curious as to what he intended to do with whatever information he was gathering.

What he wasn't going to do was make her beg—at least not yet. Give it another five to ten minutes, she thought in resignation, and she'd probably be willing.

Instead she let her fingers play against her stomach, where her hand had rested after he laid her on the mattress. She scraped her nails back and forth over the soft skin, her breath catching at the piercing pleasure that shuddered through her.

This only happened with Crowe. She couldn't give herself this much pleasure, not without his touch as well. And she knew no other man could even come close.

"So damned pretty," he groaned, sending a flood of warmth washing through her. "I've never seen anything prettier than you, especially when you're flushed with pleasure and aching for my touch."

How the hell was she supposed to hold on to any self-control, let alone any part of her soul when he said things like that?

Then it didn't matter. Crowe reached out, his fingers touching hers, easing them aside; then he ran the tips over her stomach as she had done.

And it was so good.

So good and so hot, causing her to arch to him, to whimper for more. More of his touches, his kisses, whatever the hell he wanted to give her.

Her hand fell from her stomach, her fingers clenching in the sheets beneath her as he ran just the tips of two fingers along the pouting, bare folds of her sex.

"I almost came in my jeans the first time I saw your pretty pussy," he rasped, his voice growing darker, huskier as his touch met the thick layer of juices gathering on the intimate folds. "All swollen, with just this tiniest patch of curls."

Finding the small triangle above her clit and brushing his fingers against the curls there, his diabolically knowing fingers also brushed the softest caress against her swollen clit.

A surge of sensation rushed from the tiny nub of gathered nerve endings and sent a punch of rapturous sensation to clench her womb. The force of it stole her breath and tightened her belly as a flood of silky juices rushed along the clenched inner channel.

"So wet and ready for me," he whispered, his head lowering to nip at her thigh. "And I can't wait to taste the softest treat I've ever had at my lips."

And she couldn't help but watch. She wanted to watch.

Pushing her weight to her elbows and staring down her body, Amelia watched as he delivered a gentle, light-as-air kiss to her swollen clit.

And nearly made her come.

Her hips jerked toward his mouth in response, desperate to hold him to her, to rush over the climactic cliff she could feel awaiting her.

"Don't tease me," she whispered desperately.

"Would I do that, little sugar elf?" he questioned her with such patently false innocence that she knew he would do exactly that.

"You would do that and more," she said, panting and catching his gaze as he looked at her through the thick, spiked lashes that nearly covered his eyes.

"Hmm" was the only response she got before his head lowered again and his tongue wiped through the narrow slit of her pussy.

Amelia fell back, unable to support her weight any longer, even to watch what he was doing to her.

Because it was so good.

It was incredibly good.

His tongue licked in one long stroke through the sensitive flesh, caressing nerve endings that had never been so sensitive, so responsive. As though the anger that had raged through her moments ago had only stimulated her senses for his touch.

Her knees lifted and bent, her feet pressing into the mattress as she thrust her hips to the tormenting lick of his tongue. It flicked through the pouting folds, probing at her tender clit, then moved to the saturated entrance of her pussy.

Just when she thought he would impale the aching flesh with his tongue, he pulled back. Tormenting her, teasing her, he flicked a heated lick through the sensitive folds once again. Probing tastes led his tongue to the burning nub of her clit, and he caressed the swollen bundle with flicks that threatened to have her begging in far less than the aforementioned five minutes.

Hell, forget begging, she would be crying. Screaming.

"Crowe. Oh God, don't tease me like this," she moaned brokenly, her head twisting against the sheets as her hands gripped his hair, holding tight just in case he decided to move or to stop. Oh God, what would she do if he stopped? She didn't think she would be able to bear it.

Rather than answering, Crowe let a low male groan rumble from his throat and vibrate against her clit as she cried out again, her body straining to get closer to his teasing tongue.

She couldn't even close her legs or escape the deliberately taunting licks of his tongue. His hands were flat against her inner thighs, holding them apart, creating the space he needed to drive her crazy with his touch.

Flashpoints of incredible pleasure reverberated through her pussy, traveled in quick zaps to her womb, then surged to her pussy with sensual little explosions that didn't even come close to release.

"Oh God, please," she moaned as he licked down the narrow slit.

The taunting licks and kisses moved to the clenched opening of her vagina again. There, he rubbed at it with the flat of his tongue until every cell in her body was poised in anticipation.

She needed his tongue doing what it was supposed to

do there. He was supposed to push it inside the painfully needy flesh and use it to stroke her to release.

And he could, so easily.

Pulsing, painfully clenched, her inner muscles throbbed with the need to be stroked, stretched, and fucked. She needed it until she felt poised on a pin edge of agonizing lust.

But did he do anything to relieve it?

Did he even try to ease the need burning through her?

Oh, hell no.

With his tongue still flattened between the plump folds, he licked back to her clit then surrounded the little bud with his lips and gave it deep, erotic kisses that almost—just almost—threw her over that edge.

"Damn you!" she cried out as he eased back to lay several kisses along the slick, soaked folds.

She couldn't stand it.

Panting, she strained to get closer to him, to convince him to give her just a second of what she needed. Just one hard licking thrust—his tongue surging inside the fluttering, gripping tissue.

"Oh my God. Crowe yes, oh my God—" Sensation exploded inside her, tossing her into a chaotic wave of incredible pleasure. Her hips tilted, lifted, desperate for the deepest touch possible.

Just as quickly as he thrust inside her, his tongue retreated.

A quick little thrust, the barest taste of her, and then he was gone.

Completely.

Her eyes opened quickly, staring down her body as his head lifted, his gaze catching hers.

His lips were swollen, damp from her juices, and as she watched he licked them with sensual enjoyment. The gold in his gaze flared as though in response to the taste of her.

"What are you trying to do to me?" she whispered. Her entire body was burning and all too aware of him as he lay between her thighs.

"Touch your breasts," he whispered. "Let me watch you play with them."

She didn't even think to refuse him or dare to negotiate. She should, she really should, but her breasts were so sensitive, so aching that any touch would have the potential to push her over the edge.

As she cupped her breasts, her breath caught in her throat, a broken, desperate cry escaping her as a low moan of tortured pleasure.

"Oh yeah, sugar elf," he breathed out roughly.

As though rewarding her for following his command, he slid one hand along the inside of her thigh before his fingers moved to the wet, swollen folds of her pussy.

Parting the aching flesh as he watched her caress her breasts, his fingers moved to the aching entrance of her vagina. Then they rubbed against it with slow, light movements that circled then pressed against the opening with flirty little touches and near thrusts into the fluttering flesh.

"So pretty," he whispered again, using his tongue for something other than what she was desperate for.

"You're driving me crazy," she cried out.

"Ah, sugar," he crooned. "Not yet. I promise, I have yet to show you what being driven crazy really means."

Or he had yet to understand what being crazy *for* her meant. Crowe wasn't certain which it was, but he knew he was having a hell of a time finding out.

The problem was, he'd started this interesting little excursion for a reason. There had been a point to it. But dammit, he couldn't remember what that point was. All he could concentrate on at the moment was the sweet, sweet, intoxication of her feminine heat and—he swore—the pleasure he could feel pouring from her.

Sweet. Hot. The most intoxicating taste he'd ever known.

Each time he touched her, pleasured her, she spilled her lush taste to his waiting lips. Her body tightened, grew warmer and became more pliable to his touch. She lifted to him, reaching for him as he rimmed the silken entrance to her pussy and teased himself with her taste.

The need to thrust inside her was becoming a hunger raging inside him. To plunge his tongue into the gripping, clenched tissue and feel it rippling around him.

His cock throbbed furiously at the thought, eager to do the same. To feel her gripping it, her snug pussy milking his release straight from his balls.

Damn her. She made him forget—

God, there was something he was supposed to do—some lesson to teach her, and he just fucking didn't care what it was anymore.

He tilted his head, his fingers parting the swollen, syrup-slickened folds as his tongue thrust inside her. His need for her overcame anything—everything—else.

The feel of Crowe's tongue pushing inside her, licking against the delicate walls of her pussy, sent desperate, aching surges of sensation of racing through her. Amelia swore she would die if she didn't come. If he didn't make the throbbing ache ease she was going to die.

Reaching, lifting to him, a strangled cry tearing from her throat, she was certain, so certain she would fly straight into that abyss of rapture if he would just speed up the licking thrusts a little. Just a little—

That body-clenching, flaming, complete-destruction-of-the-mind pleasure that she'd only found in Crowe's arms had to be within reach.

It was right there.

"Crowe, please!" she gasped, fighting to twist in the grip he had on her hips, tortured, desperate to meet the chaos reaching out for her.

And still, it remained just out of reach.

Torturing her.

Teasing her with that elusive promise of rapture. Hinting at the burning pleasure that was becoming more addictive to her than any drink or drug could ever be.

Just as quickly as she was pushed to that brutal edge, his tongue retreated, his lips leaving the desperate ache between her thighs as he rose between them.

One hand gripped his cock, his fingers guiding the heavy stalk of flesh as he came over her. As he fit his hips between her thighs, his gaze locking on hers, Amelia felt her breath catch.

Fiery hot, throbbing, pulsing with demand, he felt so much fuller, thicker than ever as the flared crest pressed against her opening.

Tilting her hips to him, her gaze following Crowe's as it slid down the center of their bodies, she watched—

Her breath caught, a whimper leaving her lips as the dark, flushed cockhead began stretching her, parting the sensitive entrance as he began working it inside her.

The swollen folds of her pussy flared out around it, cupping the very tip of his cock until it penetrated her. Slick, glistening with her juices, the snug flesh of her entrance began cupping the crest little by little as he worked it against her.

Sensual flames ignited as she struggled to accept him, her sex tightening, clenching then releasing around the wide crest working its way into the suckling heat.

Lifting her knees to grip his hips, Amelia was unable to turn away from the sight of it. She could not help herself as she both felt and watched the steady impalement of her pussy. The blistering eroticism of the act amped her own arousal to a height she couldn't have imagined reaching before.

She wasn't going to just fly into release when it came. When it came, she was going to explode into it.

"Fuck yes," he moaned, a dark, rough groan that caressed her senses as the head of his cock disappeared inside her greedy flesh.

Where it was stopped by the heavy, flexing muscles inside her sensitive vagina.

Not that Crowe was about to let that actually stop him.

The pleasure increased for both of them as she was forced to stop watching the penetration, her head falling back and a cry whispering past her lips.

"Fuck me," she moaned, her need for him obliterating everything, anything else. "Please, Crowe. Hard. Fuck me hard. Now."

She wanted that bite of pain. She needed to feel it, as she had before, as his cock slid inside her hard and fast.

"Are you sure, baby?" His lips fell to her neck; he was unable to watch himself possess her for even another second but desperate to tease them both with the pleasure just a little longer. "Are you very sure this is what you want?"

"Damn you, fuck me," she cried out.

His hips stilled, bunched.

"Yes. Yes." He was going to give it. She could feel him tensing, preparing to surge inside her.

There was no way to prepare herself for the coming sensations. Pleasure. Pain. A fiery combination of both sensations so extreme she knew a part of her wouldn't survive it.

Blazing.

The first, hard thrust buried him only inches inside her, not even half of the hardened length of his cock filling her. It struck a match to the already fiery wash of feelings and sent ecstatic pleasure careening through her body.

Before she could process one sensation, he retreated then returned, amplifying it, throwing her so hard, so fast into another level of sensation that she couldn't even process the full scope of how each felt.

They clashed together in burning, surging waves of pleasure so extreme that pleasure and pain merged.

Stretching, agony and ecstasy, burning heat and a heavy, erotic stroke that almost eased it, then suddenly made each sensation glow brighter, erupt with greater intensity than any other time he'd touched her.

Her hips writhed beneath each heavy thrust, her breath rasping in her throat as she gasped, whimpered, and couldn't find the breath to cry out.

All she could do was hold on to Crowe and pray she lived through the ride.

Coming over her fully, he let one hand grip her thigh, his elbow braced at her shoulder, as his powerful knees spread her thighs wide. His knees dug into the bed, his muscular hips powering every fierce penetration of his body into hers and pushing her closer to an edge she was already poised to race over.

Closer.

Each hard stroke of his cock shafting to the depths of her pussy dragged an agonized cry from her lips. Pleasure screamed through her. Each penetration ratcheted sexual tension deeper, higher, until every cell was at peak reception, peak sensitivity.

"Please, please—" She was crying the word, barely aware of it slipping past her lips as a chant, a plea, the only way she had of begging for release.

"God yes," he groaned, his breathing rough and heavy as his lips parted at her neck, spreading kisses over the sensitive flesh there.

"So fucking good. So fucking good and so fucking tight. And so fucking—ah God, Amelia. Baby—"

His lips reach the uplifted curve of her breast, the brutally tight tip of her nipple—

Covering the hard peak and sucking it into the heat of his mouth, he set off a chain reaction inside her body that destroyed her.

The lightning stroke of sensation began at her nipple, struck with brutal pleasure to her womb, her tightening pussy, then the painfully swollen bud of her clit.

Each strike of agonizing pleasure sparked a reaction until that chaotic abyss she'd been reaching for so desperately finally enveloped her.

Sensation shot from her sex through the rest of her body. It exploded, blazed, exploded again and surged through her like a tidal wave.

Ecstasy tore through her system at the impact.

Complete. Perfect. Pleasure.

Rapture.

Her eyes flew open. Her gaze caught with his, locked, widened, and felt that rapture detonate as two hard, deep thrusts buried Crowe to the hilt inside the tightening flesh, the milking, fluttering waves of her release trigging his own.

Fiery jets of semen ejaculated fiercely inside the sensitive depths of her vagina. Hard waves of pulsing sensory overload had yet another wave of sensation trigging through her body.

It was brutal.

It was a swirling, whirling storm of orgasmic bliss. And she knew, after being taken, possessed, and completely overcome by such ecstasy, she would never—no, she *could never* be the same again.

CHAPTER 26

He was supposed to teach her a lesson.

Sitting next to her on the bed, Crowe gently cleaned the semen from the inside of Amelia's thighs after using the damp cloth to erase the drying remnants of their perspiration from her slender body.

She was asleep.

Son of a bitch, the second he'd forced himself to ease from her, long after her pussy had stopped throbbing and pulsing around his cock, she'd slipped into a sleep so deep he wondered if she ever slept when she was alone.

Or did she lie awake in the bed, as he'd seen her in Kimmy's room, staring into the darkness, wondering when the monster would strike?

Crowe pulled the sheet and quilts over her body, then tucked them over her shoulders before rising from the bed to find his clothes.

His next stop was the security control room where Cameron, Jase, and Ivan were still working with the security system. Mike had been either a genius or a fucking moron; Crowe couldn't determine which. Either way, he had created more problems than the three techs could figure out together.

Ivan Resnova had become their protector. His money and the tech gurus he had at his command had saved their asses more than once since the Resnova family had come into Brute Force. Add in Crowe's military knowledge, Logan's surveillance abilities, and Rafer's knowledge of the mountains and tracking skills, and they were steadily tracking Wayne Sorenson and ensuring he lost each hidden haven he thought he possessed.

They'd nearly caught him at the last one. High above Sweetrock, Wayne had installed a telescope in the window of a small hunting cabin and managed to find a direct line of sight to front door of the house.

The house was the first one on the corner of the last block before you headed out of town. Running deep and hard in a series of heavy ripples and light rapids, Sweet Water Gorge opened and leveled off outside town, while the heavy course of water continued to flow past within sight of the house.

Directly across from the house a path had been clear cut halfway up the mountain by a logging company intent on building a road through the trees it intended to log. John Corbin had produced a deed to the mountain that trumped the one the logging company possessed. It had effectively ensured the company was driven straight out of the county and the mountains were left almost as pristine and gorgeous as they had been before the company arrived.

Except for that one clear cut path, which went straight up then stopped. And through that path, Wayne had found the line of sight he needed to watch Amelia the way a cat watched a particularly attractive mouse.

He had left detailed notes of her movements and months' worth of insane ramblings written in a wrinkled composition book that looked as though it had been chased through the mountains right along with Sorenson.

They had scored a major hit against him when they

found and struck the cabin. Unfortunately, only minutes before the team had poured through the trees surrounding the cabin, he'd discovered they were coming.

The back door had still been open. In the cabin they had found the four cameras Wayne had managed to hide by burying the wires several inches beneath the dirt before running them up the trees the cameras were positioned in. The setup had allowed him to glimpse the movement in the forest and escape before the cabin was surrounded.

But they had his notebook, and they had a hell of a lot of his supplies.

For a man nearing his sixties the son of a bitch was in damned good shape to have escaped them so quickly.

Now, if Crowe were Wayne, he'd want plenty of places to hide, and he'd want each of them stocked with whatever he needed. If each of his hideaways was well stocked, then Wayne wouldn't have to worry about carrying supplies if he had to run. Each of those hideaways would have the same system of cameras as well, though they would be positioned differently. Wayne would want to ensure his pursuers weren't prepared to evade his cameras if they found another of the hunting cabins.

If Wayne actually managed to get into the house and Amelia came face-to-face with him, Crowe was terrified Wayne would kill her before they could get to her. Or worse yet, if Wayne managed to find Kimmy.

It was one of those insane, rambling plans he'd detailed in the composition book: to get into the house, to get Amelia, and—if it appeared he couldn't escape with her—to kill her before killing himself.

But that was before Amelia had brought their daughter, and the wife Wayne had believed he'd killed, to the house.

Until then nothing had mattered to Wayne but taking Amelia.

Nothing mattered but destroying her.

Amelia had, as Wayne had written, committed the ultimate sin. She'd not only slept with a Callahan, but had betrayed him for Callahan.

She had, Wayne had written, loved a Callahan, and for that, she had to die.

As Crowe entered the communications room, his gaze was caught by movement on one of the cameras. Amelia was leaving the bedroom. Dressed now in loose cotton pants and a T-shirt, she moved to Kimmy's room.

Crowe watched as she entered their daughter's room. Kimmy sat up in bed, a wide smile filled with love on her face. She jumped to her knees in bed and wrapped her arms around her mother.

Amelia cradled their daughter, her expression so serene, so incredibly beautiful in its maternal grace that Crowe felt his throat tightening with a surge of emotion he could barely contain.

He wanted to be there with them. He needed to be there with them. The instinct was so deep, so overwhelming he was tensing to turn and leave the room.

"Mr. Callahan, this damned system is driving me fucking crazy." Cameron stopped him as he cursed the flickering of another screen, tapped the monitor, then blew a heavy breath of irritation. "Son of a bitch, I even changed the power packs this morning and had new cameras brought in. I swear, I get up with Mike and I'm killin' the little son of a bitch."

"Let's see if we can figure out what the hell he did." Biting back the irritation rising inside him, Crowe sat down and powered up the laptop he'd placed there earlier.

They were running out of time, he could feel it. The knowledge of it tore at his senses and drove him to immerse himself in the electronics that were his first line of defense in protecting Amelia against the bastard.

The monster.

"Monsters do exist, son." His father nodded somberly as he sat next to Crowe's bed. "But they're not invisible. They're right there in plain sight, smiling, laughing, convincing you that they're not monsters just before they strike." The weight of knowledge in his father's eyes convinced Crowe to the soles of his feet that there really weren't monsters under his bed as his grandpa John had claimed.

"Why did Grandpa lie to me?" he asked his father, feeling betrayed.

His father sighed heavily. "Grandpa didn't lie to you exactly. He just doesn't know how they hide. I do."

"Have you seen them?" Crowe whispered, his eyes widening as his father suddenly seemed ten feet tall and as strong as the mountains. If he fought monsters, then Dad had to be really strong, didn't he?

"I've seen them." There was a look in his father's eyes that had Crowe's heart beating faster. "And they look just like anyone else, son. It's what's inside a man that makes him a monster, not what's on the outside. It's not the slimy aliens or the hairy wolf men you have to watch out for. Those are for television and for some little boys"—he gave his son a stern look—"scaring their younger cousins with."

Crowe got the hint and shook his head. "I won't no more," he promised, wanting to hear more about the real monsters. "Did you find a monster, Dad, that looked like me or you?"

"Not like you, son," David Callahan promised with a hint of a smile at his lips. "But one that looks like a man. Remember that, Crowe. Monsters walk on two legs, and they're crafty. They're real good at fooling even the smartest of men. Don't forget that. Because sometimes, you don't realize monsters are stalking you until it's too

late. It's far better to be smart, to be safe, and to watch for monsters in everyone you know."

"Even Logan and Rafe?" he whispered, suddenly wondering if somehow his cousins were monsters.

He couldn't hurt his little cousins. He'd promised Dad he'd always watch out for them, and for his baby sister. What was he supposed to do if one of them was a monster?

His father gave him one of those small, man-to-man smiles Crowe always tried to get.

"Well, maybe not Logan and Rafe," his father amended. "It's hard to imagine a Callahan as a monster, don't you think?"

Crowe nodded quickly. "They're just dumb kids sometimes," he sighed. "But I make sure to tell them when they're dumb so they'll get smart."

His father chuckled at that. "You keep doing that, son."

Reaching out, his father ruffled his hair as Crowe tried to duck and act like he didn't want his hair messed up. After all, Kiely Moss down the street really liked his hair when he brushed it just that certain way. But Crowe swore that when his dad did that, he was treating Crowe like he was growing up. After all, hugs and kisses were for moms. Dads patted their sons' shoulders or ruffled their hair.

Well, except for daughters, Crowe remembered. His dad said his baby sister, Sarah, would always need his hugs, but he'd wait until Crowe asked for one. That was after Crowe had told him hugs were for sissies, though.

"Dad." He stopped his father as he moved to stand up from the bed.

"Yeah, son?" his father asked softly.

Crowe cleared his throat, a little uncomfortable, but suddenly overwhelmed by a need he didn't understand.

Refusing to allow his face to go all hot, though, he asked, "Can I have one of those hugs now?"

His father's face gentled. Crowe wondered if maybe his dad liked giving him hugs.

"You sure as hell can, son."

Crowe met that hug halfway. Rising to his knees, his skinny arms wrapping around his father's neck, he felt his father's strength enfold him.

"I love you, Dad, but you said a bad word," he reminded his father, fighting against the tears that suddenly filled his young eyes and a fear he couldn't explain.

"I love you, too, son." His dad's voice sounded a little strange, like it did when he and Mom had been reading those papers the night before and Crowe had seen his dad's eyes get kind of wet. "I love you, too."

Pulling back, Crowe lay back down, staring up at his dad. The monster slayer, he decided. His dad was a monster slayer.

"Go to sleep," his dad told him firmly.

"Can we go get Mom's Christmas present tomorrow?" Crowe asked then. "I saw what I want to get at Pierson's."

His dad shook his head slowly. "Not tomorrow, son. Maybe the next day. I have to take your mom to the lawyer tomorrow. But if nothing comes up, we'll definitely go the next day."

"Be careful, Dad." His dad always said that when Crowe and his cousins went outside to play. "The news said it might snow."

His dad smiled. "I'll definitely be careful."

Then he reached over, turned out the light, and, as Crowe watched, left the room.

It was the last time he'd seen his father, Crowe realized as the memory faded.

Strange how the memories he'd been certain he'd forgotten over the years were surging back with the realization that he now had his own child to watch out for.

As he tracked electronic glitches, cursed some and rerouted others, in the back of his mind was the knowledge that he wanted to see Amelia pregnant. He wanted another child with her. He wanted to watch the changes in her body, be there when his child was born, hold it as an infant and shelter both children as they grew.

Working, he kept check on the monitor displaying his daughter and his woman. He'd maintained a distance between himself and his daughter that was killing him. And today, he saw, it was killing his daughter as well.

You lied to my mommy. You are not my daddy. Her voice echoed in heart.

He was her daddy, and he prayed to God he could prove it. Soon.

Very soon.

CHAPTER 27

It was after midnight before Crowe was able to leave the security room and head to bed.

He hadn't forgotten he was heading to an empty bed, though. Amelia had been sleeping with Kimmy in the room tucked between hers and the one her parents slept in. The small bedroom was connected to Ethan and Thea's room, giving them a security Crowe was suddenly thankful for.

The glitches in the electronics had finally been tracked to a disconnected sensor on the first floor an hour before. After this was reconnected, the flickering in the screens had stilled, and the diagnostics had finally come up clear.

He was going to kill Mike, he thought again. As soon as they found him.

As soon as he managed a few hours' sleep.

First, there was something he had to do though, he decided. Something that wasn't going to wait another night.

The memory of that last night his father had been alive had haunted Crowe. What had made his father come into his room that night? Had he somehow sensed the danger moving closer to him and his family? Was that why he'd changed his mind at the last minute about taking both his children with him, as he normally did?

Whatever the reason, his father had taught him not to ignore the urge that sent him to find his daughter, and the woman who had protected her for him until he could protect them both himself.

Moving purposely to the room Kimmy slept in, Crowe opened the door silently and stepped into the bedroom. Closing the door without so much as the softest snick he stared at the sight that met his eyes.

Amelia lay next to their daughter, her delicate body curled protectively around the tiny girl with the heavy mass of thick, black waves falling from her head. Those odd brown-and-amber eyes were hidden now, sleep stealing the sight of them as Crowe moved to the small chair next to the bed and sat down slowly. Propping his elbows on his knees and wiping his hands over his face, he wondered how the hell he was supposed to deal with this.

If he'd known Amelia was pregnant, he'd have had a minute to get used to the fact that there was another life depending on him.

That wasn't the case, though.

Kimberly Crowe Callahan Roberts was a too tiny little fireball ready to kick Daddy's chops for being all too human, and he couldn't even blame her.

Hell, once this was over, he'd even let her do it.

Reaching out, almost terrified of waking either of them, he let the tip of his finger curl around one heavy wave of hair that had fallen over the blanket covering them. With his thumb he tested the texture of it, realizing with a sense of wonder that it felt just like her mother's did. Soft and warm and filled with life. It even gleamed with that heavy blue-black sheen only Rafe's hair held. Both Logan and Crowe had inherited a bit of their mothers' coloring as well, dulling that Irish rich sheen their fathers had possessed.

God, what was he going to do?

How the hell was he going to protect them, keep them from being hurt, keep life from dimming that innocence in both their eyes?

That was his job, he realized with a thoughtful frown. Wasn't that what his father had once said about his wife and daughter?

Another memory surfaced, like the first, forgotten and left to lie in wait until it was needed.

As fresh as it had been the day it happened, Crowe remembered standing next to the open hood of his father's car when he'd been no more than eight.

David Callahan wore his Stetson and cowboy boots, faded stained jeans, and a western work shirt with the sleeves rolled up his muscled, tan forearms.

As Crowe had stared into the mystery of the motor his father was working on, his dad ruffled his hair.

"What are you doing out here, son?" Gruff, yet always filled with affection, his father had smiled down at him with eyes the same color as his own.

"Mom told me to come out and play with you." Crowe grinned back up at him. He'd felt like a man, standing there with Dad and mimicking his thoughtful expression as he stared into the car's innards.

"Why did she do that?" his dad asked, his voice firm and patient.

But it was a tone that demanded an answer.

Crowe breathed out heavily. "She says I got too much tostrone, or something." He frowned up at his father. "What's tostrone, Dad? Will it make me sick?"

His father laughed, his eyes crinkling in a way that assured him he hadn't done anything wrong, but maybe

Mom had done something that was going to cause his dad to give her a kiss and get all goofy with her.

"It's testosterone, Crowe," he answered, the laughter still in his voice. "And you just might have your share and more besides. Only time will tell. But no, it won't make you sick." His dad chuckled then. "Though it might end up making the women in your life a little irritated with you as you get older."

Oh well, that was okay then. He liked irritating his mom sometimes, especially when she was spending too much time with that bratty little girl across the street.

"Well, Mom says I got too much now." Gripping metal frame, he tried to lift himself up to see the motor better. "But Mom's actin' all girlie again anyway, like she's gonna cry or something." He looked up at his father again. "Like I said, actin' weird again, Dad."

A hint of sadness touched his father's eyes. "Mom's just a little sad sometimes, Crowe. We'll make it all better for her later, huh?"

Crowe nodded, but he was a little sad now. "Because Grandpa was yellin' at you last night?"

His father's gaze had hardened for just a moment before he blew out a hard breath, his big hand rubbing at the back of his neck the way he did when he was trying to figure out why the motor sounded funny.

He stooped down until he could stare in Crowe's eyes with a look he only used with other adults. "Crowe, son, one day you'll understand," he said, his voice kind of sad as Crowe tried to listen to him with the same expression his uncles used. As though he understood, when at the time he hadn't really. "It's a man's job to see the world, to climb his mountains and learn all he can about the rules. You learn all you can so that when you find that special girl you love, and you have a daughter of your own, you know how to protect all that innocence that fills their hearts. Because that's our job. To make sure, no matter what we have to do, that the women we love are always innocent. That the monsters of the world never touch them. But sometimes, the monsters get sneaky, Crowe, so you have to be on your guard all the time. Ya know? I think Mom just gets worried sometimes that those sneaky little problems are going to get past us, and touch you, or even me. When she gets worried, she tends to get a little sad. That's what grown-ups do."

"Not real monsters, though, right, Dad?" he asked somberly, wondering if real monsters existed.

"Not the kind that hide under beds," his father promised.

Crowe nodded, trying to understand. He wanted to be grown up like Dad, and he wanted to climb a mountain, and learn all the grown-up rules, and help Dad fight the monsters so Mom wouldn't get all sad or worried.

"I'll be grown up soon, Dad," he promised. "I'll help you watch for the monsters, okay?"

His dad smiled. A smile that reached his eyes, and Crowe knew his father trusted him to do just that.

Had his father known he'd fail to protect his wife and children from the monsters? Crowe wondered. Or had he just feared it and done all he could to prepare his son for a world without the parents who would have tried to shelter him?

Staring at Amelia and Kimmy now, his hands hanging between his spread knees, Crowe felt the same deep sense of failure that he'd felt the day his parents, and the tiny form he'd believed was his sister, were buried.

He hadn't helped his father protect his mother and sister, and he hadn't been able to protect Amelia or the child he hadn't known existed.

He'd climbed the mountains, learned the rules of the world, and had learned to navigate the world of monsters.

Yet here he sat, unable to eliminate the danger stalking his woman and his child. Still, though, both of them retained their innocence. Now keeping that innocence in their eyes was paramount.

He couldn't fail.

His father hadn't known the identity of the monsters. It was a knowledge Crowe had, and staring at the two most important people in his life, Crowe swore he wouldn't fail.

"I'll make sure the monster is destroyed. I know who it is now," he whispered, confident they slept. "I swear to both of you, I won't fail."

Rising to his feet and leaning over the bed, he laid a whisper-soft kiss against the top of Amelia's head before laying his head next to the tiny form of his daughter.

"Sleep, sprite," he whispered. "Daddy's here now. And I promise you, you'll never have to hide again."

Straightening and moving to the door, he left the room silently and made his way to bed.

He was enjoying his own form of protection, a backup no one would know existed but himself.

As he'd gone over the system the day Mike had been sent back to the office, Crowe had remembered one of Wayne's first victims. Her security system had included several highly expensive cameras inside her home. Wayne, or one of his partners, had managed to completely disable it. Crowe had been working for days to ensure that none of the cameras, mics, or security alarms could be breached so easily.

Never again, he swore to himself, would he allow Wayne to strike out and take anything from him.

Sure as God was his witness, he would not allow Wayne to steal the woman who carried his soul or the child she'd died for precious minutes to protect.

No one, not even Ivan, realized what Crowe had been doing to the equipment Mike's careless installation had apparently rendered useless. Programming, wiring, as well as electronics had been so sloppy it had been all Crowe could do not to find the bastard and kill him.

Mike still hadn't been found. Once he had time, Crowe thought, he and Ivan would deal with him. Until then, Crowe would ensure that the tech's carelessness remained, to anyone interested, irreparable.

Unless it was needed.

Should it be needed, then that tech would die the same painfully slow way Crowe intended to ensure Wayne suffered.

One bloody bullet at a time.

"Mama, you awake?" Kimmy whispered, her voice so soft it was barely audible as she turned in Amelia's arms, her drowsy gaze meeting her mother's as she fought to blink back her tears.

"I'm awake, baby." Staring into the somber, damp depths of her daughter's gaze, she sent a quick thank-you heavenward for the short visit Crowe had made to the room.

"Daddy loves me," she whispered, awe filling her voice.

"I told you he loved you, Kimmy," she reminded her. "Sometimes we just have to let Daddy get used to things, right?"

Kimmy nodded before cuddling into her mother's arms again. "Next time, I'll give Daddy time, I promise." Then she looked up at her mother again. "But I still get to act like I don't know, right? Just a little bit?"

Amelia had to laugh, though softly. "Just a little bit, Kimmy. Don't overdo it, huh?"

"I promise." Kimmy nodded, then lay back against her mother.

She yawned as Amelia wrapped her arms tighter around her, tucked her closer, and felt the tear that slid down her cheek.

Sometimes Crowe just needed a minute, that was all.

Lying next to the child they created together, Amelia let a small smile tug at her lips.

God, she loved him. Loved him until her heart felt ready to burst.

Memories she had held back over the past years surged through her mind. That first summer that had resulted in Kimmy's birth was filled with memories she'd had to bury to survive. But she didn't have to hide them any longer.

That first night at the Spring Social. She'd been the coordinator's assistant since she was sixteen, until she took over as coordinator herself at age twenty.

That first Fairy Ball had been her idea, but the coordinator hadn't understood the magic that could have been created. Amelia's dress had been the creation she envisioned, though.

The russets, golds, and dark browns had been perfect for her coloring.

That night she had teased Crowe into one of the secluded grottoes to slip to him the information that she'd seen a part of a file Wayne was gathering on him and his cousins. While he was there, she convinced him to dance with her. Then she'd convinced him to take her to a secluded area in the Sweet Water Gorge where they could talk.

The little glade set back from the swiftly flowing river held calmer waters that lapped at a sandy shore. Huge boulders, natural grottoes, and small caves dotted the horseshoe-shaped canyon. That night the full moon had glowed overhead, spilling its golden rays to the hidden glade.

It was there, in his pickup truck, that he'd kissed her for the first time.

Staring into the dimly lit room now, she realized something. In the weeks they had been together that spring and summer, and the weeks that he had come back into her life, she had never told him she loved him.

Kimmy shifted in the bed, the little bed hog deciding that three nights with her mother wrapped around her was plenty. A sharp little elbow dug into Amelia's arm and a skinny foot kicked at her shin.

Amelia rolled her eyes.

Rising, she tucked the blankets around her daughter's shoulders and slipped quietly from the room to return to her own.

Crowe was awake as she entered. His dark eyes watched her as she moved to him, his expression somber and intent.

He'd already showered. His damp hair lay around his face, thick and dark, emphasizing the natural beauty of his powerful body and the savage features of his face.

The blanket was pulled to his hips, one hand lying on his tight, hard abs, the other curled behind his head. He looked lazy and indolent, though she knew he was anything but. That he was a sensual, sexual being intent on pleasure at any given moment was far closer to the truth.

He was a proud man. A strong man. He was a man in every sense of the word, and one with a code, an inborn sense of honor that might sometimes offend the letter of the law, but understood justice.

They hadn't talked about Stoner or how Crowe had ensured he never hurt another young girl since the night she had learned he was definitely dead. Amelia had worried about that at first. Now, she realized, there simply was nothing to talk about. Crowe wasn't scarred by the experience, or resentful. It was something that had to be done, he'd believed, and he was the one there to do it.

She wouldn't change him.

He might bend for her. He might compromise a time or

two, but at no time would he change a decision he felt had to be made simply to please her.

"How long have you been awake?" he asked.

She could see the other question in his eyes, though. Had she heard what he'd said?

"I haven't been sleeping well without you," she admitted. "And Kimmy flops around like a fish when she's asleep so I was only dozing when you came in."

He lifted his hand from where it rested against his tight stomach and held it out to her, his fingers curling around hers as she laid them against his palm.

"I never meant to hurt her."

"Shh." Placing her fingers against him as she sat on the side of the bed, she refused to hear an apology. "You've done what you've believed was best to protect her. No one could ever ask for more."

"You should have told me, Amelia," he whispered, though the statement lacked anger or resentment. "I would have helped you protect her. It shouldn't have fallen to you alone to make the decisions you've had to make."

Laying her hand against his chest as she stared down at him, she knew she, too, had done the only thing she could.

"It would have tortured you," she whispered. "You were out of the country, doing whatever you did in the military that had every woman's instinct inside me terrified for you. The knowledge that Kimmy was there, protected only by the fact that the Slasher didn't know about her yet, would have killed you, Crowe. I knew that, even when I went to Clyde to try to contact you."

He shook his head. "You were too young to have to do it alone, Amelia."

"But I wasn't alone," she reminded him. "You may hate it, I may regret every moment it was necessary, but even you and your cousins couldn't have done more than Dad and Uncle Jack did to ensure no one followed me when I went to see her. Just as they made certain no one learned she existed. I knew the day would come when you'd be back. That one day the Slasher would be gone forever. I made sure Kimmy knew that the only reason you weren't with us was because there was a very bad man trying to hurt you, one who would have hurt me and her as well, if he'd known about her. She accepted that, and she's awaited the day she'd know you. But." She stopped him when regret flashed in his gaze and he would have spoken. "Don't think Kimmy isn't enjoying the hell out of the little confrontations the two of you are having. She loves to argue. She loves to push her boundaries. She's a feminine replica of you, Crowe, and she terrifies me with her courage. Just as you've always terrified me with yours."

CHAPTER 28

Pride snapped in his gaze so fast Amelia couldn't help but smile.

"Does it please you, knowing your daughter is so much like you that it's damned scary?"

"She's already giving me gray hairs," he sighed. "Logan actually started playing with her this afternoon to keep her off that damned stair banister. The little minx would have broken something if I hadn't made it to the bottom in time when she came flying down it."

Amelia laid her head against his chest, groaning. "She's already broken her arm climbing a tree on the estate that Dad's group owns in France. She's fearless, Crowe."

"She's beautiful," he whispered.

Lifting her head, she gazed down at him, seeing a man aching for the years he had lost with his child.

"Do you realize," she whispered. "We were together over three months that summer. And nearly as long now. You've killed a man to protect me, you've watched over me when you could, but you've never told me you loved me?"

His expression softened, not a lot, but a bit. The gold in his eyes gleamed brighter, though.

"I told you I loved you every night we were apart," he

whispered then. "Every time I've touched you, I've told you with every cell in my body how much I love you, Amelia. I'm only surprised Wayne never realized it over the years. That each time I was within sight of you, every part of me that mattered was screaming out how much I loved you."

Tears filled her eyes, her lips trembling at the emotion that thickened his voice.

"I always loved you," she whispered. "So much that sometimes I swore my soul was bleeding with the wound punched into it when you left me."

His hand cupped her cheek, his thumb whispering over her lips. "I know you did," he told her gently. "You didn't have to say the words, Amelia. Your eyes, your touch, they said it."

A tear slid slowly down her cheek and touched his thumb, binding them further together.

"I want more kids," he surprised her by saying. "As many as you want to have, but at least one more little girl. Maybe a boy, too."

"At least two more," she agreed, wondering what he would think if he knew she wanted at least three more children. Enough children that if, God forbid, their parents be taken from them, they would always have someone to hold on to. Another part of their parents that would ensure they always knew they were loved.

"Whenever you're ready," she promised. "You know, I conceived that first night, Crowe."

His eyes widened. "We were together three months."

She nodded. "The night you left, I'd just taken one of the home pregnancy tests. I'd only realized then that as irregular as my periods were, they weren't *that* irregular. So I doubt it will take long to ensure Kimmy has a little brother or sister."

Before she could guess his intention he grabbed her,

pulling her atop him as he rolled over and pinned her to the bed. Staring down at her, his gaze heated with arousal again, his expression now filled with so much love that the wound she'd carried eased and began healing.

"As soon as Wayne's dealt with," he demanded.

Amelia sobered, nodded. "As soon as he's dealt with."

His head lowered, his forehead touching hers as his hand cupped her cheek again. "I love you, Amelia. Every day, every hour, every minute we've been apart, I've loved you until I wondered if I would survive another second away from you."

His lips touched hers, gently. It wasn't a sexual kiss. It was an intimate kiss. The kiss of a man who knew and understood so much more than he ever spoke of, so much more than he ever explained. A man who knew the woman in his arms and the fears that often held her.

He grimaced at the sound of his cell phone pinging. "Hell," he groaned, rolling from her and grabbing the phone from the bedside table. "What is it?"

As Crowe listened, he sighed heavily. "Those fucking computers in the security room." The call didn't sound like an emergency or hold any hint of danger if his voice was anything to go by. When he rose from the bed, Amelia realized he'd been totally naked beneath those blankets.

Damn. Her thighs instantly softened, her inner flesh melting and preparing for him.

"One of the monitors is acting up again," he explained to her after he disconnected, moving to the clothes he'd laid out on the chair next to the bedside table.

Amelia remained in the bed, covering a yawn. "I'll wait for you."

She would always wait for him, she realized.

He dressed quickly, then sat on the bed and pulled on his boots before lacing them quickly. "I won't be long," he promised, leaning to her, his lips moving over hers.

Taking hers.

He parted them, his tongue tasting her as he took deep, heated kisses that rocked her to the tips of her toes. Lifting her hands she buried them in his hair, holding him close, letting him pull her into the dizzying heat that surrounded her each time he touched her.

When he pulled back, she realized he was breathing just as hard as she was, the touch of just their lips enough to bring them both to full, blazing arousal.

"Rain check?" he whispered.

"Rain check," she agreed, staring up at him, praying the team she'd learned was out searching for Wayne found him soon.

Watching him leave she smiled at the look in his eyes as he left the room. She'd seen it often, she realized, just as she realized that her heart had heard the words her ears had missed.

They were there in his eyes, pouring from his soul.

I love you.

He had whispered the words the only way he could, the only way he knew would keep her safe from the danger that stalked him and any lover he was suspected to have.

Exhaling deeply to calm her breathing and the arousal that had begun building in her, Amelia moved from the bed and straightened the loose shirt she wore. While Crowe checked his monitors, she wanted to check on Kimmy. She could spend hours just watching her daughter sleep.

She'd been forced to spend so much time away from her that now Amelia found it hard to allow her baby out of her sight.

Leaving the bedroom she glanced along the hall, her lips twitching. Ivan's cousin, the hall guard, was dozing where he'd been sitting in the large wingback chair, the newspaper he was reading still in his hand.

Ivan would have his head for that, just after Crowe finished kicking his ass. She'd wake him when she returned to her room.

Gripping the doorknob she opened the door, stepped inside—

She entered hell.

"Close the door, sweetheart," Wayne ordered, his voice soft, almost gentle as he held a knife to her daughter's throat.

Amelia was dying inside.

She felt the ice forming in her soul, the silent screams of pain and denial unlike anything she'd ever felt in her life as her entire world crashed in on her soul.

Closing the door softly, she stared at her daughter's innocent face, the long lashes that lay against her sleep-flushed face, the tangled waves of her hair that her daughter refused to bind when she slept.

Crowe's daughter. And she was so much like him. Courageous and daring, without fear, without hesitation when she decided on something.

Amelia had wanted nothing more than to ensure that the evil she knew existed on the edges of her life never touched her daughter. She'd sent her baby away to France when she was just an infant, with her own mother and father. She'd stayed away from her as much as possible. She'd died inside over and over again without the man she loved, and the daughter they had created together.

Only to become so desperate to give Crowe the gift she had saved for him that she had convinced herself the evil couldn't get to her as long as she stayed in the house. As long as Kimmy was surrounded by Crowe's and Ivan's security agents, not mention her father's team, then she would be safe.

Her gaze was held by the glint of steel against her daughter's throat. She knew Wayne meant to take her baby, Crowe's baby, away from them.

"You won't get out of here with her," she whispered, desperate to make certain Kimmy remained asleep. "Just leave, Wayne. I won't let anyone know you're here. I swear."

He chuckled, a low, demented sound of amusement. "You'd do anything to keep this child, wouldn't you, Amelia? No matter what."

"I always have," she assured him.

"Tell me, how did you hide this precious little treasure from me?" He stroked Kimmy's neck with the blade. Amelia felt her heart burst in her chest.

Her breath hitched on a sob as his smile widened. "Come on, Amelia, tell me how you did it."

"She was premature." Her voice was strangled. "I wasn't showing much, and I would have left had I begun showing more. But she came early."

He nodded. "I've been doing the research I should have done years ago." He shook his head, staring back at her with a gleam of anger in his eyes. "You shouldn't have kept this from me, Amelia."

"You threatened to kill me," she whispered. "I didn't know you were the Slasher and you kept threatening to make certain everyone knew the information you found in Cami's journal. I didn't want to die."

She didn't want to leave her baby to be raised without either parent and she hadn't wanted her death on Crowe's conscience. Something had told her he couldn't have survived it.

"Ah yes," he nodded. "I did do that. But what has me thinking that the only reason you stayed in Sweetrock was to protect your lover?" Then he sneered. "And your whore mother."

She shook her head desperately. "I didn't know about Mom until after Crowe left. She wanted me to leave with her, and I wouldn't. I stayed . . ."

"To protect Crowe?" he snapped.

"What does it matter why?" she begged desperately. "I stayed." Tears fell from her eyes as she clenched her hands in her robe. "Oh God, please move the knife. Please. She's asleep."

She was dying. Sobs were trapped in her throat; screams were strangled inside her as her knees threatened to collapse beneath her.

He only smiled back at her.

"Wayne, Crowe won't let you out of here alive, you know that. If you just go, I'll help you. I'll go with you," she sobbed, fighting to keep her voice low. "The guard is sleeping outside. He won't know . . ."

"He's actually dead."

She froze. "What?"

"Dearest, you couldn't wake that Russian moron if you tried. He's dead. I killed him."

Dead?

She hadn't even asked his name when Ivan brought him in earlier. All she knew was that he was Ivan's cousin, and Kimmy had teased him about his accent.

And he had seemed to be charmed by her.

Ivan would never forgive her. He would never forgive any of them for his cousin's death.

"Do you think no one else is here?" she asked him, fighting back her screams as another muffled sob escaped. She felt strangled by her own breaths, her heart so tight, filled with such agony she didn't know if she would survive if he actually managed to get away with her baby.

From the corner of her eye she saw Kimmy's lashes twitch and she began to pray harder. Desperately.

Please God, don't let her wake. Don't let her memories be touched by the monster standing over her.

"What made you believe I'd let you keep his child once I did find out?" Wayne sighed as he stared down at her daughter. "Of all the Callahans, Crowe is the one you had to choose. What made you think I'd actually allow it, Amelia?"

Reaching out, he caused a low whimper of terror to leave her lips as he ran his fingers down the back of her daughter's hair before looking up at her again.

"Really, Amelia? Did you believe I wouldn't punish you for this?"

She shook her head jerkily. "I thought you would focus on Mom," she admitted. "Not on my daughter."

She had never imagined Wayne would get past a house filled with trained agents. She had never imagined she was risking her precious daughter.

"I heard what you said about me after you were rescued," he told her quietly. "That you loved me once?"

She had told a journalist she had loved him as a child who believed all fathers loved their daughters. When she was very young. Before her mother was taken from her.

As he stared at her, his gaze turned heavy as he seemed to regret the past.

Amelia watched him, tracking the knife as it lifted marginally from her daughter's neck.

"I was a child," she whispered, fighting to breathe past her tears.

"And I was cruel to you." He nodded, smiling back at her again. "I promise to try to be nicer to this little darling, though." He stared down at Kimmy again as Amelia found herself sobbing silently, desperately. He whispered, "Pretty little Callahan. Crowe's precious little daughter."

A ragged cry tore from her as Wayne touched her baby's cheek with that blade again.

"Let her go, Wayne. There's no way you'll get her out of here alive. You know you won't," she begged.

"There's no way you would risk your child by screaming," he retorted knowingly. "And once I leave, you'll never find me."

"I won't let you leave with her, Wayne." From the corner of her eye she watched as the eyes of the stuffed teddy bear that lay on Kimmy's pillow seemed to blink with a confusing faint blue sheen.

"Amelia, dear, you can't stop me," Wayne chuckled cruelly. "You may have gotten away with protecting that bastard over the years, but you may as well forget this precious child. She's mine now."

"Never." The tone he used, the words he used, filled her with a horrifying knowledge. Nothing else existed inside her now except ensuring he didn't leave the room with her daughter. "That's my daughter. I won't let you take her away from me." She couldn't, not and survive. It was her job to protect her daughter, to keep this from happening. She would not compound it by allowing Wayne to actually get away with her baby.

"How did you get in here?" she demanded, her voice still thick with tears, the sobs trapped in her throat still echoing in her voice. "Someone had to have helped you. If you could have accomplished it on your own you would have already done so."

He smiled back at her benignly. "Darling daughter, just as you were unable to figure out how I slipped in and out of this house when the Slasher was having fun, you won't figure it out now. With that being said, kindly have a seat in that chair next to you so I can ensure I get away with no trouble."

From his side he lifted the weapon Amelia hadn't seen. A handgun with a silencer attached at the end.

Oh God. Oh God.

She was barely aware of the whimpering sob that tore from her throat.

She had to stop him. She couldn't let him leave with her baby. *Oh God, please, please help me.*

As the prayer whipped through her mind the bedroom door opened.

"Oh God, no." Amelia reached out as though she could stop Wayne from pressing the barrel of the gun against Kimmy's head when Crowe stepped into the room.

Crowe didn't say a word. His gaze swiveled from Wayne, to Kimmy, then to Amelia.

His eyes were flat and hard, devoid of a single emotion for her to hold on to.

This was the man who'd killed Stoner, the one who'd tracked him, saved the two teenagers he would have raped, then shot him with no remorse whatsoever.

Whatever happened to Wayne tonight, Crowe would never lose so much as a moment's sleep over it.

She stared back at him in desperation. Wayne would take them both from her. She could see it in his eyes, in his smug smile. In the way that gun slowly turned on Crowe.

"Ah, how kind fate is being," Wayne sighed, pleasure gleaming in his eyes as his gaze went over Crowe. "I keep thinking how much better it would have been had I killed your sorry ass when you were bawling at your mama's grave the night they buried her."

"After you killed her," Crowe reminded him, moving closer to Amelia as Wayne watched him with malevolent eyes.

"I put her out of her misery," Wayne snapped.

"But she wasn't miserable, Wayne," Crowe reminded him without any sense of gloating. "You killed her because of your jealousy, greed, and insanity."

"I killed her because your father was a nosy fucking bastard," Wayne snarled. "He just had to keep picking, just had to keep probing where he didn't belong. The day they signed those papers with the lawyer, he and his fucking brothers just had to take their wives to talk to that coroner about the bodies that were stolen from the morgue after I thought I'd killed that bitch wife of mine and her lover." Wayne shook his head, regret flashing in his expression. "How I loved her, Crowe. And how she wanted to destroy me."

"Why would she want to destroy you?" Crowe asked coolly. "You took her from me, Wayne. The least you could tell me is why rather than spouting pathetic excuses."

What was he doing?

Amelia stared at her daughter as the gun remained trained on Crowe. Could Kimmy roll from the bed fast enough? She was awake, Amelia could *feel* it. Yet Kimmy lay there, quietly, to all appearances still sleeping.

"Pathetic excuses?" Wayne retorted furiously, his anger growing now that Crowe was in front of him. "I loved her. I loved her until I wanted to die when I learned she was screwing that damned Callahan bastard."

"Would it have mattered who it was?" Crowe asked, sliding his hands into the pockets of his slacks as he tilted his head and watched Wayne the way a cat watched a mouse.

Wayne took a single step away from Kimmy, then stopped.

"It wouldn't have mattered who it was." The gun trembled in his hand as his attention became focused solely on Crowe. "I still would have done everything I could to destroy it."

"Even kill her?" Crowe said softly, musingly.

"Even kill her," Wayne spat, enraged. "A thousand times over I would have killed her for daring to allow another man to touch her. Another man's brat to fucking invade her body. I'd kill her again if I could."

"That isn't love." Crowe shrugged carelessly as though what Wayne felt, or didn't feel, didn't really matter. "You can kill to protect the woman you love. You can die for her. But you can't hurt her. You can't take from her. And you would die before you see her hurt."

"Like you love this little bitch?" Wayne sneered, waving his gun in Amelia's direction.

"Yes actually." Crowe nodded slowly. "Just like that."

"And if I killed her?" Wayne drawled, leveling the gun on Amelia's head.

"I wouldn't suggest that." Crowe sighed as though growing weary with the conversation.

"And why wouldn't you do that?" Wayne's gaze snapped back to him.

Crowe smiled. "Whoever's helping you forgot to mention that Thea didn't arrive at this house alone."

Wayne's eyes narrowed.

"She arrived with that lover you thought you killed when you thought you killed her," Crowe said softly. "Tell me, did you know he was a sniper?"

The second the words left Crowe's throat, the window behind Wayne shattered.

Amelia jumped for her daughter even as Kimmy was rolling off the side of the bed to the floor. The connecting door to Amelia's parents' room was thrown open, Ivan and Jack jumping forward, grabbing Amelia and Kimmy, and jerking them to safety.

"Crowe," Amelia cried out, desperate to know if he was okay, to know what was happening.

Turning, she tried to jerk out of her uncle's grip and reach the bedroom door. She was hustled into the hall just as quickly.

"Don't you fucking distract him." Ivan was suddenly in her face, snarling down at her. "Your father couldn't get into the proper position. At the most, Wayne has only been wounded and that makes him even more dangerous. Distract Crowe, and you could cause his death."

Her arms wrapped automatically around her daughter as Kimmy threw herself into the embrace. Amelia felt herself begin to crumple.

"Hey there, Little Bit." Her uncle caught her, his voice, his arms gentle as he steadied her on her feet. "Crowe's the best. Remember that." Lifting her face, he stared down at her, confident, certain in what he was saying. "Remember that, Amelia. When he walks out that door, it's going to be over."

CHAPTER 29

Wayne wasn't dead.

Crowe heard Ethan's report as he managed to get himself into the best position possible, more than a mile away, and set his sights on the window and Wayne.

"No mark," he snarled into the link. "Get that bastard to move."

Crowe had only managed a few inches away from Kimmy.

"I can distract him, possibly wound him," Ethan snapped, fury rasping in his voice. "That fucker."

"Take the shot," Logan commanded, following the orders Crowe had given him before he stepped into the bedroom.

"It fucking doesn't work like that," Ethan growled. "I could end up hitting Crowe."

"Crowe said take the fucking shot," Logan snapped into the link before he could second-guess the orders Crowe had given. "Take the goddamned shot or he said he'll kick all our fucking asses. Starting with yours."

Crowe had been prepared.

He was aware of Kimmy rolling just as Jack had promised she would do, and Amelia jumping for her, just as she had been taught to do by her father and uncle. At the same time, the bedroom door had opened and Jack and Ivan had pulled them both to safety.

Leaving Crowe with Wayne, because he didn't want Amelia see who he was. What he was.

Crowe stared at the dead man in the middle of his uncle Sam's living room floor. He swallowed back the need to vomit. His dad didn't vomit, neither did Uncle Ben, and they were standing there, too, staring at the man with cold, hard eyes.

Crowe knew his eyes weren't cold and hard. He was only twelve and all he wanted to do was puke. But he managed to hold it back.

"Is he a monster, Dad?" he asked, embarrassed that his voice was shaking.

"God, Crowe." His dad knelt beside him. "You okay, son? You sure you're okay?" His dad ran his hands over him quickly as Crowe stared back at him, seeing fear in his dad's eyes for the first time in his life.

"I'm okay, Dad." He took in a deep breath. "Did I do okay?"

His dad had started teaching him how to fight monsters. His uncles helped by always jumping from behind doors or trees, trying to scare him.

When the man had moved from the sliding doors and tried to grab Crowe, he'd done what his father had taught him. He'd buried his fist in the guy's balls.

"Did I kill him, Dad?" he asked, his voice kind of funny sounding. Like it wasn't his voice at all.

"No, son, you didn't kill him." His dad stared into his eyes. Holding his head still, making Crowe just stare at him. "Look at me, Crowe." His dad's voice was soft now, firm. That kind of firm don't-you-dare-disobey voice. "Did you hear me? You didn't kill him. You understand me?"

Crowe's eyes moved to the side involuntarily as he detected movement.

"Look at me, Crowe." His dad's voice got a snap to it, and Crowe didn't dare not look at him.

"I am, Dad." He tried not to, but his father was holding his head. "I see you."

"Good boy," his dad approved. "When I let you go, I want you to forget about this, you hear me." His dad kept staring into his eyes. "You can't ever let Mom know, Crowe. Not ever. You're going to have to be a real man this time, son. You can't ever tell Mom. You can't tell anyone. Ever. Promise me."

He wouldn't dare tell Mom. She might cry or something. He'd hate it if he made her cry.

His eyes widened. "No way, Dad." His voice cracked as he made the promise. "No way will I tell."

"Swear it, Crowe," his dad urged, his eyes filled with so much pain and sorrow that Crowe swallowed tightly.

"I swear it, Dad."

"Good boy." His dad nodded, slowly releasing his head as he straightened. "You're going to be a fine man, Crowe. A good man."

Crowe nodded and looked around.

He frowned.

There was no body. There was no blood.

His head swung back to where his father watched him sadly.

"Dad?" His voice trembled.

"It was a bad dream, son," his dad whispered. "Remember that, it was just a bad dream. You okay?"

A bad dream?

He narrowed his gaze on his father, seeing the desperation in the other man's eyes, and he nodded slowly. He didn't believe it, but he knew his dad.

His dad said it was his job to protect his family, and

he would feel like he wasn't protecting Crowe if he thought Crowe didn't believe him.

"It was a really bad dream, Dad," Crowe whispered, a little scared now, but knowing his dad needed him to believe it. "A really bad dream."

Relief filled David Callahan's gaze as he reach to ruffle Crowe's hair, then stopped. His hand fell on his shoulder instead, like he did with Crowe's uncles. He gripped it briefly. That was a "man hug," his dad had told him once.

Did that make him a man now?

Keeping a secret not just from his mom, but from his dad as well? The secret that he knew, to the soles of his feet: His dad had killed a man that night. And his dad would never forgive himself if he thought Crowe would never forget the sight of it.

"Come on, son." David guided him toward the stairs. "I'll go upstairs with you. Maybe tonight we'll talk about those monsters you have to watch out for."

Crowe leveled his own weapon on Wayne's head, staring down at him icily.

"You can't do it," the other man sneered. "You're as weak as your old man."

Crowe grinned. "Remember the night your father disappeared, Wayne?" he asked softly, all too aware of the other two men who stepped into the room behind him.

Wayne's nostrils flared, his gaze going to Logan and Rafe as they came to Crowe's side.

"That man you're calling weak," Crowe stated softly. "He killed that bastard with his bare hands. Ripped his head half off his neck when he broke it. I thought I was going to puke at the sight of his head torn like that, blood going everywhere. Then I remembered." He aimed the gun right between Wayne's eyes as they widened and feral, cunning fear filled them. "I remembered, Wayne, monsters don't count."

He pulled the trigger.

Staring down at Wayne's body, his eyes wide and glazed, the scent of death beginning to fill the air, he bent, cleaned his prints from the weapon, placed it in Wayne's hand, ensured his prints were in place, then let the gun fall to the floor.

Rising, he turned to his cousins, his gaze narrowed on them, knowing the men they were, and knowing that even though either one of them would have pulled that trigger if he had to, still, it would have kept them awake at night.

Just as he accepted that he wouldn't lose a second's sleep over it.

"He killed himself," he stated.

His cousins stared back at him.

They were men.

The type of men who knew monsters existed and knew they had to be destroyed to save the innocent lives they fed on.

Both nodded.

"He sure did," Rafe murmured, placing his hand on Crowe's shoulder and giving it a brief, hard squeeze. "Thank God."

"He saved me the trouble." Logan did likewise, placing his hand on Crowe's shoulder and squeezing.

A man hug.

"Do you think they know?" It was Rafe who spoke the question, his voice soft, filled with regret that the parents who had fought so desperately to ensure their safety when they were younger hadn't lived to see the day that their sons had avenged them.

Them, and every innocent life Wayne had taken.

Crowe nodded. "They know."

Stepping from the bedroom, he faced Amelia and their child. As Amelia stared back at him, shaking, Crowe saw the fear in his lover's eyes that he'd been forced to kill again. It would hurt her, he thought, finally realizing the lessons his father had taught him and why. It was a man's responsibility to be gentle, loving, to be a man who fought monsters, not be a monster himself, in his family's eyes.

"Crowe?" Amelia whispered. "Is he . . ." She swallowed. "Is he dead?"

"He shot himself with his own gun," he lied and didn't even hesitate. He'd sworn to her once he'd never lie to her, but this was one of those lies that didn't count. This lie would ease her, and it would ensure his daughter didn't have nightmares of monsters with her father's face.

He bent, resting on his haunches in front of his daughter as she stared back at him—and by God, he had to grin. There wasn't so much as an ounce of fear in her eyes.

"I knew you would get him," she said softly as she held on to her mother. Her brown-and-amber eyes were suspicious, though.

She didn't believe him.

Maybe Amelia didn't, either.

He lifted his head, staring up at her.

Whether she did or not, it wasn't in her eyes. All he saw there was love.

He turned back to his daughter, opening his arms. As she flew into them, he whispered, "There's my girl."

His arms wrapped around her, tight. Holding on to her, tears filling his eyes, he felt Amelia next to him, her love surrounding both of them.

"My baby girl," he whispered against Kimmy's hair.

"I love you, Daddy . . ."

EPILOGUE

News of Wayne's "suicide" exploded around the county just as Thea's return from the dead and Crowe's six-year-old daughter were being reported.

Journalists were once again flooding Corbin County and camping on the doorsteps of anyone who may or may not have been involved. The reporters were told Sorenson had managed to access his former home through a hidden door, where he'd managed to use a silencer to kill the security agent outside the bedroom door of the child Crowe Callahan was claiming as his own. When he found the room empty, then came face-to-face with the Callahan, he'd put the gun to his head and pulled the trigger rather than be taken.

No one suspected how he'd really died.

No one, least of all the security agent paid to arrange it, was aware that the experts who had spent a week going over the equipment had figured out exactly how he managed to get past their defenses.

Crowe knew the mettle of the man he'd partnered with when he went into business with Ivan Resnova. From the moment they'd realized Mike had allowed Wayne to slip past their security and kill Ivan's cousin, Crowe had suspected Mike's body would disappear just as completely as Stoner's had.

No one was more surprised the next morning when Archer called with news of Mike's arrest, though. Crowe wouldn't have blamed Ivan; the young man who'd died had been close to the Russian. Crowe would have considered helping had Ivan asked, because even if Kimmy didn't have nightmares for years to come, Crowe knew he would have them where that night was concerned.

He was waiting for Ivan as he stepped into the house that afternoon, his dark, aristocratic face heavy, his gaze brooding.

"Uncle Ivan." Kimmy appeared at the doorway, stepping slowly into the foyer, her big dark eyes solemn as she stared up at the man.

She'd been picking out her own clothes since she was three, Amelia had told Crowe that morning when he first caught sight of Kimmy skipping through the house. She wore black leggings and a knee-length sweater dress of some sort paired with furry boots.

She was celebrating, she'd informed them all solemnly. The bad man was gone and now they were all just going to live happily ever after like the princesses do in the fairy tales.

Ivan sighed deeply then squatted down and stared back at the little girl with the air of a man facing a battle he wasn't certain he wanted to fight.

"Kimmy . . ." he started, resigned.

"I'm very sorry about the bad man killing Rico." Her voice was soft, the compassion Crowe was beginning to glimpse in her filling it. "I liked him a lot."

Ivan's face softened immeasurably, and for a moment Crowe was given a glimpse of the father Ivan must have been to his own daughter.

"Thank you very much, Kimmy," he said softly. "I appreciate your kindness."

"If you need to talk, Uncle Ivan, I'm always here." She nodded sagely.

For a moment, Ivan looked a little bemused. "Kimmy, your papa has told you I'm not your uncle, has he not?" he asked the girl.

Kimmy stared back at him with a quiet, solemn wisdom. "But you're my uncle because I picked you to be. But I understand you're upset with me and Mommy right now, 'cause you think we were mean to Daddy." She reached out to touch his cheek with her tiny hand. "I promise, we're gonna make Daddy very happy, though."

His lips quirked sadly. Crowe realized that perhaps Kimmy was right, in some ways. Ivan had been furious since the night Kimmy had arrived.

"Yes, I know you make your papa very happy," he said softly. "And perhaps it's not so much anger I feel as it is jealousy, because my beautiful little girl no longer needs her papa."

"All little girls need their daddy," Kimmy promised him then. "Just sometimes." She gave Crowe a very firm look before turning back to Ivan. "Our daddies just get silly and hurt our feelings really bad and don't know it. Did you hurt your little girl's feelings, Uncle Ivan?"

"I would hope I did not," he answered, almost amused.

"Well, I think you should ask her." Kimmy crossed her arms and stuck out one little sneaker-shod foot as she nodded wisely. "And just ask her nice, like you would ask her if she wanted ice cream. Maybe have ice cream when you ask her." She nodded again as she gave this advice.

Ivan blinked back at her, then lifted his gaze to Crowe.

"You, my friend, are in so much trouble," he murmured.

Kimmy turned back and flashed a Crowe a grin so innocent he nearly winced.

Oh Lord—

"Yeah," he answered Ivan. "I am."

"Come, little one." Focusing on Kimmy once more, he held out his hands. "You may call me Uncle Ivan then."

An infectious giggle fell from her lips as she threw her arms around his neck and hugged with all the exuberance of an emotionally confident six-year-old.

"I didn't ask for permission, Uncle Ivan." She smacked a kiss to his cheek. "I already knew it was okay."

Then she turned and bounced out of the room just as quickly.

Straightening, Ivan shook his head as a small grin played at his lips. Then, straightening the belted band of his slacks at his hips, he focused on Crowe once again.

"I hear you turned Mike in to the FBI?" Crowe asked as the other man slowly slid his hands into the pockets of his slacks and stared back at Crowe for long, silent moments.

"Unfortunately, Amara and her friend Grace arrived as my men arrived at the offices with him." Ivan grimaced. "I do try to keep my true nature hidden from my daughter." His gaze slid to the doorway Kimmy had disappeared into. "I'm certain you understand."

His daughter Amara was twenty-one rather than the seventeen or eighteen most assumed she was. She was also making her father insane with her awareness of his former job description.

"I do." Crowe nodded.

"Ah well, time to get the agents home," Ivan stated. "I'll have them begin packing and get them out of here so you and your family have a chance to spend time together."

Tilting his head, Crowe saw the flicker of anger in his gaze then.

"Are you angry with Amelia, Ivan?" Crowe asked the question softly as the other man turned to leave.

Ivan paused then turned back slowly, that air of resignation, of quiet acceptance surrounding him.

"I believe *anger* would be the wrong word." Ivan's lips quirked with a hint of mockery. "I would say instead, I was a bit put out with her. You see, she did what no one else has been able to do. She kept her secrets hidden from me. No matter my suspicions that the child existed, I could not prove it. I was a bit . . . perturbed."

That sounded more like Ivan.

"She was good." Pride filled Crowe. He couldn't help it. He hated that she'd done it, that the need had been there.

"She is a woman to be extremely proud of," Ivan said nodding. "No training. She is no agent, no officer, she is a woman of ultimate strengths and feminine weaknesses. She is a woman to always have the greatest pride in, my friend. You are very lucky."

There was a hint of sadness in his friend's eyes, Crowe thought. A shadow of a hunger, or perhaps a fear that flickered there for a second.

"Lucky is an understatement," he replied.

"I will begin the preparations of removing security now." Ivan turned away.

He paused again, but this time he didn't turn to meet Crowe's gaze.

"We have a problem," he said, shoulders tense.

"Of what sort?"

The line of Ivan's jaw tensed. "I am considering removing one of the men from the home office and sending him to the field instead."

Crowe's brow arched.

Hell, he knew what was coming.

"Rory?" he asked.

Ivan turned back slowly. "Were you aware of the situation?" Anger flashed in his eyes now.

"Wrong move, my friend," Crowe sighed. "But I won't fight you over it. I wouldn't appreciate your interference. Though, I need to point out"—Crowe shrugged—"you *would* interfere."

"Perhaps now, I will not," Ivan's voice was a rasp of anger now. "He will be leaving for Europe in two days' time. A request for security has come from a contact I have there. His team will be heading out as soon as possible."

Crowe frowned at that information. "His family helped us here, Ivan," he felt the need to point out. "His brother and uncle supplied immeasurable intel, not to mention the backup their friends gave us. Don't send Rory out to die."

Fire flashed in Ivan's eyes. "No matter the rumors of my blackened soul, Crowe, I would not send him to die."

With that, the other man stalked across the foyer and up the stairs, his steps heavier than normal.

"Problems?" Amelia stepped from the kitchen, moving to his side as Crowe pulled her into his embrace.

God, she felt good against him. She felt like he'd finally come home.

"He's the father of a twenty-one-year-old daughter who's interested in a man he feels is wrong for her," he sighed.

"Ouch," she whispered.

"Yep. Ouch." He chuckled.

Wrapping both arms around her, he pulled her closer, his lips lowering to her ear in a heated caress.

"Shall we let your parents watch Kimmy for a bit?" he suggested. "You and I could slip away, maybe sin a little."

"Sin a little, huh?" She softened against him, her breath becoming heavier, her heart racing against him. Crowe was a second from the kiss he'd been aching for all morning.

"Oh please!" Childish disgust had them jerking back quickly.

Turning to his daughter, Crowe let his eyes narrow in mock warning until he saw the complete vulnerability that filled her face. Something Amelia saw as well if the tension in her body was any indication.

"Kimmy?" Soft, gentle, Amelia's voice held all the soul-deep love she had for her daughter. "Did you need something, baby?"

"Yes, I do." She nodded hesitantly. "Mommy, I want to go home."

For a second, Crowe felt his world collapse.

"France?" Confusion filled Amelia. "You said you didn't like France, baby."

Kimmy was shaking her head quickly, her eyes moving to Crowe then. "You said we would go to Daddy's home, in the mountains," she said softly. "Where the wolf and her puppies are. Where his big house is buried in the mountain. I want to go home, Mommy. I've just always wanted to go home."

Amelia lifted her hand to her lips to hide their trembling before she could speak. "Baby, we need to discuss all this first."

"Why?" Crowe and Kimmy asked the question at once, each of them turning to her.

Her eyes widened. A second later, a grin began tugging at her lips.

"Well, then I guess that's what we're doing . . ."

"I'm packed." Pure excitement filled Kimmy's face and her rich amber-flecked brown eyes. "Grandma and Grandpa are all packed, too. Can we go now? Please, can we go?"

"Kimmy . . ." Amelia laughed, and Crowe could hear the gentle request for patience in her voice.

"I can't wait to take you and our daughter home," he said softly, bending his head to her ear. "Let's take our sprite home, fairy-girl. Now."

"Now?" Surprise, pleasure filled her expression as she turned to him. "Right now?"

"Pack a bag, fairy." He grinned. "We're going home."

Kimmy's whoops filled the air, drawing Thea, Ethan, Jack, and the rest of the team from the kitchen.

"We're going home, Grandma." Kimmy flew to her grandparents, staring up at them in joy. "I'm going home."

Turning, she ran back to her father, jumped into his arms, and gave him a hug that he swore weakened his knees.

His daughter.

Sweet God, his precious daughter.

Turning to his fairy-girl, Crowe found himself overwhelmed with the knowledge of what he would have been without her. The icy, unemotional killer who had taken out Stoner, who had killed for his nation, who had seen only what had to be done.

Until his Amelia, until she brought him what his soul had lacked, Crowe knew he would have died on the inside.

"Thank you," he whispered.

"For Kimmy?" Laughter gleamed in her eyes.

"For Kimmy, but even more." Drawing her to him, his daughter in one arm, soul in the other. "Thank you for bringing me magic."

Love filled her expression then. It flowed from her, wrapped around him and Kimmy, and warmed them. From the inside out, she warmed everyone she touched.

Slowly, she shook her head. "It took both of us to make the magic, Crowe."

His lips touched hers, gently, lovingly. The warmth wrapped around them, magic sparked in a child's laughter, and in that moment Crowe realized the ice he'd carried inside him was gone. Not even a chill remained in the deepest corner of his spirit.

His fairy had burned it away, and with the child they created she filled it with warmth, with love and hope.

They hadn't committed the ultimate sin when they loved. They'd given birth to the ultimate joy instead.

Don't miss these other novels of seduction and suspense by #1 *New York Times* bestselling author

Lora Leigh

"Leigh's books can scorch the ink off the page."
—*Romantic Times BOOKreviews*

THE CALLAHANS
MIDNIGHT SINS
DEADLY SINS
SECRET SINS

THE ELITE OPS series
LIVE WIRE
RENEGADE
BLACK JACK
HEAT SEEKER
MAVERICK
WILD CARD

THE SEALs trilogy
KILLER SECRETS
HIDDEN AGENDAS
DANGEROUS GAMES

BOUND HEARTS
WICKED PLEASURE
FORBIDDEN PLEASURE
ONLY PLEASURE

Anthologies
LEGALLY HOT
MEN OF DANGER

AVAILABLE FROM ST. MARTIN'S PAPERBACKS

New York Times bestselling author Lora Leigh keeps the sensational reads coming…

Don't miss:

TAKEN

Featuring some of Leigh's most sought-after short stories—together, for the first time, in this sizzling collection!

And the novels in the sensational Bound Hearts series:

DANGEROUS PLEASURE
GUILTY PLEASURE
ONLY PLEASURE
WICKED PLEASURE
FORBIDDEN PLEASURE

AVAILABLE FROM ST. MARTIN'S GRIFFIN

31901055658233